The New St. Martin's Workbook

The New St. Martin's Workbook

Lex Runciman
LINFIELD COLLEGE

BEDFORD/ST. MARTIN'S
BOSTON / NEW YORK

For Bedford/St. Martin's
Developmental Editor: Kristin Bowen
Senior Production Supervisor: Dennis Conroy
Marketing Manager: Karen Melton
Art Director: Lucy Krikorian
Text Design: Anna George/Dorothy Bungert
Cover Design: Anna George
Composition: Jan Ewing, Ewing Systems
Printing and Binding: R. R. Donnelley & Sons Co.

President: Charles H. Christensen
Editorial Director: Joan E. Feinberg
Editor in Chief: Nancy Perry
Director of Editing, Design, and Production: Marcia Cohen
Managing Editor: Erica T. Appel

Copyright © 1999 by Bedford/St. Martin's

All rights reserved. No part of this book may be reproduced, stored in a retrieval system, or transmitted in any form or by any means, electronic, mechanical, photocopying, recording, or otherwise, except as may be expressly permitted by the applicable copyright statutes or in writing by the Publisher.

Manufactured in the United States of America.

4 3 2 1 0
f e d c b

For information, write: Bedford/St. Martin's, 75 Arlington Street, Boston, MA 02116   (617-426-7440)

ISBN: 0-312-18851-X

Acknowledgments
Definition of *compose.* *The American Heritage Dictionary of the English Language, Third Edition.* Copyright © 1996 by Houghton Mifflin Company. Reproduced by permission.
Anne Bradstreet. Excerpt from *In Memory of My Dear Grandchild.* From *A Book of Women Poets from Antiquity to Now* by Aliki Barnstone and Willis Barnstone, editors. Schocken Books, 1980.
Rachel Carson. Excerpt from *The Sea Around Us,* Revised Edition, pp. 83–84. Copyright © 1950, 1951, 1961 by Rachel Carson; renewed 1979 by Roger Christie. Used by permission of Oxford University Press, Inc.
Clifford Odets. "Joe and Edna," Scene I from *Waiting for Lefty* by Clifford Odets. Copyright © 1935 by Clifford Odets; renewed 1962 by Clifford Odets. Used by permission of Grove/Atlantic, Inc.
Dana Owens, Simone Johnson, Mark James, Anthony Peaks, and Shane Faber. Excerpt from *Ladies First* (Shane Faber, Queen Latifah). © 1989 T-Boy Music Publishing, Inc. c/o Lipservices obo itself & Queen Latifah Music, Forty-Five King Music, Forked Tongue Music/Warner Chappell Music, Inc. International copyrights secured. All rights reserved. Used by kind permission.
Dylan Thomas. 13 lines from "Fern Hill." Taken from *Poems of Dylan Thomas.* Copyright © 1945 by the Trustees for the copyrights of Dylan Thomas. Reprinted by permission of New Directions Publishing Company and David Higham Associates.

Preface

The New St. Martin's Workbook is designed as a multifaceted resource for both teachers and student writers. Everything in this book proceeds from two basic assumptions: first, that every college student can become a skilled and successful writer; and second, that successful writing proceeds from both a knowledge of how English works and a knowledge of what writers do.

This workbook is devoted to discussion and exercises dealing with the formal complexities and conventions of written English as it is typically used in college writing. A working knowledge of these conventions encourages writers to believe that English is indeed their language and can be used to serve their own purposes—in a college essay, a research paper or technical report, a job application, a short story, or a poem.

The New St. Martin's Workbook shares its organization with Parts 1-7 and 11 of *The New St. Martin's Handbook*: The books' chapter and part numbers and titles parallel each other, and the numbers that follow major text heads in the *Workbook* (1a, 1b) correspond to numbered *Handbook* sections in which the same material is covered. The two texts can easily be used together, with the *Workbook* providing many additional exercises. Like the *Handbook*, the *Workbook* highlights the twenty errors most commonly found in college essays, providing explanations and exercises to enable student writers to identify such errors and to correct them. The *Workbook* may also be used alone, as either a primary or a supplemental text.

The *Workbook* has been redesigned and revised throughout to be a better companion for *The New St. Martin's Handbook*. New to this edition, the *Workbook* includes exercises opening each chapter that focus on everyday use, linking the material in the *Workbook* with students' lives beyond the classroom. All together, approximately 60 percent of the *Workbook's* exercise questions are new to this edition. Finally, four new chapters in Part Eight—For Multilingual Writers: Mastering the Nuances of English—pay special attention to the needs of multilingual writers.

To accompany *The New St. Martin's Workbook*, an Instructor's Manual is available, containing suggested answers and strategies for using the *Workbook*'s exercises. Teachers who wish to may use exercises in this book as the basis for classroom discussion and as the basis for work in small groups; the Instructor's Manual identifies exercises that particularly lend themselves to this approach. Such collaboration is widespread in business and professional writing and is encouraged in many rhetoric texts; it is time for such strategies to find their way into workbooks.

Most importantly, this book attempts to give student writers a realistic image of the good writer. Students tend to think that good writers write effortlessly, quickly, and perfectly. That is simply not so. All writers struggle with questions of content, purpose, and audience. All writers must sometimes look up fine points of grammar and punctuation. And when at last we see that our words communicate almost precisely what we wish them to, when we have worked through and conquered the confusions, looked up misspellings and nailed down every comma, the elation we feel is real and well earned. *The New St. Martin's Workbook* aims to make such success more practically and more frequently attainable.

Books of this type and size depend on the collaboration and cooperation of many individuals, and I want to thank at least a few of them here. First, thanks must go to all the good people at Bedford/St. Martin's. Special thanks to Marilyn Moller and Kristin Bowen, who shepherded this edition through the revision process. Thanks also go to Diana Puglisi for her skill and patience, and continued thanks go to *The New St. Martin's Handbook* authors Andrea Lunsford and Bob Connors.

Writers, like everyone else, need human encouragement, and it helps immensely to work among folks with similar interests. So thanks to my colleagues at Linfield College for your encouragement and friendship. Finally, thanks to my family—to Debbie, Beth, and Jane. You are wonderful, fascinating people; what can I say—we have a good time.

Lex Runciman

Contents

PART ONE The Writing Process   1

1 Understanding the Writing Process   3
Considering the process of writing (1a)   3
Planning, drafting, revising (1a3–5)   4
Remembering the importance of talking and listening (1d)   6
EXERCISES   9

2 Considering Rhetorical Situations   13
Analyzing assignments (2b, 2c)   13
Determining your stance (2d, 2g)   15
Focusing on your audience (2h)   17
EXERCISES   21

3 Exploring, Planning, and Drafting   27
Exploring a topic (3a)   27
Establishing a working thesis (3b)   30
Gathering information (3c)   31
Organizing information (3d)   32
Producing a draft (3f)   34
EXERCISES   37

4 Revising and Editing   45
Revision strategies (4a, 4b, 4c, 4d, 4e)   45
Editing strategies (4f, 4g, 4i)   48
- Checking your writing for the top twenty errors found in student writing   51

Consider your final format (4h)   52
Proofread the final draft (4j)   53
EXERCISES   55

5 Thinking Critically: Constructing and Analyzing Arguments   *61*

Recognizing argument (5b)   *61*
Understanding the purposes of argument (5b1)   *62*
Formulating good reasons (5d)   *62*
Establishing credibility (5f)   *63*
Appealing to logic (5g)   *64*
Appealing to emotion (5h)   *67*
Using the Toulmin System (5j2)   *67*
EXERCISES   *69*

6 Constructing Paragraphs   *77*

Understanding paragraphs   *77*
Constructing unified, coherent, and fully developed paragraphs (6a, 6b, 6c, 6d, 6e)   *78*
Special-purpose paragraphs (6f)   *83*
EXERCISES   *85*

PART TWO   Sentences: Making Grammatical Choices   97

7 Constructing Grammatical Sentences   *99*

Recognizing the parts of speech (7b)   *99*
■ Common error: Wrong or missing preposition   *104*
Recognizing the parts of a sentence: Subjects and predicates (7c)   *106*
Classifying sentences according to function and form (7d)   *112*
EXERCISES   *115*

8 Understanding Pronoun Case   *139*

Using the subjective case (8a)   *139*
Using the objective case (8a2)   *140*
Using the possessive case (8a3)   *141*
Using *who, whoever, whom,* and *whomever* (8b)   *142*
Using case in compound subjects or objects (8c)   *143*
Using case in appositives (8c)   *144*
Using case in elliptical constructions (8d)   *144*
EXERCISES   *147*

9 Using Verbs   *159*

VERB FORMS   *159*
■ Common error: Wrong or missing verb ending   *160*

Using auxiliary verbs (9a) *162*
Using regular and irregular verbs (9b) *163*
Using *lie/lay, sit/set*, and *rise/raise* (9c) *165*
VERB TENSES *166*
- Common error: Wrong tense or verb form *166*
Using the present tenses (9d) *167*
Using the past tenses (9e) *168*
Using the future tenses (9f) *169*
Using verb tenses in sequence (9g) *170*
VOICE *172*
MOOD (9h) *174*
EXERCISES *177*

10 Maintaining Subject-Verb Agreement — 197

- Common error: Lack of agreement between subject and verb *197*
Making verbs agree with third-person singular subjects (10a) *198*
Making the subject and verb agree when separated by other words (10b) *198*
Making verbs agree with compound subjects (10c) *199*
Making verbs agree with collective-noun or indefinite-pronoun subjects (10d, 10e) *200*
Making verbs agree with relative-pronoun subjects (10f) *201*
Making linking verbs agree with their subjects (10g) *202*
Making verbs agree with subjects that are plural in form but singular in meaning (10h, 10j) *203*
Making verbs agree with subjects that follow them (10i) *203*
EXERCISES *205*

11 Maintaining Pronoun-Antecedent Agreement — 215

- Common error: Lack of agreement between pronoun and antecedent *215*
Making pronouns agree with compound or collective-noun antecedents (11a, 11b) *215*
Making pronouns agree with indefinite-pronoun antecedents (11c) *217*
Checking for sexist pronouns (11d) *217*
EXERCISES *219*

12 Using Adjectives and Adverbs — 223

Distinguishing adjectives from adverbs (12a) *223*
Using adjectives and adverbs after linking verbs (12b) *224*

Distinguishing between *good* and *well*, *bad* and *badly*, *real* and *really* (12c) *225*
Using comparative and superlative forms (12d) *226*
EXERCISES *231*

PART THREE Sentences: Making Conventional Choices **237**

13 Maintaining Clear Pronoun Reference **239**

■ Common error: Vague pronoun reference *239*
Matching personal pronouns to unambiguous antecedents (13a) *240*
Keeping pronouns and antecedents close together (13b) *240*
Checking for troublesome pronoun reference (13c, 13d, 13e, 13f) *241*
EXERCISES *245*

14 Recognizing Shifts **253**

Recognizing shifts in tense (14a) *253*
■ Common error: Unnecessary shift in tense *253*
Recognizing shifts in mood and voice (14b, 14c) *254*
Recognizing shifts in person and number (14d) *255*
■ Common error: Unnecessary shift in pronoun *255*
Recognizing shifts in tone and diction (14f) *256*
EXERCISES *259*

15 Identifying Comma Splices and Fused Sentences **267**

■ Common errors: Comma splice and fused sentence *268*
Separating independent clauses into two sentences (15a) *268*
Linking independent clauses with a semicolon (15c) *269*
Linking independent clauses with a comma and a coordinating conjunction (15b) *270*
Linking independent clauses with a semicolon and a conjunctive adverb or transitional phrase (15c) *270*
Recasting two independent clauses as a single independent clause (15d) *272*
Recasting one of two independent clauses as a dependent clause (15e) *273*
Can independent clauses ever be joined using commas? *273*
EXERCISES *275*

16 Recognizing Sentence Fragments **287**

■ Common error: Sentence fragment *287*

Recognizing and revising phrase fragments (16a)   *288*
Recognizing and revising compound-predicate fragments (16b)   *289*
Recognizing and revising dependent-clause fragments (16c)   *290*
Using fragments sparingly for special effect   *290*
EXERCISES   *293*

17 Placing Modifiers Appropriately   **297**
■ Common error: Misplaced or dangling modifier   *297*
Identifying and revising misplaced modifiers (17a)   *297*
Identifying and revising disruptive modifiers (17b)   *299*
Identifying and revising dangling modifiers (17c)   *300*
EXERCISES   *303*

18 Maintaining Consistent and Complete Grammatical Structures   **309**
Making grammatical patterns consistent (18a)   *309*
Making subjects and predicates consistent (18b)   *310*
Using elliptical structures carefully (18c)   *311*
Checking for missing words (18d)   *312*
Making comparisons complete, consistent, and clear (18e)   *312*
EXERCISES   *315*

PART FOUR   Sentences: Making Stylistic Choices   **323**

19 Constructing Effective Sentences   **325**
Emphasizing main ideas (19a)   *326*
Being concise (19b)   *327*
EXERCISES   *329*

20 Creating Coordinate and Subordinate Structures   **335**
Using coordination to relate equal ideas (20a)   *335*
Using subordination to distinguish main ideas (20b)   *336*
Using coordination and subordination for special effect (20a, 20b)   *338*
EXERCISES   *339*

21 Creating and Maintaining Parallel Structures   **345**
Using parallel structures in a series (21a)   *345*
Using parallel structures with pairs (21b)   *346*
Including all necessary words in parallel constructions (21c)   *347*
EXERCISES   *349*

- Common error: Unnecessary comma(s) with restrictive modifier 463
- Omitting unnecessary commas with restrictive elements (30j) 463
- Omitting commas between subjects and verbs, and between verbs and objects (30j) 464
- Checking for other unnecessary commas (30j) 464

EXERCISES 467

31 Using Semicolons   483
- Using semicolons to link independent clauses (31a) 483
- Using semicolons to separate items in a series (31b) 484
- Checking for overused semicolons (31c) 485
- Using semicolons with other punctuation (31e) 485

EXERCISES 487

32 Using End Punctuation   493
- Using periods (32a) 493
- Using question marks (32b) 494
- Using exclamation points (32c) 494

EXERCISES 495

33 Using Apostrophes   501
- Common error: Missing or misplaced possessive apostrophe 501
- Using apostrophes to signal possessive case (33a) 501
- Common error: *Its/it's* confusion 502
- Using apostrophes to signal contractions and other omissions (33b) 502
- Using apostrophes to form the plural of numbers, letters, symbols, and words used as words (33c) 504

EXERCISES 505

34 Using Quotation Marks   511
- Using quotation marks to signal direct quotations (34a) 511
- Using quotation marks with other punctuation (34e) 512
- Using quotation marks to signal titles and definitions (34b) 515
- Using quotation marks to signal irony and coinages (34c) 516

EXERCISES 517

35 Using Other Punctuation Marks   525
- Using parentheses (35a) 525
- Using brackets (35b) 527

Using dashes (35c) *527*
Using colons (35d) *528*
Using slashes (35e) *530*
Using ellipses (35f) *530*
EXERCISES *533*

PART SEVEN Understanding Mechanical Conventions — 541

36 Using Capitals — 543

Capitalizing the first word of a sentence or line of poetry (36a) *543*
Capitalizing proper nouns and proper adjectives (36b) *544*
Capitalizing titles of works (36c) *546*
Capitalizing *I* and *O* (36d) *547*
Checking for unnecessary capitalization (36e) *547*
EXERCISES *549*

37 Using Abbreviations and Numbers — 555

ABBREVIATIONS *555*
Abbreviating personal and professional titles and academic degrees (37a) *555*
Using abbreviations with years and hours (37b) *557*
Using acronyms and initial abbreviations (37c) *557*
Checking for appropriate use of abbreviations (37d) *558*
NUMBERS *559*
Spelling out or using figures for numbers (37e, 37f, 37g) *559*
EXERCISES *561*

38 Using Italics — 565

Using italics for titles (38a) *565*
Using italics for words, letters, and numbers referred to as words (38b) *566*
Using italics for foreign words and phrases (38c) *567*
Using italics for the names of vehicles (38d) *567*
Using italics for special emphasis (38e) *568*
EXERCISES *569*

39 Using Hyphens — 573

Using hyphens to divide words at the end of a line (39a) *573*
Using hyphens with compound words (39b) *574*

Using hyphens with prefixes and suffixes (39c) 576
Using hyphens to clarify meaning 577
EXERCISES 579

PART EIGHT For Multilingual Writers: Mastering the Nuances of English 589

40 Understanding Nouns and Noun Phrases 591
Distinguishing count and noncount nouns (53a) 591
Stating plural forms explicitly (53b) 592
Using determiners appropriately (53c) 592
Choosing articles appropriately (53d) 594
Arranging modifiers (53e) 596
EXERCISES 599

41 Understanding Verbs and Verb Phrases 605
Forming verb phrases (54a) 605
Using present and past tenses (54b) 607
Understanding perfect and progressive verb phrases (54c) 608
Using modals appropriately (54d) 609
Using participial adjectives appropriately (54e) 611
EXERCISES 613

42 Understanding Prepositions and Prepositional Phrases 621
Using prepositions idiomatically (55a) 621
Using two-word verbs idiomatically (55b) 622
EXERCISES 625

43 Forming Clauses and Sentences 627
Expressing subjects explicitly (56a) 628
Expressing objects explicitly (56a) 628
Using English word order (56b) 628
Using noun clauses appropriately (56c) 629
Choosing between infinitives and gerunds (56d) 629
Using adjective clauses carefully (56e) 630
Understanding conditional sentences (56f) 631
EXERCISES 633

Answers to Preview Questions 643

Index 645

A Note to Students

Think about the word *writing*, and you will realize that it has two basic meanings. Writing is what you're reading now, but writing is also the activity writers go through as they write. It's an activity that involves considerable thinking: thinking about what you want to say, thinking about who you're saying it to, thinking about how the material can be organized, and so on. Writing teachers often distinguish these various activities by calling them planning, drafting, and revising. Put that way, it sounds like writing—the activity—is a straight-line process; you plan first, then you draft, then you revise. That's a neat model for what writers do, but it makes the process look orderly and predictable, when in fact most writers will quickly acknowledge that the activity of writing often means planning, drafting, revising the plan, drafting some more, researching answers to unanticipated questions, drafting again, revising some more, and so on. Notice how often the word *revising* gets mentioned. If you depend on one draft, you can be smart only once. If you revise, you can be smart many times.

If you are a student opening *The New St. Martin's Workbook* for the first time, you will find that it focuses most of its attention (and therefore most of yours) on making revision easier and less troublesome and more correct. The majority of the explanations and writing activities you find here will help you understand and practice the ways that sentences and paragraphs can be put together accurately and concisely. And the hope is that completing exercises in this book will give you the understanding and the confidence to use these same strategies and techniques when you write and revise your own sentences.

Good writing needs to be substantially correct; it needs basic clarity, or its readers will be lost. But good writing is the result of much more than a concern for sentence-by-sentence correctness. Good writing begins with a decision to think, a decision to engage yourself in a process of discovery and learning, a process that will make clear to you what you want to say and how it ought to be said. This edition discusses large questions of strategy and approach in Part One, but these chapters are not meant to be complete by themselves. See them as introductions, useful as such.

The very term *college writing* can provoke a certain amount of worry. Sometimes people aren't sure they can measure up. Sometimes people fear that they just weren't born with the right equipment. This book knows otherwise. It knows that college writers are made, not born; and it knows that the key factors are study and practice; to become a better college writer, you must write. If you don't now consider yourself "a college writer," you can become one, and this book will help. If you already know you can excel as a college writer, this book will help you add to your set of tools for using that astonishingly versatile and powerful set of conventions called the English language.

PART 1

THE WRITING PROCESS

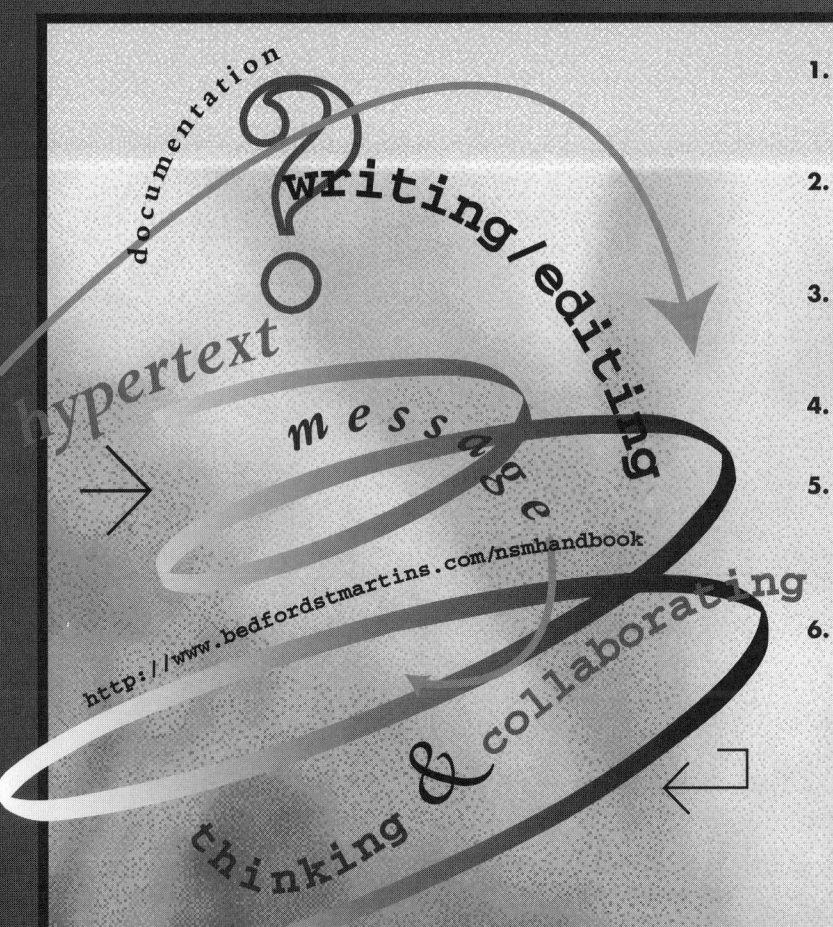

1. **Understanding the Writing Process** 3
2. **Considering Rhetorical Situations** 13
3. **Exploring, Planning, and Drafting** 27
4. **Revising and Editing** 45
5. **Thinking Critically: Constructing and Analyzing Arguments** 61
6. **Constructing Paragraphs** 77

PART 1

PREVIEW QUESTIONS

These questions are designed to help you, the student, decide what you need to study. Read the following statements and indicate whether they are true or false. (Answers to preview questions are found at the back of the book.)

1. Skillful writers do not need to revise. _____

2. Those who do not demonstrate marked writing skill before college are not destined to become successful writers. _____

3. Freewriting allows a writer to think on paper without worrying about the correctness of the ideas or of the writing itself. _____

4. Writers should never consider the nature of their readers when writing. _____

5. Comparison and contrast and cause and effect are the only two logical relationships that can form the basis of an essay's organization. _____

6. The drafting process demands time, concentration, and the flexibility to follow where our thought processes lead us. _____

7. Revision helps writers understand what they want to say, and how readers are likely to interpret their words. _____

8. Experienced writers never discuss their work with others. _____

9. An outline is useful because it allows writers to see an entire paper's organization, so that they can spot inconsistencies. _____

10. An arguable statement presents assertions for which no certain answers or solutions exist. _____

11. Tone is an important element in an essay's persuasiveness. _____

12. Successful arguments rely solely on emotional appeals to convince readers. _____

13. Deductive reasoning moves from a general principle to a specific instance. _____

14. A *non sequitur* ties together two logically related ideas. _____

15. A paragraph is a group of sentences focusing on one main point. _____

16. Transitional words and phrases help both the writer and the reader make connections and achieve clarity in a paragraph. _____

▼ Understanding the Writing Process

Considering the process of writing (1a)

Consider all that we read. We read billboards, news magazines, daily comics, and the front covers of whatever is stacked near the grocery checkout counter. We read weather forecasts, advice columns, building directories, transit schedules, box scores, editorials, and advertisements on the insides or the outsides of buses. We read neon signs, cereal boxes, product directions, romance novels, thrillers, biology textbooks, *People* magazine, recipes, and poems such as Robert Frost's "Stopping by Woods on a Snowy Evening."

All of these are finished pieces of writing. Very little of what we read is not a final product. It is not surprising, therefore, that when we think of the writing *process*, we forget just how much of it consists of *getting to* those final products. Many of us even think that practiced, skillful writers produce polished prose immediately, in a single draft. From time to time, a very experienced writer will manage this. But much more often, such writers spend hours and hours making notes, jotting down ideas, scribbling aimlessly just to get some thoughts on paper, rewording, reorganizing, starting all over, going back and looking for more information.... This sort of work makes up the real writing process.

This book will give you many opportunities to experience every part of the writing process—those just listed and others as well. You will be able to reflect on each stage and to hone your own unique writing process to suit you and to help you improve as a writer.

This book will add to your knowledge about writing and language; it will also help you understand and refine your own writing habits. It begins, however, with two basic assumptions:

1. Writing is a **process**, a set of many actions that *eventually* lead to a finished product. Whether you are conscious of it or not, you already have experience with many of these actions.
2. You are a writer. You use written language to produce grocery lists, notes to yourself, and letters. You have written school assignments, you will write more of them, and your job will probably require you to write such things as business letters, memos, evaluations—perhaps even proposals or reports. Above all, it is within your power to learn how to write all these things more easily and with better results.

THE WRITING PROCESS IN EVERYDAY USE

Deciding which college to attend and going through the process of applying and enrolling called on you to do some important reading, writing, and researching. You may remember doing some research on possible colleges, poring over campus descriptions and university homepages to determine which schools would be appropriate, and writing up the final applications. Think for a moment about how you have used reading, writing, and research in other decisions you've made recently—what computer to buy, where to vacation, and so on. Select one of your recent decisions, and write out a list of the ways in which it involved reading, writing, and research.

Planning, drafting, revising (1a3–5)

In this book, when we speak of writers, we are speaking of ordinary people who use written language to teach themselves and to communicate with others. How do these ordinary folks write? They think; they struggle; they use pen, pencil, keyboard, paper. And you can be sure of this: few writers sit down and effortlessly compose a perfect sentence, followed by another, followed by another. To do so would be roughly equivalent to sitting down at a piano for the very first time and playing, effortlessly and expertly, a Mozart sonata or a blues improvisation.

Put in the simplest terms, writers plan, draft, and revise (each of these major activities will be discussed in a following chapter). This sounds like it should be a straight-line process: plan first, then draft, then revise. Actually, though, the process is rarely that simple. More often, it looks like this: a writer *plans* (thinks, researches, takes notes, brainstorms), *drafts* (writes quickly, letting the thoughts take their own shape), *rereads*, then perhaps *plans* some more (conducts more research, for example), *keeps drafting,* or *revises* what has been drafted before and then *drafts* some more. Any one of these activities might occupy a writer for hours or days; a writer could just as easily be involved with all these activities in the space of only a few minutes.

This movement from drafting to revising to planning to more drafting is called *recursion*; hence, writing is often called a *recursive activity*.

Experienced writers may involve others in these activities. They brainstorm with others, talking out part of a draft as a way of provoking additional thought; often they seek response from unbiased readers to focus the revising process and make it more efficient. But whether alone or in concert with others, writers typically engage in the three main processes or activities of planning, drafting, and revising. Let us look at each briefly.

Planning

How should I begin to write? What do I know about this topic? What else do I need to know? What will be easy about this particular writing task? What will cause me

UNDERSTANDING THE WRITING PROCESS

trouble? Should I try brainstorming or freewriting? These are all planning questions. Planning includes asking such questions. It also includes everything you do as you prepare to write words readers might actually read. Many writers use writing as a way to plan. That is, they write notes or outline or freewrite. No one else reads this material. Many writers plan with others, sharing information as they go and using the responses to help shape the planning process.

The planning stage for an in-class essay exam might last only a few minutes. The planning stage for a lengthy research paper might extend over several weeks. As writers plan, they work toward an understanding of both what they want to say and how they will organize those thoughts. Chapter 3 will address the planning part of the writing process in considerable detail.

Drafting

Suppose your class has spent the last week reading Zora Neale Hurston's novel *Their Eyes Were Watching God*, and your instructor has assigned a three-page response paper in which you are asked to discuss your first reactions to this book. Your planning for this writing might lead you to reread the journal entries you wrote earlier (if you kept a reading journal). Or you might just make a list of single words that begin to describe your reactions, trusting that this planning will carry you directly into drafting: writing words in sentences. Or you might simply sit down and start writing anything that comes to mind as you think about that book. You'd be writing for yourself, trying to tell yourself what you think. Drafting an essay or paper means trying to think it onto paper. And drafting is a part of the writing process that you will return to again and again as you think and rethink and add to your drafts. Chapter 3 will discuss a number of useful strategies to make drafting easier.

Revising

As you draft, sometimes the words spill out so quickly you have trouble getting them onto the page (or onto your computer screen). But eventually you stop. Either you finish a train of thought and don't quite know what to say next, or something else in your life demands that you stop and attend to it. So writing often feels like an ebb and flow between getting the words down and reading those words. As you read over what you've written, you will almost inevitably see that you want to make changes. A word seems poorly chosen, so you change it. Let's go back to that response paper for *Their Eyes Were Watching God*. Let's say that in one twenty-minute burst you wrote a page of prose that talks about your first reactions. Part of your page of writing talks about how the dialogue in the book started out as a problem: you weren't used to reading it on the page. But after a while, this problem seemed to disappear. And after reading forty pages or so, you didn't notice this as a problem at all. In fact, by that time the dialogue became something positive. It added realism, so that you felt you could actually hear the characters talking.

As you read over your page that sketches all this, you realize that you haven't included any examples at all. So you plan to go back to the book and choose something brief to quote, something that illustrates your point. Once you actually look through the book and find an appropriate passage, you write it into the page you already have. If you use a computer, adding some sentences is easy; if you write on paper, then you might draft this example on a second piece of paper and make a note on your original draft that reminds you to insert these new sentences. As you see, revising means reading and rereading. It means making decisions about what to keep, what to add, what to cut, what to rephrase, and what to move to make your logic clearer.

Remembering the importance of talking and listening (1d)

While writing can sometimes feel like something you do entirely on your own, remember that you can easily involve other people in your writing process. In fact, virtually all practiced writers make a special effort to do just this. Researchers seek out colleagues to discuss possible approaches to a problem. Technical writers ask consumers whether or not their manuals are useful. And novelists and poets often seek the responses of other readers they trust. As a college writer, you can help yourself and help other writers in your class by talking about and exploring what you think, by reading your drafts out loud, by listening to what others think, and by telling others what their drafts communicate to you. Involving other people helps topics and issues come to life.

Talking, listening, and planning

If you are assigned a paper on Friday and have a week to finish it, then you'll be planning during much of that week, making decisions about when you will work as well as making decisions about how you will begin. As the week progresses, you'll be making other decisions about how to continue working on the paper, and all of these decisions can involve talking with others and listening to what they have to say.

Suppose, for example, that your assignment asks you to write a response to a newspaper editorial—a response that clearly shows why you agree with the editorial or why you disagree. Here are some ways that talking and listening can help you once you've read the editorial:

- Form a small group (two to four people), and take turns summarizing the editorial. What's the issue that it discusses? What are the sides or options or ways of looking at this issue? Make sure that as you discuss the editorial and what it means, you include all its major points; don't leave anything out. As a group, see if you can write a three- or four-sentence summary of the editorial's main points. Make sure that each member of the group has a copy of this summary.
- Once your group understands what the editorial says, see how many good reasons you can find for disagreeing with it. Make a list of all these reasons. Then make a list of all the good reasons you can think of for agreeing with the editorial.
- Once you've done this preliminary work, form pairs for a little while, with one of you being the designated talker and the other being the designated listener. If you are the talker, tell your partner your current thinking about the editorial.

Include both what you are sure of and what you still need to consider, mentioning as much of your current thinking as you can. If you are the listener, take notes so that you will be able to repeat what you have heard. If you do not understand something, make a note of that, but try not to interrupt your partner. Once the talker has finished, the listener explains what she or he has heard. The listener can then ask questions about whatever seemed unclear. Then the two of you switch roles. This way, both members of the pair get a chance to talk out their own response to the editorial, and both get a chance to hear someone else's responses.

Talking, listening, and drafting

Once you have discussed a topic or issue and your plans for writing about it with other people, you will usually find it easier to begin writing some of what you think. In fact, you can often begin drafting by mentally continuing your discussion on paper. Don't worry about spelling errors or sentence punctuation; just focus on getting your thoughts onto the page. Make it just clear enough that you can read it to someone later.

Talking, listening, and revising

After you have discussed a topic or issue and have begun putting some of your own ideas into words on the page (or on the computer screen), you can easily continue this process by reading what you've written aloud to yourself or to others. Reading out loud can be especially useful if you change partners or groups so that you are reading to someone who knows nothing about your thought process but hears only what your words say. Remember that early drafts almost inevitably leave out parts of what you think or some of your reasons for thinking that way, and they almost always get written in a somewhat jumbled order. So don't read more than a page before asking for some response.

When you listen to someone read a draft, take notes. Listen for the main logic. Watch for the main point and for whatever supports that main point. See if you can identify examples or explanations, and see if you can link these to the main points. If you can find such links, then that's what you should tell the writer. If you cannot see the links and cannot really see the main point, say that. In short, explain what you understand (even if it is only a part or a fragment) and what you do not understand. As a listener, your goal is to report as accurately as you can what you heard. And you should also be asking questions—"Did you mean ___ here?"—as a way of showing the writer how the words could be interpreted.

Listening to what others understand and don't understand about your draft should help you see what parts of the draft need your attention. Maybe you need to add some sentences. Maybe you need to make your transitions sharper by adding phrases such as *in contrast* or *on the other hand*. Maybe you need to reorder what you've written so that your main point is expressed earlier. Maybe you need to explain how your examples lead you to your main assertion. These are never easy decisions, and seeking the responses of other people offers no guarantees, but talking with actual readers is better than trying to imagine what they would say.

EXERCISE 1.1   REVIEWING YOUR OWN WRITING PROCESS

Assume that you have been asked to write a short essay that discusses your own history as a writer and tells readers what you normally do to complete a writing task. Assume that you have been given several days to complete this assignment. *Do not write that essay.* Instead, use your own paper to answer the questions below. Use several sentences to answer each question, making your answers as specific and as candid as they can be. It is important, as you begin this book, that you know your own writing habits and attitudes.

1. Would you be eager to begin this assignment? Would you begin working on this writing assignment right away, or would you put it off? Explain why.
2. Describe the step-by-step process you would be most likely to use to complete the assignment. Include any procrastination that you might be prone to. Be as detailed as you can be: What would you do first? second? after that? Include all significant steps. This answer will be the longest of the four you write for this exercise.
3. Are you entirely happy with the process you just described? Would that process enable you to produce your absolutely best work? Would your final reader give your writing the response that you would want? Explain.
4. Would you consider the writing process you described typical of the way you normally work as a writer? Explain why or why not.

EXERCISE 1.2   ANALYZING YOUR OWN WRITING PROCESS

Use Exercise 1.1 to help you analyze your own writing process further. Use your own paper to answer the following questions.

1. Review your answer to the second question from Exercise 1.1. Which parts of your step-by-step process would you classify as planning?
2. Which parts of your process would you consider drafting?
3. Which parts of your process would you consider revising?
4. Of these three stages of the writing process, which is your strongest and which is your weakest? Use several sentences to explain your answers.

EXERCISE 1.3   REVIEWING YOUR WRITING HISTORY

Answer the following questions with full sentences. There are no right or wrong answers here, only incomplete ones. Use your own paper for this exercise.

1. What kinds of writing have you been most frequently asked to do? Have you most frequently written history papers? papers analyzing literary works? memos for a job? personal experience papers? essay exams? Use at least two examples to illustrate your answer.

2. How have your final readers (teachers, employers) usually judged your writing in the past? Do you agree with their judgments? Why or why not?

3. All writers have their strengths and weaknesses. What are your strengths as a writer? Use examples to illustrate your answer.

4. What are your weaknesses as a writer? Use examples to illustrate your answer.

EXERCISE 1.4   TALKING ABOUT AND LISTENING TO YOUR WRITING HISTORY

Find a partner in the class, and ask that partner to tell you a story that has something to do with his or her writing history. It could be a story about elementary school or high school or work, as long as it has something to do with writing. It could be a story with a happy theme, or it could be a horror story. Work with your partner so that you can write his or her true story. Use the discussion under "Remembering the Importance of Talking and Listening" to help you with this process. Take several days if necessary to understand the story and to make sure that your partner agrees that your written version is accurate.

Once you've actually finished writing your partner's story, write a paragraph on your own paper that discusses the whole process. What did you learn in working with your partner?

EXERCISE 1.5   TALKING ABOUT AND LISTENING TO YOUR READING STORY

Read Exercise 1.4, but instead of telling your partner a story based on your writing history, focus on some reading assignment given to you by your instructor. Once you have done this reading, tell your partner the story of your reading. Tell your partner what you understand, what you don't understand, what you find interesting, what you agree with and disagree with, and what new questions or thoughts the reading has given you.

Then switch roles and listen to your partner's reading story.

Your overall task here is, first, to do the assigned reading (taking whatever notes will help you); second, to tell your partner the story of your reading; and third, to listen to, understand, and write up the story of your partner's reading. Accomplishing these steps may easily require you to spend several sessions with your partner.

Finally, once you have finished the three steps above, use your own paper to write a one-page discussion of what this entire process has taught you about reading and writing.

◤ Considering Rhetorical Situations

Analyzing assignments (2b, 2c)

As you know if you have worked through Chapter 1, writing is more than something others read—it is also something writers *do*. Experienced writers know what kinds of activities and writing strategies work for them, and they have learned the importance of beginning early. They begin thinking about writing as soon as the task is assigned. And in doing that thinking, they often begin by considering the **audience** they're writing to (the person or group that they most want to reach) and the **purpose** they have in writing (the goals established by the writing task, the person assigning the task, and the writer).

As a writer, you will have occasion to write for many purposes and to address many audiences—to amuse your friends, to reassure your parents that you are still alive and well, to inform a credit-card company about an error in your bill, to explain a sales campaign to employees, to persuade your local government to lower its assessment of the value of your house, and so on. Here are five questions you can use to help you understand any new writing assignment in terms of its audience and its purpose.

1. Who will read what you write?
2. What do your readers already know or believe?
3. What is it that only you can tell your readers?
4. What judgments or actions do you want your readers to make?
5. What information will effectively convince your readers to make these judgments or take these actions?

Suppose, for example, that your teacher's first assignment asks you to introduce yourself by telling a story about yourself. You can choose to write a story about some big event, or you can choose to write about something that happens virtually every day but that still shows readers something significant about you. Since your teacher plans to ask you to read over your rough draft with others in the class, you're supposed to think of your readers as being your teacher and your classmates. Here is how you might use the questions above to decide whether or not you've chosen a good story.

1. Who will read what you write?

My teacher and classmates will read this.

2. What do your readers already know or believe?

   My readers here really don't know anything about me, except for what I give them to read. They sure don't know anything about the car wreck—where it happened, how it happened, who was in the car.

3. What is it that only you can tell your readers?

   I'm the one who knows this story. Since they don't know any of it, I'm going to have to think about how much background to give. I could start by talking about how the afternoon was so much fun. I need to make sure they know who Treavor and Lea are—how long we've known each other. I'll have to make sure that I answer the readers' questions.

4. What judgments or actions do you want your readers to make?

   First of all, I want my readers to understand how the events went—what happened first, second, and so on. And I want them to understand how I felt that evening, how it seemed that I should have been hurt and not the others (since I was driving). I want them to know how humiliating it was to fail the breath test, and how scared I was about Treavor. So I want my readers to understand, and then I guess I want them to see how this should never have happened.

5. What information will effectively convince your readers to make these judgments or take these actions?

   If I leave out the details, I'm in trouble. Then they'll have to stop reading and try to figure out the part I didn't include. And that means they're not reading the story, not staying inside it. The accident itself and what happened just after it—this is crucial. The woman with her shopping bag, the police officer, how at first I couldn't move, seeing the blood, how quiet it was after the skidding....

RHETORICAL SITUATIONS IN EVERYDAY USE

You can probably remember a time when something you wrote failed to achieve your purpose or, worse yet, backfired on you. Even a fairly routine thank-you note calls for careful thinking about its audience and its purpose—such a note sent to a grandparent in response to a birthday present will differ considerably from a note thanking a prospective employer for an interview or a note expressing gratitude to club members for their help on a group project. Make a list of some thank-you notes you have either sent or received. Then briefly explain how these notes differed according to their purposes and audiences.

As you can see, these five questions can be tremendously useful. As you answer them, you make real progress toward understanding how your audience and your purpose affect what you write.

Determining your stance (2d, 2g)

Although your audience and its needs will be important any time you write, it is also important for you to consider your own opinions, your own understandings, and your own purposes—in short, your own **stance**. You may start with no stance at all, especially if the assigned topic is new to you. In other situations, you might begin with a well-developed stance, especially if you can bring to the topic some personal experience or earlier study. Suppose, for example, that because of tight budgets your school was considering dropping certain sports programs—rugby, swimming, and volleyball. Suppose further that your composition teacher asked you to write a paper arguing either to save such sports programs or to cut them. What's your stance? If you have played on a volleyball team, for example, then your experience—assuming it was positive—might immediately give you a stance: save the volleyball program. Examining your stance even further here will help you understand what you have to say.

However, suppose that you begin the assignment with little or no prior knowledge, little or no opinion. Your task then is to develop a stance. In fact, that becomes one of your central purposes in writing.

Here are five questions to help you analyze your own stance:

1. What knowledge or experience do you already have on this subject?
2. What are your feelings about this topic? strong opinion? curiosity? dislike?
3. What interests you most about this topic? Why?
4. What interests you least about this topic? Why?
5. What do you expect to conclude about this topic?

Here's how a volleyball player in the situation mentioned earlier might use these questions to more fully develop a stance.

1. What knowledge or experience do you already have on this subject?

   Since I've been on volleyball teams for over three years, I bring considerable knowledge to this subject. I know the kind of camaraderie that a team sport can build. My first year here, I was homesick and unsure about college. It was the volleyball team and the support they gave me that made me feel like I could make it. And I know about the kind of personal dedication that sports can foster. Volleyball has taught me a lot about my own potential; I know that hard work can pay off.

2. What are your feelings about this topic? strong opinion? curiosity? dislike?

   Strong opinion. I really feel that I'm right about this topic.

3. What interests you most about this topic? Why?

   Now that I think about it, I guess I'm interested in how much volleyball has given me—things that a fan in the stands would never be able to see. It's so much more than just winning or losing. And I'm also curious about the reasons other people have for dropping these sports. Is their argument only about money? Should it be only about money? This topic is a good one for me because I bring so much of my own interest to it.

4. What interests you least about this topic? Why?

   I guess the budgetary questions interest me the least: How much do these sports cost? How much do they cost compared to big spectator sports like basketball or football? Are there ways to trim the budgets and still keep the programs? I know that budgetary questions are probably important, but my own interest comes from having actually played on one of these teams. I want people to see how important that experience has been (and still is) to me.

5. What do you expect to conclude about this topic?

   I expect to conclude that these sports should be kept, not cut. I'll want to say whatever I can to support that.

Clearly, these answers show a writer with a strong stance. Answering the questions helps clarify it, and answering the questions helps this writer develop a personal interest and motivation; what might have started out as just another writing assignment becomes an activity with some personal interest and passion.

But suppose you start with little or no prior knowledge. Suppose you're asked to write a paper outlining the controversy over the death penalty. While we've all had some exposure to this question via the media, maybe you haven't really studied it, nor do you have any direct experience with it. The assignment seems boring. Again, answering these questions should help you begin to develop a personal stance and the personal interest that goes with it. And if you're starting with virtually no knowledge or initial interest, question 3 becomes crucially important in helping you analyze your stance. Your answer to this question must be something useful, rather than a one-sentence indication that nothing about this topic is interesting. The key here is to take advantage of the chance to explore and learn.

1. What knowledge or experience do you already have on this subject?

   I have no direct experience with this topic, no knowledge beyond what I've heard on television or seen in the papers.

2. What are your feelings about this topic? strong opinion? curiosity? dislike?

   My own feelings at this point are somewhere between dislike and curiosity.

3. What interests you most about this topic? Why?

   I guess I have always thought it was weird that the law could call murder a horrible crime, yet make killing a justified, legal punishment. There's something inconsistent here, isn't there? I remember seeing the daughter of someone who'd been shot. She was interviewed after a jury had sentenced her mother's killer to death, and she was glad! She said it made her mother's death worth more. I'm not sure what she meant. So, what interests me most about this topic? Part of it is the emotion of it all. How can anyone not be emotional about killing someone? And I'm interested in finding out what *I* think. I'm a citizen of this state, and if the state uses the death penalty (notice we don't say *if the state kills someone*), then in some ways do I share responsibility for this?

4. What interests you least about this topic? Why?

   The extremists are least interesting to me. They're sure. And I think they often make complicated issues too simple. Besides, I don't know where I stand on this issue. I want to focus on the reason and the values here, and I have a feeling they're pretty complicated.

5. What do you expect to conclude about this topic?

   I may not conclude anything, and I'm glad now that this assignment is supposed to be an overview. I won't have to advocate a position in the paper. Still, I hope the reading and thinking I do will help me decide what I privately think.

Focusing on your audience (2h)

Almost all the writing we do is read and used by other people. Instructors read what you write and use it to help measure your course performance. Prospective employers will read your job application letters. Once on the job, you may be asked to write a variety of requests, memos, evaluations, and so on. Thinking about your audience will often make your writing task clearer. Remembering your readers' point of view will also help you determine an appropriate tone and even in some cases an effective organization for what you write.

Think about how closely audience and purpose are linked. Suppose, for example, that in an introductory physics course you are asked to write out an explanation for what happens when a baseball is hit for a home run. In this case, you can probably assume your audience has seen a baseball game and knows what's meant by a home run. But can you assume your audience understands specific concepts of physics—things like accelerations and velocity—or should your writing take the time to explain these terms? If you're writing to explain this to your roommate, a history major, then you'd better explain the terms.

Considering your audience becomes especially important whenever you're trying to argue or convince. The first test of a written argument is whether or not readers actually read it. If an argument loses readers after the first paragraph, then it's a failure, despite the shining logic on page 3. Thinking in terms of your audience should help you make useful decisions about your writing.

Here are some questions you can use to help you analyze your audience and make decisions that will help you reach them effectively:

1. Who will read and use your writing? If you can see more than one group of readers, what group should you consider your first (or primary) audience?
2. As they finish reading your writing, what do you want your audience to see or feel or understand or agree to?
3. What is your relationship to your audience? Can you approach your readers as friend to friend? expert to novice? expert to expert? novice to novice?
4. What assumptions do you make about your audience's beliefs and about what they think and value?
5. What assumptions will your audience make about your topic or about you as a writer on this topic? Are these useful assumptions? If so, how can you take advantage of them? If they are problematic assumptions, how can you neutralize them?

As you consider these questions, see if you can arrive at a tentative decision about your writing. For example, suppose that as a student in a community college you want to convince voters in your community college district to support the latest tax levy so that your college can stay open. You know the budget doesn't allow for any expansion—only for maintaining current quality. Here's how the questions just listed might help you write a persuasive letter to the local paper.

1. Who will read and use your writing? If you can see more than one group of readers, what group should you consider your first (or primary) audience?

   Although my instructor will read this and grade it, I should think of local newspaper readers as my primary audience here.

   Decision: Write to local newspaper readers.

2. As they finish reading your writing, what do you want your audience to see or feel or understand or agree to?

   I want readers to decide to vote yes on the tax levy.

3. What is your relationship to your audience? Can you approach your readers as friend to friend? expert to novice? expert to expert? novice to novice?

   I live in the same community, so I can approach readers as a neighbor. But I also go to the community college, so I have some inside information. And I'm a taxpayer, too, so I can talk to readers as one taxpayer to another.

Decision: The taxpayer-to-taxpayer relationship is the one to make use of here. That relationship stresses the connection I have with readers. I can bring in the student–taxpayer relationship after the taxpayer–taxpayer relationship is established.

4. What assumptions do you make about your audience's beliefs and about what they think and value?

I assume people don't want to pay more taxes. I also assume that they believe education is important. I assume that my readers don't want me to just tell them how wrong they are.

Decision: Maybe begin by agreeing that taxes are high, that it would be easy to just vote no without really looking at what the tax money supports.

5. What assumptions will your audience make about your topic or about you as a writer on this topic? Are these useful assumptions? If so, how can you take advantage of them? If they are problematic assumptions, how can you neutralize them?

Since I want to increase the votes for the tax levy, I want to talk particularly to those readers who would be inclined to vote the other way. I suppose some of them are tired of hearing about any tax levy. Once they find out I'm a student at the community college, they might dismiss what I say. They might also think the community college is doing too much already and that some parts of the curriculum could be cut.

Decision: Maybe begin with something that diverts attention away from the tax issue itself. Whatever opening I use shouldn't sound dull; it should hook people into reading. And the editorial needs to talk about why the college offers such a diversity of programs.

EXERCISE 2.1 ANALYZING AN ASSIGNMENT

NAME _____ **DATE** _____

Suppose your composition teacher gives you the assignment below. Read the assignment carefully, then use the five questions provided to help you analyze it.

> Pick a consumer product or service that you frequently use. Identify the product or service, and tell your readers why it is important to you. For this assignment, assume that you are writing to the other members of the class.

1. Who will read what you write?

   _____

2. What do your readers already know or believe?

   _____

   _____

   _____

3. What is it that only you can tell your readers?

   _____

   _____

   _____

4. What judgments or actions do you want your readers to make?

   _____

   _____

   _____

5. What information will effectively convince your readers to make these judgments or take these actions?

   _____

   _____

   _____

EXERCISE 2.2 DETERMINING YOUR STANCE

NAME _____ **DATE** _____

Use the given questions to help you analyze your stance for each of the two writing assignments.

ASSIGNMENT 1

Identify some out-of-school activity that you enjoy—some hobby or sport or other activity. Talk about this activity, and show your readers why you find this activity enjoyable or rewarding. Ultimately, your paper should encourage readers to give your activity a try. Your audience is other college students who are unfamiliar with your topic.

1. What knowledge or experience do you already have on this subject?

   _____
   _____

2. What are your feelings about this topic? strong opinion? curiosity? dislike?

   _____
   _____

3. What interests you most about this topic? Why?

   _____
   _____

4. What interests you least about this topic? Why?

   _____
   _____

5. What do you expect to conclude about this topic?

   _____
   _____

ASSIGNMENT 2

Now try a bigger, less well defined topic: violence in America. Write a paper that gives your sense of how violence (or the fear of violence) affects your life. Your audience here is very wide. Assume you're writing a feature piece for a local magazine or newspaper.

1. What knowledge or experience do you already have on this subject?

   _____

   _____

   _____

2. What are your feelings about this topic? strong opinion? curiosity? dislike?

   _____

   _____

   _____

3. What interests you most about this topic? Why?

   _____

   _____

4. What interests you least about this topic? Why?

   _____

   _____

5. What do you expect to conclude about this topic?

   _____

   _____

EXERCISE 2.3   FOCUSING ON YOUR AUDIENCE

NAME _____ **DATE** _____

Use the following questions to help you analyze your audience for the writing assignment below. Note that you should make some decisions based on questions 1, 3, 4, and 5.

> Your school (or your place of work, if you wish) has continued to have trouble articulating a policy on sexual harassment. The policy makers say it has to define sexual harassment, offer consideration and protection both to those who feel they've been sexually harassed and to those who have been accused, and set up a workable set of procedures. You have been asked to write a three-page "As I See It" paper, explaining what you think policy makers need to understand in order to arrive at the best policy.

1. Who will read and use your writing? If you can see more than one group of readers, what group should you consider your first (or primary) audience?

   _____

   _____

   Decision: _____

   _____

2. As they finish reading your writing, what do you want your audience to see or feel or understand or agree to?

   _____

   _____

   _____

3. What is your relationship to your audience? Can you approach your readers as friend to friend? expert to novice? expert to expert? novice to novice?

   _____

   _____

   Decision: _____

   _____

4. What assumptions do you make about your audience's beliefs and about what they think and value?

Decision: _____

5. What assumptions will your audience make about your topic or about you as a writer on this topic? Are these useful assumptions? If so, how can you take advantage of them? If they are problematic assumptions, how can you neutralize them?

Decision: _____

Exploring, Planning, and Drafting   3

Exploring a topic (3a)

Analyzing your assignment, your stance, and your audience are crucial steps toward a rough draft. But after such an analysis, you may not be sure what to do next. Should you go directly to a rough draft? Should you go to the library to look up every single bit of information on your topic? Should you try to talk to your teacher or a classmate to find out what others are doing? Or should you just hope you'll get some ideas by the time your paper is due?

Faced with such questions, experienced writers frequently use some sort of strategy to explore this new, perhaps strange, topic systematically. Four such modes of exploration will be discussed here: brainstorming, freewriting, looping, and questioning. Each of these methods will help you explore a topic, as well as help you determine your interest in and level of knowledge about the topic.

EXPLORING, PLANNING, AND DRAFTING IN EVERYDAY USE

If you have ever written a love letter, you probably know all about exploring a topic and working hard on a draft. You might have spent days, even weeks, exploring the ideas you wanted to convey and considering the effects your language might have. And you may have drafted, torn up the draft, and then drafted some more, searching for just the right words to express something deeply felt but difficult to put down on paper.

Thank goodness few writing tasks are as demanding as a love letter, but most of the writing you do will call on you to give some serious thought to what you want to say and how you want to say it. Make a list of some other occasions outside of school when you thought long and hard about something you needed to write—a letter to a friend asking for a special favor, a personal statement to accompany a job application, and so on. Then, for one of these occasions, briefly explain how you went about exploring your topic and planning what to say.

Brainstorming

To **brainstorm**, simply make a list of words or phrases that seem connected to your topic. The idea here is to push yourself to focus on the topic without judging your results. Work fast, and do not censor yourself. At the top of a notebook page, jot down your topic; then note under it anything that comes to mind. Figure 1 shows what a brief brainstorming session might produce after some reading or class discussion of the Industrial Revolution.

Brainstorming works best when writers already have some knowledge of their topic. It is even more effective in a group. Even two people brainstorming together will normally produce much more material than an individual. And talking with others, tossing out ideas, is a way to hear what you already know and what you need to find out more about.

>Industrial Revolution
>new machines to speed up production
>all kinds of products → like what? textiles - weaving
>   mass productions - clothes, household goods
>"Sweatshops" working conditions - long hours
>safety - child labor
>
>Shift from country to city
>less reliance on agriculture / weather / forces of nature / God
>more dependence on mill owners, market forces
>- lives out of control?
>standardized products, not unique hand-made ones
>
>Pollution rich get richer / poor get poorer
>   less self-sufficiency
>transportation vastly improved

Figure 1 Brainstorming

Freewriting and looping

Like brainstorming, **freewriting** asks writers to suspend judgment, banish hesitation, and simply think on paper. Instead of making notes, freewriting involves writing sentences, or something approximating sentences. What do you write? You write whatever comes into your head after you have thought for a minute. The key to freewriting is to keep right on going, even if all you are writing is, "I don't know what to say now." If you have written "I don't know what to say now" two or three times and you really seem stuck, go back to the last substantive sentence and recopy it. But keep writing. How long should you keep going? Plan on no more than ten minutes. Set a timer if you like. Write nonstop for ten minutes, and if there is more to say, keep right on saying it.

Here is a freewrite on "one aspect of the Industrial Revolution."

I'm supposed to write on one aspect of the Industrial Revolution. That's a big one. There's what happened to technology—all those machines doing things that people used to do. Tremendous efficiency in comparison with the old ways. I need some examples here. But what's the price? the consequences of all this? Were people better off? happier? Some probably were, some not. So which ones were happier and which ones were not? Fine, all I'm coming up with are questions. And now I'm running out of things to say about the Industrial Revolution. Except that word revolution revolution revolution revolution—something→connected to other revolutions. These are big changes we're talking about here—generation gaps. TVs with 2-inch screens, and my grandparents didn't know tv at all as kids. Not to mention space travel.

Not everything this student has written would go directly into her European History paper; the instructor is probably not interested in reading about space travel. But that's fine—nobody grades your freewriting. It's intended to help you get started. When this student looked back over what she had written, she found herself most interested in going back to a question she had posed, then dropped, in the middle of freewriting: Who was better off, and who suffered, as a consequence of the Industrial Revolution? She had found a way into her topic and a starting point for exploration.

Freewriting can be effective as you begin a writing task, and it can be equally effective later on as you explore a subtopic. Since freewriting is easy, you can try it on several possible topics as a way of helping to settle on one.

Writers can also see freewriting repeatedly in a method that the writer and educator Peter Elbow calls "**looping**." Say you have written a freewrite that looks something like the one just shown. Choose a sentence in it that for some reason appeals to you—for instance, "So which ones were happier and which ones were not?" These words now become the starting point for your second freewrite, with your goal being to explore further the ideas contained in that sentence.

Questioning

One of the oldest ways to explore a topic is to ask questions about it systematically. You can pose and answer questions entirely on your own, or you can use any of the sets of questions in this section as a basis for group discussion.

The ancient Greek philosopher Aristotle first proposed these four questions as a way to generate information:

1. What is it? (definition or description)
2. What caused it? (cause and effect)
3. What is it like or unlike? (comparison/contrast)
4. What do others say about it? (testimony)

The journalistic questions *who, what, when, where, why,* and *how* are also widely used and are particularly helpful if your overall purpose is to explain.

Finally, the modern philosopher Stephen Toulmin designed a way to help writers analyze their thinking when their aim is to persuade. Toulmin's analytic model is shown here in modified form as a series of brief questions.

1. What is the *claim* I am making?
2. What are the *grounds* or *good reasons* that support my claim?

3. What *underlying assumptions* support the grounds of my claim?
4. What *backup evidence* do I have or can I find to add further support?
5. What *refutations* can be made against my claim?
6. In what ways is or should my claim be *qualified*?

Note that these question sets may require that you perform research to answer them thoroughly. Such research may be useful and necessary, but there is no point in conducting research until you have some idea of how you will use the information you gather. At an early stage in the writing process, you may not need to answer any of these questions completely. Their value lies in their ability to focus your thinking so that you can begin to determine what you know and what you need to find out.

Establishing a working thesis (3b)

As writers explore a topic, their major goal is to develop a working thesis to guide them as they begin to draft. A **thesis** is a one-sentence statement that presents an essay's main point and suggests the writer's purpose for that essay. A **working thesis** is tentative and subject to change or refinement. Your working thesis evolves as you explore your topic and ultimately becomes your final thesis. Although a working thesis is likely to change, establishing one early makes the drafting process smoother.

A good working thesis has two parts: a topic portion and a comment portion. The **topic** portion states the subject, and the **comment** portion makes an important point about that subject.

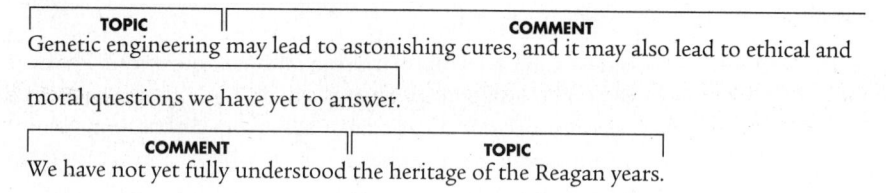

| TOPIC | COMMENT |

Genetic engineering may lead to astonishing cures, and it may also lead to ethical and moral questions we have yet to answer.

| COMMENT | TOPIC |

We have not yet fully understood the heritage of the Reagan years.

Note that both of these examples aren't yet well focused. What are the astonishing cures? What are the ethical questions? How many of each will be discussed? And what exactly is the heritage of the Reagan years? Is this paper going to talk about changes in the tax code? Will it discuss President Reagan's vision of America as defined by his speeches and campaign commercials? In short, a working thesis gives you a place to start. Once you have written a working thesis, you can begin looking at what it promises that your paper will do. As you think about your thesis, you will almost certainly change it somewhat. Remember, the point of a working thesis is to get you working.

FIRST VERSION   My friend Rosa is an important friend I have known for years.

- *Interest.* Certainly this must be interesting to the writer, someone who has known Rosa for a long time and presumably shared many experiences with her.

Readers might not yet find this interesting. Readers (strangers, after all) do not know Rosa and may not know the writer. So this working thesis seems to leave readers out of the picture.

- *Specificity and clarity.* The topic focus on Rosa is clear. The comment section, however, is very vague. Why is Rosa important? Is it just that the writer has known her for years? The writer needs to answer this question and then rephrase the working thesis to make it more specific.
- *Manageability.* Right now it is difficult to judge the manageability of this working thesis. If the writer plans to discuss the entire friendship with Rosa, the topic is probably too large.
- *Conclusions.* This working thesis needs revising, particularly so that the comment part is more specific. That specificity should help make the working thesis more interesting to readers and should also limit the topic so that it can be reasonably handled by the writer.

REVISED WORKING THESIS   I learned what friendship is from Rosa, particularly in the two weeks I roomed with her after my apartment was burglarized.
[TOPIC] [TOPIC]

Notice that now the topic has shifted to "what friendship is," a topic with much broader interest. Notice, too, that the comment part has been focused much more specifically. The writer of this working thesis has moved to a much clearer and more carefully defined plan. This revised working thesis tells the writer what to write about: the burglary, those two weeks with Rosa, and what those two weeks taught the writer about friendship.

Gathering information (3c)

Once you have carefully considered your audience, explored your topic, and established a working thesis, ask yourself whether or not you already have enough information to begin writing a draft. Your working thesis can be a guide here. If it is tightly focused and specific, it may mean that you already have enough information to feel comfortable drafting. However, if your own sense of your topic is still vague or somewhat confused, then you probably need to gather additional information.

Begin your information-gathering process by listing the questions that you need to answer. Let's say you've been assigned to write a report on a job or career that interests you (your audience being other college students), and you've decided to write on photography. You have a topic; you may have a vague, still-unfocused working thesis such as "photography can be an interesting and profitable career." Here are some questions you might still need to answer.

- What exactly do I mean by "interesting"?
- What career options are open to photographers? Do I want to talk about all of those options?

- How much do photographers make?
- What kind of hours do they keep?
- What do they think is the best part of their job?

Listing questions like these helps you decide what information you're looking for, and it should help you figure out where to look.

One option is to consult written sources. In many academic writing situations, the textbooks you already have will provide the information you need in order to begin drafting. If you need additional information, consult your school or community library. (If you use written sources, you *must* document your research by citing your sources. Ask your instructor for information on documenting sources.)

Information can also be obtained through interviews, field observation, and surveys. If, for example, you want to know what photographers think of their job, one obvious thing to do would be to interview some local photographers.

Don't forget the important role that your audience plays in deciding what information you need. If your audience is other college students, they won't understand (or have the patience for) a chemically precise description of how color prints are made. As someone interested in photography, you may find this fascinating, but you will probably have to stay away from that sort of highly technical discussion with this audience.

Organizing information (3d)

When writers actually start drafting depends on their own inclinations. Some writers won't begin drafting until they have written an outline; they use the outlining process to help them decide on their organization. Other writers just begin drafting; they use the drafting and revising process itself to help them understand and organize what they are writing about.

Whatever your inclinations, you should be aware of some common organizational patterns. Recognizing these patterns in the information you gather will often help you organize your essay.

The simplest organizational pattern is based on time: first this, then this, then this. Whenever you have to tell a story, you're using this organizational pattern. Sometimes this **chronological** pattern can be used for an entire piece of writing—an account of your auto accident for your insurance company, for instance. Sometimes chronological organization will be part of a larger structure.

Several common essay forms are based on logical relationships. The **cause-effect** pattern can work in either of two ways: by trying to explain why something happened (thus working from effect back to cause) or by trying to forecast something that is likely to happen (thus working from current causes to possible effects). A newspaper article that tries to explain a politician's defeat may begin by acknowledging an effect (the defeat), then discuss its probable causes. A business report analyzing a proposed price change would discuss the price change (the cause) and its probable effect on sales.

The **problem-solution** pattern identifies and describes a problem, explores possible solutions, and typically ends by recommending one solution as preferable. Such a pattern would be appropriate, for example, in a paper urging commuters to solve their parking problems by taking the bus.

An essay employing **illustration** provides concrete examples to support the essay's main idea. If your essay's purpose is to describe the promising future awaiting liberal arts graduates, you might well begin by proposing that thesis and then using examples to illustrate it.

Closely related to the illustration essay is the **definition** essay, which describes what something is and, often, what it is not. For example, an essay that sets out to define the character of people raised in the Midwest would essentially be a definition essay. This same topic could also be organized as a **comparison/contrast** essay. By its nature, a comparison/contrast essay focuses on two main topics or subjects, examining their similarities and their differences. Thus a writer might contrast midwestern cultural values with southern cultural values.

Writers can organize comparison/contrast essays in two ways. Using **block comparison**, an essay would speak about one topic (one block), then discuss the second topic in light of the first (the second block). Here is an organizational sketch for a paper comparing and contrasting American factory working conditions in 1898 with those in 1998:

A. Introduction
B. Block 1: Working conditions in 1998 (hours, pay, safety)
C. Transition
D. Block 2: Working conditions in 1898 (hours, pay, safety)
E. Conclusion

The other possibility is to organize according to major points, comparing each point separately and then moving on to the next. This is called **alternating comparison**:

A. Introduction
B. Working hours in 1998 vs. working hours in 1898
C. Brief transition
D. Pay scales in 1998 vs. pay scales in 1898
E. Brief transition
F. Workers' safety in 1998 vs. workers' safety in 1898
G. Conclusion

Two other logical relationships can also form the basis for essay organization: **division** and **classification**. An essay based on division begins by examining an idea in its entirety, then proceeds to identify and discuss parts of it. Suppose you are asked to write an essay that describes "the good teacher." You might identify and discuss the components that you believe go into a good teacher—knowledge of subject, enthusiasm, respect for students, and so on. You might then follow this discussion with your explanation of how these various traits are related to one another.

To classify means to group according to categories. You might choose to describe your particular college courses this term by classifying them as science/math or liberal arts.

Writers often use some combination of several of these organizational strategies. Considering this question of organization before beginning a rough draft should give you a sense of direction, control, and confidence as you begin drafting.

Producing a draft (3f)

At some point, your thinking, information gathering, and planning must lead you to writing sentences and paragraphs that will eventually add up to a rough draft of your essay. Where should you begin? You could begin with the introduction if you know what it should say. But if beginning with the introduction seems difficult (as is often the case), start drafting some middle part of the paper—some part you know well. But do begin. (For more on writing introductions, see Chapter 4.)

What, in general, can be said about the drafting process?

- *Drafting demands flexibility.* As you write, you are thinking—concentrating with more intensity and interest than earlier. As a result, you will probably find it necessary to revise your plan as you go along. This should not surprise you or dismay you; in fact, you should expect that as you draft you will probably not follow your own plan to the letter.

- *Drafting demands paying attention to your content and to your process.* What should you do if you realize as you draft that you lack certain information or that you are not making use of information that you spent hours gathering? All writers encounter such situations at one time or another. They are normal and must be accepted. Sometimes that means continuing to draft but writing a note to yourself that you have skipped over a key point and will have to come back to it later; or it might mean that you will simply omit some information to provide a tighter, more manageable focus for your paper. Such adjustments should not be cause for panic or frustration.

- *Drafting demands time.* No matter how much planning you have done or how much information you have gathered, chances are that your drafting will proceed fitfully and will require more than one sitting. If your drafting goes forward without a hitch, consider yourself lucky. The advice here is to anticipate that your drafting will take longer than you want it to, so be sure to avoid last-minute, hurried drafting if you wish to rise above mediocrity. Also realize that juggling other concerns and responsibilities is part of the writer's lot. Even full-time writers cannot entirely escape the sometimes chaotic reality of their daily lives.

Perhaps the most important advice about drafting is this: generate a train of thought and stay with it. Do not stop to look up words in the dictionary (circle them and come back to them later). Do not stop to ponder paragraph breaks or the rules regarding quotation marks. Write in bursts of at least ten minutes—longer, if the words are coming easily. If you have access to a computer, consider drafting at the keyboard.

If you cannot finish a draft in one sitting, stop at a point where you know what you will say next. Suggest that information with a couple of phrases jotted on the page. You will be grateful for those notes to yourself when you next look at the draft.

What if you get absolutely stumped and can see no way to proceed? Do not panic. Reread what you have written, looking for wrong turns or imprecise expressions in the last page or so of your writing. If you are still stumped, set the draft aside and do something entirely different, something that will allow you to forget the writing task altogether. Jog. Do laundry. If your deadline allows you to stay away from the writing overnight, do so. A brief time away will often give you a new perspective and enable you to resume drafting. One more possibility is to skip the section that is giving you trouble. This may be possible if you know what you want to say further on. By the time you have written the rest of the paper, you will probably have figured out how to address the problem portion of the draft.

All of these tactics you can try by yourself, but perhaps the best remedies involve other people. Talk to someone about your writing. If your campus has a writing center, talk to one of the writing assistants. Talk to your instructor. Talking about a draft helps you see that draft more objectively, and that new outlook may be all you need to continue drafting.

EXERCISE 3.1 EXPLORING A TOPIC

NAME _____ **DATE** _____

Read the assignment below, and then use the specified strategies to help you explore the assigned topic.

> Write a personal essay about some aspect of prejudice—age, race, religious upbringing or affiliation, sex, physical appearance, sexual orientation, life-style choices—any sort of prejudice. In your essay, you should answer this question: How have you personally experienced prejudice? Since this is such a wide-open topic, begin by finishing the sentence below and then freewriting for at least five minutes.

When I think of experiencing prejudice, the first thing that comes to mind is

_____

_____

_____

_____

_____

_____

_____

_____

_____

_____

_____

_____

_____

_____

Now use the journalistic questions below to help you continue exploring the question, "How have you personally experienced prejudice?"

1. Who was involved?

2. What happened?

3. When did it happen?

4. Where did it happen?

5. Why did it happen?

6. How did it happen?

Based on your initial freewrite and your answers to the journalistic questions, explain to a partner (or small group) what you think you will write about in your personal essay about prejudice. Listen to your partner's (or your group's) questions, and make notes about whatever you think you need to add or make clearer. Then switch roles and be the listener. Listen to what your classmate might write about, and try to help that classmate make his or her story clearer and more complete. Once this discussion process is finished, write a paragraph explaining how it was useful to you to freewrite, to use journalistic questions, and to discuss your topic with others.

EXERCISE 3.2 ESTABLISHING A WORKING THESIS

NAME _____ **DATE** _____

A. For each of the five working theses below, underline the topic part of the thesis, and circle the comment part. Remember, the topic portion answers the question "what is this about?" and the comment portion makes a claim or description or other important point about the topic.

EXAMPLE   For a report to appear in a general-interest magazine: <u>Drift-net fishing</u> is (an efficient method but an environmentally disastrous international problem.)

1. For a paper aimed at other new students: The first week of college is filled with unexpected challenges.

2. For a campus newspaper: Volunteering is a rewarding way to share campus resources with the larger community.

3. For a paper in your international politics class: The unintended consequences of international decision-making processes may be far-reaching, as a recent law-of-the-sea negotiation illustrates.

4. For a brochure issued by an environmental organization: The Amazon rain forest constitutes one of the most ecologically diverse habitats in the world.

5. For an opinion piece in a film class: Although the special effects hold our eyes, it is the contest between good and evil that truly holds our interest in the *Star Wars* movies.

B. For each of the topic areas below, write out a possible working thesis. Underline the topic part, and circle the comment part.

    EXAMPLE TOPIC AREA   Pollution in your area (for a feature article in the local newspaper).

    EXAMPLE WORKING THESIS   <u>Cleaning up after the bankrupt United Chrome Company</u> (continues to be a time-consuming and expensive process.)

1. Topic area: Local or campus issues (to be written for your local or campus newspaper).

   Working thesis: _____

   _____

2. Topic area: The importance of work experience (to be written for students entering college).

   Working thesis: _____

   _____

3. Topic area: Choosing a college (to be written for high school seniors).

   Working thesis: _____

   _____

4. Topic area: Childhood experiences (to be written for other college students).

   Working thesis: _____

   _____

5. Topic area: A popular television or radio program (to be written for critics of the program).

   Working thesis: _____

   _____

C. Use the questions below to help you test your working thesis for any one of the topic areas in part B. Then revise your working thesis accordingly.

1. *Interest.* Why are you interested in this topic? Does your thesis statement make this interest clear to readers?

   _____

   _____

   _____

   _____

2. *Specificity and clarity.* Is the topic focus clear and specific, or is it so vague that readers will have to guess at it? Is the comment section clear, or will it leave readers guessing?

   _____

   _____

   _____

   _____

3. *Manageability.* Can this topic and comment be handled in five pages, or will it require a more lengthy report? If the topic and comment seem to require more than five pages, how can the topic and comment be made more manageable?

   _____

   _____

   _____

   _____

   Your revised working thesis:

   _____

   _____

   _____

EXERCISE 3.3 ORGANIZING AND PLANNING A DRAFT

NAME _____ **DATE** _____

Respond to the questions below to help you see your own methods for planning and drafting.

1. This chapter identified four methods for exploring a topic: brainstorming, freewriting, looping, and questioning. Of these four, which one seems most useful to you? Why?

   _____

   _____

   _____

2. Suppose that in your American studies class, Women and Men, you are assigned a paper that asks you to contrast your generation's attitudes about sex roles and expectations with the attitudes held by students your age in 1905. What two techniques from this chapter would you use in drafting a working thesis? Be specific.

   First technique: _____

   _____

   _____

   Second technique: _____

   _____

   _____

3. Suppose that for the American studies assignment above, you've been asked to bring your working thesis to class. Your instructor has collected the assignments and redistributed them, and the thesis you have in front of you reads this way: "If we could transport ourselves back to a college classroom in 1905, some of our fellow students' attitudes would seem very foreign to us." Would you encourage the writer of this working thesis to begin drafting, or would you encourage this writer to refine the working thesis? Explain your recommendation in a helpful way.

   _____

   _____

   _____

Revising and Editing

Revision strategies (4a, 4b, 4c, 4d, 4e)

We revise and edit all the time—even in our conversations. Directions to a child on how to measure the ingredients for cupcakes may have to be revised on the spot if the child isn't understanding. A story told to friends may be revised in the telling to get the sequence of events right. Like speakers, writers are likely to find that their first efforts are often sketchy or wandering or incomplete, which is hardly a surprise since they are first efforts. Good writers don't confuse first drafts with final copy; they know those first drafts will need reworking. For experienced writers, **revising** may include rethinking the thesis, assessing the draft's logic and organization, adding or changing material, gathering more information to develop or support a point, or reshaping sentences. Typically, writers revise for two main reasons. Revision helps them understand what they really think, what they really want to say. And revision helps writers make their prose communicate clearly to readers.

Revising often goes hand in hand with drafting. In fact, every time you reread what you've written (which you probably do often as you draft), you are using one of the most important revision strategies.

REVISING AND EDITING IN EVERYDAY USE

You may well remember a time when you consciously edited what you were saying in order to be tactful or considerate of someone's feelings. For example, a woman seeing a new baby for the first time was stuck for what to say, for the baby struck her as anything but cute. Revising and editing rapidly in her head, she stumbled on what she hoped was a tactful as well as an honest response. "What a baby!" she exclaimed. "What a baby!"

For a portion of a day, listen carefully for revising and editing in conversations you hear or take part in. Then analyze what kinds of revisions you heard and what seemed most interesting about them. Summarize your analysis of each conversation in a sentence or two.

Revision strategy 1: Reread to see what you've said

As you reread, pay attention to your thoughts, and don't worry about small errors in punctuation or spelling (you should fix them, but later in the process). As you reread, do so with a reason in mind. You might have the nagging sense that your draft has veered off somewhere; reread to see if you can find the wrong turn. Or you might have a sense that even though your draft is only two pages long, it has said everything it should; however, your teacher has asked for five pages. In that case, reread to look at your examples or illustrations to decide whether or not they really tell readers all that those readers will need. Remember that rereading should lead you toward revising—adding or changing—what you already have. Here are some questions to keep in mind as you reread.

1. What does the opening paragraph promise that the rest of the paper will discuss? Is this promise clear and focused? How can this opening be sharpened or clarified?
2. Can you tell what the assignment is just by reading the draft? Can you identify the intended audience for this assignment? If not, what should be added or rephrased?
3. As the draft moves from point to point, can you understand its logic? If the paper seems to jump around, where are the jumps? Where do you get lost? What needs to be added or rearranged?
4. What conclusion is the draft working toward? What makes this conclusion clear to you? What doesn't?
5. How will your readers react to this draft? Will they find enough explanation? Will they draw the conclusions you want them to draw?
6. What is the best, clearest, most compelling part of the draft now?

Revision strategy 2: Ask objective readers to mirror, question, and discuss your content

Whenever you write, your first reader is yourself. But virtually all your college and work-related writing will be read and acted on by others. Thus, asking for objective response to a draft is a tremendously powerful revision strategy. Outside readers will only have what is on the page to read and understand. They are often able to spot incomplete explanations or missing transitions.

Before you ask for a response, identify some questions to help guide your reader. Saying "Will you read this and tell me what you think?" will probably give you a response such as "This is good" or "I like most of it." Hearing those things might make you feel good, but those responses don't help much when it comes to revising. As you work on your own draft, you will naturally feel more confident about some parts, more uneasy about others. Ask readers to help you with the problem areas. For example, you could say something like "This part on the top of page 2 has been giving me trouble; what does it say to you?" You may have a number of such questions. And the questions listed earlier, under strategy 1, will also work here to help outside readers give you specific feedback.

Above all, get your outside readers to talk about your draft. Ask them to explain the paper's purpose. Ask them to identify its major points. Ask them what has been left out. Their answers will help you see your own draft and hear its strengths and weaknesses in someone else's words.

Revision strategy 3: Make a revision plan

Sometimes it is easy to feel lost in the writing process, especially if you are writing about new material or writing with a new purpose (say, your first scholarship application). When this sense of being lost hits, stop and review what you've done. Take out a sheet of scratch paper, and begin by briefly writing out your assignment: What are you writing? Why are you writing it? Who will read it? Underneath that, list the things you've already done to make progress. What parts have you drafted so far? What questions have you researched, and what sources have you consulted? As you read your draft, what questions are you yourself sure of? Which ones are you still unsure about? What answers do you need to find? You might, for instance, realize that you need to reread something or that you need to locate some new answers.

Once you've begun to take stock in this way, identify what specifically you will do next. Will you reread something before you try to do more drafting? Will you skip to another section and work on it for now? Will you head to the library to look for some specific answers? Will you ask an objective reader for some input and response? What can you do next to make progress?

Revision strategy 4: Chart the organization of your draft

Sometimes with short writing assignments, and especially with longer ones, writers have trouble keeping track of their logic and organization. The simple solution here is to use some method to make that logic clear to yourself. Outlining is one way to accomplish this, for by outlining your draft you will see how it is put together. Alternatively, you might try numbering each paragraph of your draft and then writing a sentence or phrase summarizing each one. Write the summaries consecutively on a piece of scratch paper. Once they are written, you should be able to see whether you need to rearrange some sections, cut some sections, or add new ones.

Revision strategy 5: Give yourself time

If you have worked hard drafting, you will eventually get tired and lose your concentration. At this point, your best revision strategy is to take a break. If you have the luxury of stepping back for several hours or a whole day, you might find that when you return, the draft—which seemed jumbled and hopeless before—now announces its flaws so that you can see how to deal with them. This strategy can be helpful even if you have only a few minutes or an hour for a break. Take a walk, do some laundry, jog—anything that's not too demanding but that will take you away from the desk for a little while. When you come back, you should come back fresh and ready to apply one of the other strategies.

here, but the list that follows identifies each error and the chapter that will help you with it. (Note that *not* included in the top twenty is by far the most common error made by student writers by a factor of three to one: misspelling. If you have trouble in this area, study the spelling tips provided in Chapter 24.)

1. Missing comma after an introductory element (see Chapter 30)
2. Vague pronoun reference (see Chapter 13)
3. Missing comma in a compound sentence (see Chapter 30)
4. Wrong word (see Chapters 25–27)
5. Missing commas with a nonrestrictive element (see Chapter 30)
6. Wrong or missing verb ending (see Chapter 9)
7. Wrong or missing preposition (see Chapter 7)
8. Comma splice (see Chapter 15)
9. Missing or misplaced possessive apostrophe (see Chapter 33)
10. Unnecessary shift in tense (see Chapter 14)
11. Unnecessary shift in pronoun (see Chapter 14)
12. Sentence fragment (see Chapter 16)
13. Wrong tense or verb form (see Chapter 9)
14. Lack of agreement between subject and verb (see Chapter 10)
15. Missing comma in a series (see Chapter 30)
16. Lack of agreement between pronoun and antecedent (see Chapter 11)
17. Unnecessary commas with a restrictive element (see Chapter 30)
18. Fused sentence (see Chapter 15)
19. Misplaced or dangling modifier (see Chapter 17)
20. *Its/it's* confusion (see Chapter 33)

Since so many students fall into these twenty error patterns, chances are that several of them may end up on your personal editing checklist. You could *begin* your checklist by looking through your writing for some of the twenty errors just listed. After all, one of the hardest things about correcting your own writing is knowing what mistakes to look for. This list can give you some ideas, but bear in mind that learning what mistakes you routinely make will take time. You will probably keep adding items to your checklist long after you finish using this book. As you do, you will be actively making yourself a stronger, more accomplished writer.

Consider your final format (4h)

Once editing has been completed and you are ready to retype or print out your final version, take some time to consider the way you want your writing to look on the page. For example, if your paper is longer than two or three pages, you might consider whether or not to use subheadings to guide your readers, showing them where your writing shifts to a new area. Thus a paper reporting on the history of the Sierra Club might begin with a subheading called "Origins," followed by "The Sierra Club to 1970," followed by "From 1970 to the Present."

REVISING AND EDITING

In addition, this is your last chance to consider whether or not you want to add any charts or illustrations. If you are working with a word processor or if you have a graphics program, you can consider using different fonts or other visual cues to change the appearance of your draft and help guide the reader.

Proofread the final draft (4j)

As a writer, you need to **proofread** to make your final draft as correct as you can make it. That means one final rereading even after you think you have caught every single error. Read aloud slowly. Check for punctuation marks, letters left out or transposed, and any other typographical errors. If you have been doing your drafting and revising on a computer, you should be able to produce an absolutely clean and error-free copy. However, if you catch any last-minute errors to correct after your final draft has been printed out, don't be shy about doing so right on the paper you're about to turn in. Your instructor would rather see you correcting your own errors than receive a totally uncluttered typescript full of uncorrected errors.

EXERCISE 4.1   ACTING AS A READER

Reproduced below you will find the first draft (written in class) of what is supposed to become a two-page essay that discusses the writer's first week in school. Read the draft, and then, using your own paper, write out your responses to the writer's questions below.

    I don't know what to say about this first week. It's been a struggle. Registration wasn't too hard—I'd expected some foul-ups. Buying my books just took a long time, standing in line to get into the bookstore and standing in line again to check out. Not much different from going to the grocery store the day before Thanksgiving. The big problem is that after all this time away from school I'm worried that I won't be able to handle it. I'm used to being busy, between working and taking care of Aaron and the kids, but I haven't had to do much deep thinking. At least I'm still used to reading—even if it's just been email at work and novels or magazines at night.

    Humanities looks OK, but the reading list is long. The books cost a lot, too, and two aren't in yet. The class starts with the Greeks, so I'll soon see if I can remember anything about mythology. My computer class sounds tough, but I'm used to debugging and solving software problems. The big difference is that I'm not used to writing much about it—just talking to my supervisor. And my writing class—well, I haven't written anything long in a long time—just grocery lists, letters, and memos. It all seems overwhelming, but I'm determined. This is something I've wanted to do for two years now. And getting through this first week means I've started. I'm nervous about it, but at least I've made a start.

WRITER'S QUESTIONS

1. This seems wandering and too informal to me, but I don't know what else to do. Can you suggest some ways to organize what I want to say?

2. I know I'm not including all that you need to know about me and about my first week back. What have I left out?

3. Is there anything good about this draft?

EXERCISE 4.2 UNDERSTANDING DRAFTING AND REVISING

Think about this chapter and about your own drafting and revising habits as you answer these questions on your own paper.

1. What kind of writing have you done most frequently in the past?

2. How would you describe the drafting and revising process for this writing? Was this kind of writing always a straight-line, clear process? What made it easy? What made it difficult?

3. Of the five revision strategies discussed in this chapter, which one is most effective for you? When you use this strategy, what is the key to making it work?

4. Of the five revision strategies discussed in this chapter, which one seems most promising to you even though you have not used it much before? Why does it seem promising?

5. When it comes to drafting and revising, what two pieces of advice would you give to less experienced writers? Why would it be important for them to follow this advice?

EXERCISE 4.3   CONSIDERING TITLES AND INTRODUCTIONS

TITLES

Five pairs of titles are given. For each pair, indicate the title that would be more likely to move you to read whatever would follow it. Then explain briefly the reason for your choice. Use your own paper for this exercise.

EXAMPLE

Looking at College Life after Two Years Away *or* Returning to College: Back in the Saddle Again

The second version, "Returning to College: Back in the Saddle Again," would be my choice. Besides giving a fairly clear indication of the essay's topic, this version suggests a somewhat humorous tone, which suits the topic. The first version does a good job of identifying the topic but does not have the human interest of the second version.

1. Low-Fat Foods *or* The Low-Fat Fantasy: Healthy or High Calorie?
2. Recovery from Pollution *or* The Columbia River: A Comeback Story
3. Federal Taxes and You *or* Do New Tax Laws Mean You'll Pay More?
4. What High Schools Don't Want Students to Read *or* Censorship
5. Occupational Death *or* English Working Conditions in Textile Mills during the Industrial Revolution

INTRODUCTIONS

You want to write a persuasive paper aimed at convincing students that they ought to learn how to perform the Heimlich maneuver. The training takes only a short time, and clear directions for the procedure are available on posters. You have statistics on the choking victims saved by this procedure. You have talked with a person who was saved from choking by a restaurant employee. You have interviewed several students with food-service jobs who are reluctant to attend the training, so you know why they are reluctant. You have interviewed the local trainer, who has explained the importance of properly performing the procedure when someone is choking.

1. Specifically identify two ways that this persuasive paper could be introduced.
2. Explain how you would begin this paper. What factors will influence your decision?

penalty is cruel and unusual punishment" is arguable because it presents an assertion with which readers could reasonably disagree. Any of these could form the basis for an argumentative working thesis (see Chapter 3) and hence, for a college-level essay. Your task in such an essay would be to give reasons that would get your reader to agree with your argument.

> **CRITICAL THINKING IN EVERYDAY USE**
>
> Perhaps the most pervasive form of argument we face in our everyday lives is advertising. From the cereal box at breakfast to the posters on the bus to a few minutes of television before bed, advertisements call out to us to buy some product, vote for some candidate, or behave in some particular way. To get a sense of how much advertising comes into your everyday life, keep a notebook with you for one day and put down a mark every time you see or hear an advertisement. Count up your total at the end of the day, and if possible, compare your count with those of others in your class. Which of the advertisements were particularly powerful, and why?

Understanding the purposes of argument (5b1)

When a 60-second commercial on television trumpets the performance characteristics of a new truck or whispers the advantages of a new perfume, we understand the goal for this argument: the advertisers want us to purchase their products. And when a politician delivers a campaign speech, we understand that the politician wants our vote. So we are quite familiar with argument that aims to win, or to convince us to do something we might not do otherwise. And since we are quite familiar with (and perhaps quite weary of) arguments with this sort of aim, we might consider all argument as little more than a cynical attempt to manipulate us.

In academic settings, however, argument can fulfill a much different role: argument can help us understand the complexity of issues. Often, only after we have examined and understood a complex question from many perspectives, can we make clear—if difficult—choices about what we think is right. And argument based on working and sharing information with others can help us see beyond our own original perspectives. Argument of this sort aims to add to our education.

Formulating good reasons (5d)

The point of a gun may temporarily persuade those at whom it is aimed; however, that persuasion does not typically last long. Real persuasion occurs only through the careful presentation of reasons, on the one hand, and careful listening, on the other. Without both, no lasting agreements can be reached. Centuries ago, the Greek philosopher Aristotle identified three kinds of **good reasons** that can make for real persuasion: reasons that establish credibility, those that appeal to logic, and those that appeal to emotion.

Establishing credibility (5f)

Whenever you write, you present an image of yourself. It is important, then, if you want to win your readers' agreement, to present an image of yourself as someone who can be trusted. You can establish credibility in several ways; let us look at the most effective methods one by one.

Demonstrating knowledge

You get your readers' attention when you show that you know a fair amount about the subject you're arguing about, whether that knowledge comes from study or personal experience. Use the following questions to help make sure you are presenting yourself as sufficiently knowledgeable:

- Can you support your claim with information from several outside sources (library materials or testimony by qualified experts, for instance)?
- Will your sources be considered reliable by your readers?
- Do any sources contradict one another? If so, can you resolve the contradictions?
- If you have personal experience relating to your claim, will your readers agree that it is applicable?

Establishing common ground

One of the best ways to convince readers to listen carefully to your argument is to establish **common ground**, that is, to discover and point out any values you may initially share. For example, it is likely that writers on both sides of the gun control issue value freedom and human life. Both sides may also agree that safety in cities is a problem. If an argument establishes these common points of agreement, even hostile readers will be more willing to listen to the entire argument. And readers who read the whole argument are probably the only readers you have a chance to convince.

Demonstrating fairness

This method of establishing credibility is an important one, of course. **Fairness** in argument is, more than anything else, a matter of being willing to take opposing views into account. To establish credibility, you have to make sure your readers can see you doing this. These questions can help you as you build your argument:

- How can you show that you have considered all the evidence?
- How can you show that you are taking into account all points of view on the issue you are arguing about?

- How can you show that you are open to further arguments?

Recognizing ethical fallacies

Fairness also has to do with the argumentative tactics writers use. Often a writer is tempted to make a point by attacking the character of his or her opponent rather than sticking to the issue. A writer who blasts the senator's health care bill because the senator has been accused of corruption is not commenting on the bill but on the senator's personal character; the point is irrelevant to the bill's merits. Such unjustified personal attacks are a convenient way to sidestep issues. Writers who use these tactics, often called **ethical fallacies**, usually give the impression that they can think of no better methods of argument.

Appealing to logic (5g)

Successful arguments do more than simply establish their credibility. Logic and emotion also play their parts. This section will discuss how writers present the logic of their arguments.

Providing examples

Well-conceived examples go a long way toward the logic of making arguments effective. Suppose that you want to change majors, but your parents are against it. Suppose further that one of your best friends changed majors last year. Also assume that this friend has done wonderfully—has, in fact, gone from being a mediocre student to being a mainstay on the dean's list. If you use your friend as an example when you present your case to your parents, then they may well be more willing to agree to your change of major.

Citing authority

In addition to examples, argumentative writers often call on **authorities** to help back their claims. A writer arguing about the appropriate treatment of AIDS patients might cite information provided by the Centers for Disease Control. Most researchers and most of us in the general populace would agree that this authority is reliable.

Citing authority is a time-honored argumentative technique, but it must still be done carefully and intelligently. The following guidelines should help you use authority effectively:

- *The authority should be timely.* A book about the impact of computers on American life may not provide the best evidence for your argument if it was published during the 1960s.
- *The authority should be qualified to judge the topic at hand.* When the American Medical Association urges a health position (say, the encouragement of AIDS education), it is arguing from authority. If the AMA advocated cars made by

one company over cars made by another, we might reasonably wonder if the AMA is qualified to act as an authority on automobiles.

- *The authority should be known and respected by readers.* Many investors will listen to advice from large investment firms such as Merrill Lynch. Not many investors will listen to an unknown stock analyst publishing a newsletter out of a garage.

Using inductive and deductive reasoning

When you work from a number of specific instances to some general statement, you are using **induction**. Reasoning inductively is one way to arrive at a cause-and-effect relationship—and showing that one event is the cause or effect of another is one way to support an argument. Say, for instance, that five times in the last month you've had a cup of coffee after dinner, and each time you had trouble sleeping that night. You will probably conclude, inductively, that coffee after dinner interferes with your sleep. Accomplished writers of argument know that inductive reasoning can be a powerful persuasive tool. If you can lead readers to understand a succession of specific facts, chances are that you can lead them to agree with the inductive generalization you arrive at. Here, for instance, are statistics (obtained from the FBI) on the number of handgun killings during a typical year in the United States and in several countries where handgun ownership is much more restricted: Great Britain, 7; Sweden, 19; Australia, 13; Israel, 25; Canada, 8; the United States, 8,915. You might present these to support your inductive generalization that legal controls on handgun ownership reduce the number of handgun killings.

Another method of reasoning works deductively. Rather than moving from a number of specific incidents to an overall generalization, **deduction** moves from general principles, or **premises**, to specific instances. Induction and deduction often work together. For instance, having arrived inductively at the major premise *Coffee after dinner keeps me awake at night,* you might combine it with the minor premise *I just drank two cups of coffee with dessert,* and arrive at the conclusion *I will not sleep well tonight.*

It is important to remember, though, that deductive conclusions are only dependable if the premises on which they are based are strong. Sometimes you will hear deductive statements based on unspoken major premises that, once examined, fall apart. *Let's not bother asking Arnold to join our study group; he's in a fraternity.* This statement, straightforward as it sounds, is based on a deduction:

MAJOR PREMISE	Men in fraternities aren't interested in studying.
MINOR PREMISE	Arnold is in a fraternity.
CONCLUSION	Arnold isn't interested in studying.

But the major premise here is certainly open to doubt. Arnold may or may not be interested in the study group; but to decide that, you need more information than a faulty premise can give you. Being able to spot the implied premises on which many arguable claims are based will help you evaluate their truth.

Recognizing logical fallacies

Logical fallacies are errors in reasoning. We have already discussed the difficulties writers often face in linking causes and effects, as well as the potential pitfalls of inductive and deductive reasoning. Several other argumentative techniques are illogical and will only anger careful readers.

BEGGING THE QUESTION

Suppose a politician roars out in a speech, "We must defeat those ultraliberal Democrats in November!" This statement is "begging the question" because it treats several unproven, debatable points as if they were settled facts. It assumes that all Democrats are "ultraliberal," that we all share the same definition of "ultraliberal," and that we all agree that being "ultraliberal" and being a Democrat constitute sufficient grounds for defeat.

THE *POST HOC* FALLACY

The *post hoc* fallacy is the assumption that because event B happened after event A, B must have been caused by A. Suppose you are driving your car down the highway and run over some broken glass. Ten minutes later you have a flat tire. You might automatically assume that the broken glass caused your flat tire. You may in fact be right, but until you actually prove this is so, you are guilty of the *post hoc* fallacy.

THE NON SEQUITUR

Non sequitur means literally "it does not follow." This fallacy is the attempt to tie together two or more logically unrelated ideas: "Since it was raining outside, I felt the book was simply not well written."

THE EITHER-OR FALLACY

A child walks up to her parents and says, "Either you give me a candy bar, or I'll be entitled to a cookie." That child has used the either/or fallacy. This type of argument is illogical because it pretends that only two options exist when in fact there are many more. In this case, the child's parents could offer her an apple or could say, "Not until after dinner."

THE HASTY GENERALIZATION

A hasty generalization bases one or more conclusions on too little evidence or on evidence not carefully analyzed; for example: "I couldn't understand the lecture today, so I'm sure this course will be impossible."

OVERSIMPLIFICATION

Oversimplification is too simple a relationship between causes and effects. "If all high school students were required to learn touch typing, they would be able to write superior papers once they got to college." That sentence grossly oversimplifies the skills required to write well. Although typing is a useful skill for writers to have, not all writers must be good typists (think, for example, of Shakespeare, who had no access to typewriters).

Appealing to emotion (5h)

Recognizing emotional fallacies

Emotional appeals constitute a valid, often necessary, and useful part of argumentative strategy. However, some emotional appeals seek to preclude the use of any logical or factual investigation or decision making. Such emotional appeals are flawed and unfair, and they should be avoided. Knowledgeable readers will see right through them.

THE BANDWAGON APPEAL

The candidate who argues that because the polls show ever-increasing support, undecided voters should "get on the bandwagon" makes an argument by appealing to the human fear of being left out or left behind. This appeal tries to eliminate any use of fact or logic, and it has no real bearing on politics.

FLATTERY

Typically, a writer using flattery praises readers for possessing certain qualities, then indicates that because readers possess these qualities, they must certainly agree with the writer's position: "As civic-minded and caring individuals, I am sure that you will want to support the sheriff's posse benefit dinner by purchasing two tickets." Such an appeal asserts that anyone who does not purchase two tickets is automatically the opposite of civic-minded and caring. The argument is thus deflected away from any logical or factual line of discussion. Is the sheriff's posse benefit dinner really a worthy cause? Why?

VEILED THREATS

The veiled threat fallacy also ignores the real issues in a question; it tries to intimidate an audience instead: "If People's Utility does not get an immediate 14 percent rate hike, it may be forced to discontinue service to its customers." The thought of losing electricity may well inspire considerable fear on the part of customers, and that is exactly the writer's intent.

Using the Toulmin System (5j2)

Philosopher Stephen Toulmin has developed a seven-step system for argument, and you may be able to use this in arguments you develop for college classes. In simplified form, the organizational scheme looks like this:

1. Begin with an introductory statement of a claim or thesis, often in large terms. ("Experts on air pollution agree that automobile exhaust accounts for much of the pollution in large cities.")
2. Restate your claim or thesis in narrower, more carefully defined terms. ("I believe we can lower pollution levels by making mass transit cheaper and by raising downtown parking fees.")

3. Discuss the good reasons behind your thesis or argument.
   (Successes in some cities using exactly these means; consumer polls indicating willingness to ride buses or rail cars if they're cheap, reliable, and safe.)
4. Discuss the underlying assumptions that support your reasons.
   (No one likes pollution. No one likes the illness it causes. No one likes how pollution looks. People are willing to change what they do if the changes are relatively easy to make and the gains seem to apply to everyone.)
5. Provide further evidence supporting your claim—statistics, testimony, examples, and so on.
   (Contrast a city without effective mass transit with a city that has made mass transit easy. Give readers a sense of frustration of individual driving vs. the ease of riding. Use statistics to show how many commuters can switch from private cars to public transportation, and thus how many pounds of pollutants would not be sent into the atmosphere.)
6. Acknowledge and respond to possible counterarguments.
   (Some downtown business owners may oppose the raising of parking fees, figuring that this might cut into their retail sales. But perhaps public transportation agencies and private businesses could share the costs of an advertising campaign highlighting the new public transportation system and explaining how it makes downtown shopping easier and more pleasant.)
7. Draw your conclusion.
   (For all the reasons discussed above, we should work to lower air pollution in our cities by raising downtown parking fees and by improving mass transit and aggressively marketing these new improvements.)

Even if your final paper doesn't correspond precisely to this format, the Toulmin organizational scheme offers a useful way for you to think more fully about any controversial issue.

EXERCISE 5.1   RECOGNIZING ARGUABLE STATEMENTS

NAME _____   **DATE** _____

Look at the following sentences. Indicate which are arguable statements of opinion and which are factual. Be ready to explain your choices.

EXAMPLE   The movie *The Commitments* focuses on how an Irish rock band formed and then disbanded. _factual_

EXAMPLE   The movie *The Commitments* offers one of the best sound tracks of any movie in the last fifteen years. _opinion_

1. The new Italian restaurant on Colfax Avenue is the best in town. _____
2. The soccer team finished the season with a 9-3 record. _____
3. The government should fund experimental medical procedures to determine whether they would benefit many patients. _____
4. Early childhood education is the highest priority in education today. _____
5. New York City receives more yearly rainfall than Nashville, Tennessee. _____
6. Terminally ill patients ought to be able to choose doctor-assisted suicide. _____
7. Several states have voted on the issue of doctor-assisted suicide. _____
8. Handgun accidents kill children every year. _____
9. The laws in this state require the use of seat belts. _____
10. Economists forecast slow but steady growth for the next six months. _____

EXERCISE 5.2 UNDERSTANDING THE REASONS FOR ARGUMENT

Use your own paper for this exercise. Working in pairs or small groups, consider the following statement:

> The death penalty constitutes cruel and unusual punishment and should therefore be replaced by life in prison without possibility of parole.

- Begin by individually writing for ten minutes or so to record your own first reaction to the statement above. Once you've written this first response, set it aside for later.
- Now consider the statement from the point of view of someone who views all killing as wrong. Develop this person's full argument even if you don't personally agree with it.
- Then consider the statement from the point of view of a prosecuting attorney, someone who has spent many years working for the government, preserving law and order. Develop this person's full argument even if you don't personally agree with it.
- Then consider the statement from the point of view of a defense attorney, someone who has spent many years defending accused individuals. Develop this person's full argument even if you don't personally agree with it.
- Then consider the statement from the point of view of a family member (a sister or brother) related to a murder victim. Develop this person's full argument even if you don't personally agree with it.
- Finally, consider the statement from the point of view of a family member related to someone standing trial for murder. Develop this person's full argument even if you don't personally agree with it.
- Now, based on your further understanding of this complicated issue, write your own current thoughts and feelings about the statement. As you write, make sure that you refer to each of the various positions and perspectives you've examined, and relate each of them to your own current understanding. Do you agree with the original statement, or do you disagree with it? If you cannot now decide, explain why you cannot.

EXERCISE 5.3   USING INDUCTIVE REASONING

NAME _____ **DATE** _____

In each of the following cases, you are provided with examples of specific information. Draw a reasonable conclusion supported by those examples.

EXAMPLE   The average class size in the local grade school has increased from twenty-two students to twenty-nine students.
Several local teachers have left to take jobs in other school districts.
The high school track program has just been cut and the two track coaches laid off.
The district has canceled all school-sponsored field trips for next year.
Test scores in the district have declined in the last two years.
Leaky roofs have caused water damage in four classrooms.

Inductive generalization: <u>The school district is underfunded.</u>

1. On January 8, 3" of snow fell.
   On January 9, the snowfall measurement was 2½".
   Although a few flakes fell, no measurable snow fell on January 10.
   The snowfall on January 11 was measured at a record 4".
   The snowfall on January 12 was 3".

   Inductive generalization: _____

2. Emile H. is a business major and lives in a fraternity.
   Christopher F. is an art history major and lives in an apartment.
   Julie N. is a business major and lives in a sorority.
   Hiroko W. is a business major and lives in married student housing.
   Jackson R. is a political science major and lives in a dorm.
   Morgan J. is a business major and lives in a fraternity.

   Inductive generalization: _____

3. Small business owner Jamal K. notes the following things during the course of a month:
   Orders for the company's goods are at an all-time high.
   The shipping department used to take three days to ship a new order; now new orders take sixteen days before they're shipped.
   Four people in the shipping department have been sick in the last two weeks.
   The company accountant says the company is making more profits than ever.
   A few customers have noticed that their orders are not arriving as promptly as they once did.

   Inductive generalization: _____

Constructing unified, coherent, and fully developed paragraphs (6a, 6b, 6c, 6d, 6e)

Developing your ability to construct effective paragraphs puts you well on the way to completing successful full-length essays. Let's take a look at three qualities that all well-written paragraphs share: **unity**, **coherence**, and **development**. A paragraph is unified if it focuses on one main idea; it is coherent if the reader can easily see how all of its parts fit together; and it is developed if its main idea is supported with specifics.

Making paragraphs unified: Focusing on a main idea

One good way to give unity to a paragraph is to include one sentence in which the main idea or topic is stated clearly. The other sentences then relate in one way or another to the topic sentence, often supporting it by adding examples and details.

Should the topic sentence come first in the paragraph? Can it come later in the paragraph? Those are good writing questions—ones that a writer must answer on the basis of both material and purpose for writing. As you continue reading this chapter, you will encounter topic sentences in many positions. Finally, however, the position of the topic sentence is less important than overall paragraph unity—the end to which the topic sentence is only a means.

Consider this paragraph:

<u>My Monday mornings are often difficult.</u> Part of the problem lies with my own internal body clock. It's set to keep me awake and alert until late in the evening. When the clock radio comes on at 6:06, my internal clock says it's way too early to climb out of bed. Since I'm groggy and not exactly eager to wake up, I tend to be grouchy. Even after I've had my shower and begun to feel conscious, I can get irrationally angry when there isn't a full bowl's worth of Grape Nuts left; never mind that there's an unopened box of Raisin Bran in the pantry. If it's raining when I go out to get the paper, I'll probably curse the weather <u>and</u> the paper.

As you can see, the topic sentence is positioned as the very first sentence in the paragraph. Every sentence that follows it adds some new example or detail to support the statement made in the topic sentence.

In a unified paragraph, all the information contributes to the paragraph's main point; nothing irrelevant is included. In paragraphs that deal with ideas, unity sometimes presents problems. Consider this paragraph:

Tracy Kidder's *Among Schoolchildren* discusses the fifth-grade class of Mrs. Chris Zajac. It focuses especially on two of her more troublesome students, Clarence (who almost never does any of his homework) and Robert (who routinely hits himself). I liked reading the book because it reminded me of my fifth grade and the time Tommy Fleming decided to take a fudge pop home to his mom. It melted in his pocket and made quite a mess. And I wonder what happened to Cornelia Hays. I was in love with her in sixth grade, before she moved away. Tommy Reily, my best friend in first grade, moved away the summer before second grade. I can still remember going into the lunchroom and not having anyone to sit with. Poor Mrs. Zajac; she tries hard in this book. She really cares about her students.

What is this paragraph about? It starts by discussing a book, Tracy Kidder's *Among Schoolchildren*. Based on just the opening sentence, you could reasonably expect that the entire paragraph would focus on the book, and especially on those troublesome students Clarence and Robert. But that's not where the paragraph goes. Instead, it wanders to the writer's own grade school experience. This kind of wandering is often what our minds do, and this kind of paragraph turns up commonly in first drafts. The only cure for such a disunified paragraph is revision. The writer here needs to make some decisions about the paragraph's main point. The writer could decide to keep the focus on the book. In that case, the paragraph needs more discussion of Clarence and Robert. Or the writer could decide to focus the paragraph on how Kidder's book awakens memories of grade school. In that case, the paragraph needs a new opening that accurately establishes this focus. But the paragraph cannot be effectively revised until the writer decides what's really important.

To analyze a paragraph for unity, first determine its topic sentence. Then ask yourself whether each of the other sentences illustrates, explains, or adds to your knowledge of the main point identified in the topic sentence. If you cannot determine the paragraph's topic sentence, the paragraph probably needs substantial revision.

Making paragraphs coherent: Fitting details together

In a coherent paragraph, the sentences are related to each other not just by their content but also by their sentence structures and word choices. As a writer, you should be aware of four important techniques for creating coherence: repetition, pronoun usage, parallelism, and transitions.

Repetition is the multiple use of key phrases or words. The following paragraph uses repetition to achieve coherence:

> Why do some college students succeed while others struggle? Some succeed because their educational backgrounds have prepared them for college-level work. Others succeed because they are effective time managers: they have set aside time for study and time for play. Others succeed because they are motivated. If a class seems too difficult, they recognize the difficulty and seek help. Successful students are also determined students. And finally, successful students do not ask themselves to be superhuman; they are aware of their strengths and not discouraged by their weaknesses.

As you can see, several words and phrases are repeated from sentence to sentence, including the word *succeed* and the phrase *successful students*. This paragraph uses just about the maximum amount of repetition that any paragraph can stand without sounding affected, forced, or insincere.

In this sample paragraph, one important noun phrase is *college students*. Three pronouns—*some*, *others*, and *they*—consistently refer to the college students named in the topic sentence. This **pronoun usage** reminds readers that the paragraph is still addressing the subject it began with. It is another way writers can link ideas and increase the coherence of their paragraphs.

The next paragraph uses the third technique to add coherence. In this example, the sentences are related by **parallelism**, the use of grammatically similar structures. Notice how many of the subjects and verbs (underlined) have been positioned right ly. In some children's hospitals, cancer wards use dogs and cats, even gerbils, as ways to provide patients with unrestricted acceptance. Kids whose hair has fallen out or who find themselves in casts or bandages sometimes wish to withdraw from contact with their family or friends because they do not wish to be seen "that way." But pets don't care. Their love is unconditional. The elderly respond in much the same way. To these people, often in pain and sometimes without nearby family or friends, pets provide instant companionship and instant distraction. As a result, some older folks take a greater interest in their own well-being and in the life around them.

■ The Specific-to-General Pattern

As you no doubt have guessed, the **specific-to-general** paragraph is organized so that the sentences providing explanations or examples come first. Positioned at the end of the paragraph, the topic sentence serves to unite the explanations and examples. This organizational format creates a quite different reading experience. A successful specific-to-general paragraph draws readers in with its specifics, then unites those specifics with a topic sentence that provides a neat summary.

> Originally they filled whole rooms, and occasionally bugs would crawl in and interfere with the circuits. Their earliest uses were mostly government sponsored, either for military purposes by such organizations as the CIA, or for space exploration efforts by NASA. Over the years they shrank in size and price, even as their usefulness and variety of applications dramatically increased. By 1980, the machine that once filled a room now filled a box smaller than a standard suitcase, and data input had shifted from the clumsiness of punched cards to the ease of keyboards and floppy disks. In this way, computers evolved from behemoths only governments or large corporations could afford to personal computers affordable to many families and individuals. What was once an obscure, unknown, and even scary piece of equipment has become a routine tool at home, in business, and in school.

■ The Problem-Solution and Question-and-Answer Patterns

A **problem-solution** paragraph states a problem first, then provides one or more solutions. Similarly, a **question-and-answer** paragraph opens by raising a question, then providing one or more answers.

■ Process Analysis Paragraphs

A **process analysis** paragraph is chronologically organized. It specifies a particular action or set of actions, then proceeds to tell readers how they regularly occur. Here, for example, is a nontechnical process analysis describing how a car is started:

> The process of starting a car begins when the driver inserts the car key into the ignition. Turning the key (typically to the right) completes a circuit and sends electricity from the car's battery to the starter motor and to the spark plugs. The starter motor sets the pistons in action. The spark plugs begin to fire, and the pistons begin to rise and fall on their own. At this point, the driver disengages the starter motor and depresses the gas pedal slightly to give the cold engine the fuel it needs.

Cause-Effect Paragraphs

A **cause-effect** paragraph examines why something happened (emphasis on causes), tries to predict what will happen (emphasis on effects), or does both (cause and effect given equal billing). The typical television weather forecast is often a cause-effect analysis with an emphasis on effects.

Comparison/Contrast Paragraphs

Another quite useful organizational pattern is **comparison/contrast** (you *compare* similar things; you *contrast* dissimilar things). This pattern is discussed in Chapter 3 as an essay organizational format.

Narrative Paragraphs

A **narrative** paragraph tells a small story in order to support some main point. The story usually moves from beginning to end in chronological order, and the ending usually forms the story's climax, making the point of the story clear to readers. For example, a writer who wants to urge readers to seek help for substance abuse problems might choose to include the story of a friend or family member who has successfully sought help. A narrative paragraph (or a series of paragraphs) presenting this story might start with the recognition of the problem, move to the decision to seek treatment, then present the treatment period itself, and end with the individual's continuing recovery. Once the story has been told, the writer then uses additional sentences to underscore the point that the story makes and to link that story to the larger issue.

Narrative paragraphs have the advantage of making large issues more personal and more immediate. Readers identify with the people in a story. However, if your aim is to persuade readers to some new understanding or new action, narrative paragraphs might not be enough by themselves. Especially with controversial issues, readers need to be convinced that a personal story—however dramatic—is typical and applies to more than just one person. Thus narrative paragraphs are often linked with statistics in order to bring the statistics and the larger issues to life.

Special-purpose paragraphs (6f)

Occasionally essays, especially narrative essays, will use **quoted dialogue** to present the actual words of several speakers. The conventions of paragraphing dialogue are simple: every time you present a new speaker, use a new paragraph. Recognizing that convention, you know how to write and how to read this exchange:

> "Want to jump rope?"
> "Nah. I'm tired."
> "Want to play gin rummy?"
> "Nah."
> "Want to watch TV?"

"We've already watched an hour's worth, and you know what Mom said."
"Well, then—"
"What about if we kick the soccer ball in the backyard?"
"I thought the ball was flat."
"It was until Mom pumped it up again."
"OK, let's go."

Short stories and novels follow the same convention for quoted dialogue: every time there is a new speaker, there is a new paragraph.

The introduction and conclusion of an essay, as discussed in Chapter 4, require special types of paragraphs that relate to the entire essay. Transitions from paragraph to paragraph also need special attention; consult the part of Chapter 4 that deals with the use of transitions.

EXERCISE 6.1 FINDING PARAGRAPH BREAKS

NAME _____ DATE _____

The passage below is taken from Rachel Carson's *The Sea around Us*. Here she discusses the way volcanic action creates islands in the sea. Read the passage and determine where you think the paragraph breaks should be. Mark each of your paragraph breaks with a slash (/). Underline the topic sentence of each paragraph you identify.

(1) Millions of years ago, a volcano built a mountain on the floor of the Atlantic. (2) In eruption after eruption, it pushed up a great pile of volcanic rock, until it had accumulated a mass a hundred miles across at its base, reaching upward toward the surface of the sea. (3) Finally its cone emerged as an island with an area of about 200 square miles. (4) Thousands of years passed, and thousands of thousands. (5) Eventually the waves of the Atlantic cut down the cone and reduced it to a shoal—all of it, that is, but a small fragment which remained above water. (6) This fragment we know as Bermuda. (7) With variations, the life story of Bermuda has been repeated by almost every one of the islands that interrupt the watery expanses of the oceans far from land. (8) For these isolated islands in the sea are fundamentally different from the continents. (9) The major land masses and the ocean basins are today much as they have been throughout the greater part of geologic time. (10) But islands are ephemeral, created today, destroyed tomorrow. (11) With few exceptions, they are the result of the violent, explosive, earth-shaking eruptions of submarine volcanoes, working perhaps for millions of years to achieve their end. (12) It is one of the paradoxes in the ways of earth and sea that a process seemingly so destructive, so catastrophic in nature, can result in an act of creation. (13) Islands have always fascinated the human mind. (14) Perhaps it is the instinctive response of man, the land animal, welcoming a brief intrusion of earth in the vast, overwhelming expanse of sea. (15) Here in a great ocean basin, a thousand miles from the nearest continent, with miles of water under our vessel, we come upon an island. (16) Our imaginations can follow its slopes down through darkening waters to where it rests on the sea floor. (17) We wonder why and how it arose here in the midst of the ocean. (18) The birth of a volcanic island is an event marked by prolonged and violent travail: the forces of the earth striving to create, and all the forces of the sea opposing. (19) The sea floor, where an island begins, is probably nowhere more than about fifty miles thick—a thin covering over the vast bulk of the earth. (20) In it are deep cracks and fissures, the results of unequal cooling and shrinkage in past ages. (21) Along such lines of weakness the molten lava from the earth's interior presses up and finally bursts forth into the sea. . . .

EXERCISE 6.2   UNDERSTANDING TOPIC SENTENCES AND PARAGRAPH UNITY

NAME _____ DATE _____

As you read each paragraph below, identify its topic sentence, and indicate any sentences that interrupt paragraph unity because they do not illustrate or relate to that topic sentence. Then briefly explain your reasoning. (The sentences have been numbered for you.)

EXAMPLE

(1) My typical Monday morning starts sometime after 6:06. (2) That's when the clock radio comes on to bring me the early traffic report and the weather forecast. (3) However, we don't set the alarm on weekends. (4) After twenty minutes of dozing and groaning about how hard it is to climb out of bed, I get up and stumble into the kitchen to make coffee. (5) Half consciously my hands know what to do: measure the water and pour it into the coffee maker, and so on. (6) But I don't really wake up until the shower water hits my face. (7) I know other people who seem bright and awake the minute the alarm sounds. (8) After showering, it's breakfast time—more coffee, vitamins, a bowl of cereal. (9) On Sunday, I usually linger and read the paper.

Topic sentence 1

Unnecessary sentences 3, 7, 9

Explanation The topic sentence identifies Monday morning as the paragraph's focus. Sentence 3 talks about weekends, not Mondays. Sentence 7 talks about people different from the writer, and again this is off the subject. Sentence 9 talks about Sunday rather than Monday.

1. (1) Identifying poison oak depends on several factors. (2) First of all, since poison oak typically grows near or under regular oak trees, look for it there. (3) Unfortunately, poison oak is hard to dig up and hard to kill. (4) Mature poison oak vines either snake along, rising only a few feet off the ground, or they loop around the other tree trunks for support. (5) Once you think you've spotted a poison oak vine, pay attention to the leaves (but don't touch them). (6) Old leaves will have the color and shape of regular oak, but the newest sprouting leaves will often have a distinct reddish purple color, especially along their edges. (7) Often these new leaves will also look wet or glossy. (8) Regular soaps won't wash poison oak oils away. (9) Autumn is the easiest time to spot poison oak. (10) Then its leaves often turn a vibrant, deep red. (11) Remember, if you burn poison oak cuttings, stay away from the smoke.

Topic sentence _____

Unnecessary sentences _____

Explanation _____

_____

_____

2. (1) By putting us inside the mind and heart of Bigger Thomas, Richard Wright's novel *Native Son* offers one of the most memorable and gripping reading experiences in all of American literature. (2) Wright makes us see how racism determines Bigger's view of his own world. (3) Reading this book, I was surprised at how racist and discriminatory that world was. (4) I hadn't really understood how completely the races were separated in the 1930s. (5) No wonder Richard Wright chose to live in France and not in America. (6) I probably would have too. (7) In Bigger's world, he can't live anywhere but the black part of town. (8) He knows he can't achieve even modest dreams such as succeeding in the army or going to school in the hopes of becoming an airplane pilot. (9) He knows that there's little hope his family will ever be able to afford more than their one-room, rat-infested apartment. (10) The story opens with Bigger having to kill a rat by throwing a skillet at it. (11) And Bigger knows that the only reason for these injustices—really no reason at all—is the color of his skin. (12) No wonder Bigger feels hate, and no wonder he acts violently. (13) His world offers him few other options.

Topic sentence _____

Unnecessary sentences _____

Explanation _____

_____

_____

EXERCISE 6.3   UNDERSTANDING DEVICES FOR AIDING COHERENCE

NAME _____ DATE _____

The paragraph below uses repetition, parallel sentences, and pronouns to achieve coherence. Read the paragraph and take note of these devices. Then answer the questions that follow. (Note that the sentences have been numbered for you.)

(1) Some people vacation at a favorite lake, whereas others choose the solitude of a mountain retreat. (2) But when we have time off, we head for the beach. (3) We prefer falling asleep each night to the ever-present sound of surf. (4) We prefer tides and the constantly changing spectacle of the beach itself. (5) One day the beach is cluttered with small pieces of debris—agates smaller than marbles, pieces of mussel shells, bits of seaweed and coral. (6) Then the next day an entire tree washes ashore, its roots looking like tangled hair. (7) We prefer the beach because it's never the same place twice. (8) In summer, mounded dunes invite picnics. (9) In winter, the scoured shore reveals an ancient seabed marked with fossilized shells. (10) Sure, we like lakes. (11) And we admire the mountains. (12) Still, we prefer the beach.

1. Identify four important words (not pronouns) that are repeated and that help give this paragraph coherence.

   _____

2. Identify four pairs of sentences using parallel structures to add coherence.

   _____

3. What pronoun is repeated, and how does that add coherence?

   _____

   _____

   _____

3. Comparison/Contrast
   Topics: doing a task (which you specify) with or without a particular tool / using the computer lab versus using your own computer / the advantages of one type of job you have held versus those of another / the different characteristics or strengths of two friends or acquaintances / the advantages of one geographical location versus another

   Topic sentence: _____
   _____

   Details and support:
   a. _____

   b. _____

   c. _____

   d. _____

4. Cause-Effect
   Topics: why your favorite local team did not win the championship this year / what makes action movies exciting (or boring) / why one type of class is or is not enjoyable / why a particular teacher or other person inspires you / why you made a particular decision

   Topic sentence: _____
   _____

   Details and support:
   a. _____

   b. _____

   c. _____

   d. _____

EXERCISE 6.6 USING TRANSITIONS

NAME _____ **DATE** _____

Read the paragraph below. You'll see that transition words and phrases have been left out. Select the most appropriate transition word or phrase for each blank from the list of possible words and phrases below the paragraph. Write the number of the blank next to the appropriate word or phrase. (You will not use every transition word or phrase in the list.)

We don't know how to argue logically anymore, ____(1)____ maybe it's true that we don't even know how to think. Instead of logic and good reasons, television offers us slogans: Coke is it; Just do it; Image is everything. ____(2)____ the news offers us sound-bite assertions, ____(3)____ it rarely offers any extended discussion to support those assertions. ____(4)____ we hear that Congress ought to pass such and such a bill because "It's right, and it's good for the country," ____(5)____ we ought to elect so-and-so, who's a "leader for tomorrow." ____(6)____ the commercials and the news blur; ____(7)____, we may not really believe any of it. ____(8)____, television doesn't encourage us to think, it encourages us to shout louder (a form of intimidation). It encourages us to act not on the basis of good reasons or any reasons at all, ____(9)____ because the advertiser's jingle stays in our heads or we like the scenery the car drives through.

or	of course	as a result	but
nevertheless	eventually	but rather	and
finally	thus	sometimes	in addition

EXERCISE 6.7 SUMMARY EXERCISE: WRITING PARAGRAPHS

This exercise asks you to draft and revise a paragraph. To begin, read the several possible writing tasks given below, and choose one that interests you. Circle your choice.

Your assignment for foods and nutrition class asks you to list the contents of your refrigerator and then arrive at a conclusion about your diet.

In your educational psychology class, you're studying learning styles. You're asked to tell the story of one instance in which you learned something very easily (or with great difficulty). Your paragraph should pay special attention to your reactions to this learning situation.

In a sociology class, you are asked to write a paragraph responding to this question: What does the word *community* mean to you?

PART 2

PREVIEW QUESTIONS

These questions are designed to help you, the student, decide what you need to study. Read each sentence, and underline the word or words specified in parentheses, or underline the correct word of the two provided within the sentence. (Answers to preview questions are found at the back of the book.)

1. Meryl drove her car to the supermarket. (nouns)
2. The Washingtons brought their pet to the doctor. (nouns)
3. Makiko will get a new dress after she finishes her exams. (verbs)
4. Juan might speak to his father about going to the ball game. (verbs)
5. Anybody could buy Prince's record, but only those who went downtown could buy his new single. (pronouns)
6. Which restaurant do you want to go to? (pronouns)
7. Until nine o'clock she waited under the bridge, but then she gave up and walked away. (prepositions)
8. Celia and (I, me) are very close friends.
9. The audience did not know (who, whom) to applaud.
10. (Who, Whom) did you call this morning?
11. Both (he, him) and (her, she) were chosen for the play.
12. They invited both John and (I, me) to the party.
13. I (be, am) a marvelous cook.
14. That woman (don't, doesn't) want anyone to help her.
15. Sarah (give, gave) John a piece of candy yesterday.
16. John (lay, lied) on the bed until he felt better.
17. If I had done better, (will, would) you be satisfied?
18. Neither I nor anyone else (want, wants) trouble.
19. The class assembled at (its, their) usual time.
20. Each student should bring (his, a) notebook to class.
21. My family (travel, travels) to India tonight.
22. The members of my family (has, have) much in common.
23. The news (is, are) always on at six o'clock.
24. She began to feel (good, well) after a few days.
25. Dave was the (more, most) handsome of the three.
26. He took a (real, really) hard exam.
27. Marianne is (more nice, nicer) than her brother, but her father is the (nicest, nicer) of all of them.

On a separate sheet of paper, list at least one of each of the following, taken from any of the sentences above: a complete subject, a complete predicate, a direct object, an indirect object, a possessive pronoun, a linking verb, a past tense verb, a future tense verb, and a compound subject. Check your answers against the material presented in the next five chapters; if you need help, ask your instructor.

Constructing Grammatical Sentences

Recognizing the parts of speech (7b)

The parts of speech are the basic building blocks of language. There are eight different parts of speech: **verbs**, **nouns**, **pronouns**, **adjectives**, **adverbs**, **prepositions**, **conjunctions**, and **interjections**. Native speakers of English learn its parts of speech and sentence patterns as young children, intuitively saying, "The bright red cardinal surprised me," rather than "Cardinal bright the surprised me red." Although you use grammar each time you speak or write, reviewing each of the parts of speech can help you refine your intuitive knowledge so that you speak and write more skillfully.

> **GRAMMATICAL SENTENCES IN EVERYDAY USE**
>
> Perhaps more than any other subject we'll ever learn, grammar comes to us almost automatically, without our thinking about it or even being aware of it. Listen in, for instance, on this conversation between two six-year-olds:
>
> > Charlotte: My new bike that Grandma got me has a red basket and a loud horn, and I love it.
> >
> > Anna: Can I ride it?
> >
> > Charlotte: Sure, as soon as I take a turn.
>
> This simple exchange features sophisticated grammar—subordination of one clause to another, a compound object, a series of adjectives—all used effortlessly. Listen to a conversation, and transcribe a few sentences as done above. Then, using this chapter, see what grammatical structures the conversation contains.

Recognizing verbs

Verbs show action (*run, sleep, scratch*) or occurrence (*become, happen*) or a state of being (*be, live*). The verb is underlined in each of these examples:

The cat <u>scratches</u> with its paw.

A tadpole slowly <u>becomes</u> a frog.

Mrs. Byron <u>is</u> Sadek's teacher.

Verbs are often combined with other words called **auxiliary verbs** to indicate time or obligation. The most common auxiliaries are forms of *be, can, do, have, may, must, shall,* and *will*. A verb combined with an auxiliary is called a **verb phrase**. In the following examples, the verb phrase is underlined.

> Josh <u>will go</u> to the store for bread.
>
> Yukiko <u>has finished</u> her letter.
>
> Tonight I <u>must get</u> some sleep!

A verb is the key word in the part of a sentence called the predicate. In a complete sentence, the **subject** tells what the sentence is about, and the **predicate** asserts or asks something about the subject. See the next section in this chapter, Recognizing the Parts of a Sentence, for more information about subjects and predicates. In addition, Chapter 9 provides a complete discussion of the forms and functions of verbs, and Chapter 10 provides a discussion of subject-verb agreement.

Recognizing nouns

Nouns name things (or places or people or ideas or concepts). The following words are all nouns: *cup, wood, paper, St. Louis, lake, Einstein, Jordan, love, gravity, justice*. **Proper nouns** such as *St. Louis* name specific people or places; their first letters are capitalized (for more on capitalization, see Chapter 36).

■ Plural Nouns

Most nonproper nouns can be changed from **singular** form (one) to **plural** form (more than one) by adding *-s* (*lake, lakes; paper, papers*) or *-es* (*church, churches; lunch, lunches*). Some nouns, however, form plurals in other ways (*child, children*). **Mass nouns** name things that cannot be easily counted and so cannot be made plural (*dust, peace, tranquility*).

■ Possessive Nouns

Nouns use a **possessive** form to show ownership; you can form the possessive by adding *'s* (for more on using apostrophes, see Chapter 33). Thus if you wished to talk about a thought that was unique to Einstein, you would refer to it as *Einstein's*, because it belonged to him.

■ Articles

Nouns are often preceded by **articles** (sometimes called noun markers): *a, an,* and *the*. Nouns always follow (rather than precede) these words, as in *a dime, an apple, the bank*.

REVIEW

- Nouns name things, places, people, ideas, or concepts.
- Proper nouns name specific people or specific places.

- Possessive nouns indicate ownership by using *'s*.
- Articles are always followed by nouns.

Recognizing pronouns

Pronouns are used in place of nouns, making repetition unnecessary. In practice, we use pronouns frequently. Consider this sentence: *Marion lost the watch, but she found ten dollars.* In that sentence, the word *she* refers to *Marion*. Without a pronoun, the sentence would read this way: *Marion lost the watch, but Marion found ten dollars.* In most cases, pronouns refer to specific earlier nouns, called **antecedents**. The antecedent of *she* in the example is *Marion*.

■ Pronoun Types

There are many types of pronouns. *She* is a **personal pronoun** because it refers to a person. Personal pronouns take different forms depending on how they are used in sentences. For now, you should simply be able to recognize the personal pronouns:

I, my, mine, our, ours, we, us

you, your, yours

she, her, hers, he, him, his, one, it, its, they, them, theirs

There are quite a few other kinds of pronouns. **Reflexive pronouns** refer to the subject:

Aimee likes *herself*.

Bertice prepared *herself* for the interview.

Myself, ourselves, yourself, yourselves, himself, herself, itself, and *themselves* are reflexive pronouns.

Indefinite pronouns do not indicate a specific individual:

Everyone saw the winning play.

Nobody likes going to the dentist.

All, another, any, anybody, anyone, anything, both, each, either, everybody, everyone, everything, few, most, much, neither, nobody, none, no one, one, somebody, someone, and *something* are indefinite pronouns. (Some of these can also be used as adjectives.)

Demonstrative pronouns single out or point to some particular thing:

That was a mean trick!

These are my best sneakers.

This, that, these, and *those* are demonstrative pronouns.

Interrogative pronouns are used to ask questions:

Which is your favorite pizza topping?

What do you think?

Who, whom, which, what, and *whose* are interrogative pronouns.

Relative pronouns introduce dependent noun or adjective clauses (more about clauses later in this chapter):

The day *that* it rained I caught a cold.

Who, whom, whose, which, that, and *what* are relative pronouns.

Note that several pronouns (*who, whom, whose, which, that, what*) appear in more than one list. How these pronouns are used determines their particular classification. (Further information and advice about correct pronoun use is provided in Chapters 8, 11, and 13.)

Recognizing adjectives

Adjectives modify nouns, which means they describe or limit them. In the following pairs of words, the underlined word is an adjective, and the second word is a noun:

<u>red</u> ball   <u>crowded</u> store
<u>sleepy</u> man   <u>empty</u> bucket
<u>beautiful</u> sunset   <u>aged</u> man

Note also that nouns may modify other nouns, as in these examples:

<u>Styrofoam</u> cup   <u>tuna</u> sandwich
<u>Sunday</u> clothes   <u>peace</u> symbol

Although the underlined words function here as adjectives, they are still considered nouns. (For more on using adjectives, see Chapter 12.)

Recognizing adverbs

Adverbs describe or limit verbs, adjectives, other adverbs, or (rarely) entire sentences. Adverbs frequently end in *-ly,* though some common adverbs, such as *always, soon, rather, very, not, never,* and *well,* do not. The adverbs are underlined in the following examples:

Renee and Adrienne <u>recently</u> visited Santa Fe. [*adverb modifies verb*]

They had an <u>absolutely</u> marvelous time. [*adverb modifies adjective*]

Adrienne had <u>not really</u> expected to like New Mexico. [*adverb* not *modifies adverb* really, *which in turn modifies verb phrase* had expected]

<u>Clearly</u>, we should consider visiting Santa Fe. [*adverb modifies whole sentence*]

Recognizing prepositions

Prepositions indicate a specific relation to nouns or pronouns in a sentence. Often, but not always, prepositions define direction, location, or time. Prepositions are combined with nouns (and their adjectives) to form **prepositional phrases**. *Under the stairs, with the boxes,* and *of old clothes* are prepositional phrases. In each case, the preposition begins the phrase. Here is a list of commonly used prepositions:

about	as	beyond	inside	onto	to
above	at	by	into	out	toward
across	before	down	like	over	under
after	behind	during	near	past	until
against	below	except	of	regarding	up
along	beneath	for	off	since	with
among	beside	from	on	through	without
around	between	in			

Sometimes prepositions are combined into compound forms:

according to	except for	in place of	next to
because of	in addition to	in spite of	out of
due to	in front of	instead of	with regard to

A prepositional phrase always has at least one noun or pronoun as the object of the preposition. In each of the following examples, the entire prepositional phrase is underlined:

<u>According to your recent letter</u>, the orders never arrived. [*The compound preposition is* according to; letter *is the noun object of the preposition*; your *and* recent *are adjectives modifying the noun.*]

Carry this painting <u>through that door</u>, <u>down the hall</u>, and <u>into Gallery A</u>. [*This example contains three prepositional phrases in a row.*]

<u>For us</u>, twenty dollars is a large sum <u>of money</u>.

→ COMMON ERROR: WRONG OR MISSING PREPOSITION

Prepositions are small words, and when working quickly, we may not pay much attention to them. This is probably why the seventh most common student writing error is a wrong or missing preposition.

MISSING PREPOSITION   Mo went the store. [*missing* to]

WRONG PREPOSITION   I took that part out *in* the story.

I took that part out *from* the story.

Checking for incorrect preposition use is a simple matter of rereading your draft very slowly to be sure that each preposition you have used is the most appropriate ("I went *to* Texas" rather than "I went *at* Texas"; "I took that part *out of* the story" rather than "*out in* the story"). Checking for missing prepositions is perhaps best done by reading your draft aloud. Reading silently, our minds often fill in words that are not actually on the page, just because we are used to seeing them there. But reading *Mo went the store* aloud makes it obvious that something has been omitted.

Recognizing conjunctions

Conjunctions introduce or join words or groups of words. In so doing, conjunctions indicate logical relationships. For example, the conjunction *but* indicates a reversal or a contradiction, whereas *and* indicates an addition. There are four kinds of conjunctions, and each will be explained briefly. (Conjunctions sometimes join clauses; this will be discussed later in this chapter.)

Coordinating conjunctions join grammatically equivalent words, phrases, or clauses. The most common coordinating conjunctions are *and, but, for, nor, or, so,* and *yet*.

In sixth grade, I ate tuna *and* pickle sandwiches for lunch. [*The conjunction* and *joins two modifying nouns—*tuna *and* pickle—*which both modify* sandwiches.]

Work *and* play are two sides of the same coin. [*The conjunction* and *joins two nouns.*]

Susan enjoys softball, *but* basketball is her favorite sport. [*The conjunction* but *works with a comma to join two sentences.*]

Correlative conjunctions come in pairs and serve to join equivalent words or word groups. The most common correlative conjunctions are *both . . . and, either . . . or, neither . . . nor, not only . . . but also,* and *whether . . . or*.

Both Monica *and* Suki will graduate this term. [*The correlative conjunctions join two nouns.*]

Either I mow the lawn now, *or* I take a nap. [*The correlative conjunctions work with a comma to join two independent clauses.*]

CONSTRUCTING GRAMMATICAL SENTENCES

Subordinating conjunctions introduce dependent clauses. A **dependent clause** has a subject and a predicate but cannot stand alone as a sentence. Instead, it is connected by a subordinating conjunction to an **independent clause**, which can stand alone. The most common subordinating conjunctions are these:

after	even though	since	unless
although	if	so that	until
as	in order that	than	when
because	once	that	where

I understood the material *once* I reread it carefully. [*The subordinating conjunction* once *introduces a dependent clause.*]

Although I enjoy writing, I also find it hard work. [*The subordinating conjunction* although *introduces a dependent clause.*]

Some conjunctions—*before, since,* and *until,* for example—can also be used as prepositions. When they are followed by whole clauses, they are considered subordinating conjunctions. When they are followed only by nouns plus any adjectives, they are considered prepositions. Compare these examples:

After the lecture, I understand the material more clearly. [After *acts as a preposition here;* lecture *is the object of the preposition;* After the lecture *is the complete prepositional phrase.*]

After I heard the lecture, I understood the material more clearly. [After *acts as a subordinating conjunction; the complete dependent clause is* After I heard the lecture.]

In contrast to subordinating conjunctions, **conjunctive adverbs** connect independent clauses, each of which could stand alone as a sentence. These conjunctions act as adverbs, describing or limiting the second independent clause. Here are some common conjunctive adverbs:

besides	moreover	similarly
finally	nevertheless	then
however	next	therefore

Pokey is an outside cat; *nevertheless,* she greets me at the front door each evening.

The political struggle pitted North against South; *however,* the economic factors brought the South to a crisis.

The political struggle pitted North against South; the economic factors brought the South to a crisis, *however.*

Notice that the two clauses must be separated by a semicolon, not just a comma. In addition, unlike other conjunctions, conjunctive adverbs can be moved to different positions in the clause.

Recognizing interjections

Interjections express emotions or exclamations. They often stand alone, as fragments (rather than full sentences). Even when they are included in sentences, interjections are not grammatically related to the rest of the sentence. The most common interjections are *Oh! No! Hey!* and *Yeah!* Interjections are most frequently used in informal writing and dialogue:

"*Hey!* Wait for me!"

Recognizing the parts of a sentence: Subjects and predicates (7c)

As you have seen, every word in a sentence can be talked about as a part of speech. The words of a sentence can also be talked about according to how they function in that sentence. But before we go further, we need a definition of the word *sentence*.

What is a sentence? Answered most simply, a **sentence** is a grammatically complete group of words that expresses a thought. To be grammatically complete, a sentence must contain at least two structural parts: a **subject**, which identifies what the sentence is about, and a **predicate**, which asserts or asks something about the subject. The simplest sentences are composed of a one-word subject and a one-word predicate—for example, *Marcellus sneezed*. Here the subject is *Marcellus*, and the predicate is *sneezed*. By now you should recognize that *Marcellus* is a noun, and *sneezed* is a verb. In this sentence, then, *Marcellus* is a **simple subject**—a noun acting as the sentence subject—and *sneezed* is a simple **predicate**—a verb acting as the sentence predicate.

Of course, most sentences contain more than two words. Consider a sentence like this one: *The drawing shows her latest design*. The nouns in that sentence are *drawing* and *design*. *Shows* is the verb. You should also be able to identify *the drawing* as the subject of the sentence and *shows her latest design* as the predicate.

SUBJECT	PREDICATE
The drawing	shows her latest design.

Note: A sentence must contain at least two parts: a subject and a predicate. A subject and a predicate that combine to express a complete thought can also be called an **independent clause**.

When a predicate contains more than a verb, as in *shows her latest design*, we call it a **complete predicate**. A **complete subject** also contains more than a simple, one-word subject. It might be *the drawing on the north wall by the door* instead of just *the drawing*.

A complete predicate may include a number of sentence elements that provide information that make the thought, idea, or action of the sentence complete. As was mentioned before, the simple subject–simple predicate pattern of *Marcellus sneezed* presents a complete thought or action. But this is not always the case. *The train was* and *Abby caught* follow the same pattern as *Marcellus sneezed*, but clearly we need more information in these sentences.

The four grammatical elements that can be added to the predicate to complete the meaning of a sentence are subject complements, direct objects, indirect objects, and object complements.

A **subject complement** is a noun, noun phrase, adjective, or adjective phrase that is used with a linking verb to describe the subject of the sentence (more about linking verbs later in this section). In the compound sentence *The train was an express, but it was late,* both the noun phrase *an express* and the adjective *late* act as subject complements.

A **direct object** receives the action of the verb. In *Abby caught the ball,* the direct object is *the ball;* it is the thing that is *caught.* Direct objects typically answer the question *what?* or *whom?* (*What* was caught? *The ball.*) *Edward slapped Mark.* (Edward slapped *whom? Mark.*)

An **indirect object** literally receives the action of the verb indirectly. It is used along with a direct object—never without one—when subject, verb, and direct object still do not tell the whole story. In the sentence *Rafael made Lisa breakfast,* Lisa is the indirect object of *made,* and *breakfast* is the direct object. Without *Lisa,* this sentence tells a very different story.

An **object complement** relates to the object in a sentence the way a subject complement relates to the subject: it describes the object, particularly with respect to the state of being that the verb establishes. Consider the sentence *Rafael's thoughtfulness made Lisa very happy. Very happy* is the object complement of *Lisa;* it describes the effect resulting from the action of the verb.

Common sentence patterns

The sentences you have just read follow patterns that are used over and over in English. Not all sentences you write are required to follow these patterns; however, it may help you to refer to them during revision of your own writing if you have trouble deciding whether a sentence is complete or not, or if you question whether you have arranged its elements in the correct order. The patterns are as follows:

subject + verb + subject complement

subject + verb + direct object

subject + verb + indirect object + direct object

subject + verb + direct object + object complement

Note that indirect objects and object complements are always used with direct objects, never by themselves. (*Rafael's thoughtfulness made Lisa* and *Rafael made very happy* are not complete sentences.)

These patterns, and the patterns of most complete English sentences, boil down to subject + verb + [more information to complete and specify the action of the verb]. Thus, in our earlier example, *late* and *an express* both answer the question *the train was what?* and *the ball* answers the question *Abby caught what?* Also, the *type* of verb used in a sentence often determines, at least in part, which of the four predicate elements must follow it.

Verb type and sentence structure

A verb can be classified as one of three types: linking, transitive, and intransitive. **Linking verbs** generally require subject complements, **transitive verbs** generally require direct objects, and **intransitive verbs** generally require neither (intransitive verbs are the ones used in the sentence pattern subject + verb; *sneezed* in *Marcellus sneezed* is an intransitive verb). Let us look at these types of verbs and how they help to determine sentence structure.

■ Sentence Structures Using Linking Verbs

Linking verbs act exactly as their name implies: they link a subject with a subject complement.

> The actress *was* Elizabeth Taylor.
>
> Coffee *is* a beverage.

In each case, the subject complement (*Elizabeth Taylor, a beverage*) is a noun or noun phrase that renames the subject (*the actress, coffee*). Nouns used in this way are called **predicate nouns**.

When the subject complement describes rather than renames the sentence subject, we call it a **predicate adjective**:

> The actress was *beautiful*.
>
> Coffee is *hot*.

These examples use *is* or *was*—forms of the verb *be*. Other verbs such as *feel, look, taste, seem, appear,* and *become* can also function as linking verbs. Note that these verbs can almost always be interchanged with a *be* verb without substantially affecting sentence meaning. For example, *The actress looked beautiful* can become *The actress was beautiful*.

■ Sentence Structures Using Transitive and Intransitive Verbs

Consider this sentence: *The door opened slowly*. You should be able to identify *the door* as the subject of the sentence and *opened* as the verb. You should also be able to identify *slowly* as an adverb modifying the verb *opened*.

Now consider this sentence: *Reynaldo opened the door*. Here, *Reynaldo* is the subject, and *opened* is the verb. But what is *the door*? It is the direct object of the verb *opened*. In this second sentence, *opened* is a transitive verb. The action implied in the word *opened* is transferred to something, in this case, *the door*. Transitive verbs transfer their action to a noun other than the sentence subject. That other noun is called the direct object of the verb. All of the following sentences have transitive verbs, which are underlined once; the direct objects are underlined twice. Remember, direct objects typically answer the question *what?* or *whom?*

Stevie <u>replaced</u> the typewriter <u>ribbon</u>. [*replaced what? the* ribbon]

The elms <u>dropped</u> their <u>leaves</u>. [*dropped what? their* leaves]

Don <u>kissed Abigail</u>. [*kissed whom?* Abigail]

How does *opened* function in the sentence *The door opened slowly*? There, *opened* is an intransitive verb. It does not take an object. It cannot transfer its action to the noun *door* because that noun is already the sentence subject.

Now consider this sentence: *The lioness gave her cubs food*. You should be able to identify *lioness* as the noun subject and *gave* as the verb—in this case, a transitive verb. What did the lioness give? She gave *food*, which makes *food* the direct object. And who received the food? *Her cubs*. In this example, *cubs* is the indirect object of the verb *gave*. Note that if a sentence contains both a direct object and an indirect object, these elements follow a typical order: subject, verb, indirect object, direct object. Here is another example:

SUBJECT	VERB	INDIRECT OBJECT	DIRECT OBJECT
John	sent	Kate	a birthday card.

Here, *a* and *birthday* modify the direct object, *card*.

Indirect objects in such sentences can easily be converted to prepositional phrases. For example, *Jack sent Kate a birthday card* becomes *Jack sent a birthday card to Kate*. In the second sentence, *Kate* is the object of the preposition *to*. One way to determine the indirect object in a sentence is to see whether it can be rephrased so that the possible indirect object becomes the object of a preposition.

Because pronouns frequently replace nouns, pronouns can also act as direct objects and indirect objects:

SUBJECT	VERB	INDIRECT OBJECT	DIRECT OBJECT
You	should give	me	that.

Direct objects and indirect objects are never parts of a prepositional phrase:

SUBJECT	VERB	PREPOSITIONAL PHRASE	PREPOSITIONAL PHRASE
They	sailed	to Africa	for a vacation.

Recognizing and using phrases

A **phrase** is simply a group of words that are associated in some grammatical way but do not contain both a subject and a predicate. There are six types of phrases: noun phrases, verb phrases, prepositional phrases, verbal phrases, absolute phrases, and appositive phrases.

Noun phrases are composed of a noun and all its modifiers. *The blue sweater, an exciting day,* and *a moderately priced air conditioner* are noun phrases. (For more on noun modifiers, see the earlier section on adjectives.)

Verb phrases are composed of a verb and its auxiliaries. (For more on auxiliaries, see the earlier section on verbs.) *Are composed, must arrive,* and *should have been explained* are all verb phrases.

Prepositional phrases are composed of a preposition plus one or more nouns or pronouns and their modifiers. (For more on prepositions and prepositional phrases, see the earlier section on prepositions.) In these examples, the preposition comes first; the nouns plus any modifiers complete the phrase: *to Grady's store, for the next assignment, after supper.* Prepositional phrases act as either adjectives or adverbs, depending on what they modify. Consider this example: *In the morning, she will call.* Here the prepositional phrase *in the morning* modifies the verb *will call* by specifying when this action will take place. Because it modifies a verb, this prepositional phrase acts as an adverb. Now, consider this example: *Your directions to the store were clear.* Here the prepositional phrase *to the store* modifies the noun *directions* by specifying which directions. Since it modifies a noun, this prepositional phrase acts as an adjective.

Verbal phrases are made from verbs but function as nouns, adjectives, or verbs. The three types of verbal phrases are infinitives, gerunds, and participles.

Infinitive phrases are made by adding *to* before the verb. Thus *to run, to sleep,* and *to enjoy the ball game* are all infinitive phrases. Here are examples:

> *To sleep late on Saturdays* is a habit at our house. [*This infinitive phrase includes a prepositional phrase; the entire infinitive functions as a noun and acts as the subject of this sentence.*]

> *To draw plans* is a good way *to begin.* [*This example contains two infinitive phrases. The first functions as a noun and acts as the subject of the sentence. The second modifies the noun* way *and so acts as an adjective.*]

> She coughed a little *to clear her throat.* [*Here, the infinitive phrase modifies the verb* coughed *and so acts as an adverb.*]

Be careful to distinguish infinitives from prepositional phrases. The word *to* is used to introduce them both. In a prepositional phrase, *to* is followed by a noun or pronoun; in an infinitive, *to* is followed by a verb.

> Though busy, Harry found time *to run.* [*infinitive as adjective modifying* time]

> Sam ran *to the store.* [*prepositional phrase*]

Gerunds are formed by adding *-ing* to a verb for use as a noun. (When an *-ing* form of a verb acts as an adjective, it is called a participial phrase; more on participles in a moment.) **Gerund phrases** are composed of gerunds and all modifying words. Since they always act as nouns, gerunds and gerund phrases may occur in any sentence position that nouns would occupy. Here are examples:

> *Running every other day* is good exercise. [*The gerund phrase acts as the subject of the sentence.*]

Alicia enjoys *running every other day.* [*Now the gerund phrase is functioning as the direct object of the verb* enjoys. *Enjoys what? Enjoys* running every other day.]

Participial phrases may be either in the present tense or in the past. **Present participles** are formed by adding *-ing*; **past participles** are usually formed by adding *-ed* or *-en*. Some past participles (*gone*, for example) have irregular forms. All participles function as adjectives. Note that the present participial form and the gerund form are identical: both are made by adding *-ing* to the verb. What differentiates gerunds and participles is their function. Gerunds always act as nouns; participles always act as adjectives. Here are examples of both past and present participles:

Tired by a long hike, the dog slept before the fire. [*The past participial phrase acts as an adjective modifying* dog.]

The stereo *blaring next door* made sleep difficult. [*The present participial phrase acts as an adjective modifying* stereo.]

Note that participial phrases may either precede or follow the nouns they modify.

An **absolute phrase** is formed by combining a noun or pronoun and a participial phrase. Absolutes modify an entire sentence and are always set off from the rest of the sentence by commas. Here are two examples:

The big cat waited, *its nostrils flaring slightly*.

Feet aching, I finally crossed the finish line.

Absolute phrases can often be moved in the sentence without destroying the meaning: *Its nostrils flaring slightly*, the big cat waited.

An **appositive phrase** is a noun phrase that renames the noun, which most often immediately precedes it. An appositive phrase is always set off by commas. Here are two examples:

Victor Atiyeh, *a former governor*, lives in Portland. [*This appositive phrase is composed of a noun*, governor, *its article*, a, *and its modifying adjective*, former.]

The police officer fed Scarlet, *the station-house mascot*.

Recognizing and using clauses

There are two types of clauses: **independent clauses**, which can stand alone as sentences, and **dependent clauses**, which cannot stand alone. Clauses always have subjects and predicates. For example, *The weather forecast calls for snow* and *I'll start the fire* are both independent clauses; they are also sentences.

Dependent clauses are always coupled with independent clauses in order to make a complete sentence. By themselves, dependent clauses are sentence fragments that do not express a complete thought. Some dependent clauses are introduced by

EXAMPLE	Will Ann pick me up after her racquetball lesson is over?
REVISED AS A STATEMENT	Ann will pick me up after her racquetball lesson is over.
INDEPENDENT CLAUSE	Ann will pick me up
DEPENDENT CLAUSE	after her racquetball lesson is over

The original question is therefore a complex sentence.

EXERCISE 7.1   IDENTIFYING VERBS

NAME _____ DATE _____

A. Underline the verbs in the following sentences.

1. I <u>washed</u> that mug yesterday.
2. Grosbeaks <u>make</u> a distinctive sound.
3. I <u>choose</u> broccoli over asparagus.
4. The alarm clock on the dresser <u>rings</u> at 6:15.
5. The librarians <u>shelved</u> the books during the afternoon.
6. Aleda, please <u>tell</u> us your answer.

B. Underline the verbs with their auxiliaries in the following sentences.

1. Tomorrow I will go to the fortune teller.
2. Fernando must bake three dozen cookies for the bake sale.
3. My, how your tomatoes have grown!
4. The next match will be more challenging.
5. The cleaning crew has not washed the floor.
6. After class we can walk to the pizza parlor.

EXERCISE 7.2   IDENTIFYING NOUNS

Underline all the nouns in the short paragraph below; remember not to confuse nouns and pronouns. The first noun has been underlined for you.

In his <u>book</u> *Hiroshima*, John Hersey tells the story of six people who survived the destruction of Hiroshima on August 6, 1945. The bomb detonated at 8:15 in the morning. When the explosion occurred, Mrs. Hatsuyo Nakamura was looking out her window and watching a neighbor work on his house. The force of the explosion lifted her into the air and carried her into the next room, where she was buried by roofing tiles and other debris. When she crawled out, she heard her daughter, Myeko, calling out; she was buried up to her waist and could not move.

EXERCISE 7.3   IDENTIFYING PRONOUNS

NAME _____ DATE _____

First, underline all the pronouns in each of the following sentences. Then, in parentheses after each sentence, use these symbols to indicate the types of pronouns being used: PER for personal; REF for reflexive; IND for indefinite; DEM for demonstrative; INT for interrogative; REL for relative. The first sentence has been done for you.

1. <u>That</u> cup, <u>which</u> <u>you</u> found on the coffee table, is <u>mine</u>. (DEM, REL, PER, PER)
2. Jeb noticed that his lawn was full of dandelions.
3. Most of us enjoy a good movie occasionally.
4. The eagle that we sighted yesterday has its nest on Sauvie Island.
5. Whom did you say she insulted?
6. The senator likes herself too much for her own good.
7. Nobody saw the bear, but the ranger said it was dangerous.
8. Which way did you say that they went?
9. Our paper was assigned on Monday.
10. Her supervisor evaluated her work after six weeks on the job.
11. Anyone who enjoys pizza should try the Armando's near campus.
12. Terri felt tired after she worked that double shift.

EXERCISE 7.4 IDENTIFYING ADJECTIVES

NAME _____ **DATE** _____

Fill in an appropriate adjective for each noun below.

EXAMPLE   <u>scary</u> movie

1. _____ volleyball team
2. _____ movie rental
3. _____ encyclopedia
4. _____ question
5. _____ park
6. _____ situation
7. _____ meal
8. _____ bus
9. _____ highway
10. _____ project
11. _____ story
12. _____ video

EXERCISE 7.5   IDENTIFYING ADVERBS

NAME _____ **DATE** _____

Underline the adverbs in the following passage.

    Recently psychologists have suggested that the pace of our lives has quickened dramatically. And this extremely busy pace means we have little time to deal with normal, daily emotions. Instead, we finish one task so that we can quickly move to the next. Our workdays often become increasingly frantic efforts to cross off another task on our lists of things to do. If we spend all week at such a hectic pace, we probably have trouble truly relaxing on weekends. Instead of leisurely taking that long walk, we find ourselves walking at an uncomfortably brisk pace as we replay the little slights and angers and frustrations of the week. But since this makes us uncomfortable, when we get home we get busy again, keeping ourselves so fully absorbed in the present that we don't notice how rushed our lives have become. The solution to this, psychologists repeatedly suggest, lies in learning to pay attention to now, to find some pleasure and joy in the process of whatever we're doing.

EXERCISE 7.6   IDENTIFYING PREPOSITIONAL PHRASES

NAME _____ **DATE** _____

Underline the prepositional phrases in the following paragraph. Circle the prepositions. The first phrase has been done for you.

Our newspapers and magazines often report problems (with) elementary education. Some of these articles argue that because class sizes have increased, teachers give attention only to students who are disruptive. Even students who are working below grade level may not get enough help from the overloaded teacher. Other writers believe that schools located in areas where poverty and crime and joblessness set the tone cannot by themselves overcome such problems. When students arrive in the morning without breakfast, when they go home to crowded living conditions that make doing homework difficult, and when the adults in their lives have little interest in education, then, say these writers, how can we expect a single teacher to succeed? Education, they assert, needs the support and active participation of all of us.

EXERCISE 7.7 IDENTIFYING CONJUNCTIONS AND INTERJECTIONS

NAME _____ **DATE** _____

Read the following sentences. Underline conjunctions once and interjections twice. Write COORD (for coordinating), CORREL (for correlative), or SUBORD (for subordinating) in parentheses after each sentence to indicate the types of conjunctions being used. The first sentence has been done for you.

1. <u><u>Hey!</u></u> <u>Unless</u> you turn the oven on, the cake won't bake! (SUBORD)
2. After we finish dinner, we can walk to the park.
3. Stop! Put the tray down first, and then open the door to the kitchen.
4. Although the payment is due today, we can give you until tomorrow to bring it in.
5. Neither the manager nor the assistant manager approved the new schedule.
6. After breakfast, either I'll rake the leaves or I'll go for a walk.
7. Jake and Sandy, Elly and Hank, and Sally Jo and Michael all plan to travel together and attend the conference.
8. Dee is arranging her schedule so that she can chair next week's meeting.
9. Our parts shipment did not arrive yesterday, so I cannot fill your order.
10. Yeah. She said she likes you, but will she like your family?
11. You performed last night and still passed the test? Wow!
12. Until I saw that movie, I never thought about daily life at that time.

EXERCISE 7.8   IDENTIFYING THE PARTS OF SPEECH

NAME _____ **DATE** _____

Identify the part of speech of each underlined word as it functions in the sentence.

EXAMPLE   The <u>car</u> <u>door</u> slammed <u>into</u> the utility pole.
car: adjective   door: noun   into: preposition

1. <u>Advertisements</u> clearly <u>and</u> directly reflect our sense <u>of</u> what <u>we</u> want.

2. <u>One</u> thing that Soloflex and NordicTrack and <u>Nike</u> agree on is that we <u>want</u> <u>fitness</u>.

3. And as the <u>frequency</u> of <u>movie</u> ads and music ads <u>suggests</u>, we <u>also</u> crave diversion: we <u>want</u> entertainment and relief <u>from</u> stress.

4. To get this <u>relief</u>, we <u>can purchase</u> a facsimile of <u>the</u> first edition of Ernest Hemingway's *For Whom the Bell Tolls*.

5. <u>Or</u> we can listen to the Beastie Boys's <u>new</u> release *Ill Communication* from <u>Grand Royal</u> records.

6. <u>In</u> addition, advertisements suggest <u>that</u> we <u>consistently</u> worry about <u>our</u> health.

2. Verb: tossed

   a. *indir. obj.* _____
   _____

   b. *obj. of prep.* _____
   _____

3. Verb: owed

   a. *indir. obj.* _____
   _____

   b. *obj. of prep.* _____
   _____

4. Verb: passed

   a. *indir. obj.* _____
   _____

   b. *obj. of prep.* _____
   _____

5. Verb: offered

   a. *indir. obj.* _____
   _____

   b. *obj. of prep.* _____
   _____

EXERCISE 7.11 USING LINKING VERBS AND SUBJECT COMPLEMENTS

NAME _____ **DATE** _____

A. With the subjects provided, construct sentences using linking verbs followed by predicate adjectives. Use linking verbs *is*, *are*, *was*, *were*, *feel(s)*, *taste(s)*, *look(s)*, *seem(s)*, or *become(s)*. Don't use any verb more than once.

EXAMPLE cup
The cup was broken.

1. fish _____

2. novel _____

3. river _____

4. bagel _____

5. painting _____

B. Using the subjects provided, construct sentences using linking verbs followed by predicate nouns. The predicate nouns may be modified by adjectives.

EXAMPLE sand wedge
A sand wedge is a golf club.

1. this car _____

2. that track star _____

_____

3. a guitar _____

_____

4. those buildings _____

_____

5. two children _____

_____

EXERCISE 7.12   UNDERSTANDING LINKING, TRANSITIVE, AND INTRANSITIVE VERBS

NAME _____ DATE _____

A. The following sentences give a subject and a verb. Complete each by adding an indirect object and a direct object. Underline the direct object once and the indirect object twice.

EXAMPLE   The school sent
The school sent <u><u>Mary</u></u> <u>her grades</u>.

1. Megan built _____.
2. Grandma knit _____.
3. Mr. Ortega made _____.
4. Chen asked _____.
5. The dog brought _____.
6. Masio passed _____.
7. Jean handed _____.
8. The salesperson gave _____.
9. The New Year brings _____.
10. The chef cooked _____.

B. Identify the underlined verb in each sentence as either transitive, intransitive, or linking.

EXAMPLE   The race <u>started</u> with a pistol shot. intransitive
This lasagna <u>tastes</u> delicious. linking
You should <u>wear</u> a coat today. transitive

1. Out on the lake, the loon <u>called</u> for a long time. _____
2. The Taylors' cat <u>seems</u> sick today. _____
3. My neighbor <u>sang</u> loudly last night. _____
4. Lily's roommate <u>moved</u> all her records into the hallway. _____
5. Keanu Reeves <u>looked</u> tough in that movie. _____
6. I <u>held</u> the phone line for hours! _____
7. This building <u>is</u> the oldest on the block. _____
8. The rubber duck <u>floated</u> in the water. _____
9. The committee <u>drafted</u> the new bill late last night. _____
10. The sales manager <u>has considered</u> your report very useful. _____

129

EXERCISE 7.13 USING PREPOSITIONAL PHRASES

NAME _____ **DATE** _____

Add a prepositional phrase to each of the following sentences. Circle the phrase you add, use an arrow to indicate the word your phrase modifies, and indicate whether the phrase functions as an adjective or an adverb.

EXAMPLE Carrie slept.
(After dinner,) Carrie slept. (adverb)

1. His lecture convinced me.

2. The barn is a local landmark.

3. Hamid felt ill.

4. The plumbers will repair that leak.

5. LuAnne announced that she was leaving.

6. Can you hand me the remote control?

7. Luciano fell asleep.

8. Your letter was rather blunt.

9. Make sure you close the door.

10. Greg hasn't been to a dentist.

EXERCISE 7.14 USING INFINITIVES, GERUNDS, AND PARTICIPLES

NAME _____ **DATE** _____

Add the specified phrase to the given sentence.

EXAMPLE I discovered the book _____. (Add a past participial phrase with *hide* to modify *book*.)
<u>I discovered the book hidden under the couch.</u>

1. _____ is to live. (Add an infinitive phrase with *run*.)

   _____

2. My cousins always enjoyed _____ . (Add a gerund phrase with *play*.)

   _____

3. The dog _____ is the liveliest. (Add a present participial phrase with *bark*.)

   _____

4. Angela enjoyed _____ . (Add the gerund form of *walk* to complete the sentence.)

   _____

5. _____ , I arrived just as class began. (Add a present participial form of *hurry* to modify the subject *I*.)

   _____

6. Alan tried _____ . (Add an infinitive phrase with *sprint* to complete the sentence.)

   _____

7. _____ , you should count calories and exercise regularly. (Add an infinitive phrase with *lose*.)

   _____

8. _____ , it is a good idea _____ . (Add two infinitive phrases, one with *improve*, the other with *practice*.)

   _____

9. The Golden Gate Bridge, _____, was astonishing to see. (Add a past participial phrase with *build*.)

   _____

10. The dentist, _____, never stopped asking me questions. (Add a present participial phrase with *drill*.)

    _____

11. _____, the car needed a lot of work. (Add a past participial phrase with *wreck*.)

    _____

12. _____ was Martina Navratilova's livelihood. (Add a gerund phrase with *play*.)

    _____

EXERCISE 7.15   USING PHRASES

NAME _____   **DATE** _____

Combine or add to the following sentences as specified.

EXAMPLE   Harold phoned Monica. (Add infinitive phrase.)
<u>Harold phoned Monica to ask her for a date.</u>

1. Albert emailed Randi. (Add only a prepositional phrase.)

2. Randi called Albert back to cancel their dinner plans. (Add a present participial phrase.)

3. Contestants must think quickly under pressure. (Add an infinitive phrase.)

4. Annie likes to play tennis every Saturday. It keeps her active. (Combine using a gerund phrase as the subject.)

5. Havre, Malta, and Glasgow were named by the railroad. All these towns can be found in Montana. (Combine using a past participial phrase.)

6. William Carlos Williams established himself as an important twentieth-century American writer. He was also a medical doctor. (Combine using an appositive phrase.)

7. Test the water. (Add a prepositional phrase with a gerund functioning as the object of the preposition.)

   _____

   _____

8. My ears were ringing, and my hands were aching. I left the concert and headed for my car. (Combine using an absolute phrase.)

   _____

   _____

9. The warehouse burned fiercely. (Add a present participial phrase.)

   _____

   _____

10. Gilbert Boyer is a chef. He specializes in regional American cooking. He will be head of the college food service starting next month. (Combine using an appositive phrase that contains a present participial phrase.)

    _____

    _____

EXERCISE 7.16   IDENTIFYING DEPENDENT CLAUSES

NAME _____ **DATE** _____

Read the following passages, and underline the dependent clauses. The first dependent clause has been underlined for you.

Dick and I remember that afternoon well. The sun glinted off the ocean <u>as we pulled into the state park</u>. Dick said that the surf looked a little high. Even so, we weren't worried. After we were seated in the kayak and headed into the waves, we began getting worried. Each wave washing over us put us lower in the water. Before we had time to think, we found ourselves underwater. It was quiet and pale blue under there. When we struggled to shore half an hour later, a man who had been watching strolled over to us. I'll never forget what he said, "Well, you made it, though for a while there I wasn't sure that you would."

Journal writing means quick writing. When I sit down to add something to my journal, I have no idea what I'll say. Maybe I'll praise the sunshine after days of fog. After another phone call requesting money or trying to sell me something, maybe I'll complain about that for two or three sentences. As I read over old entries, I see that in the last month I've talked about airplane travel, music that I like to listen to, my frustration with technology that doesn't work, the sound of rain on the roof at night, and the people who ride my bus. Although most writing takes time and effort, journal writing is quick, and I don't usually revise it.

EXERCISE 7.17   UNDERSTANDING FUNCTION AND FORM

Underline each independent clause once and each dependent clause twice in the sentences that follow. Then identify each sentence according to function and form.

EXAMPLE   Will you take me to the store when I get home from school?
Function: *interrogative*
Form: *complex*

1. Either you take me to the store, or I'll run away!
Function: _____
Form: _____

2. Jason finally scored a goal!
   Function: _____
   Form: _____

3. Had Sylvie heard the news that the Starlight Drive-In closed?
   Function: _____
   Form: _____

4. My favorite cartoon show features Scooby Doo.
   Function: _____
   Form: _____

5. Although the region had heavy rains during April, the drought is not over.
   Function: _____
   Form: _____

6. While we were sleeping, Alec went to the store for us, and he has even fixed us dinner!
   Function: _____
   Form: _____

7. I can still taste the delicious Cajun chicken that you prepared for us last night.
   Function: _____
   Form: _____

8. After playing a tough game of racquetball, participants must always shower.
   Function: _____
   Form: _____

9. Jenny traveled to exotic lands while she was away on leave, and she ate many new foods.
   Function: _____
   Form: _____

10. You should apologize to your mother before you go on your trip.
    Function: _____
    Form: _____

11. If the feeling moves me, I will go to the jeweler and I will buy a ring.
    Function: _____
    Form: _____

EXERCISE 7.18   USING CLAUSES

NAME _____ **DATE** _____

A. Determine whether each of the following clauses is dependent (DEP) or independent (IND). Then make a sentence by adding a clause of your own.

EXAMPLES   when lightning hit the roof <u>DEP</u>

(Make into a complex sentence.) <u>Every bulb in the place blew out when lightning hit the roof.</u>

the alarm sounded <u>IND</u>

(Make into a compound sentence.) <u>The burglar shattered the window, and the alarm sounded.</u>

1. Bruce caught the ball on the run _____

   (Make into a compound sentence.) _____
   _____

2. the class that you suggested _____

   (Make into a complex sentence.) _____
   _____

3. when the police arrived _____

   (Make into a compound-complex sentence.) _____
   _____

4. a gentle wind blew the leaves _____

   (Make into a compound sentence.) _____
   _____

5. the abandoned car was covered with rust _____

   (Make into a complex sentence.) _____
   _____

6. the paper was nowhere to be found _____

   (Make into a compound sentence using any coordinating conjunction except *and*.) _____
   _____

7. she closed the file drawer _____

   (Make into a complex sentence.) _____
   _____

SENTENCES: MAKING GRAMMATICAL CHOICES

PRONOUNS AS SUBJECTS OF SENTENCES AND CLAUSES

Excited and eager, *we* drove to the hospital. [*In this simple sentence with one independent clause*, we *acts as the subject of the verb* drove.]

Although *they* were tired, the chorus sang well. [*In this complex sentence with one dependent and one independent clause*, they *acts as the subject of the verb* were.]

PRONOUNS AS SUBJECTS OF SUBORDINATE CLAUSES

Nobody knew that *she* had arrived. [*subject of noun clause*]

When *he* arrived, the store had already closed. [*subject of adverb clause*]

Irwin returned the book *he* had borrowed. [*subject of adjective clause*]

Predicate nouns follow linking verbs and rename the subject. Because they rename the subject, they traditionally take the subjective case, although this usage is often not preserved in spoken English.

USING PERSONAL PRONOUNS AS PREDICATE NOUNS

The only students who didn't get the flu were Barbara and I. [Barbara *and* I *are predicate nouns renaming the subject*, students.]

Using the objective case (8a2)

When pronouns function as objects of a verb, a verbal (an infinitive, gerund, or participial word or phrase), or a preposition, they take the **objective case**. The objective case forms for personal pronouns are as follows:

SINGULAR	PLURAL
me	us
him, her, it	them

Following are examples of pronouns used as objects.

PRONOUNS AS DIRECT OBJECTS OF VERBS

Al caught the ball and threw *it* to Robert. [It *acts as the object of the verb* threw.]

Gordon asked Debbie and *me* to go to the party. [Me *acts as one of the objects of the verb* asked.]

PRONOUNS AS INDIRECT OBJECTS OF VERBS

Thursday's unexpected blizzard gave *us* an unscheduled holiday. [Us *acts as the indirect object: the blizzard gave what?* holiday (*direct object*); *gave a holiday to whom?* us (*indirect object*)]

PRONOUNS AS OBJECTS OF VERBALS

It has taken me years to know *him* well. [Him *acts as the direct object of the infinitive* to know.]

Wishing *us* luck, Professor Decker said we could begin the final exam. [Us *acts as the indirect object of the participle* wishing.]

In helping *us* this way, Professor Ede showed real concern for students. [Us *acts as the direct object of the gerund* helping.]

PRONOUNS AS OBJECTS OF PREPOSITIONS

Andre handed the graphite racquet to *her*. [Her *acts as the object of the preposition* to.]

With *him* and Jack, no two hunting trips were ever the same. [Him *acts as one of two objects of the preposition* with.]

Using the possessive case (8a3)

Possessive case pronouns are used to indicate ownership or possession. Such pronouns take one form when they are used alone to replace nouns and a separate form when they are used as adjectives to modify nouns. The possessive case personal pronouns are as follows:

SINGULAR		PLURAL	
Noun Form	*Adjective Form*	*Noun Form*	*Adjective Form*
mine	my	ours	our
yours	your	yours	your
his, hers, its	his, her, its	theirs	their

(Note: The possessive pronoun *its* is often confused with the contraction *it's*. If you share this confusion, try reminding yourself that *it's* is a shortened form of *it is*.)

Possessive forms as adjectives

The adjectival forms are used only before a noun or a gerund, as in these examples:

Her aerobic dancing keeps her fit. [Her *precedes the gerund* dancing.]

Your shoes are worn, especially at the heels. [Your *precedes the noun* shoes.]

Their sleeping late caused them to miss the train. [Their *precedes the gerund* sleeping.]

Be careful to distinguish between gerunds and participles. Gerunds always act as nouns, so when pronouns precede gerunds, they always take the possessive case. But the same word may function as a gerund in one sentence and as a participle in another. Consider this example: *I remember his singing well.* Here, *singing* is a gerund; it functions as a noun and is the direct object of the verb *remember*. Thus the possessive pronoun *his* is accurate. The singing is *his*. The original sentence could be arranged in this way without changing its meaning: *I well remember his singing.* After all, *well* is an adverb, and adverbs cannot modify nouns.

Now consider this example: *I remember him singing well.* Only one word has changed, but the pronoun *him* creates a sentence with a very different meaning. Now the adverb *well* must modify the participle *singing*. Here we know the quality of his song: he sang well.

Possessive nouns

Functioning like the nouns they replace, possessive pronouns may also be used by themselves, often appearing in sentences using some form of the verb *be*. Here are two examples:

Theirs was the toughest schedule in the league. [*possessive noun as subject*]

The one coat left must be *hers*. [*possessive noun as predicate noun*]

Using *who, whoever, whom,* and *whomever* (8b)

Using *who* and *whom* to begin questions

Although everyday speech often does not preserve the distinction between *who* and *whom*, much formal and academic writing still does. Thus *who* and *whom* often give writers trouble. The rule is simple enough: use *who* as a subject, and use *whom* as an object. However, that rule is sometimes difficult to apply when the sentence is a question. Should you write *Whom did the consultant interview?* or *Who did the consultant interview?*

You can determine which pronoun to use by constructing a possible answer for the question and using a personal pronoun in that answer. The case of that personal pronoun will tell you the case of the interrogative pronoun. Though this sounds confusing, it is really not very difficult. The following examples should help:

Who/Whom is a good teacher? [*Answer: He is a good teacher. He is the subject; therefore, the pronoun must be the subjective form:* who.]

Who/Whom did the consultant interview? [*Answer: The consultant interviewed* her. *Her is the object; therefore, the pronoun must be the objective form:* whom.]

Who/Whom should I send this report to? [*Answer: I should send this report to* her. *Her is the object of the preposition* to. *Therefore, the pronoun must be the objective form:* whom. *In a formal writing situation, this sentence would probably be reordered to read* To whom should I send this report?]

Using *who*, *whoever*, *whom*, and *whomever* to begin dependent clauses

The pronouns *who*, *whoever*, *whom*, and *whomever* are called **relative pronouns**; often they begin dependent clauses. How the pronoun functions *inside that clause* determines which form should be chosen. If the pronoun is the subject of the dependent clause, use the subjective form *who* or *whoever*.

> I'll award a prize to *whoever* can recall the name of the first Russian cosmonaut.

How can you tell that *whoever* is the subject in that subordinate clause? One simple way is to write out only the subordinate clause. Doing that, you get *whoever can recall the name of the first Russian cosmonaut*. The verb in this clause is *can recall*; the subject of that verb must be the subjective case pronoun *whoever*.

A second test is again to isolate only the subordinate clause and then substitute a personal pronoun in place of the relative pronoun:

> She identified the clerk _____ had given her the wrong change.

The relative pronoun is the subject of the verb *had given*. By itself, the subordinate clause reads _____ *had given her the wrong change*. Substituting the objective pronoun *him* makes the clause read *him had given her the wrong change*. Clearly the objective case *him* is incorrect in this clause. The correct choice here is the subjective form: *who*.

The objective forms of these relative pronouns are *whom* and *whomever*. The same methods and criteria apply for identifying the correct use of these pronouns; the function of the pronoun within the dependent clause determines the choice. If the relative pronoun functions as an object, the correct choice is either *whom* or *whomever*.

> At the party, Alice talked to _____ she found interesting.

By itself, the subordinate clause reads _____ *she found interesting*. This is a somewhat awkward word order; a more normal word order would yield *she found _____ interesting*. The accurate personal pronoun here would be *them*, which is the objective form. Thus the correct relative pronoun here is the objective *whomever*.

Using case in compound subjects or objects (8c)

You will often encounter personal pronouns used as **compound subjects** (two or more subjects that have the same verb, generally joined by a coordinating conjunction such as *and* or *or*) or **compound objects** (two or more objects of a verb, a verbal, or a preposition, also generally joined by a word such as *and* or *or*). If you simply drop the other half of the compound, you should have no trouble determining the correct pronoun case. For example, take the sentence *Margaret and her went to the movie*. Keep the pronoun, drop the other half of the compound subject, and you have this sentence: *Her went to the movie*. That sounds wrong, and it is wrong. You now know that the correct case is the subjective: *Margaret and she went to the movie*.

Using case in appositives (8c)

Sometimes an **appositive** (a noun that renames) will follow a pronoun. In such sentences, dropping the appositive should make the case of the pronoun clear.

> Those of we/us baseball players who attended the reunion were glad we did. [*The appositive phrase is* baseball players. *Dropping it produces this sentence:* Those of we/us who attended the reunion were glad we did. *Here the pronoun is the object of the preposition* of; *hence, the correct pronoun with this appositive is the objective form* us.]

> After lunch, we/us sun worshipers sunbathe on the south lawn. [*The appositive phrase is* sun worshipers. *Dropping it produces this sentence:* After lunch, we/us sunbathe on the south lawn. *Here the pronoun acts as the subject of the verb* sunbathe; *hence, the subjective pronoun* we *is the proper choice*.]

In other sentences, you may find a pronoun as part of an appositive. When this happens, the pronoun takes the case of the noun it renames. Here are two examples:

> Two great fishermen, my father and me/I, were skunked again today. [*The appositive phrase is* my father and me/I. *This phrase renames the noun* fishermen. *Since* fishermen *is the subject of this sentence, the pronoun in the appositive must also be the subjective form*. I *is the proper choice*.]

> That one coastal cedar defeated two great tree climbers, Beth and I/me. [*The appositive phrase is* Beth and I/me. *This phrase renames the noun* climbers. *Since* climbers *is the direct object of the verb* defeated, *the pronoun in the appositive must also be the objective form*. Me *is the proper choice*.]

Using case in elliptical constructions (8d)

Elliptical constructions are sentence patterns in which one or several words are omitted because the writer assumes that readers will understand without them. Such constructions are used often; if we never left any words out, our writing would be very repetitive indeed. But leaving out words can make it easier to make mistakes, especially with pronoun usage. Consider this sentence: *Jason is younger than me*. Is the pronoun *me* used correctly? To find out, you must determine which words have been left out of the sentence and put them back in: *Jason is younger than me am*. Clearly that sounds incorrect. *Me* is an objective case pronoun; we never hear it used as the subject for a verb, so it sounds unnatural to us. The correct pronoun to use in this sentence is the subjective case pronoun *I*—*Jason is younger than I (am)*—because this pronoun is the subject of the dependent clause *than I am*.

Using the correct pronoun case in elliptical constructions is often crucial to your readers' understanding of your sentence meaning. Consider these two sentences:

> I like Fred better than he. [*If fully written out, this sentence would read* I like Fred better than he likes Fred.]

> I like Fred better than him. [*If fully written out, this sentence would read* I like Fred better than I like him.]

As you see, changing the pronoun from *he* to *him* alters the meaning considerably.

8. Though even the idea of hang gliding made her nervous, she gave it a try.

___

9. Harry called she before him left the house.

___

10. To know she is to love she.

___

EXERCISE 8.3 USING SUBJECTIVE, OBJECTIVE, AND POSSESSIVE CASE PRONOUNS

NAME _____ **DATE** _____

A. Substitute pronouns for the nouns shown in parentheses after each blank.

EXAMPLE The basketball team made <u>its</u> (the team's) way on to the court.

On the first play, Micki and Jenni guarded _____ (Micki and Jenni's) two opponents. Micki aggressively blocked the opposing player so that _____ (Micki) and Jenni could keep the other team's forwards from going after the ball. Meanwhile, Melanie passed the ball to _____ (Melanie's) teammate, Rosie. _____ (Rosie) dribbled around _____ (Rosie and Melanie's) opposing guards. Then Rosie completed _____ (Rosie's) pass to Carrie. Now it was up to Carrie to make the shot, so _____ (Carrie) took careful aim. The ball followed _____ (the ball's) usual perfect arc. Carrie did what _____ (Carrie) almost always did. _____ (Carrie) sank _____ (Carrie's) shot. All the team members shouted _____ (the team members') delight at taking the lead. The crowd, eager for the team to win, roared _____ (the crowd's) approval. As the fans jumped and shouted in the stands, _____ (the fans) all knew that _____ (the fans') team would play a spectacular game, setting new records and outdoing even _____ (the team members).

B. Now rewrite each of the following sentences on the lines provided, adding the pronouns specified in parentheses.

> **EXAMPLE**   I prefer a table by the door, but Carlos insisted that we take one in the back. (Add an intensive pronoun modifying *I*).
>
> I *myself* prefer a table by the door, but Carlos insisted that we take one in the back.

1. I spent the day at the library. (Add an intensive pronoun modifying *I*.)

2. You said that there was no chance of winning the game. (Add an intensive pronoun modifying *you*.)

3. The judge reviewed the case. (Add an intensive pronoun modifying *the judge*.)

4. The students prepare everything served in their cafeteria. (Add an intensive pronoun modifying *the students*.)

5. Jake asked how his own garden could have become so productive. (Add a reflexive pronoun modifying *Jake*.)

6. The cat washed and licked until its fur gleamed. (Add a reflexive pronoun modifying *the cat*.)

7. The crowd was standing, and their screams made it impossible for the players to hear. (Add an intensive pronoun modifying *players*.)

_____

_____

8. Nang built up by weight lifting. (Add a reflexive pronoun modifying *Nang*.)

_____

_____

9. When actors get nervous, they can calm down by looking in the mirror and saying, "You are a beautiful person." (Add a reflexive pronoun modifying *they*.)

_____

_____

10. I like going to restaurants where the head chefs prepare everything. (Add a reflexive pronoun modifying *chefs*.)

_____

_____

EXERCISE 8.4 USING *WHO, WHOEVER, WHOM,* AND *WHOMEVER*

NAME _____ **DATE** _____

Underline the correct pronoun choice in each of the following sentences, and briefly explain the reason for your choice.

EXAMPLE   The woman who/<u>whom</u> I met is, I discovered today, the sales manager.

Whom functions as the object of the verb *met*.

1. Who/Whom finished the math assignment?
   _____

2. By tomorrow Jasmine will decide about who/whom to promote to supervisor.
   _____
   _____

3. Whoever/Whomever the registrar sent a transcript to also received an explanation of the grading system.
   _____
   _____

4. Whoever/Whomever disagrees with this motion must vote against it.
   _____

5. The teacher who/whom you recommended doesn't teach the film course this term.
   _____

6. Callers who/whom phone during dinner and cannot pronounce my name do not get my full attention.
   _____

7. You can spend the afternoon with whoever/whomever you want.
   _____

8. People who/whom listen to talk radio enjoy its unpredictability.
   _____

9. Who/Whom will be our designated driver Friday night?
   _____

10. To who/whom should I make out this check?
    _____

EXERCISE 8.5 USING *WHO, WHOEVER, WHOM,* AND *WHOMEVER* TO BEGIN DEPENDENT CLAUSES

NAME _____ **DATE** _____

Work through the following sentences to determine whether to use a subjective or an objective relative pronoun. The first sentence has been done for you.

1. Richard said he would be glad to speak to _____ showed up to listen.

   The subordinate clause by itself is <u>showed up to listen</u> _____.

   Inserting a personal pronoun (he/she/him/her/they/them) yields <u>he showed up to listen</u>.

   Does this personal pronoun act as the subject or as an object? <u>subject</u> _____.

   Thus the correct relative pronoun in this sentence is <u>whoever</u> _____.

2. You'll wink at _____ comes your way!

   The subordinate clause by itself is _____.

   Inserting a personal pronoun (he/she/him/her/they/them) yields

   _____.

   Does this personal pronoun act as the subject or as an object? _____.

   Thus the correct relative pronoun in this sentence is _____.

3. That party was a drag, and _____ stayed was stupid.

   The subordinate clause by itself is _____.

   Inserting a personal pronoun (he/she/him/her/they/them) yields

   _____.

   Does this personal pronoun act as the subject or as an object? _____.

   Thus the correct relative pronoun in this sentence is _____.

4. The representatives with _____ she spoke told her a new credit card was on the way.

   The subordinate clause by itself is _____.

   Inserting a personal pronoun (he/she/him/her/they/them) yields

   _____.

Does this personal pronoun act as the subject or as an object? _____.

Thus the correct relative pronoun in this sentence is _____.

5. _____ she talks to immediately becomes a friend.

The subordinate clause by itself is _____.

Inserting a personal pronoun (he/she/him/her/they/them) yields

_____.

Does this personal pronoun act as the subject or as an object? _____.

Thus the correct relative pronoun in this sentence is _____.

6. The chef shared the recipe with those _____ he trusted.

The subordinate clause by itself is _____.

Inserting a personal pronoun (he/she/him/her/they/them) yields

_____.

Does this personal pronoun act as the subject or as an object? _____.

Thus the correct relative pronoun in this sentence is _____.

7. _____ he asked to investigate this story certainly did not do a thorough job.

The subordinate clause by itself is _____.

Inserting a personal pronoun (he/she/him/her/they/them) yields

_____.

Does this personal pronoun act as the subject or as an object? _____.

Thus the correct relative pronoun in this sentence is _____.

8. Today's weather forecast should please anyone _____ enjoys skiing on fresh powder.

The subordinate clause by itself is _____.

Inserting a personal pronoun (he/she/him/her/they/them) yields

_____.

Does this personal pronoun act as the subject or as an object? _____.

Thus the correct relative pronoun in this sentence is _____.

EXERCISE 8.6 USING CORRECT PRONOUN CASE WITH APPOSITIVES

NAME _____ **DATE** _____

In each of the following sentences, underline the pronoun form that should be used, and circle the appositives. Write the entire correct sentence on the lines provided. The first sentence is done for you.

1. To we/<u>us</u> (New Englanders,) hurricanes are a bigger worry than tornados.

   To us New Englanders, hurricanes are a bigger worry than tornados.

2. The two newcomers, Vivian and I/me, found the subway station without any trouble.

3. When we/us classmates gather on Saturday, we'll celebrate five years since graduation.

4. Lute Johannson always claimed he was the best of us/we chili cookers.

5. For once, we/us two brothers agree on something.

6. After almost ten kilometers, us/we runners all had trouble with that last hill.

7. The casting director chose two unknowns, Alexi and me/I, for the new speaking roles.

8. Even to two good cooks, Marina and he/him, the beef stew tasted delicious.

9. Going to the company picnic gave we/us employees some well-deserved relaxation.

10. Two volunteers, Jeremy and she/her, arrived early to organize the teams.

Using Verbs

VERB FORMS

Verbs identify action, occurrence, or state of being. They are crucial to our understanding of experience, and using them well is central to mastering English grammar. We use verbs to tell what we do: *sleep, wake, yawn, eat, talk*. We use them to tell what is or was or will be: *The sunshine* is *warm. The rain showers* felt *refreshing. The weekend* will be *partly cloudy.* As these examples begin to indicate, we change a verb's form to make it agree grammatically with its subjects and to indicate tense, voice, and mood. Understanding how verbs work will allow you to select the form that communicates your meaning precisely.

> **VERBS IN EVERYDAY USE**
>
> **Choose some kind of text that you read regularly—perhaps the sports section, a cookbook, a magazine, email, or a piece of your own writing—and have a look at the verbs. Jot down some interesting examples that convey lively action.**

Verb mistakes are very common. These mistakes take many forms and represent any number of confusions about verb use that trouble the writers who make them. Pay careful attention to the material that follows: some of it may be new to you, some of it may be things you once knew but have forgotten, and some of it will help you to become more sure of yourself as a verb user.

Except for *be* (more about this irregular verb later), all English verbs can take five forms. Examples of regular verbs follow. (Irregular verbs deviate from this pattern; they will be discussed later in this chapter.)

BASE FORM	-S FORM	PRESENT PARTICIPLE FORM	PAST-TENSE FORM	PAST PARTICIPLE FORM
cheer	cheers	cheering	cheered	cheered
type	types	typing	typed	typed
discuss	discusses	discussing	discussed	discussed

The **base form**, sometimes called the present form, is the form found in the dictionary. Writers use this form to indicate action that is happening now—in the present. The base form (without -s or -es) is used whenever the subject is a plural noun or the pronoun *I, we, you,* or *they*. Here are two examples:

Dogs *howl*. [*plural noun subject*, Dogs]

I *howl*. [*pronoun subject*, I]

The -s form is simply the present form with the addition of -s or -es. The -s form is used whenever the subject preceding it is a singular third-person noun, as in *The dog howls*. (For spelling rules indicating whether to add -s or -es, see Chapter 24.) The -s form is also used with many indefinite pronouns (*everyone* and *someone*, for example). The -s forms are italicized in the following chart.

	SINGULAR	PLURAL
FIRST PERSON	I wish	we wish
SECOND PERSON	you wish	you wish
THIRD PERSON	he/she/it *wishes*	they wish
	the child *wishes*	children wish
	everyone *wishes*	

→ **COMMON ERROR: WRONG OR MISSING VERB ENDING**

Some speakers use the base form instead of the -s form with a third-person singular subject. However, in all but the most informal writing situations, and especially in college writing, readers will expect the -s form with third-person singular subjects; when it is not present, they will assume the writer has made a mistake.

DIALECT	She *live* in a high-rise apartment.
ACADEMIC	She *lives* in a high-rise apartment.

The **present participle form** is made by adding -*ing* to the base form. By itself, a present participle forms a verbal, which acts to modify something (see the discussion of verbal phrases in Chapter 7). So, in fact, many times a participle does not function as a verb. But a participle can also be combined with an auxiliary verb (often some form of *be* or *have*) in order to indicate continuing or prolonged action. Here are two examples:

Barking all night, the dogs disturbed the neighbors. [*The participle* barking *acts as a verbal; it modifies* the dogs.]

Those dogs *were barking* all night. [*Present participle* barking + *auxiliary verb* were *form the predicate, the main verb of the sentence.*]

The **past-tense form** indicates action that happened in the past, as in *Dogs barked*. As you can see, the past-tense form is made in regular verbs by adding *-ed* (again, more on regular and irregular verbs later in this chapter).

The **past participle form** of regular verbs is identical to the past-tense form; irregular verbs have different past participle forms. Like present participles, the past participle form may function as a verbal when used alone (see Chapter 7). Consider this example:

Encouraged by her own success, Erin *encouraged* Mary Lou and Jeanette to study harder.

The first *encouraged* is a past participle and functions as a verbal; it modifies (tells us about) Erin. The second *encouraged* is the past-tense form and functions as the main verb of the sentence; it tells us what Erin did. Now consider this example:

Erin's parents *were encouraged* by her success.

Here the past participle form, *encouraged*, has been combined with an auxiliary verb (a form of *be* or *have*, in this case, *were*) to form the predicate (main verb) of the sentence. (More on auxiliary verbs later in this chapter.)

Using the verbs *be* and *have*

Since these verbs are commonly used as auxiliaries and since they possess several forms, the verbs *be* and *have* require special attention.

BASE FORM	-S FORM	PRESENT PARTICIPLE FORM	PAST-TENSE FORM	PAST PARTICIPLE FORM
be	am	being	was	been
	are		were	
	is			

As you see, *be* takes eight different forms. In addition, *be* is the one verb that takes present-tense forms that are different from the base form. The base form and the present-tense form of *cheer* are the same: *I cheer for the Cubs*. But the present-tense form for *be* may be any of three forms: *am, are,* or *is*.

■ Present-Tense Forms of the Verb Be

	SINGULAR	PLURAL
FIRST PERSON	I *am* a Cubs fan.	We *are* Cubs fans.
SECOND PERSON	You *are* a Cubs fan.	You *are* Cubs fans.
THIRD PERSON	She *is* a Cubs fan.	They *are* Cubs fans.

Be also takes two different forms in the past tense, *was* and *were*:

■ **Past-Tense Forms of the Verb Be**

	SINGULAR	PLURAL
FIRST PERSON	I *was* a Cubs fan.	We *were* Cubs fans.
SECOND PERSON	You *were* a Cubs fan.	You *were* Cubs fans.
THIRD PERSON	She *was* a Cubs fan. Joe *was* a Cubs fan.	They *were* Cubs fans.

The verb *have* presents fewer complications than *be*. With the exception of the third-person singular, the present tense is regular:

	SINGULAR	PLURAL
FIRST PERSON	I *have* an idea.	We *have* an idea.
SECOND PERSON	You *have* an idea.	You *have* an idea.
THIRD PERSON	She *has* an idea.	They *have* an idea.

The forms of *have* are as follows:

BASE FORM	-S FORM	PRESENT PARTICIPLE FORM	PAST-TENSE FORM	PAST PARTICIPLE FORM
have	has	having	had	had

Using auxiliary verbs (9a)

We use **auxiliary verbs** (some instructors and textbooks call them *helping verbs*) in combination with other verb forms to create a variety of specific verb tenses and meanings. The most commonly used auxiliaries are forms of *be, have,* and *do,* as well as *shall* and *will*.

> I *am working* hard. [*present progressive tense*]
>
> Candice *has been working* hard. [*present perfect progressive tense*]
>
> Carlo *will approve* of that concept. [*simple future tense*]
>
> Aaron *does* not *enjoy* wearing a tie. [*simple present tense to form a negative*]
>
> You *will have seen* your present by this time on Friday. [*future perfect tense*]
>
> One commissioner *did* not *agree*. [*simple past tense to form a negative*]

Although some speakers use the base form *be* as an auxiliary, this is generally not appropriate for academic or formal writing. In addition, sometimes speakers leave out the auxiliary when academic or formal writing would require it:

DIALECT   I *be working* hard today.
                       I *working* hard today.

ACADEMIC WRITING   I *am working* hard today.

In academic or formal writing situations, you should also be careful to distinguish between the contractions *doesn't* and *don't*. Use *doesn't* only with third-person singular subjects; use *don't* with everything else.

DIALECT   The character *don't understand* her situation.

ACADEMIC WRITING   The character *doesn't understand* her situation.
                       The characters *don't understand* their situation.

Several other auxiliaries, called **modal auxiliaries**, are used to indicate necessity, obligation, or possibility. The most commonly used modal auxiliaries are *can, could, may, might, must, ought, should,* and *would*.

I *could* not *work* harder.

Deshon *can substitute* for me.

The government *must address* issues of poverty.

The Mets *ought* to *win* tonight. [*The preposition* to *almost always accompanies* ought.]

The Mets *should have won* last night.

Using regular and irregular verbs (9b)

Most English verbs form their principal parts in the same way: the past-tense and past participle forms are made by adding *-d* or *-ed*. These are known as **regular verbs**. There are several hundred English verbs that do not follow this regular pattern. Called **irregular verbs**, these special cases must simply be memorized or their forms looked up in a dictionary.

As you look over the following list of commonly used irregular verbs, you will notice several patterns. Some irregular verbs change forms by altering an interior vowel (as in *begin, began, begun*). Other verbs do not change at all (as in *hurt, hurt, hurt*). Still others make quite radical changes (as in *go, went, gone*). For convenience, only the base, past-tense, and past participle forms are listed.

BASE FORM	PAST TENSE	PAST PARTICIPLE
arise	arose	arisen
awake	awoke/awaked	awoke/awoken/awaked
beat	beat	beaten
become	became	become
begin	began	begun
bite	bit	bitten/bit
blow	blew	blown
break	broke	broken
bring	brought	brought
build	built	built
burn	burned/burnt	burned/burnt
buy	bought	bought
choose	chose	chosen
come	came	come
cost	cost	cost
dive	dived/dove	dived
do	did	done
draw	drew	drawn
drink	drank	drunk
drive	drove	driven
eat	ate	eaten
feel	felt	felt
fly	flew	flown
forget	forgot	forgotten/forgot
freeze	froze	frozen
get	got	gotten
give	gave	given
go	went	gone
grow	grew	grown
hear	heard	heard
hide	hid	hidden
hurt	hurt	hurt
keep	kept	kept
know	knew	known
lead	led	led
let	let	let
lose	lost	lost
mean	meant	meant

meet	met	met
pay	paid	paid
put	put	put
ride	rode	ridden
ring	rang	rung
run	ran	run
say	said	said
see	saw	seen
set	set	set
shake	shook	shaken
shoot	shot	shot
shrink	shrank/shrunk	shrunk/shrunken
sink	sank	sunk
sleep	slept	slept
speak	spoke	spoken
spend	spent	spent
spread	spread	spread
spring	sprang/sprung	sprung
stand	stood	stood
swim	swam	swum
swing	swung	swung
take	took	taken
teach	taught	taught
tear	tore	torn
tell	told	told
think	thought	thought
throw	threw	thrown
wear	wore	worn
write	wrote	written

Using *lie/lay*, *sit/set*, and *rise/raise* (9c)

These particular verbs often cause writers trouble. Does the book *lie* on the table or *lay* on the table? Do I *sit* that record on the stack or *set* it on the stack? Does the sun *rise* in the sky or *raise* in the sky? The key to using these words correctly is the ability to distinguish between transitive and intransitive verbs.

To review, if a verb is **transitive**, it can take an object. *Kicked* is a transitive verb, as in *Wally kicked the empty can*. Kicked what? Kicked the can. The object of the verb *kicked* is *can*. In the pairs of verbs under discussion, *lay*, *set*, and *raise* are transitive verbs; they take objects.

I *lay* the plate on the table. [Lay *means "to put or place."*]

I *set* the plate on the stack. [Set *means "to put or place."*]

I *raise* the fork off the plate. [Raise *means "to lift or bring up."*]

As you might guess, if a verb cannot take an object, it is an **intransitive** verb. *Lie, sit,* and *rise* are intransitive verbs; they do not take objects.

I *lie* on the bed. [Lie *means "to recline."*]

I *sit* in the chair. [Sit *means "to be seated."*]

The bird *rises* into the air. [Rise *means "to go up."*]

One other complication with these pairs of verbs is that they are irregular. Here are their principal parts:

BASE FORM	-S FORM	PRESENT PARTICIPLE FORM	PAST-TENSE FORM	PAST PARTICIPLE FORM
lie	lies	lying	lay	lain
lay	lays	laying	laid	laid
sit	sits	sitting	sat	sat
set	sets	setting	set	set
rise	rises	rising	rose	risen
raise	raises	raising	raised	raised

Finally, you should recognize that of all these verbs, the forms of *lie* and *lay* can be the most confusing. The base form of *lay* is the same as the past-tense form of *lie*. And you should also be careful to distinguish between *lie* meaning "to recline" and *lie* meaning "to tell a falsehood." When used to indicate a falsehood, as in *Eric lied to his friend*, the verb is regular. Its forms are as follows:

BASE FORM	-S FORM	PRESENT PARTICIPLE FORM	PAST-TENSE FORM	PAST PARTICIPLE FORM
lie	lies	lying	lied	lied

VERB TENSES

→ **COMMON ERROR: WRONG TENSE OR VERB FORM**

Another error that is easy to fall into is using verb tenses inaccurately. Verb tense is important, because by using the different tenses correctly, writers can tell readers exactly when things occur in relationship to one another. If you have studied the forms that verbs can take, you have already begun to study verb tenses. The following material will examine in further detail how you can learn to tell one tense from another and know when to use each one.

Tenses are forms of a verb that indicate when the action named by the verb takes place. Here is a list of the tenses a verb can come in, illustrated by the regular verb *talk*. (Remember that the various tenses of an irregular verb may be formed differently.)

SIMPLE PRESENT	talk *or* talks
SIMPLE PAST	talked
SIMPLE FUTURE	will talk
PRESENT PERFECT	has talked *or* have talked
PAST PERFECT	had talked
FUTURE PERFECT	will have talked
PRESENT PROGRESSIVE	is talking *or* are talking
PAST PROGRESSIVE	was talking *or* were talking
FUTURE PROGRESSIVE	will be talking
PRESENT PERFECT PROGRESSIVE	has been talking *or* have been talking
PAST PERFECT PROGRESSIVE	had been talking
FUTURE PERFECT PROGRESSIVE	will have been talking

Using the present tenses (9d)

Simple present

The **simple present tense** can show action happening at the time of speaking or writing:

Marilyn *loves* her sisters.

He *shoots*! He *scores*!

More typically, it is used for habitual actions, for actions likely to be true at all times, or in discussions of literary or artistic works:

Wayne *calls* everyone "Dude."

I *work* at a radio station.

Water *boils* at 100 degrees centigrade.

Hamlet *hesitates* to kill his uncle.

The simple present may indicate a scheduled event in the future, if a time is indicated:

The Grateful Dead *play* in Cleveland next week.

Present progressive

The **present progressive tense** shows action that is ongoing or repeated at the time it is being written or spoken about:

I *am pushing* on the brake, but the car *is* not *stopping*.

She *is running* five miles a day.

It can also be used to indicate a scheduled event in the future:

We *are going* to New York this summer.

Present perfect

The **present perfect tense** shows an action begun in the past and either completed at some unspecified time or continuing into the present:

I *have painted* my masterpiece.

She *has talked* about her boyfriend so much I can't stand it anymore.

Present perfect progressive

The **present perfect progressive tense** shows an ongoing or repeated action begun in the past and continuing into the present:

I *have been thinking*.

He *has been eating* here for years.

As you can see, a knowledge of verb tenses enables you to specify a wide variety of time relationships.

Using the past tenses (9e)

The past tenses all discuss events that are over. Understanding the various relationships of these past tenses will allow you to present events in their proper time order.

Simple past

The **simple past tense** shows completed action:

> Last night I *dreamed* about flying.
>
> The United States *bombed* Hiroshima on August 6, 1945.

Note that the simple past tense shows actions that occurred at a specific time and do not continue into the present, unlike the present perfect tense.

Past progressive

The **past progressive tense** shows ongoing or repeated actions occurring in the past:

> I *was wondering* what to do until you came along.
>
> Clyde *was smoking* two packs a day.

Past perfect

The **past perfect tense** shows actions completed in the past before the occurrence of some other action, also in the past:

> I *had tried* everything; then a new idea struck me.
>
> She looked around and saw that the other *had vanished*.

Past perfect progressive

The **past perfect progressive tense** shows ongoing or repeated action occurring in the past and continuing up until the point of some other action, also in the past:

> We *had been driving* for six hours when we ran out of gas.
>
> When the escapee surrendered, he *had been hiding* for nearly twenty years.

Using the future tenses (9f)

The future tenses discuss events that have not yet occurred. As with present and past tenses, understanding the full variety of future tenses allows writers to indicate time relationships accurately.

Simple future

The **simple future tense** shows action still to occur:

The store *will open* next week.

(Note: The auxiliary *shall* is still occasionally preferred over *will* with the first person pronoun subjects *I* or *we* in formal and academic writing. Most American usage, however, now accepts *will* everywhere.)

Future progressive

The **future progressive tense** shows ongoing action to occur in the future:

As the population ages, we *will be paying* more for health care.

Future perfect

The **future perfect tense** shows action that will be completed before some other action in the future:

I *will have eaten* by the time you get here.

Future perfect progressive

The **future perfect progressive tense** shows a continuing action that will be completed by some specified time in the future:

This June, Sherman *will have been going* to college for three years.

Using verb tenses in sequence (9g)

Writers frequently need to indicate a particular sequence of items or actions. This is often accomplished by employing dependent clauses or verbals. The simplest sequence involves actions happening at the same time: *Debbie looked at me, and I looked at her.* The two actions were happening in the past. Whenever two actions happen at the same time (present, past, or future), the tenses of the verbs or verbals stay the same.

The matter gets more complicated when sentences contain verbs that express actions that happened at different times. In such complex sentences, the tense of the main verb often differs from the tense of the verbs in dependent clauses. In general, you may use whatever tense you need in order to communicate your meaning, so long as your tense sequences stay logical and reasonable. Study the following examples.

LOGICAL SEQUENCES

| SIMPLE FUTURE | | SIMPLE PRESENT |
He *will lend* her the money because he *loves* her.

| FUTURE PERFECT | | SIMPLE PRESENT |
We *will have repaired* your typewriter by the time you *arrive* tomorrow.

ILLOGICAL SEQUENCES

We [SIMPLE PAST] *ate* all the dessert by the time he [SIMPLE PRESENT] *arrives*.

I [PAST PERFECT] *have ridden* bicycles since before you [SIMPLE FUTURE] *will walk*.

The door bell [SIMPLE PAST] *rang* just after Jack [SIMPLE PRESENT] *finishes* talking on the phone.

Infinitives and participles also play an important role in communicating time relationships to readers. There are two infinitive forms: the **present infinitive** (the base form of the verb plus *to*, as in *to swim*) and the **perfect infinitive** (the past participle form of the verb plus *to have*, as in *to have appeared*). These infinitive forms are used as follows:

- The **present infinitive** indicates an action occurring *at the same time as* or *later than* the main verb.

    Alec and Frank like *to play* double solitaire. [*The liking and the playing occur at the same time.*]

    Kyrie will decide *to hire* a specialist. [*The decision comes first, then the hiring.*]

- The **perfect infinitive** indicates action occurring *earlier than* the main verb.

    He was reported *to have left* his fortune to his bulldog Jake. [*The leaving of the fortune came before the report.*]

The three participial forms each indicate a different time in relation to the main verb. The use of these participles is illustrated next.

- The **present participle** formed by adding *-ing* to the base form of the verb indicates action occurring at the same time as that of the main verb.

    Trying to see over the crowd, Ariel stood on her chair. [*The trying and the standing occur at the same time.*]

    Seeking shelter from the hail, we ran to the porch. [*The seeking and the running occur at the same time.*]

- The **present perfect participle** formed by combining the auxiliary *having* with the past participle form indicates action occurring before that of the main verb.

    Having finished her finals, she decided to take a long nap. [*The finishing of finals occurs before the decision to nap.*]

Having predicted rain, the forecaster was embarrassed by the sunshine. [*The prediction comes before the embarrassment.*]

- The **past participle** indicates action occurring either before or at the same time as that of the main verb.

Surprised by the first question, I decided to move on to the next one. [*The surprise comes before the decision.*]

Flown by an expert pilot, the plane turned to a northerly course. [*The flying and the turning happen at the same time.*]

VOICE

Minnesota Fats pocketed the last ball with a two-cushion bank shot.

The last ball was pocketed by Minnesota Fats with a two-cushion bank shot.

If you consider those two sentences, you will see that in the first one, a person is doing something. The person is Minnesota Fats, a legendary pool player. He is the subject of the first sentence. Since Fats is performing the action, we can say that the first sentence is written in the **active voice**.

In the second sentence, the subject is not Minnesota Fats; it is the word *ball*. The verb is *was pocketed*. And in that second sentence, Minnesota Fats is the object of the preposition *by*. This is an example of the **passive voice**: something is done to the subject; the subject does not act but is instead acted upon.

All the examples used so far in this chapter to indicate tense and verb sequence are written in the active voice. The passive voice is formed by using the appropriate auxiliary (some form of *be*) plus the past participle form of the main verb. In the Minnesota Fats example, the auxiliary is *was* and the past participle form of the verb is *pocketed*. To compare active and passive forms, see the following:

	ACTIVE	PASSIVE
SIMPLE PRESENT	She reads the paper.	The paper is read by her.
PRESENT PERFECT	She has read the paper.	The paper has been read by her.
SIMPLE PAST	She read the paper.	The paper was read by her.
PAST PERFECT	She had read the paper.	The paper had been read by her.
SIMPLE FUTURE	She will read the paper.	The paper will be read by her.
FUTURE PERFECT	By noon, she will have read the paper.	By noon, the paper will have been read by her.

In considering the merits of either active or passive voice, writers must recognize several points. Even a quick glance at the comparison chart shows that writing in the active voice produces shorter, more direct sentences. In many kinds of writing, readers appreciate this directness. Sentences in the active voice are also livelier and more vibrant.

The difference between active and passive voice is partly a matter of emphasis. In active voice, the subject performs the action; both the performer (the subject) and the action (the verb) receive emphasis. However, in passive voice, the originator of the action is not the sentence subject. In fact, in passive voice, the originator of the action can be omitted altogether, as in this example:

The last ball was pocketed with a two-cushion bank shot.

Here the *action* receives the emphasis; the force responsible for the action receives no mention at all. Passive construction of this sort is common and appropriate in scientific reporting. A paragraph describing experimental procedures should rightly focus on the procedures themselves rather than on the lab assistants who performed them.

Measurements of water temperature were taken every three minutes for one hour. These temperatures were then compared to measurements taken during phase one. . . .

But passive constructions also make it impossible for readers to learn who or what is responsible for the actions reported. Consider this example:

The monthly rate for day care has been increased another $50.

Who is responsible for implementing this increase? To whom should you complain? The passive construction of the sentence allows those responsible to remain unnamed.

- To change from active to passive, convert the object of the verb into the sentence subject.

  ACTIVE   Tom chased the cat. [*Object of the verb is* cat.]
  PASSIVE   The cat was chased by Tom. [Cat *has become the subject.*]

- To change from passive to active, convert the subject of the verb into a direct or indirect object and find a new subject.

  PASSIVE   The cake was baked for forty minutes. [Cake *is the subject.*]
  ACTIVE   Scott baked the cake for forty minutes. [Cake *has become the direct object and a new subject,* Scott, *has been added.*]

MOOD

The **mood** of a verb reflects how the message of that verb is conceived by its writer. If the verb is meant to express a fact or to ask a question, it takes the **indicative mood**. Verbs used to express commands or requests take the **imperative mood**. Verbs used to express requirements, desires, suggestions, or conditions contrary to fact take the **subjunctive mood**.

Of these, the most common is the **indicative mood**, which is used to convey facts or ask questions. Virtually this entire workbook is written in the indicative mood. All the examples of tense and voice given earlier in this chapter are written in the indicative mood.

The second most common mood is the **imperative mood**, which is used to express commands or requests. Many of the exercise directions in this workbook are written in the imperative mood. Such directions typically omit the sentence subject and use the base form of the verb, as in *Analyze the following sentences*. As you can see, the subject, *you*, has been left out.

The **subjunctive mood** may be used to express requirements, requests, desires, suggestions, or conditions contrary to fact. The subjunctive is used primarily in clauses beginning with *if*, *that*, *as if*, or *as though*. See the forms and examples that follow.

The **present subjunctive** uses the base form of the verb. The present subjunctive form of the verb *be* is simply *be*.

> Contest rules require that you *be* present to win. [*subjunctive expressing a requirement*]
>
> The teacher asked that one volunteer *stay* after school. [*subjunctive expressing a request*]

Note: Third-person singular present subjunctive verbs—such as *stay* in the second sample sentence—do not end in -*s* like third-person singular verbs in other moods.

The **past subjunctive** is the same as the past tense except for the verb *be*, which uses *were* for all subjects.

> If I *were* you, I would vote for the other candidate. [*subjunctive expressing a condition contrary to fact:* If I were you (but I am not you) . . .]
>
> The chimp scratched its head as if it *were* human. [*subjunctive expressing a condition contrary to fact:* . . . as if it were human (but it is not human, it is a chimpanzee); notice the *as if*, which requires the subjunctive in formal writing]
>
> We wished we *were* in Texas. [*subjunctive expressing a desire*]

Note: Because the subjunctive mood often creates a formal tone, some writers and speakers substitute the indicative mood in less formal writing or speaking situations. However, for academic writing, you should still use the subjunctive whenever required.

INFORMAL	That commercial says that if I *was* a real man, I'd own a truck.
ACADEMIC	That commercial implies that if I *were* a real man, I would own a truck.

EXERCISE 9.1 USING APPROPRIATE FORMS OF *BE* AND *HAVE*

NAME _____ DATE _____

Circle the appropriate form of *be* or *have* for each of the following sentences.

1. Grandma Berry am/be/is the oldest living member of the family.
2. I was/were thinking about her this afternoon.
3. She was/were raised in Colorado before World War I.
4. I is/be/am related to her by marriage.
5. Her maiden name is/be/am Boone.
6. Daniel Boone been/was/were her great-great-grandfather.
7. She have/has lived quite a life.
8. About having a large family she said once, "At least you was/were never bored."
9. She also said, "I can't tell you how proud I is/be/am of my children."
10. According to her, "A parent's job is/be/am a lifelong job."
11. Her life has/have been an example to us.
12. She has/have taught us that to am/be/is honest am/be/is a virtue.

9. a sentence using any appropriate noun as its main subject and the past participle form of *freeze* as its main verb

___

10. a sentence using *I* as its main subject and the past participle form of *pass* as its main verb

___

EXERCISE 9.5 DISTINGUISHING BETWEEN *LIE/LAY, SIT/SET,* AND *RISE/RAISE*

Underline the correct verb in each of the following sentences. The first one is done for you.

1. Alice sat/<u>set</u> her cup of tea on the counter.
2. The cat had lain/laid there so long that it was stiff when it stood up.
3. Emmett couldn't remember where he'd sat/set his glass.
4. The class began to fidget because they had sat/set so long.
5. Once the race ended, Becky wanted to sit/set on the grass and rest.
6. If we lie/lay the wrench here, will we remember to put it away?
7. Where is the chicken that lain/laid the golden egg?
8. The children are going to lie/lay themselves down for a nap.
9. The children are going to lie/lay down for a nap.
10. Lois sat/set down at her sewing machine and sat/set the material out in front of her.
11. As the flag rose/raised, a trumpeter played "Taps."
12. The dough bubbles as it rises/raises.

EXERCISE 9.6   USING THE PRESENT TENSES

NAME _____ **DATE** _____

For each specified verb and tense, write a sentence. If the verb is irregular, you may need to consult the list of irregular verbs or a good dictionary.

EXAMPLE   *run*, present perfect   <u>The new car has run every day without fail.</u>

1. *confuse*, present progressive _____

_____

2. *answer*, present perfect _____

_____

3. *watch*, simple present _____

_____

4. *wait*, present perfect progressive _____

_____

5. *lie* (tell an untruth), present progressive _____

_____

6. *sit*, present perfect _____

_____

7. *discuss*, present progressive _____

_____

8. *drink*, present perfect progressive _____

_____

9. *decide*, simple present _____

_____

10. *draw*, present perfect progressive _____

_____

11. *confuse*, simple present _____

_____

12. *exercise*, present progressive _____

_____

EXERCISE 9.7   USING THE PAST TENSES

NAME _____ DATE _____

For each specified verb and tense, write a sentence. If the verb is irregular, you may need to consult the list of irregular verbs or a good dictionary.

EXAMPLE   *swim*, past perfect progressive   <u>I had been swimming for years before the injury.</u>

1. *explain*, simple past _____

2. *forget*, past perfect _____

3. *steal*, past perfect _____

4. *drive*, past perfect progressive _____

5. *unwrap*, past progressive _____

6. *take*, simple past _____

7. *protest*, past perfect progressive _____

8. *conclude*, past progressive _____

9. *know*, past perfect _____

10. *choose*, simple past _____

11. *dream*, past perfect progressive _____

12. *delight*, past progressive _____

tense of dependent clause verb: _____

_____

_____

10. Brad was just beginning to do his Spanish assignment when he has dropped his book.

   main verb: _____

   tense of main verb: _____

   dependent clause verb: _____

   tense of dependent clause verb: _____

   _____

   _____

EXERCISE 9.10   USING VERB TENSES IN LOGICAL SEQUENCE

NAME _____   **DATE** _____

Read each sentence below. If the sequence of tenses is logical, place an *L* on the line following the sentence. If the sequence of tenses is illogical, rewrite the sentence on the lines that follow.

EXAMPLE   When the family cat got hungry, she decides to climb the window screen and look inside.

<u>When the family cat got hungry, she decided to climb the window screen and look inside.</u>

1. Chaunta has surgery last month and hopes to begin training again next week.

2. Some Civil War historians would love to live in 1860.

3. I had just finished spading the garden when you come out with the cold drinks.

4. On the first sunny Saturday in February, we decided to have taken a hike.

5. The evergreens began to grow where the meadow grass ended.

6. Mark had just stepped out of the shower when the lights started to have flickered.

7. Before we started to have eaten dinner, we emptied the dishwasher.

8. David will mow your lawn if you will have called him about it.

9. The coach announced the team's travel schedule after the players finish practice.

10. The student senate needs to have decide about this issue.

11. Next semester I will be traveling to Italy and will have been studying Roman art and architecture.

12. Pleased about finishing her weaving project, Shauvelle decided to take a break.

EXERCISE 9.11   IDENTIFYING ACTIVE AND PASSIVE VOICE

NAME _____ DATE _____

A. Underline the main verb in each sentence, and indicate whether it is active or passive.

   EXAMPLE   The azalea blossoms <u>nod</u> in the wind. <u>active</u>

1. The next section of this report analyzes the experimental data. _____
2. The experimental data are analyzed in the next section of this report. _____
3. My paper was put in your mailbox yesterday afternoon after lunch. _____
4. My roommate put my paper in your mailbox yesterday afternoon after lunch. _____
5. A variety of factors contributed to the outbreak of the Civil War. _____
6. The play was directed wonderfully by Mr. Wallcrown. _____
7. Did Moira tell you about our house rules? _____
8. Branches of trees in every part of town were snapped by the high winds last night. _____
9. Within hours, snow drifted across the field and against the fence. _____
10. During final exams, the library will be closing at 2 A.M. _____
11. The morning weather report predicts a high of 86 degrees. _____
12. Jeff's umbrella had been found in the dining hall. _____

B. The following paragraph contains five examples of the active voice and six of the passive voice. Circle each example and mark an *A* or a *P* over each one.

   Martin Scorcese makes wonderful films. Each frame is shot carefully, and each set includes the smallest of details. That is because Scorcese demands excellence from his crew. And the crew is expected to fulfill their filmmaker's vision. Each actor is directed by Scorcese with sensitivity and skill. The director choreographs every move, every word. Yet it is all made to appear completely natural. That is the mark of a truly great director. And that is why his work is treasured by moviegoers and critics alike. The movies made by Scorcese will surely distinguish themselves for many years to come.

EXERCISE 9.12 ANALYZING THE USES OF ACTIVE AND PASSIVE VOICE

Below is the paragraph from Exercise 9.11. Rewrite it on your own paper, changing the active voices to passive voices and vice versa. Underline each verb in your rewritten version. As you rewrite, pay attention to which voices you think sound better for each sentence. Which voice do you think holds the reader's interest more?

> Martin Scorcese makes wonderful films. Each frame is shot carefully, and each set includes the smallest of details. That is because Scorcese demands excellence from his crew. And the crew is expected to fulfill their filmmaker's vision. Each actor is directed by Scorcese with sensitivity and skill. The director choreographs every move, every word. Yet it is all made to appear completely natural. That is the mark of a truly great director. And that is why his work is treasured by moviegoers and critics alike. The movies made by Scorcese will surely distinguish themselves for many years to come.

EXERCISE 9.13 IDENTIFYING VERB MOODS

Read the following short paragraph from a letter. Above each underlined verb, pencil in the mood of that verb. The first verb mood has been identified for you.

The year 1994 <u>marks</u> [*indicative*] an anniversary in American art: one hundred years since Norman Rockwell's birth. Some commentators <u>argue</u> that Rockwell <u>remains</u> the most popular American artist of the twentieth century, yet they expect that this anniversary <u>will be celebrated</u> by few museums. This neglect <u>arises</u> because Rockwell's paintings <u>have been judged</u> too sentimental to merit critical praise. They cite Rockwell's own words, "I <u>paint</u> life as I <u>would like</u> it to be," as evidence of his escapism. Others argue that such judgments <u>have been made</u> simply because Rockwell's work was so popular. But real judgments <u>can be made</u> only by looking at the art—the paintings themselves. <u>Look</u> at his work in person if you get the opportunity.

EXERCISE 9.14 USING VERB MOODS

NAME _____ **DATE** _____

Circle the correct form of the verb to be used, and write in the blank whether the verb is indicative, imperative, or subjunctive.

EXAMPLE Whenever he sees a cat, our Doberman bark / (barks) _indicative_

1. It would be best if you study / studies more tonight instead of going out. _____

2. Lemurs climb / climbs trees much better than gorillas. _____

3. Whenever that screen door close / closes, it slams. _____

4. Take / Takes a left at the next light, and the station is on your right. _____

5. If Lamont were / is / was here, he would know what to do. _____

6. Go ahead, make / makes my day. _____

7. Your cooperation is / were requested at the hearing. _____

8. Peanut butter make / makes the best sandwich. _____

9. Hand / Hands me that light bulb on the shelf, will you? _____

10. My coach made it seem as if I were / was / is ready to set a new record. _____

10 Maintaining Subject-Verb Agreement

Just as friends agree about going to a favorite restaurant, you and your boss agree about your responsibilities at work, and countries agree to honor a treaty, so must subjects and verbs agree in **number** (singular or plural) and in **person** (first, second, or third). Similarly, pronouns must agree with their antecedents in number, person, and **gender** (feminine, masculine, or neuter). This grammatical accord or **agreement** allows readers to associate subjects with verbs correctly (and thereby to understand correctly what writers intend to say). Lack of agreement in these word relationships will often leave readers confused and irritated. Yet errors in agreement appear twice on the list of the top twenty student writing errors. Studying the points presented in this and the next chapter should help, if you too find agreement a difficult skill to master. This chapter will focus on agreement between subject and verb; Chapter 11 will deal with agreement between pronoun and antecedent.

> **SUBJECT-VERB AGREEMENT IN EVERYDAY USE**
>
> Subjects and verbs are at work in almost every statement you make, and you make them "agree" effortlessly most of the time. Look, for instance, at three sentences from a recent broadcast of a baseball game. The subjects and verbs are italicized.
>
> *Guzman powers* another blistering curveball over the plate.
>
> *The Yanks move* on to Milwaukee tomorrow.
>
> *The duel* of the no-hitters *continues* into the eighth.
>
> Listen to someone reporting an event—perhaps a play-by-play announcer or an on-the-scene reporter. Then jot down some of the subject-verb combinations used by this person. Do you find any that don't sound right, that might not "agree"?

→ **COMMON ERROR: LACK OF AGREEMENT BETWEEN SUBJECT AND VERB**

The general rule for subject-verb agreement is simple: singular subjects take singular verbs, and plural subjects take plural verbs. Most often, you make a verb singular by adding *-s* or *-es* to the base form. See the examples in the sections that follow.

Making verbs agree with third-person singular subjects (10a)

In the present tense, a third-person singular noun subject takes a verb ending in *-s* or *-es*. The third-person pronoun subjects *he, she,* and *it* also take verbs ending in *-s* or *-es*. (Note that the verbs *be* and *have* are exceptions to this rule. See Chapter 9 for a discussion of these verbs.)

EXAMPLES   A Madras shirt fade<u>s</u> when washed. [Shirt *is the third-person singular noun subject of the verb.*]

The projectionist watch<u>es</u> the movie. [Projectionist *is the third-person singular noun subject of the verb.*]

She swim<u>s</u> every other day. [She *is the third-person singular pronoun subject of the verb.*]

These *-s* or *-es* endings are not always easy to hear in speech and are not a part of some spoken American dialects of English. However, writers using standard written English should always use these endings. (Of course noun and pronoun subjects that are not third-person singular do not require an *-s* or *-es* ending. Be careful to write *we swim* and *you swim* rather than *we swims* and *you swims*, for instance.)

Making the subject and verb agree when separated by other words (10b)

Do not let words that come between subject and verb confuse subject-verb agreement. In the following example, the noun nearest the verb is *baskets* (plural). However, *baskets* is not the sentence subject; the subject is *contestant*.

RIGHT   The contestant who makes the most consecutive baskets wins four free pizzas.

WRONG   The contestant who makes the most consecutive baskets win four free pizzas.

In that example, a clause comes between the subject and the verb. Sometimes the intervening words are other sentence elements, such as prepositional phrases, as in this example:

RIGHT   One of his bodyguards accompanies him at all times.

WRONG   One of his bodyguards accompany him at all times.

Occasionally a sentence meaning will appear to conflict with its actual grammar. This is especially true when a sentence subject is followed by a phrase beginning with *as well as, along with, together with, in addition to,* or any similar expression. In such sentences the meaning becomes plural, though grammatically the sentence subject stays singular. Here is an example:

Senator Kutz, along with her aides, travels the state in a large van.

Here the grammatical subject (*Senator Kutz*) is in the third-person singular and so takes a singular verb (*travels*). Even though that sentence is grammatically correct, it may sound awkward to you. To eliminate such awkwardness, some writers will simply revise the sentence in this way: *Senator Kutz and her aides travel the state in a large van.* Now the subject is *Senator Kutz and her aides*; this is grammatically plural and takes a plural verb, *travel*. (More on such compound subjects appears later in this chapter.)

When proofreading to check on subject-verb agreement, reducing the sentence to only its subject and verb should make any such errors easier to spot.

The cook who baked these pizzas knows what he's doing. [cook . . . knows]

The coach, together with the team members, arrives in Salt Lake City at 9:36 P.M. [coach . . . arrives]

Making verbs agree with compound subjects (10c)

You may well understand the general rule that singular subjects take singular verbs and plural subjects take plural verbs yet still have some difficulty deciding when a subject is singular and when it is plural. Consider this example:

Jack and Jill run up the hill.

The word *Jack* by itself is singular; so is *Jill*. Yet the sentence has the two people running up a hill. This sentence is formed around a **compound subject**, two subjects (or more) joined by *and*. As you see from the following rule, most of the time, sentences with compound subjects take plural verbs.

- Subjects joined by *and* are usually plural and take plural verbs. However, if two or more parts of a subject form a single idea or refer to one person, those parts are considered to be singular and take a singular verb.

    EXAMPLES   Jack and Jill *run* up the hill. [*Subjects joined by* and *take a plural verb.*]

    Bacon and eggs *is* the most commonly ordered breakfast. [*Subjects combine to form a single item; thus the verb is singular.*]

- If the adjective *each* or *every* precedes a compound subject, the verb following that subject is usually singular.

    EXAMPLE   Each bud and flower *is* a sign of spring.

Now let us look at several other agreement rules.

- Compound subjects joined by *or* or *nor* take singular verbs if they are both singular, plural verbs if they are both plural.

    EXAMPLES   Neither the lifeguard nor the instructor *is* responsible for providing towels. [*singular subjects, singular verb*]

    Either the pool employees or the parents *are* responsible for providing towels. [*plural subjects, plural verb*]

- When one part of a subject joined by *or* or *nor* is singular and the other part is plural, the verb agrees with the part of the subject closest to it. (Common practice is to place the plural part of the subject last in these constructions, making the verb also plural.)

    EXAMPLE   Typically, either rain or cold temperatures *ruin* March weekends.

- When the parts of a subject differ in person, the verb agrees with the nearer subject.

    EXAMPLES   Either Trent or you *were* lying.

    Either you or Trent *was* lying.

Since sentences of this sort often sound awkward, writers often split the subjects, giving each its own verb: *Either Trent was lying, or you were.*

Making verbs agree with collective-noun or indefinite-pronoun subjects (10d, 10e)

Collective nouns also cause some writers trouble when it comes to agreement because these nouns (such as *family* and *team*) are singular in form even though they refer to collections of many people or things. Should such nouns be considered singular or plural? Should they take singular or plural verbs? The answers to these questions hinge on the writer's intentions.

Commonly used collective nouns are *family, team, audience, group, jury, crowd, band, class, flock,* and *committee.*

- When used as subjects, collective nouns take singular verbs when they refer to the group as a whole; they take plural verbs when they refer to parts of the group.

    EXAMPLES   My family generally *eats* dinner at six o'clock. [family *as one unit: singular verb*]

    That committee *makes* the policy decisions. [committee *as a unit: singular verb*]

My family *were* all born in the United States. [*individual family members: plural verb*]

By their nature, **indefinite pronouns**—pronouns that do not refer to specific things or persons—cause writers trouble when it comes to agreement. Often these pronouns can be used as both singular and plural, and some sound plural but are considered grammatically singular. Here is a list of pronouns that are singular in meaning and thus take singular verbs:

another	each	everything	no one	somebody
anybody	either	much	nothing	someone
anyone	everybody	neither	one	something
anything	everyone	nobody	other	

EXAMPLES *Neither* of the children *enjoys* broccoli. [Of the children *is a prepositional phrase; therefore,* children *cannot function as the grammatical subject of* enjoys.]

Another of the Barlows *enters* school next year.

Something about his voice and delivery *seems* particularly convincing.

Other indefinite pronouns are always plural. These include *both, few, many, others,* and *several*.

Several of the graduates *take* vacations after their graduation ceremony. [*Several is plural; hence, the plural verb* take.]

Still other indefinite pronouns—*all, any, enough, more, most, none,* and *some*—may be singular or plural, depending on the noun they refer to.

Most of the members *are* satisfied. [Members *is plural; thus* most *is considered plural.*]

Most of the cake *is* gone. [Cake *is singular; thus* most *is considered singular.*]

Making verbs agree with relative-pronoun subjects (10f)

So far, the discussion of subject-verb agreement has focused mostly on simple sentences without dependent clauses. Now it is time to shift attention to dependent clauses, especially ones that are introduced by **relative pronouns** (*who, which,* or *that*). Often (though not always) these relative pronouns act as subjects of the clauses they introduce.

Notice, first, that by themselves, relative pronouns are neither singular nor plural; the singular form of *who* is no different from the plural form. Thus writers must determine what the pronoun refers to in order to decide whether the verb should be singular or plural.

VERB	**SUBJECT**	
Is	a duck-billed platypus	a mammal?

(As a declarative sentence, the word order would be: *A duck-billed platypus is a mammal.*)

Writers working on rough drafts also commonly use another kind of sentence inversion. These sentences typically begin with *there*, followed by a form of the verb *be*. In such cases, the subject follows the verb. *There* never acts as the subject of a sentence.

>There are many Vietnam veterans who are still haunted by the war experience.
>[*The verb* are *agrees with the subject* veterans.]

Stylistic note: Sentences beginning with *there are* bury their most important content in dependent clauses. A more forceful wording would be *Many Vietnam veterans are still haunted by their war experience.*

EXERCISE 10.1   MAINTAINING SUBJECT-VERB AGREEMENT

NAME _____ **DATE** _____

Read the following paragraph. Then go back and look at each sentence. Circle the sentence subject, and underline the main verb. (Ignore dependent clauses.) If the sentence subject and verb do not agree, write in the accurate verb. The first sentence has been done for you. (*Hint:* Remember that sentence subjects cannot be the objects of prepositions.)

                    continue

(Computers) continues to change business practices. The use of photographs are one example. Before computers, the process worked something like this. A news photographer take a picture of an athlete. The photograph captures the essence of determination and hard work. Several of the competing newspapers decides to buy the picture for their Sunday editions. In each case, the photographer sells only one-time reproduction rights. Thus each of these sales generate new income. Now, however, many photographs have been digitalized and recorded on CD-ROMs. Anyone who owns the CD-ROM also own access to the photographs. The question that arises are this: how do CD-ROM manufacturers make sure that photographers receive fair payment?

EXERCISE 10.2   MAINTAINING AGREEMENT WITH COMPOUND SUBJECTS

A. Read the following sentences. Circle each subject, and underline each verb. If subjects and verbs agree, write a *C* on the line below the sentence. If they do not, write a corrected version.

    EXAMPLE   Neither the (lawyer) nor her (clients) <u>shows</u> any worries about winning the case.
                          <u>Neither the lawyer nor her clients show any worries about winning the case.</u>

1. Neither the witnesses nor the police officers was able to identify the hit-and-run driver positively. _____

   _____

2. Neither the witnesses nor the police officer were able to identify the hit-and-run driver positively. _____

   _____

3. Neither the car nor its occupants were seriously harmed. _____

4. Either you or the other driver were responsible for the accident. _____

5. Either the insurance company or you is going to pay for repairs. _____

B. Below you are provided with compound subjects and base-form verbs. Use these to write a sentence in the present tense, taking particular care that subjects and verbs agree.

EXAMPLE   subject: *budding flowers and freshly cut lawns*   verb: *remind*

   <u>Budding flowers and freshly cut lawns remind me of spring</u>.

1. subject: *papers and midterms*   verb: *require*

2. subject: *each paper and midterm*   verb: *challenge*

3. subject: *my best friend and confidant*   verb: *work*

4. subject: *Maria and Emilio*   verb: *prepare*

5. subject: *either the teacher or the students*   verb: *select*

EXERCISE 10.3 MAINTAINING VERB AGREEMENT WITH COLLECTIVE-NOUN OR INDEFINITE-PRONOUN SUBJECTS

NAME _____ DATE _____

In each sentence below, circle the subject, and underline the main verb. Indicate whether the subject is a collective noun or an indefinite pronoun. If the subject and verb agree, place a C on the line below the sentence; if the subject and verb do not agree, rewrite the sentence so that the verb agrees with its subject.

EXAMPLE   (None) of the employees is able to substitute for you on Friday.

Subject is <u>an indefinite pronoun.</u>

<u>None of the employees are able to substitute for you on Friday.</u>

1. A group of twelve students in my apartment building form a grocery shopping co-op.

   Subject is _____

   _____

2. Both buying food in large amounts and paying a low price is our goal.

   Subject is _____

   _____

3. Most of our purchases each month reflects the best produce buys available that season.

   Subject is _____

   _____

4. Some of the purchases result from the food preferences of the two shoppers that month.

   Subject is _____

   _____

5. Each of the shoppers spend about half a day buying bulk food.

   Subject is _____

   _____

11 Maintaining Pronoun-Antecedent Agreement

Denied the use of pronouns, writers would have to use the same nouns over and over; that would make for dull repetition. In a description, for example, the name of the person or thing described would have to be repeated. A dog would have to scratch "the dog's back" instead of "its back," and Robert would have to put on "Robert's raincoat" instead of "his raincoat." Fortunately, we can use pronouns. But we do need to be careful that every time we do so, readers understand the pronoun's antecedent. The **antecedent** is simply the noun (or noun phrase) that the pronoun replaces, the one to which it refers. Writers must make sure that both noun and pronoun agree in *gender, number,* and *person.*

EXAMPLE The rain forced Melissa to leave her bicycle at home. [*The pronoun* her *refers to Melissa. The gender is feminine; the number is singular; the person is third.*]

PRONOUN-ANTECEDENT AGREEMENT IN EVERYDAY USE

Look—or listen—for pronouns in some everyday situation such as checking the instructional manual for an appliance, explaining how to do a household chore, or giving directions for finding a destination. Record what you find. If you wish, compare written and spoken directions to see how pronouns are used differently, and whether writers are more careful than speakers.

→ **COMMON ERROR: LACK OF AGREEMENT BETWEEN PRONOUN AND ANTECEDENT**

Many cases of pronoun-antecedent agreement are easy to achieve, and we may manage that agreement without giving it a thought. But some special cases often prove confusing and can give even experienced writers some difficulty. Let us look at these cases now.

Making pronouns agree with compound or collective-noun antecedents (11a, 11b)

Compound antecedents, two or more nouns or noun phrases joined by *and*, usually require plural pronouns.

EXAMPLE   It was such a hot afternoon that Beth and Jane left their coats at school. [Their *refers to* Beth and Jane.]

However, note two exceptions:

1. If a compound antecedent follows *each* or *every*, the indefinite pronoun acts as the antecedent, and the following pronoun is singular.

    EXAMPLE   Each undergrad and grad student carries his or her own student ID. [His or her *refers to the singular pronoun* each.]

    Every mother and daughter should fill out her own questionnaire. [Her *refers to the singular pronoun* every.]

2. If a compound antecedent joined by *and* refers to a single thing or person, the following pronoun is singular.

    EXAMPLE   This writer and student has achieved his success through discipline and diligence. [His *refers to one person*, this writer and student.]

- When two or more antecedents are connected by *or* or *nor*, the pronoun should agree with the part of the antecedent closest to it.

    EXAMPLES   Either one or several chapters will arrive in their folders. [*Pronoun* their *agrees with* chapters.]

    Neither the suitcase nor the golf clubs were recovered in their original condition. [*Pronoun* their *agrees with* clubs.]

(Note: In the second example, the plural noun antecedent *clubs* follows the singular noun antecedent *suitcase*. This reflects the common practice of putting the plural antecedent second, nearer the verb.)

Compound antecedents of different genders can pose problems for writers. Consider this sentence: *Either Dave or Holly will bring _____ own guitar.* What pronoun should go in the blank? Using *her* would seem to eliminate Dave; using *his* would seem to eliminate Holly. Using *their* would imply that they own one guitar jointly, and perhaps they do. But if the sentence means to indicate that both Dave and Holly own separate guitars, no single pronoun will fit in that blank. The best solution here is to rewrite the sentence: *Either Dave will bring his guitar, or Holly will bring hers.*

Agreement problems arise for some writers when they use **collective nouns**, nouns that are singular in form but refer to collections of things or people. These nouns include words like *army, audience, committee, crowd, class, family, group,* and *team.*

- Collective nouns with singular meanings take singular pronouns; collective nouns with plural meanings take plural pronouns.

When you are referring to a group as a single unit, use the singular pronoun. When you are referring to individual members of that group, use the plural pronoun.

EXAMPLES The crowd erupted with applause as it demanded an encore. [Crowd *as a single unit takes the singular pronoun* it.]

After the encore, the crowd drifted away to their cars. [Crowd *focusing on its members is plural in meaning and takes the plural pronoun* their.]

Making pronouns agree with indefinite-pronoun antecedents (11c)

If you have already worked through Chapter 10 of this book, you may recall that **indefinite pronouns** may be always singular (*anybody, each,* and *someone* are examples), always plural (*many, few, several*), or either singular or plural depending on context (*all, more, some*). Pronouns referring to indefinite pronoun antecedents must agree in number with their antecedents. See the examples that follow.

Each of the women in the bridal party wore a dress that *she* herself made. [Each *is the singular pronoun subject of this sentence.* She *is singular and refers to* each.]

Many of the visiting swimmers won *their* races. [Many *is a plural indefinite pronoun;* their *is also plural and refers to* many.]

All of the remaining sale items should be returned to *their* original storeroom locations. [*Since* all *refers to* items, *it is considered plural; hence, the plural pronoun* their.]

Not *all* of the recovered oil could be cleansed of *its* impurities. [*Here* all *refers to an uncountable quantity,* oil; *hence,* all *is considered singular.* Its, *a singular pronoun, refers to* all.]

Checking for sexist pronouns (11d)

Indefinite pronouns such as those discussed in the preceding section often present problems of sexist usage. Consider this example:

An usher stood at the front of the movie theater and asked, "If *anyone* here is a doctor, would *he* please come forward?"

This sentence uses what is called *the generic he* to refer to people of either sex. Although grammatically acceptable, today this usage is often criticized because it seems to ignore or exclude half the human race. The best remedy for sexist usage is rewording:

5. Callahan and Larson syndicated their cartoons nationwide.

   Pronouns/antecedents: _____

6. This speed skater and disciplined athlete has achieved her goals.

   Pronouns/antecedents: _____

7. Sarah or she called their parents with the good news.

   Pronouns/antecedents: _____

8. The jurors have agreed to tell the story of its deliberations.

   Pronouns/antecedents: _____

9. Neither Jeremy's wallet nor its contents were recovered by police.

   Pronouns/antecedents: _____

10. Either Ruben or Jeanette will give their oral presentation Tuesday.

    Pronouns/antecedents: _____

EXERCISE 11.2 MAKING PRONOUNS AGREE WITH INDEFINITE PRONOUNS, AND AVOIDING SEXIST USAGE

NAME _____ **DATE** _____

Some of the sentences in the following paragraph use pronouns that unnecessarily identify the gender of an antecedent and thereby seem to exclude one sex. Some sentences may also contain errors of agreement between pronouns and indefinite-pronoun antecedents. In either case, circle the incorrect or sexist pronoun, and write the correct one above it. If you need to alter the antecedent or any other words, feel free to do so. If the sentence does not need revision, write a *C* next to it.

EXAMPLES

Doctors study
(A doctor) studies for years in order to provide the best care for (his) patients. *their*

their rounds
All golfers should be finished with (his or her) round by 5:30.

Anybody who works for a small company has to learn how to do his job well. Only a few people in such businesses are able to rely on his relatives to help him keep a job, and many eventually lose their jobs trying to replace competent work with political favors or friendship. In a small company, each person has to do their job correctly because nobody else is available to redo their work if it is sloppy or finish their work if it is late. A secretary who wastes time and does not finish her typing cannot expect her boss to be sympathetic. He has other work to do and cannot add the job of typing. On the other hand, a small business may allow more flexibility than a big company if a parent has to pick up her sick child or an employee needs to leave early to get to his class on time. This flexibility is likely to build loyalty so that more of the employees will want to devote his or her full energies to the job.

12 Using Adjectives and Adverbs

Writers use adjectives and adverbs to describe, limit, qualify, or specify. Without such modifiers, we would find it hard to say precisely what we want to say: instead of *medium-rare steak*, it would be just *steak*; instead of *fresh, New England–style clam chowder*, it would be just *chowder*. Without adjectives and adverbs, we would not be able to do justice to the fascinating and necessary details of our lives. (Note: This chapter does not discuss verbals used as adjectives or adverbs, nor does it discuss prepositional phrases functioning as adjectives or adverbs. For discussion of these matters, see Chapter 7.)

ADJECTIVES AND ADVERBS IN EVERYDAY USE

Adjectives often carry indispensable shades of meaning. In basketball, for example, there's an important difference between a *slam dunk* and an *alley-oop dunk*, a *flagrant foul* and a *technical foul*, a *layup* and a *reverse layup*. Consider as well the distinction between *talk* and *trash talk*, or *color commentary* and *play-by-play commentary*. In each case, the difference is in the adjectives. Look in the newspaper or a magazine for examples of adjectives that carry significant meaning in a sport or other activity that you know well. Make notes about what you find. Which of these adjectives add vividness to the writing, and which ones add essential information?

Distinguishing adjectives from adverbs (12a)

Adjectives can modify nouns (*blue* marble, *desperate* clients, *sleazy* proposal) and pronouns (*Stylish* and *confident*, he arrived for the trial). Some adjectives are formed by adding endings to nouns or verbs. These endings include *-al*, *-ive*, *-ish*, *-able*, *-less*, and *-ful*:

form (noun)	formal (adjective)
act (noun or verb)	active (adjective)
style (noun)	stylish (adjective)
comfort (noun)	comfortable (adjective)
rest (noun or verb)	restless (adjective)
rest (noun or verb)	restful (adjective)

Some adjectives are formed by adding the *-ly* ending to a noun (as in *lovely*, *earthly, ghostly*). This is, however, an uncommon way to form adjectives. Regardless of how they are formed, adjectives usually answer one of these questions: *which, how many,* or *what kind?*

Adverbs modify verbs, adjectives, and other adverbs:

> The cat *patiently* waited for its dinner. [*modifies verb* waited]
>
> Phil waited for an *especially* hungry fish to take the bait. [*modifies adjective* hungry]
>
> After dinner, the cat rested *quite* comfortably on the sofa. [*modifies adverb* comfortably]

Occasionally adverbs modify whole clauses, as in this sentence: *Garcia said that, regrettably, he would be late.* Here, *regrettably* modifies the clause *he would be late.*

As you can see, adding *-ly* to adjectives is the most common way of forming adverbs. However, there are also quite a number of adverbs (*very* and *quite,* for example) that do not have the *-ly* ending. Other examples of these are *here, fast, there, now, then, often, soon,* and *late.* Regardless of how they are formed, adverbs usually answer one of these questions: *how, when, where,* or *to what extent?*

REVIEW

- Adjectives modify nouns or pronouns.
- Adverbs modify verbs, adjectives, other adverbs, or (occasionally) entire clauses.

Using adjectives and adverbs after linking verbs (12b)

As you have seen, a word may often have both an adverbial and an adjectival form. Consider *bright,* for example. As written here, *bright* is an adjective. Adding *-ly* makes the adverb *brightly.* Partly because informal speech often does not distinguish between these two forms, writers sometimes have trouble deciding which form to use in a given sentence. The only certain way to choose correctly between *bright* and *brightly* is to determine the part of speech of the word being described. If the word is a noun or a pronoun, the modifier must be an adjective, *bright.* If the word (or phrase or clause) functions as a verb, as an adjective, or as an adverb, the modifier must be an adverb, *brightly.*

> The sun shone *brightly* through the window. [*adverb modifies the action verb* shone]
>
> The *bright* sun shone through the window. [*adjective modifies the noun subject* sun]

Adverbs can often change position in a sentence without destroying its meaning:

> The sun shone *brightly* through the window.
>
> The sun shone through the window *brightly*.

Adjectives, by contrast, must usually either precede closely the nouns or pronouns they modify (*rainy* morning, *yellow* paper, and so on) or follow linking verbs. If they follow linking verbs, they are called predicate adjectives. Recall that **linking verbs** are various forms of the verb *be* (*is, are, was, were, will be,* and so on), as well as verbs such as *look, sound, become, appear, taste, feel, seem, smell, remain,* and *prove*. In general, if you can replace a verb with some form of *be* without substantially changing the sentence meaning, the verb is probably a linking verb. Consider the sentence *The doughnuts tasted delicious*. Is the verb *tasted* a linking verb? If we substitute a past plural form of *be*, we get this sentence: *The doughnuts were delicious.* The test works; *tasted* functions here as a linking verb.

It is necessary to pursue this question in order to determine whether the word *delicious* should be an adjective or whether it should be the adverbial form *deliciously*. The rule is simple:

- Modifiers following a linking verb modify the sentence subject and must therefore be adjectives.

Here are two more examples:

CORRECT   After three hours in a warm keg, the beer tastes *flat*.

INCORRECT   After three hours in a warm keg, the beer tastes *flatly*.

CORRECT   Sorenson felt *angry* that the elevator was broken again.

INCORRECT   Sorenson felt *angrily* that the elevator was broken again.

Distinguishing between *good* and *well*, *bad* and *badly*, *real* and *really* (12c)

These adjectives and adverbs can cause writers trouble because common speech often blurs the distinctions between them. If you are writing dialogue or quoting someone speaking informally, you may also blur those distinctions. But if you are writing in a formal or academic setting, you should be careful to observe the distinctions outlined here.

- *Good, bad, well,* and *real* are adjectives and may follow linking verbs. (Note that *well* here means "in good health.")

Our June weather has been *good*. [Good *describes the subject*, weather.]

This leftover tuna smells *bad*. [Bad *describes the subject*, tuna.]

After treatment, the patient felt *well* again. [Well *describes the subject*, patient.]

That pearl looks *real*. [Real *describes the subject*, pearl.]

Remember that some linking verbs can also act as action verbs, as in *I looked really carefully at the fine print*. Here *looked* functions as an action verb; *carefully* is an adverb modifying *looked*; *really* is an adverb modifying *carefully*.

- *Well* may also function as an adverb to modify a verb, an adjective, or another adverb. (Note that when functioning as an adverb, *well* has nothing to do with health.)

    A chef for over eight years, she cooks *well*. [Well *modifies the verb* cooks.]

- *Badly* and *really* are adverbs and should be used to modify verbs, adjectives, or other adverbs.

    A chef for over eight years, she cooks *really* well. [Really *modifies the adverb* well.]

    They bungled that first experiment *badly*. [Badly *modifies the verb* bungled.]

Using comparative and superlative forms (12d)

Most adjectives and adverbs have three forms. The **positive** form is the simple dictionary form:

The mouse is a *small* mammal.

Alyce arrived *early*.

The **comparative** form is made either by adding the ending *-er* or by adding *more* or *less* (intensifiers). The comparative form literally compares the modified thing with some other thing:

The mouse is *smaller* than the hedgehog. [*comparative form of the adjective* small]

Hank arrived *earlier*. [*comparative form of the adverb* early]

The **superlative** form is made by adding the ending *-est* or by adding *most* or *least* (intensifiers). The superlative form compares the modified thing with at least two others and declares it to be the most extreme:

Of the mouse, the hedgehog, and the wildebeest, the mouse is the *smallest*. [*superlative form of the adjective* small]

Josie arrived *earliest*. [*superlative form of the adverb* early]

How do you know when to add an ending (*-er* or *-est*) and when to use an intensifier (*more, most, less, least*)? *-Er* and *-est* are used for most—though not all—one- and two-syllable adjectives. Longer adjectives and most adverbs use the intensifiers (*more/less, most/least*). Sometimes intensifiers are used with the shorter adjectives; the effect in these cases is greater emphasis and formality.

POSITIVE FORM	COMPARATIVE FORM	SUPERLATIVE FORM
tall	taller	tallest
early	earlier	earliest
imposing	more imposing	most imposing

There are some two-syllable adjectives that do not take *-er* or *-est* (*careful, honest,* or *scattered,* for instance). If you are not sure whether a particular adjective or adverb has *-er* and *-est* forms, look up the positive form in a college dictionary. If the *-er* and *-est* forms exist, they will be listed following the positive form.

- When comparing two things, use the comparative degree.

When speaking informally, we are often tempted to use the superlative; however, formal or academic writing normally requires the correct comparative form.

CORRECT	The painting is taller than I am. [*comparison of two things: a painting's height and the speaker's height*]
INCORRECT	Of woodworking and painting, painting is the most difficult. [*comparison of two things: the difficulty of painting and the difficulty of woodworking*]
CORRECT	Of woodworking and painting, painting is the more difficult.

- Use the superlative degree when comparing three or more things and to indicate that the modified word is the most extreme—the largest or smallest, best or worst, most intense or least intense—of those things.

Of the three dogs we know, we like Tom the *best*.

My personal opinion is that *The Shining* is Stephen King's *best* novel. [King wrote more than two novels.]

Now consider this example:

Elise was least interested in art history and most interested in mathematical group theory.

Are only two things being compared here? If so, the example is incorrect as given. If Elise is interested in several things, the sentence is technically correct as written; it is also open to misinterpretation by readers. Solution? Rewrite the sentence to clarify the terms of the comparison.

Of all her college courses, Elise was least interested in art history and most interested in mathematical group theory.

Of her two courses that term, Elise was less interested in art history and more interested in mathematical group theory.

Recognizing irregular forms

Note the following irregular forms for some commonly used adjectives and adverbs.

POSITIVE	COMPARATIVE	SUPERLATIVE
good	better	best
well	better	best
bad	worse	worst
ill	worse	worst
little [quantity]	less	least
little [size]	littler	littlest
many	more	most
some	more	most
much	more	most

As you can see, many comparative and superlative forms overlap. Thus it is accurate to write *Graf played better today than she played yesterday* (*better* here functions as an adverb modifying the verb *played*), and it is also accurate to say *She feels better today than she did yesterday* (*better* here functions as a predicate adjective following the linking verb *feels* and modifying the subject *she*).

Selecting adjectives and adverbs when using comparative forms

REVIEW

- Adjectives modify nouns or pronouns.
- Adverbs modify verbs, adjectives, or other adverbs.

When we talk, we frequently blur the distinction between comparative adverbs and comparative adjectives. Thus we might say, "I finished this race easier than the last one." In that sentence, *easier* is an adjective incorrectly modifying the verb *finished*. Writers should preserve the adjective-adverb distinction, making the sentence read, "I finished this race more easily than I finished the last one."

Checking for double comparatives and superlatives

Do not use an intensifier with an *-er* or *-est* ending.

INCORRECT	Helen is more smarter than I am. [*double comparative*]
REVISED	Helen is smarter than I am.
INCORRECT	Jack is the most quietest student in the class. [*double superlative*]
REVISED	Jack is the quietest student in the class.

Making comparisons complete

In the shared context of everyday speech, we may often make ourselves clear without completing the second half of a comparison. For example, if you and your spouse are shopping for a used car, one of you might well walk up to the fourth car you've looked at and say, "This looks better to me." Such statements are not effective in writing. The reader can only wonder, "Better than what?" The context of your shared experience with the earlier three cars would probably make that comparison clear. But in formal or academic writing (or whenever a reader or listener does not share your experience), the audience can easily misunderstand. Thus it is important to make the terms of your comparisons absolutely straightforward.

| **INCOMPLETE** | When considering capital punishment, some people argue that its deterrent effect is more important. [*more important than what?*] |
| **COMPLETE** | When considering capital punishment, some people argue that its deterrent effect is more important than the moral argument against the taking of human life. |

EXERCISE 12.1   WRITING WITH ADJECTIVES AND ADVERBS

NAME _____ **DATE** _____

Rewrite the sentences below, adding your own words to modify various elements. Indicate after the sentence whether you added an adjective or an adverb.

EXAMPLES   Teresa sang last night. (Modify the verb *sang*.)
<u>Teresa sang loudly last night. (adverb)</u>

I like that car. (Modify the noun *car*.)
<u>I like that yellow car. (adjective)</u>

1. Writing tells readers what they need to know. (Modify the noun *writing*.)

   _____

2. For example, suppose your Dodge dies on the freeway. (Modify the verb *dies*.)

   _____

3. The uneven ride tells you that a bald tire has finally gone flat. (Modify the adjective *bald*.)

   _____

4. Once you have pulled out of the traffic, you rummage through the glove compartment looking for the manual. (Modify the noun *traffic*; modify the verb *rummage*.)

   _____

   _____

5. On page 55, you see a diagram that shows where the jack is stored. (Modify the noun *diagram*; modify the verb *shows*.)

   _____

   _____

6. After you have blocked the wheels as the instructions direct, you begin jacking up the car. (Modify the verb *have blocked*.)

   _____

   _____

7. The clear manual spells out every step of the procedure. (Modify the adjective *clear*.)

   _____

8. After fifteen minutes, you finish removing the old tire and attaching your spare. (Modify the noun *minutes*; modify the noun *tire*.)

9. Though you have lost fifteen minutes, you may still make your appointment. (Modify the verb *lost*; modify the noun *minutes*.)

10. The manual's illustrations and explanations have told you what you needed to know. (Modify the noun *illustrations*; modify the noun *explanations*.)

EXERCISE 12.2 USING *GOOD*, *WELL*, *BAD*, *BADLY*, *REAL*, AND *REALLY*

Underline the correct adjective or adverb in each of the following sentences. Be ready to explain your choices.

EXAMPLE   A chef for over eight years, she cooks good/<u>well</u>.

1. A strong introduction is real/really important in a technical report.
2. After a weekend of rest, Dan looked good/well again.
3. Raising the sea chest proved real/really difficult for the divers.
4. After sitting out all night on the counter, the pizza tasted bad/badly.
5. Jessica skated good/well in the competition.
6. Getting a back massage feels real/really good/well.
7. The twins look good/well in their costumes for the play.
8. The parents treated their three children real/really bad/badly.
9. The ski team hopes that the weather will be good/well for tomorrow's practice.
10. He repaired that door bad/badly.

EXERCISE 12.3 IDENTIFYING AND CORRECTING ADJECTIVE-ADVERB ERRORS

NAME _____ **DATE** _____

Read the paragraph below. There are several errors in the usage of adverbs and adjectives. Underline those errors, and write in the correct forms. The first error has been underlined and corrected for you.

slowly
A natural gem <u>slow</u> develops over long periods of time. It may form where moltenly rock has slow cooled, where both intensely heat and greatly pressure have produced metamorphic rocks, or where mineral deposits have collected in layered rocks formed by slowly but persistent erosion. In contrast, a synthetic gem can be quick produced in a laboratory using extreme high heat. The ingredients for the synthetic gem are rapid melted and raised to highly temperatures, but the process takes only hours rather than countlessly years. A synthetic gem of highly quality will look beautifully and will glitter as bright as a natural stone. It also will complete share the same chemical properties and structure. Even a gemologist, a trained expert, may not easy distinguish natural from synthetical gems. The consumer, however, will find that the reputable jeweler proper identifies the synthetic ruby or emerald and sells it for perhaps a tenth of the price of the natural gem.

EXERCISE 12.4 USING COMPARATIVE AND SUPERLATIVE FORMS

The sentences that follow contain various kinds of comparisons. In each case, determine what is being compared and whether or not the correct form of adjective or adverb has been used. If the sentence is correct as written, write C in the space after the sentence. If the sentence is incorrect, underline the incorrect form and write in the correct form.

EXAMPLE Compared to Pizza Gallery's crust, the Downtowner's was <u>thickest</u>. *thicker*

1. Three local pizza restaurants—Dumbo's, Pizza Gallery, and the Downtowner—compete for the larger share of the area's pizza business. _____

2. Of the three restaurants, only two, Dumbo's and Pizza Gallery, provide home delivery, with Dumbo's delivery time being the slowest. _____

233

6. *rewarding*, superlative form

   _____

   _____

7. *well*, comparative form

   _____

   _____

8. *bad*, comparative form

   _____

   _____

9. *ill*, superlative form

   _____

   _____

10. *easy*, comparative form

    _____

    _____

PART 3

SENTENCES: MAKING CONVENTIONAL CHOICES

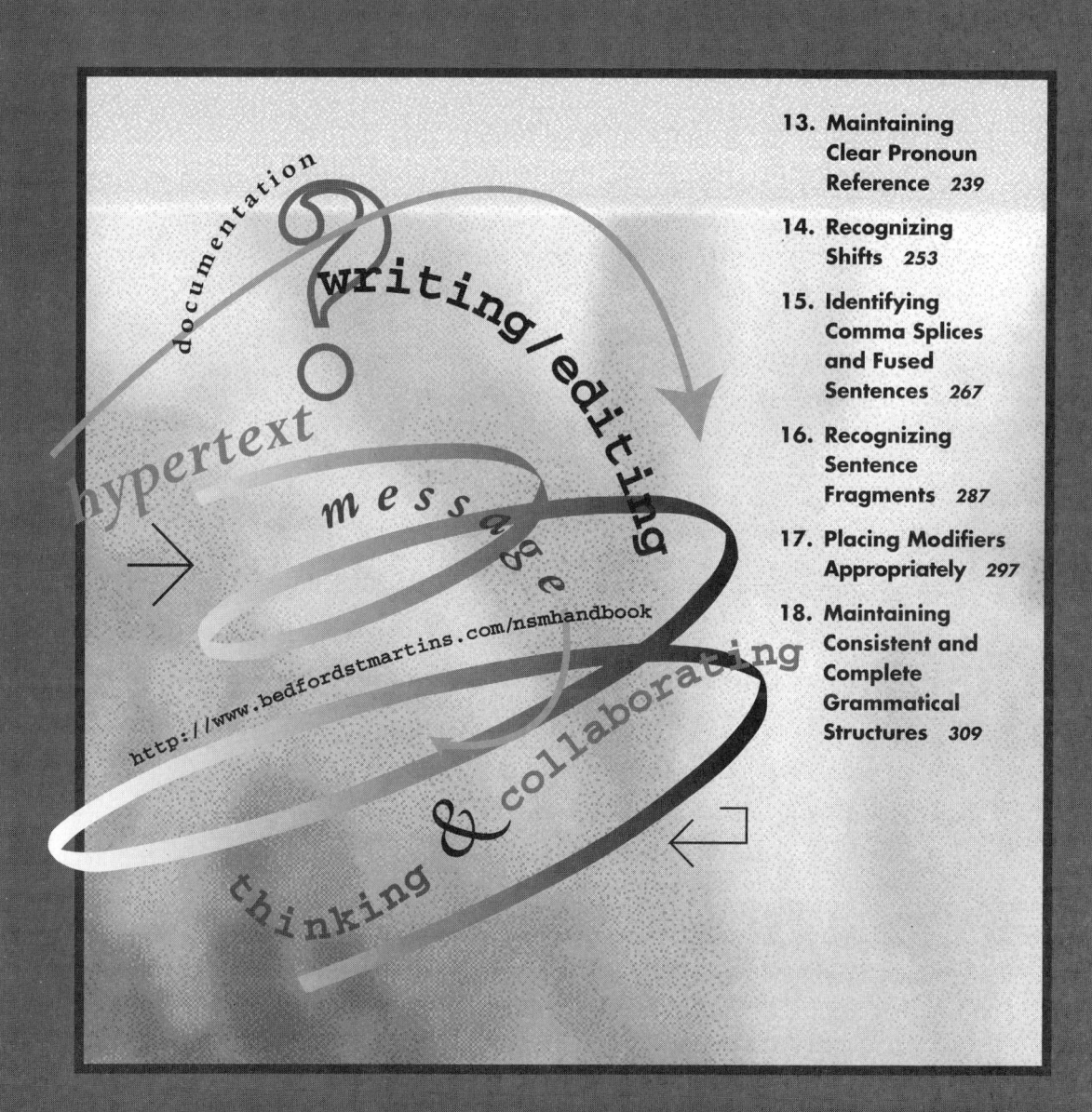

13. Maintaining Clear Pronoun Reference 239

14. Recognizing Shifts 253

15. Identifying Comma Splices and Fused Sentences 267

16. Recognizing Sentence Fragments 287

17. Placing Modifiers Appropriately 297

18. Maintaining Consistent and Complete Grammatical Structures 309

PART 3

PREVIEW QUESTIONS

These questions are designed to help you, the student, decide what you need to study. (Answers are found at the back of the book.)

1. Are the pronouns in these sentences used correctly? Mark *yes* or *no*.
   a. My father asked Joe if he was needed at the store. _____
   b. During the concert, they made a lot of noise. _____
   c. In Shakespeare's *Macbeth*, he makes Macbeth's motivation clear. _____
   d. When Jack saw how much the repairs would cost, he vowed to junk the car. _____

2. Do these sentences contain any unnecessary or confusing shifts in person, number, tense, mood, subject, or voice? Mark *yes* or *no*.
   a. Everyone brought their favorite food to the class potluck banquet. _____
   b. Students should bring their identification cards to the library. _____
   c. To revise a paper, one should first read it yourself and then give it to someone else. _____
   d. We planned to go by bus, but then it was decided that the subway would be quicker. _____

3. Are these independent clauses correctly joined? Mark *yes* or *no*.
   a. The snow piled up, but we went to school anyway. _____
   b. Elizabeth did not like the music, she listened politely. _____
   c. My mother put the cake by an open window a bird landed on it. _____
   d. The door was closed; my brother came in anyway. _____

4. Do these examples contain sentence fragments? Mark *yes* or *no*.
   a. Some kinds of guitars sound better than others. _____
   b. I think we could get there in an hour. If we hurry. _____

5. Do these sentences use modifiers correctly? Mark *yes* or *no*.
   a. Created under conditions some might think impossible to survive, this anthology of Eskimo poems is a testament to the human spirit. _____
   b. After calling the doctor, the pills started to work. _____
   c. The report was full of mistakes that I gave my manager. _____

6. Do these sentences have garbled grammatical structures? Mark *yes* or *no*.
   a. This book claims that in such large cities as New York and San Francisco, AIDS should be everyone's concern. _____
   b. Two days after the torrential rain, the earth seemed to come alive like never before the plants were so green. _____
   c. John owns many records, and CD player. _____
   d. Bart wanted chocolate, but Eileen orders vanilla chocolate chip, and they were all out anyway. _____

Maintaining Clear Pronoun Reference   13

Pronouns are little words that can carry a lot of weight in communication. Speakers of English rely constantly on clear pronoun choices in a wide range of situations: explaining to a service person what it is your computer will *not* do, describing to an insurance agent precisely the kinds of coverage you need, or directing a friend to your home. When used effectively, pronouns speed readers along; when used ineffectively or inaccurately, pronouns may actually stop the reading process by forcing readers to work backward to track down unclear references.

CLEAR PRONOUN REFERENCE IN EVERYDAY USE

Here's an exchange between a driver and a mechanic that illustrates pronoun reference in use:

MECHANIC: So, what's the problem?

DRIVER: On rainy days, it really acts weird.

MECHANIC: It won't start on rainy days?

DRIVER: Sometimes it won't start. But there are other problems, too. All those little lights on the dashboard light up all at once. That white needle goes all the way over, and the little gauge there jiggles around nervously.

MECHANIC: Hmmm. Does it crank?

DRIVER: The little gauge?

MECHANIC: The car. The engine.

In this conversation, the one breakdown in communication occurs because the driver assumes that the mechanic's last question—"Does it crank?"—refers to the last thing the driver mentioned—"the little gauge." The mechanic, however, is using *it* to refer to *the car*, not the gauge. Listen for conversations like this one in which unclear pronouns might lead to confusion, and then transcribe what you find.

→ **COMMON ERROR: VAGUE PRONOUN REFERENCE**

Chapter 6 discussed how you can use pronouns to help create paragraph coherence, and Chapter 8 focused on pronoun case. This chapter looks carefully at the impor-

EXERCISE 13.1 IDENTIFYING AND REVISING CONFUSING PRONOUN USAGE

NAME _____ DATE _____

Many of the sentences that follow contain potentially confusing pronoun usage. Rewrite those sentences to clear up any such confusion. If the sentence is clear as written, write a C on the line below the sentence.

EXAMPLE   Denise trusted Nancy because she had worked for her before.

REVISION   Denise trusted Nancy because she had worked for Nancy before.

1. The commission, the mayor, and the city manager agree that her management style must change.

   _____

   _____

2. The union representative called me last night at home and asked me if I was ready to go on strike today; I told him I still wasn't sure.

   _____

   _____

3. When Winona and Naomi sang together on the video, you could tell she was really enjoying it.

   _____

   _____

4. Of all the three stooges—Moe, Larry, and Curly—I like him the best.

   _____

   _____

5. Mandy had a silver dollar from 1892 and a penny from 1929, and she said it was very valuable.

   _____

   _____

6. When the Olympic games are televised, with all the athletes competing, I like watching them.

7. Farida told a secret to Teresa, but then she told it to Victor.

8. Albert still dated Yolanda but found Marie intriguing; finally, he decided to ask her to the party.

9. Because the mayoral race between Jensen and Wilson was so close, the debates forced him to state his position on airport expansion.

10. When Natalie and Stephen first met with the specialist, he did not know how distressing the meeting would be.

EXERCISE 13.2 IDENTIFYING AND REVISING VAGUE, AMBIGUOUS, OR WORDY PRONOUN USAGE

NAME _____ **DATE** _____

A. Read the following portion of a letter written by a first-year college student to a school board member. The letter has been altered to include several kinds of pronoun errors. Underline all problematic pronouns. Then rewrite the letter to eliminate problems of pronoun usage. You can use the space below or a separate sheet of paper.

I am a former student of Hoover High School that is now attending Valley University as a first-year student in engineering physics. Several friends which graduated in my class are also attending V. U. and are having a hard time with their classes. To graduate from high school, they took the bare minimum requirements, and they are not enough to prepare them for college. After all, most college classes build on what you have already learned. And if they don't already know the foundations, it is going to be hard to pass the class. One example is Chemistry 204. It is a class that starts off with the basics, but after two weeks, they are 200 pages into the book. Without a good high school chemistry class as background, they're lost. It is important that each school board member consider his duty to students and look into this lack of preparation. Action is needed to improve new students' chances for success in college.

B. Read the following paragraph and underline any pronoun errors. Then rewrite the passage, using specific and concise language.

Justin and Rachel decided to make pizza for dinner. First they got the packaged dough, the mozzarella cheese, the green pepper, and the pepperoni out of the refrigerator. The parmesan cheese, the mushrooms, and the tomato sauce all came out of the cupboard along with the olive oil, basil, oregano, and other seasonings. They were the secret ingredients that made their pizza so delicious. Next they rolled out the dough and began layering the toppings. They were always thickly spread so that the tomato sauce and seasonings made a flavorful base, the meat and vegetables were arranged in a design, and the cheeses were generously sprinkled on top. They were proud of their homemade pizza, and everyone always enjoyed eating it for dinner.

EXERCISE 13.3 MAINTAINING CLEAR PRONOUN REFERENCE

NAME _____ **DATE** _____

Read the sentences below. If a sentence uses pronouns in clear, concise, and unambiguous ways, write a C on the line below the sentence. Revise any sentences that use pronouns in vague, wordy, or ambiguous ways. Make sure your revision is clear, concise, and unambiguous.

EXAMPLE When Sherri discussed wages with Mari, she understood she would get a raise.

ACCEPTABLE REVISIONS When Sherri discussed wages with Mari, Sherri understood Mari would get a raise.

When Sherri discussed wages with Mari, Mari promised her a raise.

1. He is driving his van past Dry Creek Reservoir, which has given him problems in the past.

2. The legislature discussed one bill to increase funding for highways and another to support mass transit; at the end of the session, they passed it.

3. Teresa and Marina went to the subway stop and waited until it arrived.

4. The neighborhood teenagers painted a mural covering the graffiti on the wall that offended local residents.

5. That year, when the delegates voted, they endorsed Wayne Morse.

Besides paying attention to verb tenses within sentences, writers should make sure that verb tenses are consistent from sentence to sentence.

CONFUSING TENSE SHIFT   First she set up her camera. Then she walked entirely around the table with its plate of fettuccine. Finally, she adds a scattering of sliced olives, adjusts the lights, checked the exposure, and began to take the pictures that were scheduled to appear in the Sunday food section of the paper.

REVISION ELIMINATING SHIFT   First she set up her camera. Then she walked entirely around the table with its plate of fettuccine. Finally, she added a scattering of sliced olives, adjusted the lights, checked the exposure, and began to take the pictures that were scheduled to appear in the Sunday food section of the paper.

(Observe that the past tense has been used throughout.)

Note: When referring to events in literary works, use the present tense:

In *Portrait of a Lady,* Isabel Archer *marries* Gilbert Osmond.

Recognizing shifts in mood and voice (14b, 14c)

As discussed in Chapter 9, writers use verbs in any of three moods: the **indicative** (to report facts or to ask questions), the **imperative** (to convey orders, instructions, or requests), and the **subjunctive** (to state wishes or conditions contrary to fact). Shifting from one mood to another without good reason will confuse your content and your readers. Here is an example:

CONFUSING SHIFT   My car repair company always requests that a customer *call* [SUBJUNCTIVE] for a service appointment, then *brings* [INDICATIVE] the car in promptly at eight o'clock.

REVISION ELIMININATING SHIFT   My car repair company always requests that a customer *call* [SUBJUNCTIVE] for a service appointment, then *bring* [SUBJUNCTIVE] the car in promptly at eight o'clock.

Writers may also make unnecessary shifts in verb voice. You already know that verbs may be in either the **active voice**, in which the subject performs the action (*Our dog Freckles chases cars*), or the **passive voice**, in which something is done to the subject (*Cars are chased by our dog Freckles*). Sometimes, shifting from passive to active (or vice versa) is justified and useful, as in this sentence: *Professor Emberson asked* (active) *for the papers, and as they were being passed* (passive) *forward, he gave* (active) *the new assignment.* Switching voices here keeps the sentence focused on Professor Emberson's actions, not on the actions of his students.

However, sometimes such shifts are unnecessary (and potentially confusing whenever the agent of the action goes unnamed). Here are some examples:

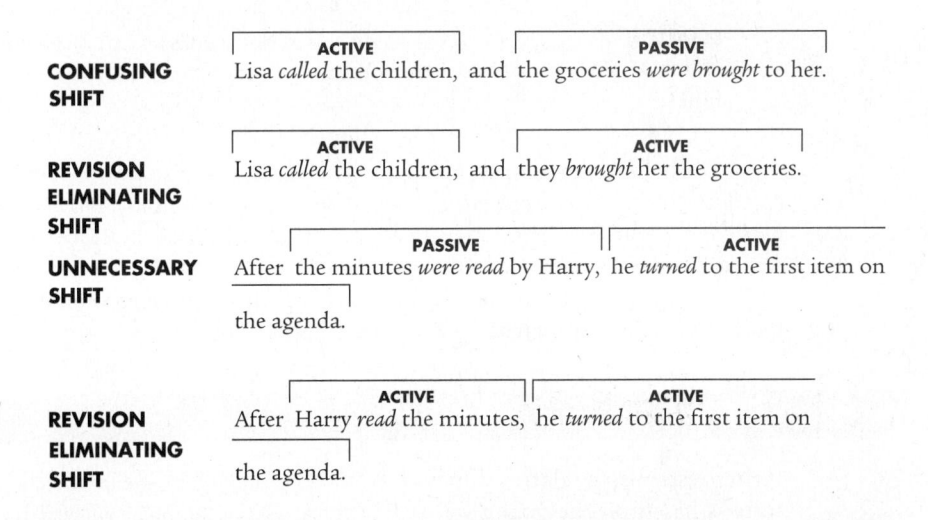

CONFUSING SHIFT Lisa *called* the children, [ACTIVE] and the groceries *were brought* to her. [PASSIVE]

REVISION ELIMINATING SHIFT Lisa *called* the children, [ACTIVE] and they *brought* her the groceries. [ACTIVE]

UNNECESSARY SHIFT After the minutes *were read* by Harry, [PASSIVE] he *turned* to the first item on the agenda. [ACTIVE]

REVISION ELIMINATING SHIFT After Harry *read* the minutes, [ACTIVE] he *turned* to the first item on the agenda. [ACTIVE]

Recognizing shifts in person and number (14d)

→ **COMMON ERROR: UNNECESSARY SHIFT IN PRONOUN**

Writers should not shift between **first person** (*I, we*), **second person** (*you*), and **third person** (*she, he, it, one, they*) unless there is good reason to do so. Be particularly careful about such shifts inside a sentence.

UNNECESSARY SHIFT *One* ought to be careful about alcohol consumption, especially if *you* plan to drive. [*The sentence begins with the third person* one *but ends with the second person* you.]

REVISIONS ELIMINATING SHIFT One ought to be careful about alcohol consumption, especially if one plans to drive. [*consistently third person*]

You should be careful about alcohol consumption, especially if you plan to drive. [*consistently second person*]

Remember that *you* should not be used in a vague or indefinite way. (For more on the vague or indefinite use of *you*, see Chapter 13.) Perhaps the clearest solution lies in replacing the problematic pronoun with a noun:

People ought to be careful about alcohol consumption, especially if they plan to drive.

Here is another example:

UNNECESSARY SHIFT	Golfers should try the new course, but you should beware of those long holes on the back nine. [Here *you* is being used as an incorrect substitute *for* they.]
REVISION ELIMINATING SHIFT	Golfers should try the new course, but they should beware of those long holes on the back nine.

Shifts from singular to plural (or vice versa) can also be confusing: *Last night the Nashville Cable Network presented a new country singer* (singular), *and they* (plural) *were a big hit.* To whom does *they* refer? The sentence should read: *Last night the Nashville Cable Network presented a new country singer, and she* (or *he*) *was a big hit.* As you can see, many shifts in person and number are actually problems with pronoun-antecedent agreement. (For more on such agreement, see Chapter 11.)

Recognizing shifts in tone and diction (14f)

Writers establish a relationship with readers by setting a tone in their writing. In part, **tone** is based on the goal a writer has for a particular piece of writing. If you want readers to laugh, you try to set a humorous, lighthearted tone. If you want readers to think about some idea or experience, you try to set a more serious, perhaps reflective, tone. The tone of a textbook should be straightforward without being stuffy. A workbook should be deliberate and trustworthy. You are not likely to find in this book (except by way of example) a sentence such as *OK, you mules, listen up!* A book written entirely that way, with a hostile and arrogant tone, would be a novelty for a few paragraphs; after that, the tone would simply be annoying.

Diction refers to word choices and to the overall level of formality or technicality that writing possesses. The several levels of diction that can be identified include *formal*, which is appropriate for many kinds of academic writing; *technical*, which is appropriate for scientific and research writing; and *informal*, which is the language of normal talk and may be appropriate for personal essays. In addition, there is *slang*, which is usually the language of banter between close friends. (For more on diction and tone, see Chapters 27, 28, and 29.)

SLANG	We stuffed that rig until it near croaked.
INFORMAL	We loaded that truck until the springs groaned.
FORMAL	We loaded the truck with the largest possible cargo.
TECHNICAL	The vehicle was loaded 112 pounds in excess of its maximum recommended weight.

Shifts in tone and diction can be sources of richness and surprise. However, when inappropriately used, such shifts may indicate that a writer is inexperienced or perhaps not entirely in control of what is being written. In general, when we talk, we mix levels of diction without creating problems. Body language and facial expression help us to do so. But readers, who have access only to sentences on a page, must be convinced that any shifts in tone or diction are controlled and purposeful.

MIXED TONE AND DICTION OF ACTUAL SPEECH

Whoa there! Hold it! This is my land and you have no permission to drive all over it willy-nilly with total impunity and rank disregard for native plant species.

CONSISTENT TONE AND DICTION OF A WRITTEN COMPLAINT

When I came upon Mr. Jones, he was behind the wheel of a Jeep stuck up to its back axle in the middle of a field. It happens that this field contains one of the few remaining undisturbed populations of a rare species of wild rose. I spoke with Mr. Jones, registering my complaint at his behavior and at his obvious disregard for the ecology of the area. I indicated that I would not allow any more four-wheel-drive vehicles on my property.

EXERCISE 14.1 IDENTIFYING AND REVISING CONFUSING SHIFTS IN TENSE

NAME _____ **DATE** _____

Read the sentences that follow, which together make up a paragraph. Underline the verbs. If the sentence is correct as written, write a C on the line below the sentence. If the sentence needs revising to eliminate confusing tense shifts, rewrite the sentence on the lines provided.

EXAMPLE   The barn swallows <u>return</u> about the same time that school <u>recessed</u> for spring break.

REVISION   The barn swallows return about the same time that school recesses for spring break.

1. World War II ended slowly in Europe as the Allies win major victories on different fronts.

   _____

   _____

2. On the French coast, General Eisenhower is leading a massive landing of American, British, and Canadian troops.

   _____

   _____

3. The code name for this Allied invasion was Operation Overlord, but it will be remembered now as D-Day.

   _____

   _____

4. The invasion was planned for many months and takes place on June 6, 1944.

   _____

   _____

5. The actual landing occurred one day later than planned because of bad weather.

   _____

   _____

6. Well over 150,000 Allied soldiers crossed the English Channel and successfully land on five beaches.

_____

_____

7. The D-Day victory was opening up Europe to Allied troops.

_____

_____

8. These troops begin working their way toward Germany.

_____

_____

9. At the same time, Soviet forces were slowly driving the German troops out of Eastern Europe.

_____

_____

10. Soviet troops will occupy Rumania, Bulgaria, Greece, Yugoslavia, Poland, Hungary, and finally Austria.

_____

_____

11. These pushes from east and west eventually result in the fall of the German capital, Berlin.

_____

_____

12. The German surrender is signed May 8, 1945, and ended the war in Europe.

_____

_____

EXERCISE 14.2 IDENTIFYING AND REVISING CONFUSING OR UNNECESSARY SHIFTS IN MOOD AND VOICE

NAME _____ **DATE** _____

Read the following sentences. Underline the verbs, and pay particular attention to any shifts in mood or voice. If those shifts appear confusing or unnecessary, rewrite the sentence. If a sentence is clear and well written in its original form, write a C on the line below the sentence. If a sentence unnecessarily employs both the active and the passive voice, convert the passive verbs to active. See the examples in the text, as well as those provided here.

EXAMPLE	Ms. MacNaught <u>read</u> the plans carefully, and they <u>were approved</u> by her. [*unnecessary shift from active to passive*]	
REVISION	Ms. MacNaught read the plans carefully, and she approved them.	
EXAMPLE	The dinner <u>was prepared</u> and <u>was delivered</u> by Fast Catering Co. [*no shift here*] C	
EXAMPLE	On race day, <u>drive</u> slowly, and you <u>should be careful</u> of the competitors. [*unnecessary shift from imperative to indicative*]	
REVISION	On race day, drive slowly, and be careful of the competitors.	

1. The graduate school requires that a master's student pass exams and defends his or her thesis.

   _____

   _____

2. The construction company delivered lumber Monday afternoon, and the wiring and plumbing materials were delivered by them later in the week.

   _____

   _____

3. Say no to their request, but you should say it tactfully.

   _____

   _____

4. Holiday traffic congested the highway and delayed the wedding party's arrival by more than an hour.

   _____

   _____

5. The credit company asks that an applicant fill out an application and returns it within fourteen days.

6. If Alysha were to become president and if Callie was elected treasurer, we would celebrate with a dinner out.

7. The coaches ask that each player registers at the table and then run a lap around the track to warm up.

8. The dogs were walked by Terrell, and then he fed them.

9. After the movie ends, pick up the popcorn boxes, and you should clean up any other trash.

10. The vice president asked that Paul present the engineering group's report and explains its recommendations.

EXERCISE 14.3 IDENTIFYING AND REVISING CONFUSING SHIFTS IN PERSON AND NUMBER

NAME _____ **DATE** _____

Many of the following sentences contain unnecessary shifts in person and number. Rewrite these sentences to eliminate those unnecessary (and potentially confusing) shifts. If a sentence is accurate as written, write a *C* on the line below the sentence.

EXAMPLE   Zoo patrons should be sure to visit the aviary, and you shouldn't miss the elephant house, either.

REVISION <u>Zoo patrons should be sure to visit the aviary, and they shouldn't miss the elephant house, either.</u>

1. You can really gain a lot of weight eating doughnuts if one is not careful.

2. Enthusiastic Super Bowl fans want to see his or her favorite team win.

3. One should avoid trapping a wild skunk in a small room, especially if they are inside that area.

4. If one visits the local art museum, you will find on display recent prints by Greg Pfarr.

5. Sea anemones thrive in coastal tidepools, but it cannot survive outside the water for very long.

263

6. When amateur photographers take pictures, he or she often enjoys the activity as much as the finished prints.

7. Lewis and Clark both kept journals, even though they wrote under less than ideal conditions.

8. A weekend runner is a prime candidate for running-related injuries, especially if they get no exercise during the week.

9. Tourists should be aware that road crews are busy on Highway 34, and a driver should expect some delay at the Oglesby Bridge construction site.

10. Whenever newspaper carriers go on vacation, you should make sure that you have arranged for a substitute to take over your route in your absence.

EXERCISE 14.4 AVOIDING SHIFTS IN TONE AND DICTION

NAME _____ **DATE** _____

A. Each of the following sentences is identified as written with a particular style of diction. Using your own paper, rewrite each sentence using the diction indicated.

EXAMPLE   Some jerkwater salesman sold me an empty box! (slang; write an informal version)

REVISION   An out-of-town salesman sold me an empty box.

1. Careful observation that leads to the reviewing of a seam before it unravels will prevent nine times as much sewing at a later date. (formal; write an informal version)

2. We spent one heck of a long afternoon in that teeny room looking through a one-way glass and watching chickens to see if they could remember which color button to peck at so as to get some of those food pellets. (informal; write a technical version)

3. The van skidded and then hit the wall. (informal; write a technical version)

4. I thought the sixteen gallons of high-gloss, fast-drying latex would easily cover the 100-square-foot surface of my home. (technical; write an appropriately formal version)

5. George Washington was the sharpest guy; he even led a bunch of his people across the Potomac and into a bunch of fights with the British. (informal; write a more formal version)

6. To be, or not to be: that is the question. (formal; write an informal or slang version)

7. Excuse me, young person, do you happen to know in which direction I should proceed in order to arrive at the food merchandising outlet? (formal; write a slang version)

8. In days to come, I would appreciate your not conversing at such great lengths with your acquaintances on the telephone. (inappropriately formal; write an informal version)

9. This is really going to bum you out, but your mother busted an artery in her head, and it bled all over in there. (informal/slang; write a more formal version)

10. In the event of unseasonable precipitation, employees are instructed to activate these toggle switches in order to deploy the large canvas awning, thereby covering the exhibition of watercolors. (inappropriately formal; write an appropriately informal version)

COMMA SPLICES AND FUSED SENTENCES IN EVERYDAY USE

While we certainly pause as we speak in order to mark off our thoughts or to add emphasis, we do not "speak" punctuation. In fact, excited conversation may contain many comma splices. In imaginative or journalistic writing, these comma splices are used in dialogue to represent the rhythms of speech. For example:

> "What about Tom?"
> "We can tell your father and Billy that Tom's mother called, he was sick, his grandmother died, anything, just so we don't have to bring him with us."
> –THOMAS ROCKWELL, *How to Eat Fried Worms!*

The comma splices in this dialogue are effective because they convey the speech patterns of two ten-year-old boys; they would not, however, be appropriate (or effective) in most college writing. Using your own paper, try revising this dialogue to make it sound more formal. You may discover some ways—and reasons—to keep comma splices out of your own writing.

→ **COMMON ERRORS: COMMA SPLICE AND FUSED SENTENCE**

Using a semicolon is just one acceptable way to link independent clauses. But there are two incorrect ways to link independent clauses, and they are discussed below. This chapter includes several options for revising them.

When commas are used to join two independent clauses, the result is a **comma splice** (two independent clauses "spliced together" with a comma). Although this construction is occasionally used in journalism and literature, most readers and academicians view comma splices as errors. Do not use a comma to link two independent clauses.

COMMA SPLICE   Grandma always kept that kitchen window open, the fragrance of those flowers filled the room.

In a **fused sentence** (sometimes also called a run-on sentence), two independent clauses have been put side by side ("fused") without any punctuation whatsoever; this is incorrect and confusing to readers.

FUSED SENTENCE   Grandma always kept that kitchen window open the fragrance of those flowers filled the room.

Separating independent clauses into two sentences (15a)

The simplest way to revise comma splices or fused sentences is to separate the independent clauses and punctuate them as two sentences.

COMMA SPLICE	Czeslaw Milosz is widely recognized as one of the finest poets of the twentieth century, his *Collected Poems* was issued in 1988.
FUSED SENTENCE	Czeslaw Milosz is widely recognized as one of the finest poets of the twentieth century his *Collected Poems* was issued in 1988.
CORRECTED SENTENCE	Czeslaw Milosz is widely recognized as one of the finest poets of the twentieth century. His *Collected Poems* was issued in 1988.

Revising by making each independent clause a sentence emphasizes the separateness of content in each sentence. However, if the two clauses are very short, converting them to two sentences may sound choppy, and another method of revision would be preferable.

Linking independent clauses with a semicolon (15c)

Comma splices or fused sentences may also be revised by inserting a semicolon as the sole punctuation between the two independent clauses. Using a semicolon in this way suggests not only a grammatical balance but also a balance between the independent clauses, showing that they carry equal importance.

COMMA SPLICE	When they met in 1992, the Democrats gathered in New York City for their nominating convention, the Republicans called their faithful together in Houston.
FUSED SENTENCE	When they met in 1992, the Democrats gathered in New York City for their nominating convention the Republicans called their faithful together in Houston.
CORRECTED SENTENCE	When they met in 1992, the Democrats gathered in New York City for their nominating convention; the Republicans called their faithful together in Houston.

Linking independent clauses with semicolons also allows you to set two ideas side by side in the same sentence. There are many possible effects to be gained from doing this. Primarily, you tell your reader that the two ideas are very closely related but that you are counting on your reader to understand the relationship without spelling it out. Here are two examples:

> I won't be able to meet you at noon today; I have an appointment at the Financial Aid office. [*cause-effect relationship implied*]

> They danced all night; they wanted to dance forever. [*the action; the impulse behind it*]

Linking independent clauses with a comma and a coordinating conjunction (15b)

You can also link two independent clauses by using a comma and a coordinating conjunction. **Coordinating conjunctions** include: *and, but, for, nor, or, so, yet*. To link independent clauses using one of these conjunctions, place the comma after the first clause, and follow this comma with the coordinating conjunction:

[Independent clause], [coordinating conjunction] [independent clause].

Following this diagram, we can revise *Margaret had a bad cold. She bought three boxes of tissues.* to read *Margaret had a bad cold, so she bought three boxes of tissues.*

Linking independent clauses by using a comma and a coordinating conjunction is the best way to show a specific relationship between independent clauses. *And* and *or* indicate continuation; *but, yet,* and *nor* indicate opposition; *for* and *so* indicate cause and effect. As the following two examples show, the choice of a coordinating conjunction can make a considerable difference in sentence meaning:

Maria felt somewhat uncomfortable, *for* she was the first guest to arrive at the party. [*Maria is uncomfortable because she is the first guest.*]

Maria felt somewhat uncomfortable, *yet* she was the first guest to arrive at the party. [*Maria is uncomfortable but arrives first despite this feeling.*]

Linking independent clauses with a semicolon and a conjunctive adverb or transitional phrase (15c)

So far in this chapter, you have seen how to join independent clauses using semicolons and using commas with coordinating conjunctions. A third method is to use semicolons with conjunctive adverbs or transitional phrases. A list of conjunctive adverbs is provided; both conjunctive adverbs and transitional phrases must be used with a semicolon, with a period, or with a comma combined with a cooordinating conjunction. Here is an example:

The test was a difficult one; *however*, Jason did well.

Note that a comma follows the conjunctive adverb *however*.

[Independent clause]; [conjunctive adverb], or [transitional phrase], [independent clause].

Here is a list of commonly used **conjunctive adverbs**:

also	finally	indeed	nevertheless	subsequently
anyway	furthermore	instead	next	then
besides	however	meanwhile	otherwise	therefore
consequently	incidentally	moreover	still	thus

Here is a list of commonly used **transitional phrases**:

after all	for example	in other words
as a result	in addition	on the other hand
even so	in fact	

Linking independent clauses by using a semicolon and a conjunctive adverb (or transitional phrase) followed by a comma allows you to specify relationships and to vary tone.

Conjunctive adverbs and transitional phrases can appear in various positions in a clause. These words and expressions are generally set off from the rest of the clause by commas.

Many questions on the test were familiar, and, *therefore,* Jason wrote most of the answers quickly.

That Simm's Grocery had to raise its coffee prices shouldn't surprise us; *after all,* Mr. Simm's prices have gone up too. [After all *indicates a cause-and-effect relationship; the tone is informal.*]

Sally was a fine golfer; *in fact,* she once shot a hole-in-one. [In fact *indicates that an example follows; the tone is more formal.*]

Common usage sometimes omits the comma following some conjunctive adverbs or transitional phrases. If you are a native speaker, you can probably hear the pause that usually follows a transitional phrase such as *in addition* or conjunctive adverbs such as *incidentally* or *besides*. Conjunctive adverbs like *then* and *thus* require less of a pause, encouraging writers to omit the comma. For more on the use of commas, see Chapter 30.

Distinguishing between coordinating conjunctions and conjunctive adverbs or transitional phrases

At this point, joining two independent clauses may begin to look confusing. After all, you use a comma with a coordinating conjunction, but you use a semicolon with a conjunctive adverb or transitional phrase. How can you tell when to use a comma

_____ 8. Despite the crowds and the excitement at a major dog show, the animals are all expected to follow commands flawlessly, the trainers, on the other hand, are expected to give their commands clearly and allow the dogs to show off their best features.

_____ 9. I love dancing the tango it is such a passionate yet formal dance.

_____ 10. Walter Cronkite was a familiar face to millions, one that brought comfort in times of crisis.

EXERCISE 15.2 REVISING COMMA SPLICES AND FUSED SENTENCES

NAME _____ **DATE** _____

Read the following passage, and underline all comma splices and fused sentences (remember the exceptions). Then use the space below to rewrite the passage. You may choose to continue to link independent clauses, or you may choose to punctuate them as separate sentences. You may add coordinating conjunctions, conjunctive adverbs, or transitional phrases as you wish. You may revise by using dependent clauses or by converting two independent clauses into one. Make sure that your revised paragraph is grammatically correct and accurately punctuated. For each comma splice or fused sentence you rewrite, be ready to explain the reason for the particular revision you choose.

Perhaps the most striking fact about people is that they make things. When early October arrives, swallows migrate dogs get heavier coats snakes go into a kind of hibernation people knit themselves caps. People without caps and people with too many caps get together and invent the set of promises we call money. Having invented money, people pay other people to make parkas and slickers or they use money to buy kits and make these things themselves. Rain pelts down deer seek the densest cover they can find people build houses with roofs. When cats get cold, they curl into tight little balls. People invent insulation or they pay sheep ranchers to provide the wool that's made into warm shirts. When caribou get hungry, they have no choice but to seek a new range. When people get hungry, they don't move eventually they invent pizza. They figure out how to cure olives they figure out how to make thick bread crusts, they experiment with anchovies and pineapple they invent beer. Indeed, people are makers.

EXERCISE 15.3 LINKING INDEPENDENT CLAUSES WITH COMMAS AND COORDINATING CONJUNCTIONS

NAME _____ **DATE** _____

In each of the following cases, two sentences are provided. Join the two sentences using a comma and an appropriate coordinating conjunction. Write these directly above the place where they should go. Reread each resulting compound sentence to make sure it sounds right to you.

EXAMPLE No biography of Shakespeare was written during his lifetime. Scholars continue to puzzle over his identity. *[, and]*

1. Jack's employee evaluation was mostly positive. He was laid off due to a shortage of orders.

2. Maybe we should plan on discussing this tomorrow at the staff meeting. Maybe we should call a special meeting that would include the other working group.

3. Alice was concerned that her books were overdue. The due date stamped in the back told her she still had two days to return them.

4. Terrence passed the literature exam. He didn't even read any of the books.

5. Perhaps this whole thing is just a joke. Then again, maybe it isn't.

6. Shredd-O-Slicers are incredibly well designed. They make great gifts, too!

7. I'd love to go to Tokyo for a year. I'm afraid it's too expensive.

8. David had finished his reading for history. He thought that world events just before World War I were quite interesting.

9. I picked roses and weeded the garden. The weather was perfect for working outside.

10. Franklin ran to catch the cable car. He was just a moment too late.

EXERCISE 15.4 LINKING INDEPENDENT CLAUSES WITH SEMICOLONS AND CONJUNCTIVE ADVERBS OR TRANSITIONAL PHRASES

NAME _____ DATE _____

In each of the following cases, two sentences are provided. Join the two sentences using a semicolon and an appropriate conjunctive adverb or transitional phrase. Write these directly above the place where they should go. Reread each resulting sentence to make sure it sounds right to you.

EXAMPLE Students returning to school after years at home or in the work force are often nervous about the transition/ With good academic counseling and with good support at home, most succeed.
  (; nonetheless,) inserted between "transition" and "With"

1. The sign urged that those of you who partake of alcoholic beverages refrain from the operation of your automobiles. If you drink, don't drive.

2. No rain fell in Iowa for more than six weeks. Grain and corn farmers suffered significant losses.

3. Biographers agree that writing the novel *Pierre* caused Melville considerable pain and difficulty. Some argue that it provoked a mental and physical collapse.

4. The 1993 Nobel Peace Prize was awarded to Mandela and De Klerk for their work in bringing political harmony to South Africa. Scattered violence continued to plague the country.

5. The events in the *Jurassic Park* novel and movie are highly improbable. Scientists are not likely to find DNA that is as complete, pure, and organized as it would be in a dinosaur.

6. Our diplomatic efforts failed. War was inevitable.

7. Preston Tucker faced widespread ridicule for building his automobiles. He completed more than fifty of them.

8. Given all the studying we need to do tonight, we couldn't possibly cook an elaborate meal. Our refrigerator is nearly empty.

9. Last month the forwards couldn't seem to shoot past the goalie. They began scoring two or three goals every game.

10. Your lab reports do not explain your procedures in enough detail. The rest of the sections are fine.

EXERCISE 15.5 DISTINGUISHING BETWEEN COORDINATING CONJUNCTIONS AND CONJUNCTIVE ADVERBS OR TRANSITIONAL PHRASES

NAME _____ DATE _____

A. Each item below presents you with a pair of sentences. Combine them as indicated using either a comma and a coordinating conjunction, or a semicolon, a conjunctive adverb (or transitional phrase), and a comma. You may wish to review the lists of coordinating conjunctions, conjunctive adverbs, and transitional phrases.

EXAMPLE   The Russian processing ship remained stationary on the horizon. Several Russian trawlers fished for hake. (Combine using an appropriate conjunctive adverb.)

REVISION   The Russian processing ship remained stationary on the horizon; meanwhile, several Russian trawlers fished for hake.

1. She awoke feeling unusually optimistic. She felt like she might sing out loud. (Combine using an appropriate transitional phrase.)

   _____

   _____

2. My diet plan says I can eat four ounces of fish for dinner. I could choose the same amount of chicken. (Combine using an appropriate coordinating conjunction.)

   _____

   _____

3. Deer are curious animals. They will often run a short distance, stop, and look back. (Combine using an appropriate conjunctive adverb.)

   _____

   _____

4. The campus was quiet late at night. The moon was shining brightly over the grassy quad. (Combine using an appropriate coordinating conjunction.)

   _____

   _____

b. _____

7. Computer technology changes rapidly, however few businesses can afford to take advantage of every new advance.

   a. _____

   b. _____

8. The airline now has a no-smoking policy on all its flights this was due to consumer demands.

   a. _____

   b. _____

9. People who wish to stay in the United States can get a green card however they are not citizens.

   a. _____

   b. _____

10. The concert was sold out the promoters added another show.

    a. _____

    b. _____

16 Recognizing Sentence Fragments

If you pay close attention to advertisements, you will find many sentence fragments like these:

> Effective pain relief.
>
> Delicious—and nutritious.
>
> Works overnight.

A **sentence fragment** is some part of a sentence (often a phrase or a dependent clause) that has been punctuated so that it looks like a sentence. Such fragments begin with a capital letter and end with a period. What is wrong with a sentence fragment? When readers see what *looks* like a sentence, they expect the full meaning that a sentence provides. Fragments are often used intentionally in advertising and in literature, but in academic prose they are normally considered errors.

> **SENTENCE FRAGMENTS IN EVERYDAY USE**
>
> Browse through the advertisements in a few magazines, or look at billboards and other signs, noting the use of fragments. Using your own paper, record a few examples of what you find. Why do you think fragments are so often used in advertising? What effects do they create?

→ **COMMON ERROR: SENTENCE FRAGMENT**

An occasional sentence fragment may tell readers that the writer has not proofread carefully. Frequent sentence fragments suggest that the writer is not fully aware of what constitutes a grammatical sentence. Many college writers have trouble with sentence fragments. This chapter discusses how to recognize fragments and how to revise them.

Sentence fragments often occur as a result of the way we think. We write something and put a period at the end of that thought. Then we remember something to add, so we add it. The result might look something like this: *Holly and Anne have definite opinions on education. And the experience to back them up.* There is nothing at all wrong with writing this in a rough draft; the writer's error here is in failing to recognize and correct the fragment before turning in the final draft. It should read *Holly and Anne have definite opinions on education and the experience to back them up.*

Perhaps the easiest way to detect sentence fragments is to read your writing backward, from the last sentence of a paragraph to the first. Reading in this way will alert you to your own punctuation.

Recognizing and revising phrase fragments (16a)

The kinds of phrases that are most often punctuated as fragments are listed here. For a review of these phrases, see Chapter 7.

- *Verbal phrases.* **Verbal phrases** are made from verbs but function as nouns or adjectives or adverbs; verbal phrases often include objects or modifiers. Infinitives (*to confuse*), present participles (*confusing*), past participles (*confused*), and gerunds (*confusing*) are all verbals.

FRAGMENT	The team lined up in punt formation. *To confuse their opponents.* [*infinitive fragment*]
REVISION	The team lined up in punt formation to confuse their opponents.
FRAGMENT	*Confused by the fake punt.* The opposing team allowed our half-back to score. [*participle fragment*]
REVISION	Confused by the fake punt, the opposing team allowed our half-back to score.
FRAGMENT	*Confusing your opponents. Is one strategy for successful football.* [*gerund subject separated from its verb, resulting in two fragments*]
REVISION	Confusing your opponents is one strategy for successful football.

- *Prepositional phrases.* **Prepositional phrases** are composed of prepositions and their objects and associated words. Such phrases do not include subjects or finite verbs. Prepositional phrases by themselves are not sentences.

FRAGMENT	*With the color of these walls.* I think we ought to choose a different rug.
REVISION	With the color of these walls, I think we ought to choose a different rug.
FRAGMENT	Meet me at 4:30. *Inside the hotel lobby.*
REVISION	Meet me at 4:30 inside the hotel lobby.

- *Noun phrases.* **Noun phrases** are formed around nouns together with any adjectives, phrases, or clauses that modify the nouns. Lacking finite verbs, noun phrases frequently appear before fragments containing verbs but no subjects.

FRAGMENT	*The children who are whining in the upstairs apartment. Should be disciplined by their parents.* [*two fragments*]
REVISION	The children who are whining in the upstairs apartment should be disciplined by their parents.
FRAGMENT	*The jumper that Donna outgrew last spring. Has been sent to Aunt Lucille for her kids to wear.* [*two fragments*]
REVISION	The jumper that Donna outgrew last spring has been sent to Aunt Lucille for her kids to wear.

- *Appositive phrases.* **Appositive phrases** consist of nouns with their modifiers. These phrases rename (or describe) other nouns. Appositive phrases by themselves are not sentences.

FRAGMENT	All Sunday afternoon, the two of them followed Arnold Palmer. *One of the most famous professional golfers in the world.* [*Note that this appositive phrase has two prepositional phrases embedded in it.*]
REVISION	All Sunday afternoon, the two of them followed Arnold Palmer, one of the most famous professional golfers in the world.
FRAGMENT	On the day of William Faulkner's burial, everything else stopped in Oxford, Mississippi. *Faulkner's hometown.*
REVISION	On the day of William Faulkner's burial, everything else stopped in his hometown of Oxford, Mississippi.

As the examples show, eliminating sentence fragments is easy and can be accomplished in either of two ways: build a new sentence to express the fragment's meaning, or combine the fragment with a sentence next to it.

Recognizing and revising compound-predicate fragments (16b)

"Compound predicate" is a technical way of saying "two verbs." A **compound-predicate fragment** is produced when the second of the verbs (plus any phrases or modifiers) is punctuated as a sentence; such fragments lack subjects. Since compound verbs are typically linked with words such as *and, or, then,* and *but,* compound-predicate fragments often begin with these words. Remember, however, that the key to a compound-predicate fragment is the absence of a subject; many perfectly good sentences (with subjects and verbs) begin with *and, or, then,* or *but.*

ACCEPTABLE SENTENCES	Julie ate her lunch. Then she began studying for a midterm.
COMPOUND-PREDICATE FRAGMENT	Julie ate her lunch. *Then began studying for a midterm.* [*The fragment lacks a subject.*]

SENTENCES: MAKING CONVENTIONAL CHOICES

As was said earlier, revising such nonsentences involves either combining the fragment with a nearby sentence or building a new sentence to express the fragment's meaning.

ACCEPTABLE REVISIONS Julie ate her lunch and then began studying for a midterm.

Julie ate her lunch. Afterward, she began studying for a midterm.

Recognizing and revising dependent-clause fragments (16c)

Independent clauses can stand alone as sentences, but **dependent clauses** cannot. Dependent clauses usually begin with words such as *after, even though, if, who, which,* or *that.* These words signal to readers that the sentence contains at least one independent clause as well as the dependent (or subordinate) clause. When readers cannot find that independent clause, the result is at least momentary confusion. In such cases, the writer's real message is this: *I didn't catch this fragment.*

A wide variety of words begin a dependent clause. They include relative pronouns (such as *who, which,* and *that*) and subordinating conjunctions (among them *after, although, because, before, even if, if, in order that, once, since, though, unless, until, when, where,* and *while*). For more complete lists of relative pronouns and subordinating conjunctions, see Chapter 7.

FRAGMENT We shouldn't forget. That we all have days that seem dark and endless.

REVISION We shouldn't forget that we all have days that seem dark and endless.

Since dependent-clause fragments are sometimes long, their length alone may make them seem like sentences. These are often the hardest fragments to catch.

FRAGMENT *After I arrived at the airport and found that the plane was late leaving Phoenix and would not depart for another hour.* I decided to buy a magazine at the newsstand.

REVISION After I arrived at the airport and found that the plane was late leaving Phoenix and would not depart for another hour, I decided to buy a magazine at the newsstand.

Using fragments sparingly for special effect

There are times when writers do use sentence fragments for particular stylistic reasons. Two guidelines are crucial here: writers must be certain that they are entirely aware of sentence-building rules before purposely using stylistic sentence fragments, and writers must be certain that their readers will not object to the use of such fragments. Many teachers and readers of academic prose look upon the use of *any* incomplete sentence as a sentence fragment. If your teachers or readers object to the use of stylistic sentence fragments, do not use them.

Stylistic fragments do function in some predictable ways. The uses listed here may appear in informal prose but almost never in more formal academic prose.

- *Fragments in dialogue.* People often speak in fragments. When such speech is faithfully reproduced on the page, the result is often a sentence fragment.

  "Really?"

  "Yes. Right there in line for the movie."

- *Fragments in answer to questions.* When questions are followed immediately by answers, repeating information presented in the questions often seems unnecessary. This is particularly so in informal writing.

  Does this mean all is lost? Not necessarily.

  What makes this sauce so special, you ask? The garlic.

- *Fragments as exclamations.* By definition, exclamations are not complete sentences.

  That home run traveled over 450 feet. Amazing!

  The model wore a swimsuit that cost over a thousand dollars. Incredible!

Writers occasionally use sentence fragments in other situations, particularly when describing or telling a story. Award-winning writer Barry Lopez uses fragments rarely but effectively. Here is an excerpt from his book *Arctic Dreams*; the fragments have been underlined.

> It was still dark, and I thought it might be raining lightly. I pushed back the tent flap. <u>A storm-driven sky moving swiftly across the face of a gibbous moon.</u> Perhaps it would clear by dawn. The ticking sound was not rain, only the wind. <u>A storm, bound for somewhere else.</u>

This paragraph occurs on page 152; by this time, Lopez has amply proved his credentials as a writer.

EXERCISE 16.1   IDENTIFYING AND REVISING PHRASE FRAGMENTS

Several of the short passages that follow contain phrase fragments. Read each passage sentence by sentence. Underline the fragments. Then revise the passage so that it contains only complete sentences. If the passage is correct as printed, write a C beside the number of that passage. Use your own paper for this exercise.

EXAMPLE   The rhododendrons bloomed like orchids. <u>Outside her window.</u> As she typed, she could see them. <u>Some of the blooms.</u> <u>Were a deep vermilion.</u> Others were the pale, off-white color. <u>Of piano keys.</u>

REVISION   The rhododendrons bloomed like orchids outside her window. As she typed, she could see them. Some of the blooms were a deep vermilion. Others were the pale, off-white color of piano keys.

1. Dancing in the rain was something Gene Kelly did in a movie. Called *Singing in the Rain*. It probably wasn't actually raining. During the filming. More likely, the movie crew rigged a rain machine over the set.

2. Designing advertising posters and brochures is great experience. It's particularly useful for journalism majors. Journalism 406 provides just such experience.

3. Like the Olympics. The World Cup soccer competition. Is held every four years. The 1994 competition was the first held. In the United States.

4. The largest crocodile ever recorded. Lived in the lakes and swamps of what is now Montana. 75,000 years ago. It measured up to 50 feet in length. And had a skull 6 feet long.

5. There are many kinds of diet soda. Available today. Some have artificial sweeteners. Others have no sweeteners. But almost all of them only have one calorie.

6. The National Basketball Association has four divisions. Grouped into two conferences. When the top teams reach the play-offs. Their games are usually fast-paced and exciting. To watch.

7. J. Robert Oppenheimer is credited with developing the first atomic bomb. It was during World War II. That a team of scientists, led by Oppenheimer, successfully exploded the weapon. In the desert of New Mexico.

8. When Shelley decided to buy a car, she asked advice about a fair price. From friends, from family members, and from competing car dealers. She also went to the library, looking for more information. In consumer magazines. And in car guides. Finally, she depended on her instinct. About which dealer seemed to offer the fairest deal.

9. The Planning Board was surprised. To see how quickly the apartment house had deteriorated. After the fire. The windows had been broken, and the floors and walls had been soaked. By the water used to fight the fire. Flames had destroyed some of the inside walls. During the blaze. The other walls were discolored and damaged. By the smoke.

10. The Environmental Committee is looking for new members. Especially people who will encourage recycling in the dorms. Or who will help assess recycling in campus facilities. Other members need to encourage the campus community. To use recycled products. In order to build a bigger market. For recycled paper and plastic.

EXERCISE 16.2 IDENTIFYING AND REVISING COMPOUND-PREDICATE FRAGMENTS AND DEPENDENT-CLAUSE FRAGMENTS

NAME _____ **DATE** _____

Read the following brief paragraphs, and underline any sentence fragments. Then revise the paragraphs to eliminate the fragments. Write your revision in the space below.

Community residents will have their final say tonight. When the city council convenes a special hearing on the proposed Sylvan Green Development Project. The project has already received preliminary approval from the council. The development proposal calls for the construction of two anchor stores in its first phase. And specifies widening McKean Boulevard to accommodate increased traffic. The developers, who have already invested over $300,000 in architectural fees and permits. Argue that all city zoning requirements have been met. Local residents and developers have clashed at two earlier meetings.

According to opposition leaders, residents worry. That nighttime deliveries might cause considerable noise. And those opposed have also voiced concern over increased traffic at the school crosswalk at Oak and Fifty-sixth. When the hearing convenes tonight at 7:30 in Council Chambers. Those opposed to the development promise fireworks.

EXERCISE 16.3 IDENTIFYING AND REVISING SENTENCE FRAGMENTS

NAME _____ **DATE** _____

Read the following passages carefully. You will notice several sentence fragments. Underline every fragment you find. Then, using the space below, revise the passages. You may combine or rearrange sentences in any way you see fit, so long as you retain the original content. You need not eliminate every single fragment; if you decide to keep a fragment, copy it after your revision. Then briefly explain that decision.

A. How people take tests says something. About them as people. Some individuals worry. And do nothing but worry. They don't reread, they don't review their notes, and they don't discuss major issues with classmates. After all this, they may still be surprised. When the test day arrives and they aren't prepared. Other people worry, but they put that worry to work. These individuals use their worry. As motivation to make study plans. In addition to reviewing notes and doing some selective rereading. These students might also try to anticipate test questions. And then construct appropriate answers. In effect, they take practice tests. Still another group of people don't worry at all. They don't take tests seriously. And probably don't spend much time in preparation. The most naturally gifted in this group. May still do reasonably well on tests. However, even the most naturally gifted may be cheating themselves. If they don't study. As my grandma used to say, "If you've never worked hard, how do you know how hard you can work?"

B. Because water supplies are limited in many areas. We need to conserve water. In as many ways as possible. Most people who have experienced water shortages have learned to take shorter showers. To avoid wasting water doing dishes, and to save water in other ways. When people do not have plentiful water to drink or to use for bathing and washing. They cannot afford to waste water on their lawns and plants. As a result. Water companies, extension offices, and nurseries encourage gardeners to select low-water plants. Adding large borders of low-maintenance, low-water shrubs and plants to a yard. That is almost all grass. Will save water. In fact, water usage may be cut in half. Besides saving water for other uses. Such changes also save money because water bills are lower. And save time and energy because less grass needs to be mowed every week.

Placing Modifiers Appropriately

17

Modifiers are words that act as adjectives or adverbs to describe or limit other words, phrases, or clauses. Modifiers add concrete and vivid details, turning an ordinary pair of jeans into faded jeans dragging on the ground, tight-fitting jeans tucked into boots, or mud-splattered jeans. The way a modifier is connected to the word it describes or limits is by its placement. The importance of placement is clear if you consider the difference between these two phrases: "Linn's silk blouse worn only on Saturday nights" and "Linn's only silk blouse worn on Saturday nights."

MODIFIER PLACEMENT IN EVERYDAY USE

You will find modifiers in abundance at any store, urging you to choose the *latest* swimsuits, *designer beach* towels, *Coppertone* lotion, and *sand* toys. In fact, you will find modifiers at work in many public places. Consider, for instance, the modifiers from a sign at a public beach: *strong* surf, *hidden* currents, *dangerous* waves, *no* lifeguard. Jot down some of the modifiers you see around you. Is the primary function of these modifiers to provide information, to make a product sound more appealing, or to do something else? Do any of these modifiers seem misplaced?

→ **COMMON ERROR: MISPLACED OR DANGLING MODIFIER**

This chapter discusses another common writing error: misplaced or dangling modifiers. Curing this problem depends first on becoming knowledgeable about it. Once knowledgeable, you should be able to identify such modifiers by carefully rereading your draft. (For background on the use of modifiers, see Chapter 12.)

Identifying and revising misplaced modifiers (17a)

Writers use modifiers to add detail. The sentence *We had a great weekend* becomes more interesting when it is made specific: *We had a great weekend waterskiing behind the Lakowskis' blue Chris Craft.* Notice that as readers we expect modifiers to be positioned next to the words they modify; we cannot move modifiers around in the sentence without creating confusion (or outright gibberish): *We Lakowskis had a blue weekend waterskiing behind the great Chris Craft.* Here is another example:

The faculty grievance board, *although it had not done so in over three years*, ruled in favor of several students who claimed they had been graded unfairly. [*clause separates subject from verb*]

She sang *in her first public concert* a selection of traditional folk songs and ballads. [*phrase placed between the subject and its object*]

REVISIONS

In the next several months, Lynn hopes to maintain her diet and actually lose weight *despite her busy schedule of entertaining*.

If it has nothing else to do and if the weather is right, a red-tailed hawk will spend most of an afternoon soaring high over the landscape.

Although it had not done so in over three years, the faculty grievance board ruled in favor of several students who claimed they had been graded unfairly.

In her first public concert, she sang a selection of traditional folk songs and ballads.

Note that all the disruptive modifiers in these examples are relatively long phrases or clauses. In some cases, single-word modifiers may effectively be inserted inside verb phrases, as in this example:

These days, employers who ask their personnel to move will *often* pay for the cost of the move.

Try shifting the word *often* to a position outside the verb phrase. In a sentence such as this one, shifting the modifier results in a new meaning.

Inserting a single-word modifier between *to* and the verb in an infinitive phrase may also be acceptable in some writing situations:

To *almost* succeed is better than to *utterly* fail.

However, some academic readers will object to such split-infinitive constructions. In such cases, revise the sentence to eliminate the infinitives:

Near success is better than utter failure.

Identifying and revising dangling modifiers (17c)

When writers use modifiers without giving them anything to modify, those modifiers just "dangle"; they are not attached to anything. Consider the sentence *After swimming for an hour, lunch was delayed*. That sentence literally says that lunch swam for an hour and was delayed. Lunches can be delayed, but they cannot swim. So the initial phrase *After swimming for an hour* is a dangling modifier. The only solution is a revision that gives the phrase something or someone to modify. That something or someone must follow the comma after the modifying phrase itself: *After swimming for an hour, the team found that lunch was delayed.*

DANGLING PHRASES   *Singing in the shower*, the water suddenly turned cold.

Dressed and ready for the dance, her car would not start.

REVISIONS   Singing in the shower, he felt the water suddenly turn cold.

Dressed and ready for the dance, she found that her car would not start.

Opening phrases as in these examples always modify the word directly after the comma.

Dangling phrases and dangling clauses are similar in appearance and in effect. A **dangling clause** is a clause that has not been completely presented; the subject or verb (or sometimes both) has been left out. (Such clauses are examples of elliptical structures. For more on careful, effective use of elliptical structures, see section 18c in Chapter 18.) In effect, a dangling clause looks like a dangling phrase; you can tell it is a dangling clause because it opens with a subordinating word (*while, after, whenever,* etc.). Turning that phrase into a complete clause is another way of clarifying sentence meaning.

DANGLING CLAUSES   *While singing in the shower*, the water suddenly turned cold.

Whenever driving, your seat belt should be fastened.

COMPLETE CLAUSES   *While I was singing in the shower*, the water suddenly turned cold.

Whenever you are driving, your seat belt should be fastened.

EXERCISE 17.1   IDENTIFYING AND REVISING MISPLACED MODIFIERS

NAME _____ **DATE** _____

Each of the following sentences contains a misplaced modifier. Underline it, and use an arrow to indicate its proper placement in the sentence.

EXAMPLE   <u>Only</u> Just Woolens sells yarn and related knitting supplies.

1. Barking, the chain link fence restrained the dog.

2. The sign said this: "Only at St. Anthony's, services are held on Sundays at 9:15 A.M."

3. Even the weather surprised the meteorologist.

4. Campers may play various games if it rains indoors.

5. That station only plays oldies until midnight.

6. The professor gave a lecture about cannibalism at Harvard.

7. I had to feed the hamster in my tuxedo.

8. The new CD player almost cost $200, but Martin had saved his bonus to pay for it.

9. Nearly riding horses all day, we circled the entire ranch.

10. Carrying blankets and wearing warm coats, the stadium was filled with fans.

EXERCISE 17.4 IDENTIFYING AND REVISING DISRUPTIVE AND DANGLING MODIFIERS

NAME _____ DATE _____

Underline any dangling or disruptive modifiers (phrases or clauses) you find in each of the sentences below. Then revise each sentence so that it reads smoothly and clearly. If the sentence is fine as written, write a *C* on the line below the sentence.

> **EXAMPLE** She sang <u>in her first public concert</u> a selection of traditional folk songs and ballads.
> **REVISION** <u>In her first public concert, she sang a selection of traditional folk songs and ballads.</u>
>
> **EXAMPLE** <u>Winded and tired,</u> the race seemed endless.
> **REVISION** <u>Winded and tired, he felt the race would never end.</u>

1. Comics, although published separately in comic books and collections, are most often read in the daily newspaper.

2. After years reading comics, the favorites are picked.

3. Telling a complete story in each segment, some people prefer the humor of the separate panel.

4. Others prefer because of its suspense and narrative interest the ongoing story.

5. The strips with separate panels may like the ongoing narrative strips have characters that appear regularly.

307

6. After reading comics for years, the conventions used are understood by most readers.

7. These conventions include as both the narrative strips and the separate panels illustrate the way the dialogue is presented in a balloon or above a character's head.

8. Sometimes the drawing alone in a strip without words conveys the point.

9. Reinforcing the humor of the drawing, other times the dialogue or written text acts as a punch line.

10. Enjoying the comics page, the newspaper supplies this popular daily entertainment for the typical reader.

Maintaining Consistent and Complete Grammatical Structures 18

Making grammatical patterns consistent (18a)

A sophisticated sentence often packs quite a bit of information between its initial capital letter and its ending period. Such sentences depend on a variety of phrases and clauses to carry all that meaning. Given the wide variety of possible sentence structures available to us as writers, it is no wonder that occasionally we begin a sentence in one way and end it in quite another way. For instance, read this sentence aloud:

> White House officials said that in most deportation cases require a more thorough investigation than many illegal aliens can afford.

The sentence begins clearly enough: "White House officials said that. . . ." The word *that* signals a dependent clause, and as readers we expect to find a subject and verb for that clause. Instead, we find a prepositional phrase beginning with *in*. Since all prepositions take nouns (or phrases or clauses acting as nouns) as their objects, as readers we look for the object—*in* what? "Deportation cases" looks like it could be the object of *in*, except that this same noun phrase acts as a subject for the verb *require*. We know that the same noun cannot act as both the object of a preposition and the subject of a verb. Clearly the grammatical pattern of this sentence is garbled. Here are three possible revisions for it:

> White House officials said that most deportation cases require a more thorough investigation than many illegal aliens can afford.

> White House officials said that most deportation cases require a thorough investigation, which many illegal aliens cannot afford.

> White House officials said that in most deportation cases, a thorough investigation is required—something many illegal aliens cannot afford.

Here is another example of a sentence that mixes grammatical patterns:

> As compact discs rapidly replace records are going to become obsolete.

Here, the word *records* tries to do two things at once: to act as the object of the verb *replace* and as the subject of the verb *are going*. The result is a confusing sentence. Once the grammatical problem has been isolated, the revision is relatively easy:

> As compact discs rapidly replace records, the latter are going to become obsolete.

Sometimes straightening out a garbled sentence requires a substantial amount of rewording:

> The increasing popularity of compact discs will make records obsolete.

COMPLETE GRAMMATICAL STRUCTURES IN EVERYDAY USE

If you listen carefully to the conversations around you, you will hear inconsistent and incomplete grammatical structures, particularly in lively or heated discussion. For instance:

> "The Bulls are . . . They must be the best team in . . . not in the league even . . . in the country."
>
> "Wait till the Lakers take them. Because you know the Magic Men, they make magic happen, in a sweep."

In the flow of informal conversation, such structures pose few problems for speakers and listeners. To verify this statement, listen carefully for inconsistent and incomplete structures in conversations, and write down an example or two. Consider what helps you understand them with ease.

Making subjects and predicates consistent (18b)

Writers also need to make sure that subjects and their predicates are carefully and accurately matched. If they are not, the result is **faulty predication**. Faulty predication occurs most frequently in sentences with the verb *be*.

FAULTY	The most important *qualification* is *applicants* with experience. [*This sentence literally says that a qualification is applicants.*]
REVISED	The most important *qualification* for applicants is *experience*.

Faulty predication can also occur when writers allow themselves to be confused by words coming between the subject and the verb.

FAULTY	The clock with the black hands circled regularly.

REVISED	The clock's black hands circled regularly.
	The clock had black hands, which circled regularly.

Sometimes faulty predication is really the result of incomplete thinking. Consider this sentence: *The elevation of Mt. Hood claimed several lives last summer.* Is this faulty? Yes, it is faulty because a mountain's *elevation* cannot *do* anything. We can arrive at a grammatically correct revision by simply dropping any mention of elevation: *Mt. Hood claimed several lives last summer.* However, this revision sacrifices some of what the writer wanted to say. The real question is this: what is it about the mountain's elevation that is important? Posing that question may lead to this revision: *Blizzard conditions at the 10,000-foot level of Mt. Hood caused the death of several climbers last summer.*

Finally, writers need to be careful of sentences built on *is when, is where,* or *the reason is because* constructions. A sentence such as *Your watch is where you left it* makes perfect sense. However, a sentence such as *Recess is where all the children play kickball* incorrectly turns recess into a place. Possible revisions include *At recess, all the children play kickball* or *Recess is the time when all the children play kickball.* A definition must have a noun or noun phrase on both sides of the verb *be.* Neither *when* nor *where* is a noun.

Sentences structured around *the reason is because* are redundant. The word *because* simply repeats the meaning of the phrase *the reason is.* Chances are, either *because* or *the reason is* can be eliminated.

REPETITIVE	The reason I ate the potato chips is because I was hungry.
REVISED	I ate the potato chips because I was hungry.
	The reason I ate the potato chips is that I was hungry.

Using elliptical structures carefully (18c)

When a sentence repeats a structure, it is often acceptable to omit repeated words *so long as the repeated words are identical to those found earlier in the sentence.* If correctly done, this type of sentence structure, an **elliptical structure**, readily makes sense to readers. In the examples that follow, the italicized word or words are identical, and the ones in parentheses can be omitted.

Beth *owns* quite a few books, and Jane (*owns*) just as many.

Canon manufactures copiers *for the* home and (*for the*) office.

Remember, the omitted words must be identical, not just similar. Here is an example of an inappropriate omission:

Phil's native talents are obvious, and his paper wonderful.

To be accurate and grammatical, the sentence must be revised to read this way:

Phil's native talents are obvious, and his paper *is* wonderful.

Even if the verbs are identical, they should be retained whenever the sentence substantially changes its meaning as it goes along. In the next example, the italicized words are identical, but none of them should be omitted.

Will *wanted* to see a science fiction movie, Melanie *wanted* to see a romance, and Brian *wanted* to stay home.

Checking for missing words (18d)

Virtually every writer working on a rough draft is liable to leave out a word or phrase from time to time. Usually the writer is capable of correcting these errors once they are identified. How does a writer identify such errors? You can ask someone to check a final draft for you; another pair of eyes can often see omissions that you have unconsciously read into your draft. (Ask for help in identifying your errors, but do not let others correct them. Instead, learn from those errors: keep a personal editing checklist. For more on the personal editing checklist, see Chapter 4.)

Read your draft aloud to yourself or someone else. Read it backward, one sentence at a time, starting at the end. Concentrate on each word, and consciously keep your eyes from going too far ahead. Learning to read this way takes practice, but it can help you catch omissions and may also help you detect spelling errors.

Making comparisons complete, consistent, and clear (18e)

Writers can also get into trouble with incomplete or carelessly phrased comparisons. Above all, comparisons must grammatically and logically compare items, qualities, or things that are comparable. As Chapter 12 discusses, the informality of speech and shared experience often allows people to form careless or incomplete comparisons with little confusion or loss of meaning. However, in formal or academic writing, readers expect both logic and completeness. Look carefully at the following examples.

INCOMPLETE	Fast food tastes better. [*better than what?*]
ILLOGICAL	Fast food tastes better than cooking. [*compares a thing* (fast food) *with an action* (cooking)]
REVISED	Fast food tastes better than what I cook.
ILLOGICAL / INCOMPLETE	This clam chowder is thicker and creamier than last week.
REVISED	This clam chowder is thicker and creamier than the one we had last week.

MAINTAINING CONSISTENT AND COMPLETE GRAMMATICAL STRUCTURES

ILLOGICAL / INCOMPLETE Bobbie Ann Mason's writing differs from Tim O'Brien.

REVISED Bobbie Ann Mason's writing differs from Tim O'Brien's.

Bobbie Ann Mason writes differently than Tim O'Brien.

EXERCISE 18.3   MATCHING SUBJECTS AND PREDICATES

NAME _____ **DATE** _____

Read the following passage. Underline any sentences with faulty or unnecessarily wordy predication. Work on revising the passage to make it clearer. Add or clarify content if you feel that will make for a clearer final version. Use the space below to revise the passage. (To make classroom discussion easier, the sentences have been numbered.)

(1) The reason people can recognize a smooth collie is because they look like collies but when they're full grown their hair is short. (2) Smooth collies are where they have the same general build as their hairier cousins (called rough collies) and the same long noses. (3) But probably their most important characteristic is where like other collies they have great dispositions. (4) The nature of collies will accept abuse that other dogs would snarl or even bite. (5) Small children can sit on collies or hold their paws as if shaking hands just like people. (6) Collies will even tolerate someone playing with their food. (7) Actually, collies are so lovable to hurt or tease them. (8) They're loyal, and they're so excited to see you in the morning that their brown eyes make you glad you got out of bed. (9) Collies are also superior intelligence.

EXERCISE 18.4 USING ELLIPTICAL STRUCTURES CAREFULLY

NAME _____ **DATE** _____

Read the following sentences. If a sentence omits words that should be included or if it repeats words that could be omitted, revise the sentence on the lines provided.

EXAMPLE Will wanted to see a science fiction movie, Melanie wanted to see a romance movie, and Brian to stay home.
REVISION Will wanted to see a science fiction movie, Melanie wanted to see a romance, and Brian wanted to stay home.

EXAMPLE Cathy arrived first, and Katie arrived ten minutes later.
REVISION Cathy arrived first, and Katie ten minutes later.

1. Jaime gets along well with Cecilia and Don with Barbara but not Bev.

2. We could clearly hear Radio Moscow yesterday, but less today.

3. Harold decided to take a nap, Michael decided to study for his chemistry test, and Susan to take a book back to the library.

4. The car's exterior is blue, but the seats black vinyl.

5. During the winter break, Matt plans to ski during the morning, he plans to snowboard during the afternoon, and he plans to ice skate in the evening.

6. As the movie continued, the audience became less attentive and interested.

7. He likes to eat fried chicken, he likes to eat mashed potatoes, and he likes to eat peas for Sunday dinner.

8. My advisor suggested that I should plan my class schedule ahead of time, I should balance difficult and easy classes, and I should take the study-skills workshop.

9. Cats eat fish and cats eat liver, but rarely steak.

10. The house is Victorian, its windows enormous.

11. Winston loved to eat, Josef loved to run, and Harry to read novels.

12. Money buys power, and money buys influence, but not happiness.

EXERCISE 18.5 CHECKING FOR INADVERTENT OMISSIONS AND FOR INCOMPLETE COMPARISONS

NAME _____ **DATE** _____

Read the sentences below, checking carefully for any omissions or faulty comparisons. If a sentence needs revising, write your new version on the lines provided. Add new content as necessary. If the sentence is accurate and acceptable as written, write C on the line below the sentence.

EXAMPLE   The small-screen color television is more expensive.

REVISION   The small-screen color television is more expensive than the 19-inch black-and-white model.

1. Antibiotics help doctors today treat infections better than the early 1900s.

   _____

   _____

2. Antibiotics are derived from bacteria and fungi, which occur nature.

   _____

   _____

3. They fight bacteria more effectively than viruses.

   _____

   _____

4. Two discoveries were more essential to this understanding of how to fight bacterial illness.

   _____

   _____

5. Once Louis Pasteur showed that bacteria did cause disease, scientists could look for better ways to fight them.

   _____

   _____

6. When Alexander Fleming found that penicillin was produced by a mold and killed bacteria, he knew that it could more effectively fight infection.

   _____

   _____

7. The problem was that recognizing penicillin's potential usefulness was easier than extracting or producing it.

   _____

   _____

8. Once the problem of producing penicillin was solved, this antibiotic gave doctors a better weapon against infection.

   _____

   _____

9. Streptomycin was the next antibiotic discovered, giving doctors more than one treatment option.

   _____

   _____

10. Now more than sixty antibiotics are available, and a doctor can prescribe one that will work better to destroy the particular bacteria causing an infection.

    _____

    _____

PART 4

SENTENCES: MAKING STYLISTIC CHOICES

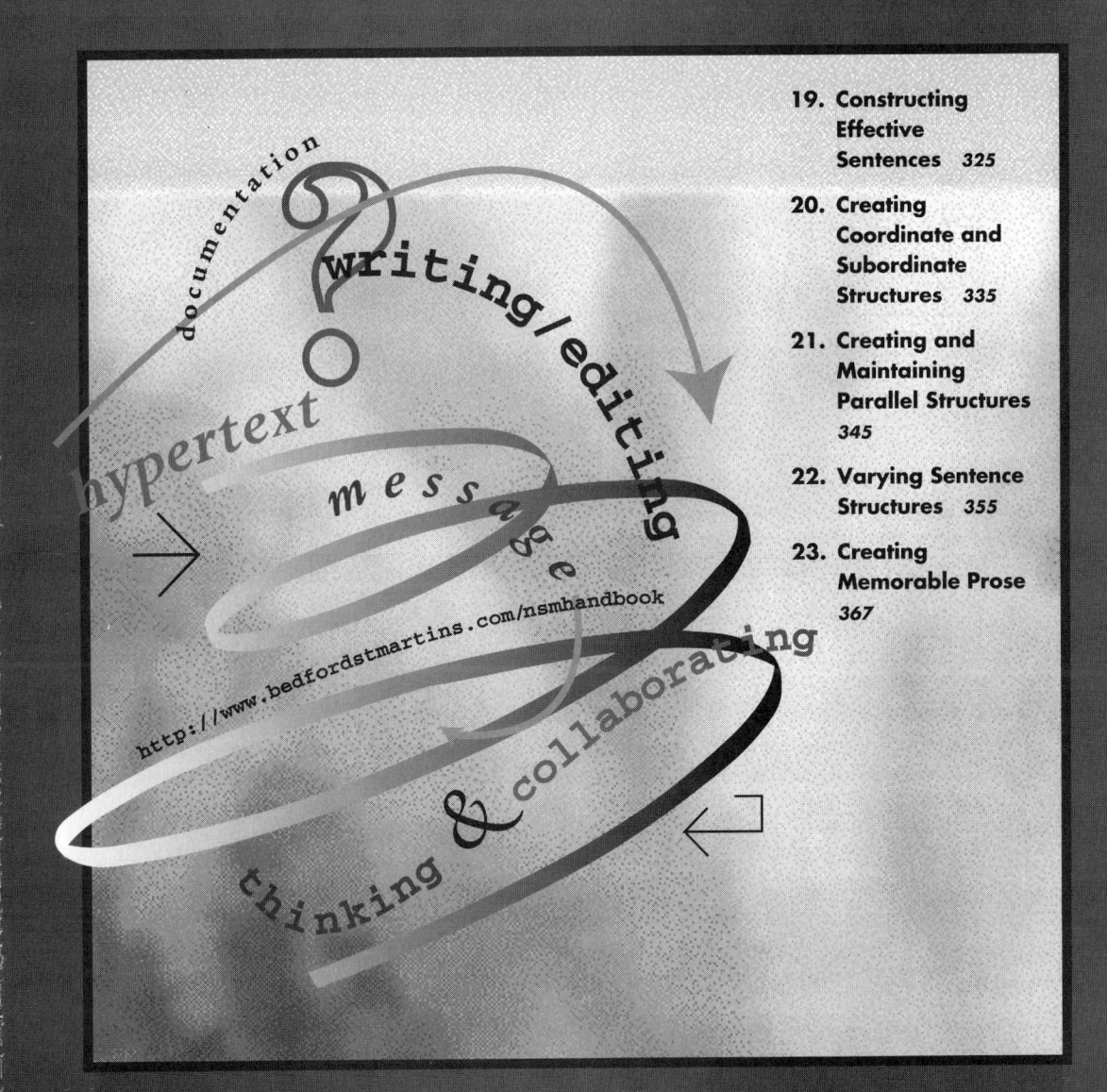

19. Constructing Effective Sentences 325

20. Creating Coordinate and Subordinate Structures 335

21. Creating and Maintaining Parallel Structures 345

22. Varying Sentence Structures 355

23. Creating Memorable Prose 367

http://www.bedfordstmartins.com/nsmhandbook

PART 4

PREVIEW QUESTIONS

These questions are designed to help you, the student, decide what you need to study. (Answers are found at the back of the book.)

1. Can the following sentences be revised to be more concise? Answer *yes* or *no*.
   a. Contemporary rock groups performing now frequently make use of synthesizers. _____
   b. The election did not resolve anything. _____

2. Underline the coordinating conjunctions in the following sentences.
   a. Siberian huskies have thick fur so they will never be cold in the winter.
   b. Usually Carolyn is never late but this time she missed her train.

3. Can a dependent clause ever stand on its own? Answer *yes* or *no*. _____

4. Underline the dependent clauses in the following sentences.
   a. When the rain started, Joyce and I took shelter in a book store.
   b. The man who gave me this watch seemed to be desperate.
   c. Carolyn was late even though she left an hour early.

5. Do the following sentences use parallel structures correctly? Answer *yes* or *no*.
   a. We will carry the fight for the ERA into the schools, the churches, and into the legislatures. _____
   b. It is better to remain silent and to have people take you for a fool than to speak and to remove all doubt. _____
   c. Hard work, long nights in the library, and constantly revising your essays will guarantee you good grades. _____

6. Identify any of these stylistic weaknesses in the following sentences: passive verbs, wordiness, weak verbs. If none of these weaknesses are present, mark a C next to the sentence.
   a. It is necessary that everyone arrive at the ticket booth at the same time. _____
   b. Pianists often wrestle with the technically treacherous passages of Bach's *Goldberg Variations*. _____
   c. Although the bronze and the silver medals were won by the other team, the gold was won by us. _____
   d. Today the weather was bad. _____
   e. My paper topic was approved by my history teacher. _____

19 Constructing Effective Sentences

As we write sentences for a rough draft, we are thinking hard about what we want to say; we are struggling with ideas and words. A rough draft about capital punishment might contain a sentence like this one: *It is true that the question of capital punishment is a complicated one because it involves a moral decision.* Getting this idea down on paper for the first time is itself an accomplishment. If you have written that sentence, you have begun to realize what you think and how you feel about capital punishment. We write rough drafts in large part precisely to make such realizations.

However, rough drafts need revising to clarify both their content (expanding sometimes, cutting at other times) and their expression. Clarifying expression means rewriting sentences to make their meaning as clear and as straightforward as it can be. In short, part of revision involves examining the wording of each sentence, making it as emphatic and concise as possible.

In the rough draft sentence on capital punishment, revision could begin with cutting *It is true that.* This kind of opening helps a writer get something on paper, but these four words add nothing to the meaning of the sentence. In addition, such a sentence buries its main points in a relative clause beginning with *that.* Cutting the opening leaves *The question of capital punishment is a complicated one because it involves a moral decision.* Can it be tightened further? *Capital punishment is a complicated question because it involves a moral decision.* Now this sentence has two parts connected with *because.* If we can figure out a way to combine those two parts, we will have an even more emphatic and concise sentence. Notice that the idea of a question is repeated in the word *decision.* Noticing that gives us a final revision: *Capital punishment is a complicated moral question.*

EFFECTIVE SENTENCES IN EVERYDAY USE

You can see the importance of emphasis and conciseness when you read directions. Directions for taking a prescription aim to state their message emphatically (to relay important information) and concisely (to fit on a small label). In the same way, a tour book tries to explain which route to take to a particular location in the clearest, briefest way. Look around for other directions that do the same—on health products, traffic signs, safety warnings, and so on. Jot down the sentences you find, and see if you can draw any conclusions about what makes language concise and emphatic.

Emphasizing main ideas (19a)

Using closing and opening positions for emphasis

Effective writing takes advantage of all we know about how readers read and remember what we write. For example, we know that readers tend to remember what we say last. This holds true for an essay, and it holds true for individual sentences. Here is a set of sample sentences; notice that the closing position is held by a different idea each time, resulting in a different emphasis each time.

> David lost six pounds following his diet this week.
>
> This week, David lost six pounds following his diet.
>
> Following his diet this week, David lost six pounds.

The first example stresses time; it comes from a paragraph discussing the time David needed to lose weight. The second example stresses his diet; it comes from a paragraph focusing on the diet itself. The third sentence stresses the number of pounds lost; it comes from a paragraph emphasizing David's achievement.

As a writer, you can use positioning to create emphasis. The results may not seem to make much difference in a single sentence, but used over the course of an entire essay, careful ordering of ideas within sentences can make the difference between merely competent writing and truly effective writing.

Using climactic order

Sentences using **climactic order** present their ideas—usually three or more—in a sequence of increasing importance, power, or drama. Sometimes this sequence also corresponds to a normal time sequence:

> Position your food in the center of the tray, program the microwave, and then push the button and wait for the bell.

Violating this normal time sequence lessens impact and may lead to confusion:

> Push the button after you have programmed the microwave and positioned your food in the center of the tray, then wait for the bell.

Sometimes climactic order has nothing to do with time and everything to do with intensity:

> Prison inmates face routine boredom, long separations from family and friends, and the risk of violence at the hands of other prisoners.

To revise sentences to take advantage of climactic order, first look for any sentences that present a series of ideas or actions. Look closely at the series to determine the most important idea or action; this one should come last. Position the remaining ideas or actions so that they proceed from lesser importance to greater importance, leading up to the most important (or dramatic or powerful) idea or action.

Three ideas were presented in our last sample sentence. Arranging them from least terrible to most terrible yielded the most dramatic sentence. Try arranging the sequence of ideas differently and you will see how much less dramatic the sentence could have been.

Being concise (19b)

Whenever you are trying to make a sentence more concise, eliminate any extra language including **redundant** wording, which unnecessarily repeats material. You can identify sentences that contain redundant material by carefully rereading your draft, looking for sentences that say the same thing twice. Here are some additional examples:

REDUNDANT	Contemporary poets writing now use rhyme more sparingly than did the poets of the forties and fifties. [*By definition, contemporary poets must be writing now.*]
REVISED	Contemporary poets use rhyme more sparingly than did the poets of the forties and fifties.
REDUNDANT	A synthetic and artificially produced material made from oil, polyester now shows up in everything from clothing to ropes to seat cushions. [*If the material is produced from oil, it must be both synthetic and artificial.*]
REVISED	Produced from oil, polyester now shows up in everything from clothing to ropes to seat cushions.

Certain common expressions are always redundant: *few in number, large in size, combine together, continue on, continue to remain, repeat again, red in color,* and *free gift.*

A number of phrases that may sound "official" are actually simply wordy. In almost every case, these phrases can be replaced with simpler ones, resulting in more concise, less pompous prose.

WORDY	CONCISE
at that point in time	then
at the present time	now, today
in the event that	if
general consensus of opinion	consensus
exhibits a tendency to	tends

Finally, you should be careful in your use of all-purpose modifiers such as *absolutely, awfully, central, definitely, fine, great, important, literally, major, quite, very,* and *weird*. Standing alone, such modifiers mean almost nothing:

We definitely had an absolutely and quite literally great time at the beach.

A sentence like this one, although it sounds emphatic, does not give readers much real information; only the writer has any idea as to what really happened at the beach to make the experience so wonderful.

EXERCISE 19.1 USING CLIMACTIC ORDER

NAME _____ **DATE** _____

Revise the following sentences so that they use climactic order.

EXAMPLE Coast Guard personnel conduct boating safety classes, sometimes must risk their own lives to save others, and monitor emergency radio channels.

REVISION Coast Guard personnel conduct boating safety classes, monitor emergency radio channels, and sometimes must risk their own lives to save others.

1. The missing child was located in the toy department after her mother called the police, alerted store security, and talked to some other customers.

2. Andrew led the cello section in the high school orchestra, played a solo with the city's youth symphony, and conscientiously practiced the cello.

3. When Max applied to college, he filled out the college application form, labored for hours writing an engaging personal essay, and requested his high school transcript.

4. Some people believe that heavy metal groups promote Satan-worship, murder, casual sex, and antisocial behavior.

5. John Kennedy became president after being elected to Congress and after distinguished service as a PT boat commander during World War II.

6. Jamaica produces many crops, including sugarcane (its most important farm product), citrus fruits, bananas, and allspice.

7. Most agree that Martin Luther King Jr.'s career as a civil rights leader reached its high point when he addressed over 200,000 protesters at the Washington Monument in August 1963; King helped establish the Southern Christian Leadership Conference in 1957 and became its first president that same year.

8. The case baffled inspectors—even though they found the killer eventually—because of the bizarre nature of the clues and the fact that no one ever heard a thing.

9. We've gone from putting a man on the moon, to orbiting the earth, to building a shuttle that can deliver satellites and return to earth in a few days.

10. The car lost traction before it whacked into the snowbank after it skidded around the corner.

EXERCISE 19.2   BEING CONCISE

NAME _____ **DATE** _____

The sentences below are all either wordy, redundant, or plagued by all-purpose modifiers. Rewrite each sentence so that it is concise.

EXAMPLE   It is believed by many PC owners that the Macintosh has definite advantages that make it superior to the IBM.

REVISION   Many PC owners believe that the Macintosh has advantages over the IBM.

1. In the event that I returned home after 9 P.M. at night, my paternal parent requested of me and asked that I leave the family vehicle with a gas tank fully and completely filled.

   _____

   _____

2. At the present time under current conditions, it truly continues to remain the case that health care reform is a really big, major, and crucial issue for the people of this great nation.

   _____

   _____

   _____

3. There can be no denying the fact that the new library reserve policy improved and made better services for off-campus students.

   _____

   _____

4. When Diana returned back to her old high school, she realized that she had previously been really unaware of just how incredibly interesting and unusual the architecture of the original building was.

   _____

   _____

   _____

5. It is believed by many experts who have studied this problem that workers who labor on graveyard shifts exhibit a tendency to commit more errors than workers commit during the shift during the day.

6. In the event that Britain had known of Hitler's plans at an earlier point in time, the war might have progressed in a different way.

7. The consensus of agreement that we have reached as a result of our discussions is that the paper originally scheduled on the calendar to be turned in on Monday will now be due on the following Friday thereafter.

8. The all-time totally best kind of vacation is one where you and your friends and maybe some other people go way down south where it's really sunny and spend a whole bunch of time outside.

9. It should be noted that Supreme Court justices wield a great deal of power given the fact that they are appointed to serve on the bench of the Supreme Court for their entire lives, or until they retire from the bench or they die.

10. Many dentists assert an argument about the use of anticavity mouthwash. They hold the position that the continued use of these oral rinses does not in fact reduce or lessen the chances of a user developing cavities.

EXERCISE 19.3   REVISING WORDY PROSE

NAME _____ **DATE** _____

Read the following passage, paying particular attention to any sentences that seem unnecessarily wordy. Work on a revision of the passage, and copy your best version onto a separate sheet of paper to hand in to your instructor. By way of example, a revision of the first sentence follows the passage.

    Modern-day experts in matters of nutrition and nutritional eating now want school cafeterias to serve healthier and more nutritious noontime lunches to children. Although it is true that the lunches at the present time are filling and serve ample amounts to children, they are not literally the most healthful. Most of the lunches served in our nation's educational institutions have an amount of fat that is too great, quite definitely well above the established guideline set at 30 percent. They also contain amounts of salt that are large in size and that may be a causal agent for later problems in being and remaining healthy. In addition to having too much of these two food components, the noontime meals also have too small an amount of more healthful vegetables and fruits. Young people, students, and school-age children really need to partake of these healthful options and choices of foods, which are especially rich in vitamins and very good sources of fiber. Even if the institutional eateries improve the healthfulness of the meals that they provide and serve, some people are concerned that children will decide not to partake of the healthier foods. Other of the involved citizenry combine together in continuing to believe that children can learn to understand the importance of making their food choices better. The general consensus of opinion is that if children are taught and educated about nutritional information and if they are given wholesome and healthful options and alternatives, they will assuredly be able to learn about how to select foods effectively for themselves.

REVISED FIRST SENTENCE   Nutrition experts now want school cafeterias to serve healthier lunches to children.

20 Creating Coordinate and Subordinate Structures

Consider these two sentences:

The sun shone.

The sky was a clear, deep blue.

Each sentence is a short independent clause: each has a subject and a verb, and each can stand alone. If you wished to combine these two sentences, you could use **coordination** to do so, joining the two sentences with *and, or, but, nor, yet, for,* or *so*. These words are called **coordinating conjunctions**. (For more on conjunctions, see Chapter 7.) Given the two sentences above, the most likely choice for an appropriate coordinating conjunction would be *and*. The two sentences combined using *and* would look like this:

The sun shone, and the sky was a clear, deep blue.

The key to understanding sentence coordination is this: both halves of the sentence are grammatically equal; both are independent clauses.

The two simple sentences *The sun shone* and *The sky was a clear, deep blue* can also be combined using **subordination**, making one sentence a less emphatic dependent clause and keeping the other sentence an independent clause.

<u>While the sun shone</u>, the sky was a clear, deep blue.

The underlined portion of the sentence is a **dependent clause**; it contains a subject and a verb, but it cannot stand alone as a sentence (*While the sun shone* is a sentence fragment). Reading that dependent clause, readers expect an independent clause to follow it. Hence, the independent clause almost always gets more emphasis. In addition, this dependent clause limits the independent clause, suggesting that only while the sun shone was the sky a clear, deep blue.

Using coordination to relate equal ideas (20a)

Although the parts of a coordinate structure are equal, the choice of coordinating conjunction can determine the meaning of their relationship. Coordination can be used to convey accumulation (using *and, or,* or *nor*), contrast (using *but* or *yet*), and

6. The sun did not come out today. The rain never stopped.

   _____

   _____

7. Karen thought she would have trouble with the math class. She earned an A on the last test.

   _____

   _____

8. After the show, we were invited backstage. We saw how all the tricks were done.

   _____

   _____

9. Try not to drop your ham sandwich in your lap. Mustard stains are hard to wash out of clothes.

   _____

   _____

10. You can buy the first car you see. You can also shop around and decide later.

    _____

    _____

EXERCISE 20.2 USING SUBORDINATION

NAME _____ **DATE** _____

For each of the items below, which together make up a passage, combine the given simple sentences by making one of the sentences a subordinate clause. (More than one correct answer is possible for each sentence.) Try to add subordination to emphasize the main ideas of the whole passage.

EXAMPLE The woman sold me a sweater. She seemed to be about Debbie's size.

REVISION The woman who sold me this sweater seemed to be about Debbie's size.

1. Many people spend every spare hour tracing family history. These people would not call themselves researchers.

2. Their interest is both a hobby and a passion. Their interest is called *genealogy*.

3. Most people begin by simply trying to identify their immediate ancestors. They often find that the family background is less a tree than a puzzle.

4. Identifying parents may be easy. Sometimes aunts and uncles are much harder to trace.

5. The aunts and uncles are eventually identified. All their children and spouses need to be tracked down, too.

6. The current generations are relatively easy to trace. Grandma and Grandpa's generation is likely to be more complicated.

7. Each relative is identified and placed on the tree. The avid genealogist wants to know the dates and places of birth and death, dates of weddings, names of spouses and children, and other such details.

8. The dates and locations for these significant events can be discovered. The genealogist may need to search diligently for church and government records.

9. The certificates of birth, marriage, and death can supply the names and dates. Family letters and diaries may add personal details.

10. Someone gets hooked on family history. Each discovery suggests tantalizing new details to trace.

EXERCISE 20.3   USING COORDINATION AND SUBORDINATION FOR SPECIAL EFFECT

NAME _____ **DATE** _____

The following paragraph uses coordination and subordination in some sentences. Other sentences can be combined using one of these techniques. Rewrite the sentences you feel would benefit from coordination or subordination.

   The world of dance has been dominated by Mikhail Baryshnikov. This has been true for nearly twenty years. He has set new standards for classical ballets. Baryshnikov has helped to define the parameters of modern dance. Baryshnikov's grace and agility were recognized by Russia's most revered instructors. From the age of eleven he was recognized. As he matured, his unique talent and body character enabled him to dance a wide range of roles. He was quickly incorporated into the Kirov Ballet's company. Baryshnikov soon grew bored with the Kirov's predictable fare. He wanted to be more challenged. Years of feeling stagnant went by in Russia. In 1974 he defected to Canada. It was his hope that in Canada and America he would find the freedom to choose his own challenges. He became a star at the American Ballet Theatre. Within days of his arrival. He became an important part of the American dance scene. He worked with many famous choreographers. He has been able to put his own imprint on many works. He was the artistic director of the American Ballet Theatre from 1980 to 1989. George Balanchine, Twyla Tharpe, and Jerome Robbins are just a few choreographers that Baryshnikov has worked with. With those people, Baryshnikov reinvented the look of modern dance in America.

▼ Creating and Maintaining Parallel Structures 21

Why do we remember (and use) maxims, or clichés, like *A bird in the hand is worth two in the bush* or *Take it or leave it* or *Red sky at morning, sailors take warning; red sky at night, sailors delight*? We use such succinct sayings because they are easy to remember, and they are easy to remember because they follow the pattern created through **parallelism**—expressing comparable elements in the same grammatical form. The diagrams below illustrate this further.

NOUN	+	PREPOSITIONAL PHRASE			NOUN	+	PREPOSITIONAL PHRASE
A bird		in the hand	is worth		two		in the bush.

VERB	+	OBJECT		VERB	+	OBJECT
Take		it	or	leave		it.

As a writer, you ought to be wary of clichés, but you ought to be aware of the effectiveness of the parallel constructions found in them. Sentences can employ parallel words, parallel phrases, or parallel clauses. Such constructions can make prose more concise, more graceful, and more readable. Many writers also carry parallel structures from sentence to sentence to create tighter, more emphatic passages.

PARALLEL STRUCTURES IN EVERYDAY USE

Jot down some examples of parallel structures that you find in everyday use—on bumper stickers, on T-shirts, in song lyrics, in advertising jingles, and so on. To explore why messages of this sort are often written in parallel form, revise one of the parallel structures you find to make it *not* parallel. Does one version more effectively catch your attention and stick in your mind?

Using parallel structures in a series (21a)

Listing items in groups of three is one common parallel construction:

We should order an appetizer to go with the *salad, fish,* and *vegetable.*

5. This company not only designs and manufactures superior hardware, but also provides first-class customer service.

6. On a clear day, you can see west to the Pacific Ocean, the Three Sisters Mountains in the east, and north to Mount Hood.

7. The firefighters asked for calm and that spectators remain a safe distance away.

8. Our system of government balances the powers of the Supreme Court, the Congress, and then there is the President.

9. She will either check into the hospital or joining Alcoholics Anonymous is her other option.

10. Some of the bloodiest fighting of World War I occurred at the Somme River, just as lots of people landing on the beaches at Normandy were killed during World War II.

EXERCISE 21.2 USING PARALLEL STRUCTURES IN REVISION

NAME _____ **DATE** _____

Read the passage that follows, paying particular attention to any sentences that could use parallel structures but do not. Remember that combining sentences will sometimes yield useful parallel structures. Underline any sentences that you would want to revise to make their structures parallel. Revise the passage, and copy your best version on your own paper to hand in to your instructor. The sentences are numbered for easy reference.

(1) In some parts of the country, summer brings sunshine, heat, and thunderstorms breaking out. (2) The appearance of a cumulonimbus or thunderhead cloud can warn that a storm is forming. (3) Inside these very tall clouds, some particles become positively charged. (4) A negative charge is what others take on. (5) When the electrically charged particles move up and down inside the cloud, they run into each other or colliding with other charged particles from the ground. (6) When these particles meet, the spark they form is visible as lightning. (7) Lightning is classified by the locations from which the charges move, such as cloud to ground, ground to cloud, cloud to air, or moving between two clouds. (8) It is also categorized by shape or appearance, including forked, streak, chain, and the kind that looks like a ribbon. (9) Whatever the lightning's direction or how it is shaped, its gigantic spark heats the nearby air, making the air expand. (10) Not only do the air molecules bounce around, motion in all directions is also produced. (11) When the molecules' movements and collidings in the air occur, they produce the sound of thunder. (12) The shape of the lightning and how far away it is determine the sound of thunder. (13) All this motion and electrical energy in the air is what produces the drama and powerfulness of a summer thunderstorm.

EXERCISE 21.3 ANALYZING PARALLEL STRUCTURES AND THEIR EFFECTS

Below are sample passages, each presented in three different versions. Some versions employ parallel structures; others do not. On your own paper, indicate whether each version uses parallel structure, and, in one or two sentences, describe how the effect of each version on the reader differs from the effects of the other two versions. Do not be concerned with which version is better but with the impressions or feelings each conveys.

1. a. The new vegetable cutter from Veggo doesn't need batteries, and the cook doesn't need to replace its blade. Also, using it simplifies cutting vegetables quickly into different shapes.
   b. When you need to cut vegetables quickly into different shapes, Veggo's exciting new vegetable cutter works without batteries, without new blades, and without complications.
   c. Veggo's Vegetable Cutter. No batteries. No new blades. No complications.

2. a. At the rodeo, the calf roping was skillful, the steer wrestling was energetic, and watching the clowns do their tricks was a real addition of enjoyment.
   b. Skillful calf roping. Energetic steer wrestling. Funny clown tricks. All exciting.
   c. With skillful calf roping, energetic steer wrestling, and funny clown tricks, the rodeo is sure to be exciting.

3. a. To Rita, Ed was a real catch; to her parents, he was an aimless drifter.
   b. To Rita, Ed was a real catch. An aimless drifter is what he seemed like to her parents.
   c. Either Ed was a real catch, which is what Rita thought, or he was just an aimless drifter, which is what Rita's parents thought.

4. a. Joe wants a big house and a fast car. Joe wants nice landscaping and a built-in swimming pool. Joe wants a lot of things.
   b. Joe wants a big house, a fast car, nice landscaping, and a built-in swimming pool; Joe wants a lot of things.
   c. Joe wants a big house. You should see the car he wants to buy. Nice landscaping is important to him, too. After he has all of that, the next thing on his list of things to buy is a built-in swimming pool. An awful lot of things is what Joe wants.

5. a. As a work of art, I thought the film failed. When one considers a movie as entertainment, one would say this movie was a success.
   b. I thought the film failed as a work of art. I would say it did succeed as entertainment.
   c. The film failed as a work of art, but as entertainment, it succeeded.

6. a. Jacques is a master chef, known around the world for his rich sauces, the baking of light desserts, and how he loves to teach others.
   b. Jacques is a master chef, world renowned for his rich sauces, his light desserts, and his ability to teach others.
   c. Known around the world for his rich sauces, Jacques is also known for his light desserts and teaching others.

7. **a.** We have to decide where we want to go for our vacation. We could ski in Colorado, dive in Florida, or camp in New Mexico.
   b. For our vacation we could either ski in Colorado, go diving in Florida, or another option is camping in New Mexico.
   c. Do you want to ski in Colorado, or do you want to dive in Florida, or would you like to go to New Mexico to go camping?

8. **a.** Watson and Crick received a Nobel Prize for discovering DNA. They were working in their lab for a long time, and finally the DNA was discovered.
   b. After years of research, scientists Watson and Crick discovered DNA. For their work, the men shared a Nobel Prize.
   c. Watson and Crick worked in their lab for a long time. They discovered DNA. They shared a Nobel Prize.

Varying Sentence Structures — 22

The length of a sentence has a strong effect on its message and its impact. Short sentences express simple, almost childlike assertions: *I want ice cream* or *This blanket's mine.* Short sentences tend to be blunt and forceful. Sometimes they crystallize complex thought or emotion: *Live free or die* or *The buck stops here.*

In contrast, longer sentences tend to depict fully the complications and complexities of experience. Notice how this longer sentence accommodates two conflicting possibilities and then resolves them: *On the one hand, I'm fond of roast beef because it reminds me of Saturday dinners when I was a kid; on the other hand, my doctor encourages me to avoid red meat: I'll order the fish.*

Sometimes alternating longer and shorter sentences capitalizes on the advantages of each—and adds variety to prose as well. *On the one hand, I'm fond of roast beef because it reminds me of Sunday dinners when I was a kid; on the other hand, my doctor encourages me to avoid red meat. Good health wins. I'll order the fish.*

VARIED SENTENCE STRUCTURES IN EVERYDAY USE

Very short capsule reviews usually contain varied sentence structures, perhaps to keep readers' attention with a snappy, fast-paced description. A *Newsweek* column included the following brief review:

> *Thelma & Louise* looks like an *Easy Rider* for women. A good idea. But this isn't going to have men lining up in droves or cheering for more.

The writer of this review varies sentence length by using a three-word fragment between two longer sentences. The writer varies sentence openings as well, beginning one sentence not with the subject but with *but*. This variety helps make the brief synopsis easy to read and remember.

Study some capsule reviews in a magazine or newspaper (or on TV), noticing the variety of sentences used, and write down an example or two. Can you draw any conclusions about the effect of sentence variety on readers?

Varying sentence length (22a)

When should you use short sentences? When should you use long sentences? You learn to make such choices for yourself, but you begin by noting what happens when different stylistic choices are made:

SHORT-SENTENCE VERSION	Live free or die.
LONG-SENTENCE VERSION	If we as people do not live under a government that allows us the basic freedom of choice, we ought to fight for that freedom of choice, just as we would fight for life itself; we ought to fight for that freedom even if it means giving our lives.

The short example is a fine rallying cry. It is easy to remember. The long-sentence version is far more complicated; it cannot be easily remembered. But it does carry its own kind of careful persuasion.

SHORT-SENTENCE VERSION	I'm fond of roast beef. It reminds me of Saturday dinners. I was a kid then. I went to the doctor not long ago. She did some tests. She says I should change my diet by avoiding red meat. So I'll order fish.
LONG-SENTENCE VERSION	On the one hand, I'm fond of roast beef because it reminds me of Saturday dinners when I was a kid; on the other hand, my doctor encourages me to avoid red meat: I'll order the fish.

The short-sentence version is grammatically correct. However, it is also choppy and sounds scattered and confusing. The long, one-sentence version is clearer because its structure and punctuation help us understand the relationships among all those independent clauses. As a result, readers have an easier time following the writer's thought. The long-sentence version unites content and form; it is a much better choice.

Choosing the length you feel is most appropriate for each sentence you write is a good way to begin thinking about varying your sentences. Even when you have thought about it, however, you may find that all your sentences have ended up at about the same length. This is because thinking about sentence lengths is sometimes not enough. If this happens to you, try selecting some of the sentences and revising them to be of a noticeably different length, even if you think this will not make them better. Many times, we stick with one version of a sentence or paragraph simply because we have not fully explored the alternatives and therefore do not realize how they might improve what we have written. This sort of experimentation will usually lead you to a more effective version than you had thought was possible.

Varying sentence openings (22b)

If you are writing to hold readers' attention, you will probably want to vary your sentence openings as well as their lengths. Such variety will add interest and pizazz to your writing. Read this passage:

The first afternoon and evening was sunny and hot. We ate dinner in a meadow overlooking the Pacific, and we watched the sun set. It was almost every shade of orange, red, and purple going down. We went to bed expecting good weather. It rained that night. We woke up in the morning and tried to make pancakes while staying warm in our sleeping bags. Some of the batter spilled onto the sleeping bags. The spill made an unpleasant mess.

What you have just read is part of a narrative of a camping trip. Every single sentence starts with a simple subject and is immediately followed by its verb. The passage carries some interest simply due to its details. But it conveys a rather boring trip overall. Why? Because its sentences all begin the same way.

Here are three ways to vary sentence openings:

- Begin with single-word transitions. (For more information about transitions, see Chapter 6.)

    Afterward, we discussed the difficulties of being a single parent.

    Hence, the board has approved your design.

- Begin with prepositional, verbal, or absolute phrases. (For further discussion of these phrases, see Chapter 7.)

    Before dawn, the mountain etches its silhouette against the sky.

    Talking around the clock, negotiators finally reached a settlement.

    Our business concluded, we decided to go out to lunch.

- Begin with a dependent clause. (For more on dependent clauses, see Chapter 20.)

    Although we could not understand the ancient script, we thoroughly enjoyed seeing an original copy of the Magna Charta.

    Once Valerie had become a vegetarian, the thought of a medium-rare steak no longer tempted her.

Varying sentence types (22c)

Are there other ways to vary your prose, making it more vibrant and lively? Certainly. Although most of the sentences you write in formal or academic situations will be declarative, you may also be able to use an occasional question, command, or exclamation. Such sentences change the routine for readers and keep them interested. Beginning a paragraph with a question (as this one does) is but one way to add such variety.

This chapter has already discussed variety in sentence lengths and openings; it is only a small step from that discussion to a larger discussion of grammatical sentence types. Here is a brief review of those types, which were introduced earlier in Chapter 7; you ought to be able to use all of them in your own writing.

- **Simple sentence** (one independent clause)

  Some people go to college to obtain a good job.

- **Compound sentence** (two or more independent clauses)

  Some people go to college to obtain a good job, but others go to gain an understanding of their values and beliefs.

- **Complex sentence** (one or more dependent clauses and an independent clause)

  While some people go to college to obtain a good job, others go to gain an understanding of their values and beliefs.

- **Compound-complex sentence** (a combination of multiple independent clauses and one or more dependent clauses)

  While some people go to college to obtain a good job and others go to gain an understanding of their values and beliefs, a significant number go to meet people with similar interests.

Two other kinds of sentences provide variety: periodic and cumulative sentences. A **periodic sentence** saves its main idea (usually expressed in an independent clause) for the end of the sentence, often using several phrases or dependent clauses to build up to the independent clause.

> For job training, for fostering an understanding of values and beliefs, for meeting other people with similar interests, for drama or forestry or philosophy, for waking yourself up—a college campus is the place.

In contrast, a **cumulative sentence** begins with the main idea (again usually in an independent clause), which is followed by several phrases or dependent clauses.

> A college campus is a place for job training, for fostering an understanding of values and beliefs, for meeting others with similar interests, for drama or forestry or philosophy, for waking yourself up.

EXERCISE 22.1 IDENTIFYING VARIOUS SENTENCE OPENINGS

NAME _____ **DATE** _____

In the paragraph below, underline the various sentence openings, and number them as (1) a single-word transition; (2) a prepositional, verbal, or absolute phrase; or (3) a subordinate clause. As an example, the first opening has been underlined and identified for you.

(2)
<u>With his appointment to the Supreme Court in 1967</u>, Thurgood Marshall became the first African American justice. Before his appointment, he was a practicing attorney. While he represented the NAACP, he argued a landmark school desegregation suit before the Supreme Court. Although it was decided in 1954, *Brown v. Board of Education of Topeka, Kansas* remains an influential case. Indeed, this case still remains the basis for the desegregation plans of many public school systems. Once he joined the Supreme Court, Marshall continued to be an advocate for liberal causes. Noted for his positions on civil rights and individual liberties, Marshall served as a justice for over two decades. In 1991, he left the Court because of poor health. Although he died in January 1993, he will be long remembered for his contributions.

EXERCISE 22.2   WRITING SENTENCES OF VARYING LENGTHS

NAME _____ **DATE** _____

Revise each of the following sentences as specified. Be ready to discuss the differences of meaning and emphasis between the original and your revision.

EXAMPLE   Since we've lost two games already and since this week's opponent has lost only one game, you can see that it's really important that we come out on top. (Summarize in a short sentence.)
REVISION   We need to win!

EXAMPLE   It was Sunday afternoon. The sun was shining. The hammock was in the backyard. It was a perfect day for resting in the hammock. (Combine into one long sentence.)
REVISION   That sunny Sunday afternoon was perfect for resting in the hammock in the backyard.

1. First you strip off the original finish, then complete any rough sanding, then smooth all of the table's exposed surfaces with fine steel wool, and then apply the new finish. (Break into several short sentences.)

2. Persistence pays. (Write a longer single-sentence version that emphasizes the importance of persistence.)

3. The clam chowder is good. The clam chowder is thick. Clam chowder and French bread make a good meal. The clam chowder is served on Fridays. It's served at lunchtime. (Combine into one or two smooth sentences.)

4. It's not a very good idea to do or say things to other people that you would find hard to accept, or that would make you unhappy, if they were said or done to you. (Summarize in a short sentence.)

5. Love hurts. (Write a longer single-sentence version that emphasizes the pain involved in a romantic relationship.)

6. The Crash Test Dummies released their second album. It was in 1993. It showed their sense of humor. Their pictures on the album cover looked like the portraits that are in art museums. Their songs also showed a sense of humor. The songs also asked deeper questions. They were very philosophical. (Combine into one or two smooth sentences.)

7. Some people find physics challenging. They may say that they study hard. They may go to all the lab sessions. Then they take the test. They may get low grades. (Combine into one smooth sentence.)

8. You should stop moving cartons around in the stockroom because a heavy box of canned peaches is falling off the top shelf right where you are standing. (Summarize in a short sentence.)

9. The most difficult part of getting a good job is following up on every lead from whatever contacts you have or whatever ads you see, sending out different application letters with your résumé, and staying optimistic even though the process may take a long time and a lot of energy. (Break into short sentences.)

10. Frank Lloyd Wright was an innovative architect. He created his prairie style during the early 1900s. He favored low, horizontal houses. He also designed open rooms that flowed into each other. (Combine into one smooth sentence.)

EXERCISE 22.3 REVISING PROSE BY VARYING SENTENCE LENGTHS AND SENTENCE OPENINGS

Revise the following passage by varying sentence lengths and sentence openings. You may combine or recombine sentences; you may add new content. Make sure that your final version is smoother than the original version. Copy your final version on a separate sheet of paper.

Land use issues are important. We don't often pay attention to them. We do pay attention when a developer decides to change the character of our neighborhood. Our family knows about this because the field behind our house has been slated for clearing, grading, and construction. Our kids have played there for years. A new shopping center will be built. That means cars, noise. It could mean new shops and a better local selection of goods. It might mean a new restaurant or two. Sometimes we think the development is a good idea. It will benefit the community and provide jobs. Sometimes we don't want that field to change. The whole family goes to planning commission hearings. We listen to the developer. We listen to our neighbors. Land use isn't some foggy, distant issue anymore. It's as close as our backyard.

EXERCISE 22.4 ADDING SENTENCE VARIETY

NAME _____ **DATE** _____

A series of sentence elements are provided below. For each grouping, create the kind of sentence named and then connect the sentences to form a paragraph. Read it back to yourself and think about how the sentence variation works as you read. Would you change any of the sentence types to create a better flow?

EXAMPLE   cat, feline (Write a simple sentence.)
              <u>A cat is also called a feline.</u>

1. what happened to me last night (Write an imperative sentence.)

   _____

   _____

2. going to pick up my laundry, ran into Lenny, old roommate (Write a complex sentence.)

   _____

   _____

3. told me he was record producer (Write a simple sentence.)

4. what he invited me to do (Write an interrogative sentence.)

5. invited to meet Paul Simon, watch him record new album (Write a compound sentence.)

6. couldn't believe it (Write an exclamatory sentence.)

7. meeting Paul Simon, hearing record, seeing studio, dream come true (Write a periodic sentence.)

8. have all his albums, been a fan for years, he has influenced my music (Write a compound-complex sentence.)

9. most exciting experience in life, inspired me to write, introduced me to people, got me back in touch with Lenny (Write a cumulative sentence.)

10. only lasted a few hours, remember it forever (Write a complex sentence.)

Creating Memorable Prose 23

The best prose accomplishes two difficult tasks: it embodies what its writer wished to say, and it moves readers to feelings, action, or agreement exactly as the writer intended. Such prose depends on a writer's sincerity and commitment, but it just as surely depends on stylistic principles that all can learn. For example, notice the use of parallelism and rhythm in the following sentence from President John F. Kennedy's Inaugural Address:

> And so, my fellow Americans, ask not what your country can do for you; ask what you can do for your country.

> **MEMORABLE PROSE IN EVERYDAY USE**
>
> Like the clothes we wear, the words we choose and the way we use them bring memorable qualities to our language. Nowhere are such choices more evident in daily life than in music. Every songwriter knows the importance of creating lyrics and rhythms that listeners will remember. Rap music, for instance, demands careful attention to stylistic choices, for its lyrics must be concise as well as memorable. Here's an example from Queen Latifah and Monie Love's "Ladies First":
>
>> I'm conversating to the folks who have no whatsoever clue
>> So listen very carefully as I break it down for you
>> Merrily, merrily, merrily, merrily, hyper, happy, overjoyed
>> Pleased with all the beats and rhymes my sister has employed
>> Slick and smooth, throwing down, the sound totally a yes
>> Let me state the position: Ladies first, yes?
>> Yes!
>
> Look at the words and structures that the writer here has chosen in order to make the lyrics memorable: the active verbs (*listen*), the inversion of normal word order (*no whatsoever clue*), the powerful use of repetition (*merrily, merrily, merrily, merrily*), and especially the repetition of *yes* that drives home both the rhythm and the point. Consider what you find most memorable about this rap.
>
> Think of some music and lyrics that you find particularly memorable. Listen to the song, and write out its exact words. What has the writer done to make the lyrics memorable?

EXERCISE 23.1   REVISING BY CHOOSING STRONGER VERBS

NAME _____   **DATE** _____

Weak verbs and unnecessarily wordy constructions plague the following sentences. Revise the sentences by substituting stronger verbs.

EXAMPLE   It is necessary that the cast arrive for rehearsal at 6 P.M.
REVISION   The cast must arrive for rehearsal at 6 P.M.

EXAMPLE   A large amount of electrical energy is a requirement for aluminum production.
REVISION   Aluminum production requires a large amount of electrical energy.

1. There are many problems that trouble cities today.

   _____

   _____

2. It is true that there are unhealthy or unpleasant conditions that make city life difficult or even frightening for residents.

   _____

   _____

3. For example, heavy traffic is a cause of pollution and is a reason why air quality is reduced.

   _____

   _____

4. A method for improving air quality is to require the development of efficient rapid transit in the city, but there are few people who will give up their cars voluntarily.

   _____

   _____

   _____

5. Other problems are also complicated and are also a challenge to the cities.

   _____

   _____

6. There is overcrowding that is of concern to everyone who needs to look for an apartment.

7. A requirement of most residents is a reasonable rent and a place to live that is well maintained.

8. In some areas gang activities are a threat to neighborhood stability.

9. When gang members are frequenting the streets, other people are fearful of violence and are wanting to protect themselves and their children.

10. If children are feeling fearful walking to school, the threat of street violence also is a disruption for their concentration in class.

EXERCISE 23.2 CHOOSING BETWEEN THE ACTIVE AND THE PASSIVE VOICE

NAME _____ DATE _____

Identify the main verbs in the following sentences as either active or passive. Then note the intended emphasis of each. If the original version accomplishes that emphasis, write *OK*. If the original version does not accomplish that emphasis, rewrite the sentence by changing the voice of its main verb.

EXAMPLES   My supervisor approved your memo.
Main verb is <u>active</u>. Intended emphasis: your memo
Your memo was approved by my supervisor.

The weather forecast was given as the last news item.
Main verb is <u>passive</u>. Intended emphasis: the weekend news anchor
The weekend news anchor gave the weather forecast as her last news item.

Kenyan coffee is grown in Africa.
Main verb is <u>passive</u>. Intended emphasis: the coffee
OK

1. During the fall, the red and yellow foliage is seen by tourists who go to New England.

   Main verb is _____. Intended emphasis: tourists

   _____

2. A gold medal was won by U.S. speed skater Bonnie Blair.

   Main verb is _____. Intended emphasis: U.S. speed skater Bonnie Blair

   _____

3. Dogs and cats are frequently disturbed by the explosions of July 4 fireworks.

   Main verb is _____. Intended emphasis: dogs and cats

   _____

4. In the next eight minutes, seismographers recorded five aftershocks.

   Main verb is _____. Intended emphasis: the aftershocks

   _____

375

5. The cards were thrown down on the table by José as the game ended.

   Main verb is _____. Intended emphasis: José

   _____

6. A mandate for social change was given by the citizens in the last election.

   Main verb is _____. Intended emphasis: the citizens

   _____

7. Pottery is a wonderfully tactile art that uses natural substances to create beauty.

   Main verb is _____. Intended emphasis: pottery

   _____

8. Your paper must be rewritten to include more facts about cloning.

   Main verb is _____. Intended emphasis: your paper

   _____

9. You are hereby summoned by Bergen County to appear for jury duty on March 16 at 8 A.M.

   Main verb is _____. Intended emphasis: Bergen County

   _____

10. Fourscore and seven years ago our fathers brought forth on this continent, a new nation, conceived in Liberty and dedicated to the proposition that all men are created equal.

    Main verb is _____. Intended emphasis: fathers

    _____

EXERCISE 23.3 COMPOSING SENTENCES THAT USE SPECIAL EFFECTS

NAME _____ **DATE** _____

The chapter identifies three kinds of sentences using structures that create special effects. One kind uses repetition, the second uses antithesis, and the third uses inverted word order. For this exercise, compose a sentence of each kind. An example of each kind of sentence is given.

EXAMPLE OF REPETITION Once I sweep out the garage, once I mow the lawn, once I wash and vacuum the car, once I pick up my sweater at the cleaner's, once I balance my checkbook and pay the bills, I will have all that free time to write letters to friends.

YOUR EXAMPLE OF REPETITION

1. _____
_____
_____
_____

EXAMPLE OF ANTITHESIS We began the project full of energy and enthusiasm; we finished weary and relieved that it was over.

YOUR EXAMPLE OF ANTITHESIS

2. _____
_____
_____
_____

EXAMPLE OF INVERTED WORD ORDER A handy, even indispensable, tool is the computer.

YOUR EXAMPLE OF INVERTED WORD ORDER

3. _____
_____
_____
_____

3. Global warming is a very serious problem. A number of troubling factors cause it. First, it is caused by an increase in the carbon dioxide existing in the atmosphere. There has also been an increase in other very harmful gases that are destroying the ozone. These gases trap heat in the upper atmosphere, and global temperatures are raised by them. And another major reason for global warming is deforestation. The decrease in the number of trees that are presently existing on our great planet Earth is having a devastating and serious effect on the amount of oxygen produced on a global level.

PART 5

SELECTING EFFECTIVE WORDS

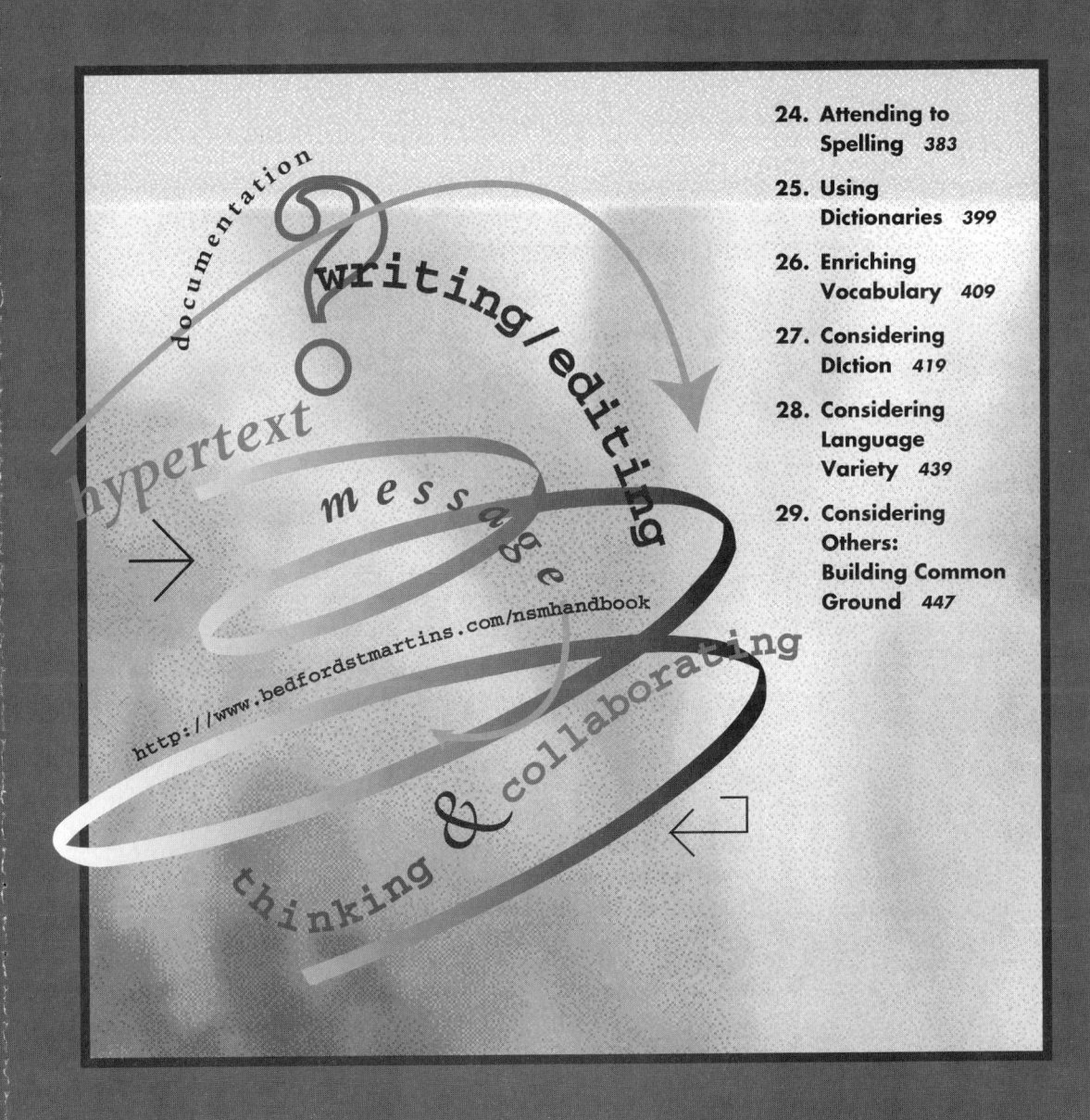

24. Attending to Spelling *383*
25. Using Dictionaries *399*
26. Enriching Vocabulary *409*
27. Considering Diction *419*
28. Considering Language Variety *439*
29. Considering Others: Building Common Ground *447*

PART 5

PREVIEW QUESTIONS

These questions are designed to help you, the student, decide what you need to study. (Answers are found at the back of the book.) First, find and correct any misspellings in the following sentences.

1. Their always telling us when they're going to have us over.
2. Harold definately never eats desert.
3. He herd the bells ringing, then he developped a headache.
4. During the rein of Queen Elizabeth I, many famous righters lived and dyed.
5. The Reagan administration concluded a nucular arms reduction treatey.

Use your dictionary to answer the following questions.

6. What is the origin of the word *adjudicate*? _____
7. What does *dementia praecox* mean? _____
8. Give at least two synonyms for *tendency*. _____
9. How many meanings does *revolution* have? _____

Respond to these questions about roots and suffixes.

10. Find two words for each of the following roots:

    a. *-bio-* = life (Gr.) _____

    b. *-jur-* or *-jus-* = law (Lat.) _____

11. What suffix indicates an *adverb*? _____
12. What are three suffixes indicating *adjectives*? _____

Underline any words in the following sentences that seem incorrectly used or inappropriate within the context. Write in the correct word if there is an error; write a C on the line after the sentence if there is none.

13. Woody Allen eludes to T. S. Eliot in his short stories. _____
14. The stink of baking apples was wonderfully appetizing. _____
15. I am continuously being interrupted by a continual stream of memos and phone calls. _____
16. This wine complements the meal perfectly. _____

Mark an X next to any of the following sentences that use language that is inappropriate for a college essay.

17. My research into the effect of television on babies requires tons of statistics.
18. Feminism and Marxism are two critical approaches frequently employed by contemporary literary critics.
19. Anyone who has studied this author's work in detail can see that he's just wrong.

Attending to Spelling   24

In the grocery store, we can decode the label for "lite" popcorn, the banner urging us to "by now," or the sign identifying "fresh tamatoes." Although some advertisers and businesses are tolerant of spelling variations—or errors—like these, people who read college or professional writing generally expect standard and accurate spellings. If you are a good speller, you may discover only an occasional spelling error in your writing. On the other hand, if you have difficulty with spelling, you may need to check carefully and regularly for spelling errors. Whatever your spelling ability, at some time or another, every writer makes spelling errors; such errors occur more frequently than any other kind. However, you can become a better speller—all it takes is time and effort on your part.

> **SPELLING IN EVERYDAY USE**
>
> President Andrew Jackson's comment "It's a damn poor mind that can think of only one way to spell a word!" is just as relevant today as it was over a hundred years ago. A short drive along an interstate turned up the following examples of alternative spellings.
>
> **Kountry Kitchen**
> **Kutz for Mutz**
> **Phat Phil's Phine Phood**
>
> Keep an eye out for fanciful or amusing spellings. Make a list of two or three examples and decide what purpose the writer might have had for the misspelling (assuming that it was intentional).

Spelling tip 1: Change your writing habits

As you draft, underline every word that you are not sure how to spell, even if you believe you have remembered it correctly. Later, look up all the underlined words at once. It is easy, once you have written a word and gone on to something else, to forget that you may have misspelled it; underlining as you go will help you remember to check. You can look up words in any standard dictionary (see Chapter 25 for advice on how to use a dictionary). Finally, if you are composing on a word processor, you may be able to make use of a spell checker. These programs are helpful in spotting *some* misspellings, but they are not a substitute for careful proofreading of your own work. For example, a spell checker will not catch typographical errors such as *form* for *from* or *king* for *kind*, nor will it know that you have written *herd* instead of *heard* or *loose* instead of *lose* because these misspellings spell words that are correct in other contexts.

Spelling tip 2: Learn to proofread for spelling errors

A final proofreading of anything you have written is essential if you want to catch your own spelling errors. The best way is to proofread sentence by sentence from the end to the beginning. Underline any questionable word as you go along. Pay little attention to content; force your eyes to study each word.

Spelling tip 3: Master commonly misspelled words (24a)

Research on college writing by the authors of *The New St. Martin's Handbook* has identified the fifty most commonly misspelled words. Chances are that at least a few of these words give you trouble, too. Here is the list:

1. their/there/they're
2. too/to
3. a lot
4. noticeable
5. receive/-d/-s
6. lose
7. you're/your
8. an/and
9. develop/-s
10. definitely
11. than/then
12. believe/-d/-s
13. occurred
14. affect/-s
15. cannot
16. separate
17. success
18. through
19. until
20. where
21. successful/-ly
22. truly
23. argument/-s
24. experience/-s
25. environment
26. exercise/-s/-ing
27. necessary
28. sense
29. therefore
30. accept/-ed
31. heroes
32. professor
33. whether
34. without
35. business/-es
36. dependent
37. every day
38. may be
39. occasion/-s
40. occurrences
41. woman
42. all right
43. apparent/-ly
44. categories
45. final/-ly
46. immediate/-ly
47. roommate/-s
48. against
49. before
50. beginning

Spelling tip 4: Recognize homonyms and similarly confusing words (24b)

Many words are **homonyms**, having the same sound but different spellings and meanings. *Deer* are wild animals; *dear* often begins a letter. *Cereal* is a breakfast food; *serial* is an adjective for things in a series. Other words sound so nearly similar that they are often confused. Here is a list of homonyms and frequently confused words; familiarizing yourself with the words in this list may help you become more sensitive to this kind of spelling problem.

accept/except	desert/dessert	plain/plane
advice/advise	device/devise	principal/principle
affect/effect	die/dye	quiet/quite
allusion/illusion	elicit/illicit	rain/rein/reign
are/our	eminent/immanent/imminent	right/rite/write
bare/bear	fair/fare	road/rode
board/bored	forth/fourth	seen/scene
brake/break	its/it's	than/then
breath/breathe	hear/here	their/there/they're
buy/by	heard/herd	threw/through/thorough
capital/capitol	know/no	to/too/two
choose/chose	later/latter	waist/waste
cite/sight/site	lead/led	weak/week
coarse/course	loose/lose	wear/where/were
complement/compliment	meat/meet	weather/whether
conscience/conscious	passed/past	who's/whose
council/counsel	peace/piece	your/you're
dairy/diary	personal/personnel	

Spelling tip 5: Be wary of spelling according to pronunciation (24c)

Spelling words according to their sounds often leads to trouble (consider a word like *enough*). Even when words are spelled as they sound, sometimes we mispronounce them (and so misspell them). We may say "reconize" when we mean "recognize," and we may carry the inaccurate pronunciation over onto the page. Here are some additional examples; in each case, the correct spelling is italicized.

nucular *nuclear*	strickly *strictly*	wich *which*
goverment *government*	artic *arctic*	suppose *supposed*
use to *used to*	liberry *library*	

Spelling tip 6: Recognize words with more than one form (24b)

In some instances, terms may be written as two words or combined to make a single word, depending on the intended meaning. Here is a list of commonly confused terms; check your dictionary for differences in meaning.

all ready/already	every day/everyday	may be/maybe
all ways/always	every one/everyone	no body/nobody

Writers also commonly misspell *a lot* and *all right*: these words are never combined. *Cannot*, in contrast, is always spelled as one word.

Spelling tip 7: Note unpronounced letters or syllables and unstressed vowels (24c)

To remember the spelling of words with unpronounced or unstressed letters or syllables, try to picture them in your mind. Or, create an alternate pronunciation that allows you to hear every letter and syllable. For example, remember *drastically* by saying to yourself "dras-tic-al-ly"; similarly, *Wednesday* becomes "Wed-nes-day." Here is a list of frequently misspelled words of this kind, with their unpronounced or unstressed letters or syllables italicized:

can*di*date	foreign	prob*a*bly
condem*n*	gover*n*ment	quan*ti*ty
diff*e*rent	int*e*rest	rest*au*rant
drastic*al*ly	mar*ri*age	We*d*nesday
Feb*r*uary	mus*c*le	

Words like *definite* contain unstressed vowels, making it hard to hear whether or not the last syllable should be spelled *-ite* or *-ate*. Sometimes picturing the word will help; remembering a related word (like *define*) should help you locate *definite* in the dictionary.

Spelling tip 8: Take advantage of spelling rules (24d)

- *I* before *e*, except after *c* or when sounded like "ay" as in *neighbor* and *weigh*.
  i before *e*: *achieve, believe, grief, friend, piece, relieve*
  except after *c*: *receive, ceiling, deceit*
  or when sounded like "ay": *neighbor, weigh, sleigh, inveigh, heinous, their*
  EXCEPTIONS: *either, neither, foreign, forfeit, height, leisure, efficient, seize, seizure, weird, science, ancient, nonpareil, conscience*

Adding prefixes and suffixes

A **prefix** is a set of letters added to the front of a word, and a **suffix** is a set of letters added to the end of a word. Sometimes the original word is spelled the same when a prefix or suffix is added to it, but many times the word changes by dropping, altering, or doubling a letter. These changes, with a few exceptions, tend to follow predictable patterns. Learning these patterns can help you spell many seemingly tricky words.

- When attaching a prefix, merely add it; do not change the spelling of the original word.

contaminate + prefix *de-* = *decontaminate*
moral + prefix *a-* = *amoral*
spell + prefix *mis-* = *misspell*

- To add a suffix for a word ending in silent *e*, keep the *e* if the suffix begins with a consonant; drop the *e* if the suffix begins with a vowel.
  snare + *-ing* (suffix begins with vowel; drop *e*) = *snaring*
  care + *-ful* (suffix begins with consonant; keep *e*) = *careful*
  EXCEPTIONS: *acreage, mileage, judgment, acknowledgment, wholly*

The silent final *e* is retained after a soft *c* (*service* + *-able* = *serviceable*) or soft *g* (*courage* + *-ous* = *courageous*). Sometimes the silent *e* is dropped when it is preceded by another vowel: in *true* + *-ly*, the silent *e* is preceded by the vowel *u*; hence, *true* + *-ly* = *truly*. The *e* is also retained occasionally to prevent confusion with other words (*dye* + *-ing* = *dyeing*).

- When adding *-ally* or *-ly*, use *-ally* if the word ends in *ic*; use *-ly* if the word does not end in *ic*.
  basic + *-ally* = *basically*
  slow + *-ly* = *slowly*
  EXCEPTION: *public* + *-ly* = *publicly*
- When adding a suffix to a word ending in *y*, keep the *y* when it follows a vowel and whenever adding *-ing*; change the *y* to *i* when the *y* follows a consonant.
  play + *-ful* (*y* follows vowel; keep *y*) = *playful*
  play + *-ing* (adding *-ing*; keep *y*) = *playing*
  beauty + *-ful* (*y* follows consonant; change *y* to *i*) = *beautiful*
  beauty + *-fy* (*y* follows consonant; change *y* to *i*) = *beautify*
  beautify + *-ing* (adding *-ing*; keep *y*) = *beautifying*
  EXCEPTIONS: Keep the *y* in some one-syllable base words: *shy* + *-ness* = *shyness*. Change the *y* to *i* in some one-syllable base words: *day* + *-ly* = *daily*. Keep the *y* if the base word is a proper name: *Kennedy* + *esque* = *Kennedyesque*.

Sometimes adding a suffix means doubling the final consonant of a word (*pin* + *-ed* = *pinned*), and sometimes it does not (*shower* + *-ed* = *showered*). Knowing when to double or not depends on your ability to identify the number of syllables in a word and your ability to hear where the stress falls when a word is pronounced correctly.

For suffixes beginning with a vowel:

- When adding suffixes to words of one syllable that end in consonants, double the final consonant only when a single vowel precedes that final consonant.
  pin + *-ing* (final consonant preceded by single vowel; double consonant)
     = *pinning*
  flip + *-ed* (final consonant preceded by single vowel; double consonant)
     = *flipped*

stream + *-er* (final consonant preceded by two vowels; do not double)
= *streamer*
curl + *-ing* (final consonant preceded by consonant; do not double)
= *curling*

- In words of more than one syllable, double the final consonant when a single vowel precedes the final consonant *and* the sounded stress falls on the last syllable of the original word.
  recall + *-ed* (final consonant preceded by consonant; do not double) = *recalled*
  begin + *-er* (final consonant preceded by single vowel, and sounded stress falls on last syllable of original word; double final consonant) = *beginner*
  invent + *-ing* (final consonant preceded by consonant; do not double)
  = *inventing*
  shower + *-ed* (final consonant preceded by single vowel, but sounded stress does not fall on last syllable of original word; do not double) = *showered*

Adding the endings *-sede*, *-ceed*, and *-cede*

The ending pronounced "seed" can be spelled in three ways.

- *-sede*: The only word in which this occurs is *supersede*.
- *-ceed*: The only words in which this occurs are *exceed*, *proceed*, and *succeed*.
- *-cede*: The ending pronounced "seed" is spelled this way in all other English words.

Forming plurals (24e)

- Form the plurals of most nouns by adding *-s*, as in *papers, clouds, dimes*.
- Form the plurals of nouns ending in *s, ch, sh, x,* or *z* by adding *-es*, as in *churches, bosses, brushes, telexes*.
- Form the plurals of nouns ending in *y* preceded by a consonant by changing the *y* to *i* and adding *-es*, as in *countries* (from *country*), *luxuries* (from *luxury*), *scarcities* (from *scarcity*).
- Form the plurals of nouns ending in *f* or *fe* by changing the *f* or *fe* to *v* and then adding *-es*, as in *leaves* (from *leaf*), *loaves* (from *loaf*), *knives* (from *knife*).
- Form the plurals of nouns ending in *o* by adding *-s* if the *o* is preceded by a vowel (as in *radios*) or by adding *-es* if the *o* is preceded by a consonant (as in *potatoes* or *heroes*).
  EXCEPTIONS: *sopranos, pros, pianos, hippos, pimentos*

Some words taken from other languages use the plurals from those languages: *phenomenon/phenomena, datum/data, medium/media, locus/loci, radius/radii*.

Spelling tip 9: Use a personal spelling chart

Spelling errors are not deliberate errors: no one sets out to use inaccurate spelling. Constructing, using, and evaluating the data from a personal spelling chart will help you see the pattern of your particular spelling problems. Once you know the pattern, you will be able to identify the specific kinds of words that give you trouble. You can then begin to anticipate which words you will need to underline (during either drafting or proofreading) and then look up. And you will also be able to concentrate on learning the appropriate rules.

The form for a personal spelling chart is as follows:

WORD (SPELLED CORRECTLY)	INACCURATE VERSION	LETTERS OR SYLLABLES INVOLVED	TYPE OF MISSPELLING
1. due	do	o/ue	homonym
2. receiving	recieving	ei/ie	letter reversal
3. response	reponse	s	missing letter
4. nastiest	nastyest	i/y	suffix rule
5. supreme	supream	e/ea	long vowel sound
6. language	langauge	au/ua	letter reversal
7. flue	flew	ue/ew	homonym
8. definite	definate	i/a	unstressed vowel
9. snoring	snoreing	e	suffix rule
10. compiling	compilling	l	suffix rule

If such words as the ten listed here appeared on your own spelling chart, you would be able to see that homonyms, letter reversals, and suffix rules consistently cause trouble. Keep such a chart over the course of a term, and you will see patterns in the errors you make. Armed with such knowledge, you will become an even more effective proofreader of your own writing.

EXERCISE 24.1 NOTING YOUR SPELLING WEAKNESSES

NAME _____ **DATE** _____

Working either individually or in small groups, read over the following list of words. Some of these words are spelled correctly, but others are not. Without consulting a dictionary, decide whether the word is accurately spelled. Mark *OK* beside those words you think are correct. If you think the word is incorrect as printed, then write your own spelling in the space provided. When you are finished, check your dictionary to see how often you identified the spellings accurately. Which words surprised you? Finally, write three or four sentences explaining the methods you use to make sure your spelling is accurate.

acceptible _____   embarrass _____

accidentally _____   Febuary _____

aquaintance _____   goverment _____

allright _____   incredeble _____

cemetary _____   necessary _____

committment _____   occurr _____

congradulate _____   oppurtunity _____

decieve _____   professer _____

diferance _____   recommend _____

drasticly _____   wierd _____

When you write a paper, how do you make sure that your spellings are accurate?

_____

_____

_____

_____

_____

EXERCISE 24.2   PROOFREADING FOR SPELLING ERRORS

NAME _____ **DATE** _____

Proofread the following passage. Underline any misspelled words or words you do not know how to spell. Check all of them and then, in the space provided below, write out a list of the misspellings you found, and the correct spelling of each.

Constructing any thing takes knowlege, time and patients. Wether you are sewwing a dress, desining a cabinet, or useing your culinery skills to make a grate omelet, chances are that your product will not be prefect the first time. So plan on makeing that first dress for youself and giving the second one as a gift; plan on staying at the workbench longer than you woud like and on hanging that first cabanet in the garage; and plan on consumeing that first omelet in privite. In this way, your expectted mistakes hurt no one. Keepping your patience, maintaining high stanards, controling your tempter—these things aren't easy. However, if you can make mistakes and lern from them, your work will improove and so wil your one estimateion of your talence.

EXERCISE 24.3   REVIEWING COMMONLY MISSPELLED WORDS

NAME _____   **DATE** _____

Reread the list of commonly misspelled words. Identify from the list five words that have given you trouble in the past. Indicate how you misspelled the word, and then use that word (correctly spelled) in a sentence. Use the space below for this exercise.

EXAMPLE   Word: apparently
In the past, I've misspelled this word by adding an extra *r*.
Sentence: Apparently, I forgot to finish the assignment last night.

EXERCISE 24.4 DISTINGUISHING BETWEEN HOMONYMS AND OTHER SIMILAR-SOUNDING WORDS

NAME _____ **DATE** _____

Twelve pairs of words are given below. For each word, write a sentence that uses the word correctly.

EXAMPLE   **a.** witch   **b.** which

a. The wicked witch wore ruby slippers.
b. I cannot decide which one of these movies to rent tonight.

1. **a.** you're   **b.** your

2. **a.** than   **b.** then

3. **a.** where   **b.** wear

4. **a.** affect   **b.** effect

5. **a.** lose   **b.** loose

6. **a.** forth   **b.** fourth

7. **a.** accept   **b.** except

8. **a.** there   **b.** their

9. **a.** its   **b.** it's

10. **a.** cite   **b.** site

11. **a.** too   **b.** to

12. **a.** later   **b.** latter

EXERCISE 24.5 USING RULES FOR *I* BEFORE *E* AND FOR SOME SUFFIXES

NAME _____ **DATE** _____

Read the following ten sentences carefully. Circle any misspelled words you find, and write the correct spelling above each misspelling.

                           Basically *proceeds*   *neighbor's*

EXAMPLE (Basicly), (procedes) of the fund-raising activities will be used to rebuild the (nieghbor's) house.

1. Members of groups such as Alcoholics Anonymous or Overeaters Anonymous work together to succede in overcomming common problems.

2. They beleive that they can control thier problem behaviores by faceing the problem personaly and by supportting each other.

3. Sucess in these programes often begins with wholley honest acknowledgment of the problem.

4. Then members usualy admit thier need of help in acheiving success.

5. They follow their consceinces in making amends for the past.

6. Each member trys to be succesful that day, encourageing others as well.

7. At regular meettings, the members publically tell thier storys.

8. In such waies, members of Alcoholics Anonymous carfuly procede through that program's twelve steps.

9. Many other programs have acheived success with basicly the same approach useing group meettings and following steps.

10. Because such a group builds personal responsibilitys and niether blames nor punishs, many people have appreciated recieving such help in controlling drinking, eatting, gambleing, drug use, and other behaviors.

395

EXERCISE 24.6 USING ADDITIONAL SUFFIX RULES

NAME _____ **DATE** _____

Based on the suffix rules discussed in this chapter, determine the proper spelling of the following new words and state the rule you applied.

    EXAMPLE   *coin + -ed*   Correct spelling: coined
                           Rule: In words of one syllable, double the final consonant only when a single vowel precedes the final consonant.

1. *control + -able*

2. *name + -ly*

3. *tragic + -ly*

4. *bounty + -ful*

5. *time + -ing*

6. *bet + -ing*

7. *like + -able*

8. *convert + -ible*

9. *employ + -er*

10. *start + -ing*

11. *refer + -ing*

12. *study + -ed*

EXERCISE 24.7 CONSTRUCTING A PERSONAL SPELLING CHART

NAME _____ **DATE** _____

Following the format given in this chapter (see spelling tip 9), begin your own personal spelling chart. Use anything you have written recently (a term paper or a letter or a list). Find and list at least ten words you have misspelled, and fill out the other three columns of the chart for each of those words. If your draft does not contain ten misspellings, complete your chart with words you have misspelled in the past. Finally, identify and list any misspelling patterns you see in your chart. What kinds of words should you look at more carefully the next time you are proofreading your writing for spelling errors?

WORD (SPELLED CORRECTLY)	INACCURATE VERSION	LETTERS OR SYLLABLES INVOLVED	TYPE OF MISSPELLING

▼ Using Dictionaries

25

Writers use dictionaries the way carpenters use hammers and cooks use pots and pans—as indispensable tools. Chances are that you have used dictionaries in the past and that you have some sort of dictionary available to you. If you are purchasing a dictionary, choose one of the hardbound "college" dictionaries. Among the most popular and well designed are the *American Heritage Dictionary* (published by Houghton Mifflin) and *Webster's New Collegiate Dictionary* (published by Merriam-Webster).

> **DICTIONARIES IN EVERYDAY USE**
>
> A dictionary can be particularly handy when you are faced with signing—or preparing to sign—a contract. For many Americans, choosing life insurance is an important decision that calls for understanding and evaluating complex and competing plans. Reading the material calls for a sharp eye and a clear knowledge of what words mean. Materials describing one such plan, for example, contain the following terms: *semiannual, net cost, underwrite, waiver, conversion, incontestability*, and *incapacitated*. How many do you understand? Which ones are generally familiar but may hold specific legal meanings in a contract? Which ones would you want to look up in a dictionary before signing the contract?

Exploring the dictionary (25a)

Dictionaries help writers check spelling, meaning, and syllabic divisions, as well as a variety of other things. Suppose that you are working on a rough draft and quoting a sentence from a speaker who said, "That should appeal to the *hoypoloy*." You underline *hoypoloy* because you are unsure of its spelling; besides, you want to look up that word because it is unfamiliar to you.

In revising, you come upon *hoypoloy* and decide to look it up. How do you look up a word that you have never seen before? First, figure out the letter combinations that could produce the word's opening sound. The first syllable could be spelled *hoy* (as in *boy*) or *hoi* (as in *noise*). Using a college dictionary, you look first under *hoy* but find nothing. Looking under *hoi*, however, does give you the entry. The word (really a phrase, as it turns out) appears this way: **hoi pol·loi**. Now you know how to spell the

7. she *explored* the issue

8. the student *endeavored* to do better

9. dinner was *tasty*

10. the howling outside was *terrifying*

11. she *hates* that place

12. his *passion* for her

EXERCISE 25.3 USING A DICTIONARY OR A THESAURUS

NAME _____ **DATE** _____

Use a dictionary or thesaurus to replace the underlined words in the following passage. Select words that have about the same meaning as the words used but are more commonly known and are more likely to be clear to a general reader. Write your selections in the space above each underlined word.

Although many people expect a writer who lived hundreds of years ago to be <u>arduous</u> and <u>irksome</u>, Chaucer is an exception. Reading his *Canterbury Tales* may be a challenge, but his characters are far from <u>tiresome</u>. They are all part of an <u>assemblage</u> of <u>the populace</u> going on a pilgrimage. They travel together and <u>enumerate</u> stories so that they are not bored on the way. They represent <u>disparate</u> levels of society from the courageous Knight who has fought many battles abroad to the <u>choleric</u> Reeve who manages his lord's farm. They also represent <u>divergent</u> social groups and occupations. Each <u>narration</u> suits the teller's social rank and personality. The drunken Miller, for example, tells a <u>scurrilous</u> tale about a carpenter and is answered by a tale about a <u>mendacious</u> miller. The tale of the Wife of Bath, <u>espoused</u> five times, argues that a wife should have authority over her husband. The Clerk's story of a patient Griselda presents the <u>antipodal</u> extreme, the long-suffering wife. Although these characters come from a different time period, they <u>manifest</u> the same human traits as people today.

EXERCISE 25.4 USING THE LIBRARY'S SPECIAL DICTIONARIES

At your local library, find special dictionaries in the reference area (ask your reference librarian for help if you need it). Select three of them. For each, on your own paper, provide the types of information shown in the example below.

> **EXAMPLE** Title: *The Oxford Dictionary of English Christian Names*
> Author or Editor: E. G. Withycombe, ed.
> Publisher: Oxford University Press
> Year of Publication: 1977
> Information Provided: 310 pages of first names together with their meanings and origins
> Sample Entry (from p. 235): OSWIN (m): Old English *Oswin,* compound of *os* 'a god' and *wine* 'friend.' It remained in use until the 14th C. and was occasionally revived in the 19th C.

Next, consulting a dictionary of usage, briefly answer the following questions. Indicate the name, all authors or editors, and the publisher of the dictionary you consult.

> **EXAMPLE** What is the difference, if any, between *further* and *farther*?
> Fowler's *Modern English Usage* says that *farther* is now common only where distance is concerned. *Further* "has gained a virtual monopoly of the sense of *moreover,* both alone and in the compound *furthermore.*"
>
> *A Dictionary of Modern English Usage*, by H. W. Fowler, 2nd ed., revised by Sir Ernest Gowers. New York: Oxford University Press (paperback), 1983, p. 190.

1. What is the difference between *libel* and *slander*?
2. Is it permissible to *allude* to someone by name?
3. What is the difference between *mendacity* and *mendicity*?
4. What is the difference between *eminent, immanent,* and *imminent*?
5. What is the proper past tense of *hang*?

26 Enriching Vocabulary

Many years ago, the famous baseball player Dizzy Dean injured his leg sliding into second base. After examining the leg, the trainer announced with a serious expression that it looked as if the leg was fractured. "Fractured, hell!" cried Dean. "The damned thing's broken!" If *fractured* wasn't a part of Dizzy Dean's active vocabulary before then, he surely figured it out quickly. So it is with all of us, for we meet new words every day. With the help of context, word roots, and dictionaries, we figure them out and make them ours.

> **VOCABULARY IN EVERYDAY USE**
>
> Think of recent times when you learned the name of something new—perhaps a new variety of plant, a computer term like *byte*, a key word used in one of your classes, or an unfamiliar food like *tapas*. Make a list of the words you learned. How exactly did you discover the meaning of each one?

Recognizing word roots (26b)

Most words possess long histories; before they became the English words we recognize, they may have been French (*ensign*, for example) or Spanish (*armadillo*, for example) or African (*banjo*, for example). Many English words come from Latin and Greek. Thus the Latin words for mother (*mater*) and father (*pater*) are the **root words** (or simply *roots*) for *maternal* and *paternal*, respectively.

Readers familiar with the most common Latin and Greek roots often find that they can determine the meaning of an unfamiliar word. Thus if you know the Greek roots *-biblio-* (meaning "book") and *-phil-* (meaning "love"), you can figure out that a *bibliophile* is a book collector—someone who loves books.

Here is a list of some common Latin and Greek roots:

ROOT	MEANING AND TYPICAL ENGLISH WORDS
-audi-(L)	to hear: *audible, auditorium*
-bene-(L)	good, well: *benevolent, benefit*
-bio-(G)	life: *biology, biography*
-duc-, -duct-(L)	to lead: *induct, conducive*

-er, -or	one who: *trainer, investor*
-ism	doctrine or belief: *Catholicism*
-ist	one who: *soloist*
-ment	condition of: *entertainment*
-ness	state of being: *cleanliness*
-ship	position held: *professorship*
-sion, -tion	state of being or action: *confusion, constitution*

SUFFIXES INDICATING VERBS

-ate	cause to be: *regulate*
-en	cause to be or become: *enliven*
-ify, -fy	make or cause to be: *amplify*
-ize	make, give, or cause to become: *popularize*

SUFFIX INDICATING ADVERBS

-ly	way or manner: *slowly*

SUFFIXES INDICATING ADJECTIVES

-able, -ible	capable of: *assumable, edible*
-al, -ial	pertaining to: *regional, proverbial*
-ful	having a notable quality of: *colorful*
-ious, -ous	of or characterized by: *nutritious, famous*
-ish, -ive	having the quality of: *clownish, conductive*
-less	without, free of: *relentless*

Analyzing the contexts of new words (26d1)

Knowing roots, prefixes, and suffixes will certainly help you determine the meanings of new words. But even if a word is entirely unknown to you, the words around it will give you clues about its meaning. We call those clues **context**. Consider the following sentence: *The clown's long face and lugubrious manner brought laughs from the crowd.* Whatever *lugubrious* means, it has something to do with laughter and with a long face. In fact, the *American Heritage Dictionary* says it means "mournful or doleful, especially to a ludicrous degree."

Becoming an active reader (26d2)

Here are four suggestions to help you become a more active reader and thus build your vocabulary.

ENRICHING VOCABULARY

- *Increase the amount of time you spend on pleasure reading.* Do not confine reading to schoolwork; save some time for reading material that interests *you*—newsmagazines, general science magazines, specialty sport or craft magazines. If you do not read a daily newspaper, start doing so. Read novels or biographies. Even the busiest schedule can accommodate twenty minutes a day for such reading.
- *Pay conscious attention to word choices in addition to content.* Reading in this way will inevitably slow your reading speed somewhat, but part of your purpose is to increase the number of words you recognize and can use.
- *Underline or otherwise note any word not entirely known to you.* You may be able to guess at some of the words you note from their context; others may be entirely baffling.
- *Copy new words into a vocabulary journal.* Make sure that your entry contains space for a brief definition and for a sentence using the word correctly. There is no need to complete the entries as you read. Simply enter the words; then, once you have finished reading, use a dictionary to check definitions and to help you write sample sentences. Here is a typical entry:

WORD	DEFINITION	USE
obdurate	hardened, unyielding	The tenants were obdurate in their decision to resist eviction.

Note that you are doing considerably more than simply consulting a dictionary; you are writing definitions and composing examples. Keeping such a journal during a time when you are also required to do considerable writing will increase your working vocabulary. Remember, reading and writing go hand in hand: to increase your writing vocabulary, you need to be reading and writing.

EXERCISE 26.1 COMPOSING USING WORD ROOTS

NAME _____ **DATE** _____

The following paragraph uses many words that are formed by Greek and Latin roots. Review the list of roots at the beginning of this chapter, and then read the paragraph, circling each root-based word you recognize. Then write out which root each word uses, and write in parentheses the meaning of the root.

EXAMPLE The (photographers) took portraits of the (biographers).
photo (light) graph (write) bio (life) graph (write)

Debate continues about whether extraterrestrial beings contact the earth, but scientific evidence of such contact is lacking. Researchers use special telescopes to search for radio waves that might be transmitted by alien beings. If audible signals were received and recorded, scientists here could try to transcribe and translate any lucid messages. Some people even envision establishing systematic communication with beings whose biology and genetics are entirely alien to our own. Such a mission, however, might benefit humankind, present unknown hazards, or generate logical but unanticipated consequences that we cannot now deduce. Whatever one's personal sentiments about the likelihood or desirability of contact, for most people the jury is still out on the issue of extraterrestrial contact.

EXERCISE 26.2 DETERMINING MEANINGS FROM CONTEXT

NAME _____ DATE _____

Try to determine the meanings of the following underlined words by studying the context of the sentences they are in. Write out what you think each word means. Then look them up in the dictionary and see how close you came.

1. She rubbed the <u>unctuous</u> lotion all over her dry, chapped skin.

   _____

2. The <u>obdurate</u> boy continued his pattern of petty crime despite his court appearances and increasingly stiff sentences.

   _____

3. The <u>viscid</u> honey coated the table, the three children, and the cat.

   _____

4. In stories by Charles Dickens, young children are often punished with a <u>ferule</u>.

   _____

5. The <u>pestilence</u> of the Middle Ages took a great toll in lives.

   _____

6. Tom's <u>languor</u> is keeping him from accomplishing any of his tasks.

   _____

7. The first and second levels were finished, then came the <u>tertiary</u> level.

   _____

8. The health inspector <u>insolently</u> raised his eyebrows and ignored all the restaurant employees.

   _____

9. The accused man was <u>exonerated</u> when another person confessed to the crime.

   _____

10. Dr. King urged his fellow marchers to keep their <u>equanimity</u> even in the event of violence.

    _____

EXERCISE 26.3 USING PREFIXES AND SUFFIXES

Drawing from the prefixes listed in this chapter and the list of common roots in this exercise, construct five new words. If you are not sure your word is in fact an English word, consult your dictionary. Write the words on a separate page, and indicate the literal meaning and the common meaning. Then use the word in a short sentence. See the example following the list of common roots. (Number your words from 1 to 5.)

COMMON ROOTS AND MEANINGS

-dict-, to say	-phon-, sound	-vid-, -vis-, to see
-vene-, to come	-graph-, to write	-duct-, to lead
-scrib-, to write	-ped-, foot	-mit-, -mis-, to send

EXAMPLE   transmit   Literal meaning: *across + to send*   Common meaning: *to send across*
Sentence: *A radio tower transmits radio waves.*

Attach an appropriate noun suffix to each of the following root words. Then write two sentences. Use the original word in the first sentence. Use the new word in the second sentence. Consult your dictionary as necessary.

EXAMPLE   king: *Henry VIII is a famous British king.* kingdom: *The daily changing of the guard reminds Britons that they still live in a kingdom.*

6. operate   7. happy   8. friend

Add an appropriate verb suffix or adjective suffix to each of the root words that follow. Then follow the instructions given for items 6 through 8.

9. broad   10. magnet   11. pass   12. emotion

27 Considering Diction

Choosing appropriate language (27a)

Choosing appropriate **diction** for college essays means choosing vocabulary and grammar that will be recognized and readily understood by your intended readers. In addition to avoiding regionalisms and dialects, college prose tends to avoid colloquial language and slang. Colloquial language (*snooze, a lot, nukes*) is informal; slang (*phat, def, rad*) is both informal and often understandable only to a few. The unconscious or haphazard use of either colloquial language or slang in college writing suggests that the writer has not really thought hard about what is being said to whom. Colloquial language or slang thus undermines an essay's credibility.

DICTION IN EVERYDAY USE

Restaurant menus provide good examples of diction at work. See how two very different menus describe fried chicken.

> Crispy-tender, finger-licking, soul-satisfyin' good chicken. Choose regular or extra spicy.

> Succulent poulet frit, with a subtle hint of garlic. Presented with steamed snow peas and potatoes lyonnaise.

Write a brief paragraph explaining what the different diction tells you about the two restaurants. What do you think each of them would be like?

Understanding denotation and connotation (27b)

Obviously, as a writer, you want to choose words that accurately convey the meaning you intend. It's important to understand, then, that there are at least two ways in which a word can carry meaning, and to be aware of both as you make your verbal choices. **Denotations** are the straightforward dictionary meanings of words, and every word has at least one. But many words carry as well certain **connotations**—suggestions of associated meanings. Connotations may be trickier to master, but they are potentially a writer's resource; by carefully choosing words for both kinds of meaning, you can communicate your meaning with precision and depth.

Unlike denotations, connotations are not often found in the dictionary; words gather connotative meanings through the ways in which they are customarily used. And words with similar denotations may carry different connotations. Think of the nouns *smell, odor,* and *aroma*. All refer to the same thing: that quality of an object that you can perceive through your nose. But different associations are attached to each because of the way people habitually use them. You might write, for instance, *I awoke to the smell of coffee*. There is nothing wrong with this; it's straightforward and efficient. Now compare it to *I awoke to the aroma of coffee*. The connotations of *aroma* suggest more delight on your part when you woke up, more anticipation of that delicious first cup. In comparison, the first sentence seems to say that you simply, neutrally noticed the smell upon waking (and maybe that is accurate). But now try this: *I awoke to the odor of coffee*. Something seems off-key here; do you dislike coffee? *Odor* seems to carry a subtle but real connotation of distaste, and unless that is what you want to express, the word is less than a perfect choice here. By the same token, you might not write *The aroma of my roommate's unwashed gym socks*, unless trying purposely for humorous effect.

Writers or speakers who aim to persuade their readers to do something—to buy a product or to take a position on an issue—often choose words to take advantage of connotative meanings. Consider the difference between *The Democrats are planning a new education bill* and *The Democrats are conspiring on a new education bill*. One might assume the second sentence was written by someone unsympathetic to the Democrats. Connotative meanings can make the difference between a nearly right word and the exactly right word, but they can also, as here, convey harsh judgments and convince a reader that the writer is not being fair-minded.

Writers often make denotative or connotative errors when using words with which they are not completely familiar—and that includes every writer sooner or later. If writers restricted themselves to words they were sure of, they would never expand their vocabularies. This means being willing to reach for new words when you write a rough draft and being willing to check those you are uncertain about, either in a dictionary or with readers or other writers.

Balancing general and specific diction (27c)

General words refer to or identify broad categories, classes, or groups of things. *Tree, book, house, emotion*—these are general words. *Elm, hymnal, bungalow,* and *anger* are more specific words. Most good writing balances general and specific words to make its content clear. Imagine the span from general to specific as a continuum:

GENERAL →	LESS GENERAL →	MORE SPECIFIC →	QUITE SPECIFIC
plant	flower	rose	tropicana rose
writing	poem	American poem	"Stopping by Woods on a Snowy Evening"

Weak writing often depends too heavily on one end of the continuum. For example, some writers forget that they are writing to readers who do not yet share their experiences or ideas. The result is prose full of summary and judgment. Here are three sentences long on general and abstract diction and short on specifics: *That ride is scary. The equipment looks old, and the ride operators seem oblivious to safety concerns. We got in, and before we could feel comfortable, the first car started moving.*

These sentences give readers emotion (*scary*) and judgment (*equipment looks old, operators . . . oblivious to safety concerns*). The only people named, *the ride operators,* are shown in only the most general terms. Readers do not get to see any of the sensory information that yields the feeling *scary* except *looks old*. Do the words *looks old* mean that the equipment needs a paint job, that it has bent supporting rods, or that it has missing or very rusty bolts? What is it about those ride operators that makes them seem *oblivious to safety concerns*? What exactly do those ride operators do (or not do)? Presumably, the writer of the passage could easily answer these questions. By not answering them, the passage actually excludes the reader from the experience it seeks to describe.

Writers can also err in the direction of too many specifics, particularly if the details are presented in what seems like random fashion. College essays should provide readers with both a general context and the specifics to illustrate it; the general statements raise questions, and the specific statements answer those questions:

GENERAL Tenants complain that their apartments are decrepit and unsanitary. [*Readers' questions: What have the tenants complained about? What are the apartments really like?*]

SPECIFIC Tenants complain repeatedly by phone and by letter that their windows will not seal and some of the window panes are cracked and loose so that the rooms are drafty, and the older tenants especially find their health jeopardized. They complain that the oil heater has been malfunctioning for months and has never been properly fixed; that the bathroom plumbing leaks consistently whether you shower, use the sink, or flush the toilet; . . . [*Readers will wish that this writer would get to the point.*]

GENERAL + SPECIFIC Tenants complain that their apartments are decrepit and unsanitary, with windows that will not seal, heaters that have never been repaired, and bathroom plumbing that leaks every time it is used. In an effort to force the owner to make repairs, the tenants have filed a suit in county court.

Using figurative language (27d)

Often, **figurative language** also plays a crucial role in conveying a writer's meaning and content. For example, few of us would really grasp the force of an ocean wave hitting a rocky outcropping if that force were expressed simply as "extreme." But we can quite readily understand the statement that such waves hit with the impact of a truck driven into a brick wall at eighty miles per hour. That comparison is one type of figurative language.

Using metaphors, similes, and analogies

Metaphors present one thing as though it were another: *The street is a carnival.* **Similes** claim that one thing *is like* another, and they make the comparison obvious by including the words *like, as,* or *as if: The ball rolled toward the hole as if drawn by a magnet.*

Metaphors and similes appear inside single sentences. **Analogies** extend the comparison to several sentences:

> Looked at in these ways, capital punishment amounts to state-sponsored murder. After all, capital punishment is the premeditated taking of another life. Like the act of a murderer, capital punishment argues that human beings have the right to deny life; it argues that human beings know how and when to exercise this right.

Metaphors, similes, and analogies help us look at things in surprising, interesting new ways. Instead of saying *We were all bored watching that movie,* a writer might say *Consider* Shoot 'Em Up III *a sleeping pill.* Metaphors such as that one carry considerable punch. Of course, no movie can actually be a sleeping pill. What the writer means is that both movie and sleeping pill have the same effect. But the use of metaphor turns an unremarkable thought into a fresh, amusing statement, the tone of which is very different from *We were all bored watching that movie.*

Using other figures of speech

If you want to comment on your friend's new Hawaiian shirt, you might say, *I could hear that shirt a block away.* Shirts do not really shout, yet your listeners understand your meaning. By giving human qualities or capabilities to something that does not really possess them, you have personified that shirt. Such **personification** gives vibrancy to what would otherwise be flat writing: *That shirt is colorful.*

Suppose that you are looking at the same shirt and you want to exaggerate in a different way. You might say (or write), *That shirt simply drips color.* This deliberate exaggeration is called **hyperbole.** On the other hand, deliberate understatement, or **litotes,** involves defining something by stressing what it is not, as in *A meal at the diner was* not *a gourmet affair.*

Allusions, indirect references to cultural works, people, or events, bring a wide range of associations to the minds of readers who recognize them. Allusions can be drawn from history, literature, current events, the Bible, or common wisdom. If you say *Your shirt gets two big thumbs up!,* your friend knows you are alluding to a common movie rating system, giving the shirt your approval.

Irony is the term for a statement that clearly means the opposite of what it says, as in *Wow, that is one drab shirt.* **Sarcasm** is a bitter or mocking form of irony, as in, *Sure, Richard, that shirt is perfect for my sister's church wedding.* Note that both irony and sarcasm depend on the audience's ability to recognize that the actual meaning is different from what is being said. In short, both irony and sarcasm depend on context. If the audience misses the irony or sarcasm, the writer has not sufficiently established the context.

■ Avoiding Clichés and Stock Phrases

Phrases such as *true blue, quick as a wink, slow as molasses in January,* and *scarce as hen's teeth* are **clichés**. Such phrases have been overused to the point that they have lost their original sparkle or wit. Similarly, we all know quite a number of **stock phrases**, all of them predictable. Here are several: *beyond the shadow of a doubt, have a nice day, dyed in the wool, climb the ladder of success, explore new horizons, have a sneaking suspicion, flagrant violations, unexpected development, raging fire.* Like clichés, stock phrases have become so commonplace that readers will find them boring and will quickly lose interest in your writing if you use them often.

Using the appropriate register (27a)

When we speak about levels of language (sometimes also called **registers**), we acknowledge the differences between the writing of a hastily written note to a roommate and the writing of a job application letter. Three levels of language, familiar, informal, and formal, will be discussed here. Most college writing uses the formal level, but you should also be able to recognize and use the other levels.

Familiar language

Familiar language—the language of nicknames, nonstandard grammar, regionalisms, slang, and sentence fragments—is almost exclusively spoken. It is sometimes the language of special groups; for instance, armed forces personnel serving in Vietnam had an intricate "second language" unique to that time and place. "In country" was their term for South Vietnam; "the world" was everywhere else, but especially the United States.

Consider this bit of talk:

> Skoochies we hit about nine. Dead. Nothing. Tried Eighty-second but too many blue lights. Makes ya nervous, ya know. And Jimmy wanting to crash. So we bailed out.

Translated into more formal language, it might read like this:

> We arrived at Skoochies, a dance club, about 9 P.M. Since the dance floor was virtually empty, we decided to try driving up and down Eighty-second Avenue. When we got there, we noticed several police cars. Just seeing police cars made us nervous. All this time, Jimmy kept saying that what he wanted to do was go home and sleep. With nothing more to do, we finally did just go home.

Although the first version is terse and somewhat dramatic, not everyone will be able to follow it. The second, more formal version is admittedly less exciting, but it is also more understandable to more readers. In fact, familiar language appears in print almost exclusively in the pages of fiction, in song lyrics, and in personal letters or

EXERCISE 27.2 CHECKING FOR CORRECT DENOTATION

NAME _____ **DATE** _____

Look for denotative errors in each of the following sentences, using your dictionary as needed. Underline every error that you find; then examine each error to determine the word intended. Write the correct word in the blank following each sentence. If there are no denotative errors in the sentence, write a C in the blank. The first sentence has been done for you.

1. Your conscious would tell you that dishonesty is not the best policy.
   conscience

2. Feeding the body and the mind is the guiding principal for the Teen Center's breakfast program. _____

3. During his military career, he served on three continents, traveling from ocean to dessert. _____

4. The current treatments for Alzheimer's are only somewhat affective. _____

5. A rabbit's foot or similar talisman gives some people the allusion of security. _____

6. She is an imminent attorney, highly regarded by her opponents in court as well as by her colleagues. _____

7. Conscientious employees typically expect promotions and regular increases in compensation. _____

8. When emergency personnel arrived, the victim was conscience and alert. _____

9. Encyclopedias often feature both biographical and geographical entries. _____

10. One literary illusion in this poem may be referring to Frost's "After Apple Picking." _____

11. Eating squid somehow goes against my native deposition. _____

12. Don't let the judges effect the way you feel about yourself. _____

EXERCISE 27.3 UNDERSTANDING CONNOTATIVE MEANINGS

NAME _____ **DATE** _____

A. Write a sentence that accurately uses the connotations associated with each word in the following pairs of similar words. If you are unsure of the connotations of a particular word, check a good dictionary.

EXAMPLE disturbing: <u>I found Anthony Hopkins's performance as the evil genius in *The Silence of the Lambs* disturbing.</u>

distressing: <u>The plight of the homeless is distressing to any feeling person.</u>

1. cute: _____

   elegant: _____

2. affection: _____

   passion: _____

3. crazy: _____

   psychotic: _____

4. cheap: _____

inexpensive: _____

_____

5. imitation: _____

_____

forgery: _____

_____

B. The sentences that follow contain words with strongly judgmental connotative meanings. Underline these words; then revise each sentence to make it sound more neutral.

EXAMPLE   The current NRA <u>scheme</u> appeals to patriotism as a <u>smokescreen to obscure the real issue</u> of gun control.

REVISION <u>The current NRA campaign appeals to patriotism rather than responding directly to gun control proposals.</u>

1. News media crackpots claim that their news reports are fair and impartial.

_____

_____

2. Liberals keep whining about the bums, the crazies, and the lazy.

_____

_____

3. Only recently have ladies landed a seat on the Supreme Court.

_____

_____

4. Each election year, packs of Republicans swarm together at a national convention, itching to finger a figurehead.

_____

_____

5. A shrieking horde of the governor's critics gathered on the statehouse steps, brandishing their signs.

   _____

   _____

6. Their grungy clothes and bizarre haircuts immediately identify them as college students.

   _____

   _____

7. Ignorant voters signed that outrageous petition.

   _____

   _____

EXERCISE 27.8 REVISING FAMILIAR AND INFORMAL LANGUAGE

NAME _____ DATE _____

Using the space below, revise the passage you examined in Exercise 27.7 so that it consistently uses formal language to establish a tone appropriate to college writing. Begin by revising the first sentence as follows:

The manager of the pizzeria on Broadway does not seem to care about his customers.

EXERCISE 27.9 VARYING DICTION AND LANGUAGE LEVEL TO FIT YOUR AUDIENCE

NAME _____ **DATE** _____

The following is a letter you received from your friend Nancy Green. After reading it, you called Nancy and urged her to write a formal letter to the restaurant about this experience. At a loss, Nancy asked for your help. Using your friend's letter, write a more formal letter to the manager of the restaurant.

> You won't believe the meal I had two nights ago. Several of us went to A Place to Eat—you know, it's new, on the West Side about a block from Sashi's. Anyway I went with the special since Frank the waiter said it was good. Good, he said! It was moldy chicken in an ancient cheese sauce. Of course, not wanting to spoil the evening, I went ahead and ate about half of it. The real fun began when I got home. We're talking big-time illness here. I still feel like I went ten rounds with somebody punching me in the stomach. Last time we darken their door. We need to get together soon. How about lunch this week? Someplace on the East Side, OK? I'll call you.
>
> Love and kisses,
>
> *Nancy*

Since Nancy sent your letter to the restaurant and subsequently received not only a refund but also a free dinner for two at the restaurant of her choice, she has become known as the local expert on self-assertiveness. Now Nancy has been asked to relate her story to the local chapters of the Boy Scouts and Girl Scouts. Once again, Nancy is at a loss and requires your help. Write the story out as you would tell it to these young audiences.

28 Considering Language Variety

Recognizing different varieties of English (28a, b)

If you think about it, the English language we share contains an amazing diversity of regional and cultural expressions, as well as words and phrases borrowed from other languages. Consider, for example, the various ways we might refer to our parents. *Mama, mom, madre, matriarch, mater, ma, mum,* and *mommy* all refer to mothers. *Papa, dad, padre, sire, pater, pa, pop,* and *daddy* all refer to fathers. These words are more than synonyms for each other; each one begins to suggest a different social, ethnic, geographical, or cultural group. *Madre* and *padre* are Spanish; if you refer to your parents using those terms, your language reflects a Spanish or Hispanic influence. Similarly, the use of *mama* is more common in southern states, less common in the Northwest. And *ma* and *pa* both sound more rural than urban in character. Each of these usages is appropriate in some context.

The language that this book teaches—the language of college writing and communication—is often called **standard academic English**. You can read standard academic English in magazines like *Time* or *Newsweek,* and you can hear it whenever you listen to nationally broadcast news. Standard academic English is the language of most of the textbooks you will read (although these books may also introduce you to highly specialized language). Standard academic English is also the language of most

> **LANGUAGE VARIETY IN EVERYDAY USE**
>
> If you attend religious services of any kind, you may have ample opportunity to observe the use of different varieties of English or, indeed, of different languages. In some religious services, Latin or Hebrew or Arabic is used in all or some parts. In others, the religious leader may use formal English for a sermon or for a reading from Holy Scriptures and then shift to more informal English for announcements. In the same way, the congregation may use highly formal or archaic English for a hymn, a chant, or a reading and then shift to regional English to make announcements.
>
> If you are familiar with a religious community, think about the way the group uses different varieties of English or other languages. In what part of the service is each used? What are the effects of switching from one to the other? What cues do these shifts provide the worshipers?

business communication—reports, proposals, and letters—reason enough for you to learn how to use it effectively. And finally, standard academic English is the language most of your other college teachers will expect when they ask you for your explanation or your opinion.

As you think about standard academic English, remember that what you are really considering is a set of **conventions**—rules that we agree to follow. In the United States, for example, we agree that c-o-l-o-r is an accurate spelling; in England or Canada (or anywhere that teaches British English), the correct spelling would be c-o-l-o-u-r. Similarly, most stores in the United States still sell sliced turkey at so much per pound. But cross the border into Canada, and you find that turkey is sold at so much per 100 grams. Knowing standard academic English means knowing—and using—a set of widely understood language conventions, as well as realizing that what constitutes the "standard" in one place or country may not do so in another.

Using ethnic, occupational, or regional varieties of English (28c, 28d, 28e)

The conventions of standard academic English are probably not the only ones that you use or have experienced: the English that you speak among your friends, for example, is probably not the English that you use in the classroom. In any job you've held, you have no doubt been exposed to English used in different ways, and have used specialized terms. In addition, if you have ever lived in or visited any large city, you have probably experienced many different regional or ethnic varieties of English—Chinese, African American, Mexican, Southeast Asian, Polish, Italian, Jewish, Native American, and Polynesian, to name only a few. Your own heritage may very well have exposed you to some of this same richness of English. Most academic writing situations ask you to set this ethnic or regional richness aside. But you will find some occasions when you can draw on your knowledge of the many varieties of English, particularly when you want to let your readers hear that language and that voice. Capturing some of that language and using it inside a larger block of academic prose can lead to some startling and effective contrasts.

Sometimes you can simply quote the ethnic, occupational, or regional English that you want to use. For example, suppose you were asked to write an analysis of Flannery O'Connor's autobiographical essay "The King of the Birds," which discusses how her family raised peacocks in Milledgeville, Georgia. In your analysis, you might write about how O'Connor varies her language, sometimes using quite formal standard academic English and sometimes using the words her family actually spoke. One paragraph begins by introducing a visitor. The language here is formal: "A man selling fenceposts tarried at our place one day and told me that he had once had eighty peafowl on his farm. He cast a nervous eye at two of mine standing nearby." This prose reads as the controlled, rather formal academic English that it is. But when the man begins to discuss what it meant to have eighty such birds on the farm, the language changes: " 'In the spring, we couldn't hear ourselves think,' he said. 'As soon as you lifted your voice they lifted their'n, if not before.' " Strictly speaking, this is not quite standard academic English. The phrase *we couldn't hear ourselves think* is really a cliché (for more on avoiding clichés, see Chapter 27), and *their'n* is not standard usage. However, this is certainly powerful English; listening to it, we can begin to visualize the person who said it. In addition, careful readers notice the contrast. It surprises them a little bit to hear such informal, everyday speech inside more formal prose. The contrast makes readers pay more attention.

In her essay "Mother Tongue," Amy Tan, author of the novel *The Joy Luck Club*, discusses the way her Chinese mother speaks English. For Tan, her mother's speech is "vivid, direct, full of observation and imagery." And even from that brief quotation, you can see that Amy Tan's essay is itself a good example of what we have been calling standard academic English. But Tan's point is that standard academic English isn't the only English that can be meaningful or persuasive, even though Tan was often called on to translate her mother's speech or to speak on her behalf. Tan illustrates the contrast between standard academic English and her mother's speech by relating an occasion when a stockbroker had failed to send her mother a promised check. Her mother expressed her complaint this way: "Why don't he send me check, already two weeks late. So mad, he lie to me, losing me money." In speaking on her mother's behalf, Tan "translated" this complaint: "Yes, I'm getting rather concerned. You had agreed to send the check two weeks ago, but it hasn't arrived."

Amy Tan's point in her essay is that in writing *The Joy Luck Club* she wanted to capture her mother on paper. In Tan's words, "I wanted to capture what language ability tests can never reveal: her intent, her passion, her imagery, the rhythms of her speech and the nature of her thoughts." To do this, Tan consciously decided to "use all the Englishes I grew up with," including her mother's "broken" English as well as standard academic English.

Using other languages in academic writing (28f, 28g)

Sometimes you may wish to use words or short phrases from languages other than English. For instance, in "Black *and* Latino," an essay about his own heritage, Robert Santiago argues against our tendency to categorize people according to easy distinctions. He explains how his dark skin color and the fact of his Puerto Rican parents confused other people and confused him, too. Most of Santiago's essay is written in standard academic English, but he does bring in some Spanish to illustrate what he means: "My lighter-skinned Puerto Rican friends were less of a help in this department. 'You're not black,' they would whine, shaking their heads. 'You're a *boriqua* [slang for Puerto Rican], you ain't no *moreno* [black].'" Notice that Santiago translates words (in brackets immediately following the original term) when he thinks some members of his audience may not understand.

You too may find college writing situations in which you can decide to include more than just standard academic English. Using ethnic, occupational, or regional varieties of English, or importing words or phrases from other languages, should be something you do to make a particular point. Used carefully and not haphazardly, these other kinds of English will enrich your prose.

EXERCISE 28.3 USING OTHER LANGUAGES

NAME _____ **DATE** _____

Working individually or in small groups, see if you can come up with five words or phrases familiar to you that are either English words or phrases heavily influenced by another language (as Amy Tan's mother uses English) or words or phrases from a language other than English (as in Robert Santiago's essay). Write out the five words or phrases as you are familiar with them, and then "translate" them into standard academic English. Once you have done this, use your own paper to write a paragraph that explains to a stranger the differences between the originals and the translations. Write this paragraph in standard academic English, but make sure that you quote from your first list.

WORDS OR PHRASES

1. _____
2. _____
3. _____
4. _____
5. _____

MEANINGS

1. _____
2. _____
3. _____
4. _____
5. _____

Considering Others: Building Common Ground

29

When we write, we want our final products to be successful; we want our writing to be read and understood by our readers. Any number of factors can make this communication more difficult and less successful, including choosing offensive words and **stereotyping**. When writing stereotypes people, it groups them and then assumes that all members of the group are the same; stereotyping doesn't recognize individual human differences. In short, speak to readers the way that you would want to be spoken to yourself. None of us enjoys being insulted or unfairly judged. When we read an assertion such as "College students are wasting their time; they don't live in the real world," we know that no such sweeping statement does justice to college students and their lives; therefore, the assertion fails.

Similarly, statements such as "Kids are irresponsible" or "Kids don't know what it means to work" assume that it's possible to group all "kids" and then accurately characterize them. Any readers (of any age) who identify with "kids" will find this stereotyping offensive, and if they find it in a piece of writing, they will probably respond with hostility. In fact, in this context, many readers may find the word *kids* itself offensive. Here, both stereotyping and individual word choice provoke anger rather than agreement.

Questions of stereotyping and word choice are particularly important whenever you are writing to persuade others. In such writing situations, choosing words carefully can make a tremendous difference in your readers' responses. Instances of obviously offensive language are easy to identify and revise. Terms such as *slob*, *dummy*, and so on are meant to hurt and to insult; terms of this sort have no place in academic writing. But other terms offensive to readers might be harder to identify. For example, some older readers object to being called "elderly" or to being labeled "the elderly." Such phrasing suggests infirmity, and these older readers often lead active lives. *Senior citizens* or just *seniors* are more neutral terms.

How can you avoid offending members of your audience? The simplest way is to ask members of your reading audience how they prefer to be identified. Be aware that these preferences evolve over time; using an old term can be just as offensive as using an intentionally malicious one. Thus *colored people* is now an offensive term; it is better to choose *African American*. In a similar vein, the native peoples once referred to as "Eskimos" now prefer "Inuit."

When you draft, and especially when you revise to make your writing even more effective, pay attention to your phrasings and word choices with these questions in mind:

- Is this writing respectful of the ideas and feelings of others?
- Does this writing treat people as unique human beings, or does it unfairly or inaccurately stereotype them?
- Might any individual phrasings or identifications offend readers?

COMMON GROUND IN EVERYDAY USE

A fourteen-year-old recently exclaimed to his aunt: "I am *not* a kid anymore, so please stop calling me that!" The nephew objected to a label that he found both inaccurate and disrespectful, one that clearly built no common ground between him and his aunt. Can you think of situations when you're not sure how someone will respond—perhaps when you're sending a letter to someone unknown, trying to describe an eighty-year-old without calling him or her "old," or addressing the woman who delivers your mail? Spend some time listening to people talking—or to television or radio broadcasters or talk show hosts. Take note of any instances in which speakers seem to make an effort to avoid language that might seem disrespectful or destructive for building common ground.

Making language choices (29b)

As you work to build common ground with your readers and to avoid offending them, and as you reread your early drafts, pay particular attention to references of these sorts:

- references to gender
- references to race, ethnicity, religion, and geographical area
- references to age, class, sexual orientation, and physical ability

Even with the best of intentions, each of these kinds of references can prove troublesome.

References to gender

These days, virtually all readers are troubled by language that makes unnecessary or sexist reference to gender. The principle here is quite simple: use language acknowledging that most human activities are just that, human activities, and not gender-specific ones. Nurse, doctor, engineer, secretary, garbage hauler, choir director, minister—all these occupations are held by women and men. Earlier in this century, commonplace sexist language often seemed to limit certain occupations to men: *policeman, fireman, chairman, congressman.* And formerly it was commonplace usage to refer to the entire human race as *man* or *mankind.* Old texts still often use *he* to refer to a representative of an entire group, as in "A doctor must know his medicine, and he must be able to communicate with patients." Such usage clearly makes the assumptions that all doctors are men and that all doctors will always be men—assumptions that were never accurate in any case and that are certainly offensive today. Readers will be similarly offended by usages such as *woman doctor* or *male nurse,* since these terms treat the persons described as if they were oddities.

You can avoid sexist usage like that in the sentence below by using any of the three listed revision methods:

SEXIST USAGE	A *judge* must consider the evidence carefully before *he* arrives at a decision.
REVISION 1	*Judges* must consider the evidence carefully before *they* arrive at a decision. [*Use plural forms.*]
REVISION 2	A *judge* must consider the evidence carefully before arriving at a decision. [*Eliminate the pronoun.*]
REVISION 3	A *judge* must consider the evidence carefully before *he or she* arrives at a decision. [*Use* he or she *or* him or her.]

Beyond these simple revisions, ask yourself whether or not gender and gender-related characteristics are actually relevant. If you are writing a news story about Dr. Shirley Clark's research, is her marital status relevant? What about the color of her hair or her physical appearance? Do these things add to readers' understanding of Dr. Clark's research? If you were writing about Dr. Charles Clark, would you identify him as husband of Shirley Clark, and would you mention the fact that he is the father of three children? Would you note that he's an attractive blond (assuming he hasn't gone bald)? In fact, if your subject is the research itself, such details simply aren't relevant and should be omitted.

Here is a checklist of questions to help you identify and revise sexist language:

- Have you used *man* or *men* or words containing them to refer to people who may be female? If so, substitute a term that is gender free.

    fireman → firefighter

    manpower → personnel

    anchorman → anchor

- Have you used terms that assume a task is performed by only one gender? For example, have you used *mothering* when what you really mean is *parenting*?
- Have you used pronouns that assume a task or occupation is performed by only one sex? If so, eliminate the sexist assumption by making your terms plural. Thus *A good cook knows how to adjust her recipe* becomes *Good cooks know how to adjust their recipes.*

References to race, ethnicity, religion, and geographical area

When referring to race or ethnicity, do so in ways that those referred to would approve and find acceptable; be particularly careful not to use such references to minimize or eliminate individual differences. And as with gender-related descriptions such as marital status or physical attractiveness, ask yourself whether race or ethnicity references are truly necessary and relevant. Does it matter that John Kowalski is the *Polish* minister who preached last Sunday? Why is it important to mention that Connie Chung is an *Asian American* newscaster? If the reference isn't crucial, omit it.

In addition, be careful not to offend your readers by confusing ethnicity and religion. For example, *Arab* generally refers to people of Arabic-speaking descent. But *Arab* is not the same thing as *Muslim*, since many Muslims (believers in Islam) live in other areas (Iran and Pakistan, for example).

Be sensitive to the ways in which you refer to residents of particular areas, and use terms they would find acceptable. For example, many residents of Scotland or of Wales would prefer not to be called British. Similarly, it is inaccurate to use *American* to refer exclusively to the United States. Canada, Mexico, Peru, Brazil, and Chile (to name but five) are also American countries.

References to age, class, sexual orientation, and physical ability

Be wary of age-related terms that might offend or carry condescending overtones. Examples include *teenybopper, well-preserved, geriatric set,* and the like. If age is specifically important to your point, report it in years.

Some terms have obvious class overtones—*aristocrat*, for instance, or *peasant*. And some of these terms have overtones that can easily alienate those to whom they refer. So be careful of terms such as *slum dweller, redneck, blue blood,* and the like.

As with any other label, reference to sexual orientation should be included only when it is directly relevant. Again, one test here is simple: would you report sexual orientation regardless of what that orientation might be? Would you, for example, say *heterosexual police officer* if that were the case? If the reference is unnecessary, omit it.

Also be sensitive to current usage regarding physical health or ability. For example, persons born with the genetic code for Down's syndrome are no longer referred to as Mongoloid. And many of those who have suffered accidents resulting in impairments to full physical functioning may object to euphemisms like *physically challenged.* If you feel the disability needs to be made clear, identify the person first, then the disability. Thus you would say *Stevie Wonder, a singer who is blind,* not *blind singer Stevie Wonder.* Again, as a writer you should ask yourself whether or not such references are even necessary. If they are not obviously and directly relevant, omit them.

EXERCISE 29.1   IDENTIFYING STEREOTYPES

NAME _____ **DATE** _____

Each of the sentences below stereotypes a person or a group of people. Underline the word or phrasing that identifies the stereotyped person or group. In each case, be ready to explain why the stereotyping may be offensive, demeaning, or unfair.

1. Why would those white-collar suburban types care about health benefits for factory workers?
2. Turning eighty-four this month, Mr. Lantana is well preserved for his age.
3. The ambulance chasers have clogged our court system.
4. Dropouts have trouble landing good jobs.
5. College kids need real-world experience.

EXERCISE 29.2   REWRITING TO ELIMINATE OFFENSIVE REFERENCES OR TERMS

Review the sentences below for offensive references or terms. If the sentence seems acceptable as written, write C on the line below the sentence. If the sentence contains unacceptable terms, rewrite it on the lines provided.

EXAMPLE   Elderly passengers on the cruise ship *Romance Afloat* will enjoy swimming, shuffleboard, and nightly movies.

REVISION   Passengers on the cruise ship *Romance Afloat* will enjoy swimming, shuffleboard, and nightly movies.

1. A good nurse needs to use her medical training as well as her skills working with people.

   _____

   _____

2. Before the plane took off, the stewardess explained safety procedures to the passengers.

   _____

   _____

3. Rolling up to the podium in his wheelchair, Dr. Franklin Benton addressed the organization on regional historical research.

4. The leaky faucet was replaced last week by a woman plumber.

5. Seventy-six-year-old Jewish violinist Josh Mickle, last night's featured soloist, brought the crowd to its feet.

6. People like mill workers probably don't listen to the classical music station.

7. Even though there's a test tomorrow, each home economics student should bring her book to class.

8. African American actor Denzel Washington appeared at a charity benefit last night.

9. A West Point cadet must keep his record clean if he expects to excel in his chosen career.

10. Acting as spokesman and speaking with a southern twang, Cynthia McDowell, attractive mother of two, vowed that every elementary school teacher in the district would take her turn on the picket line until the school board agreed to resume negotiations.

_____

_____

_____

PART 6

UNDERSTANDING PUNCTUATION CONVENTIONS

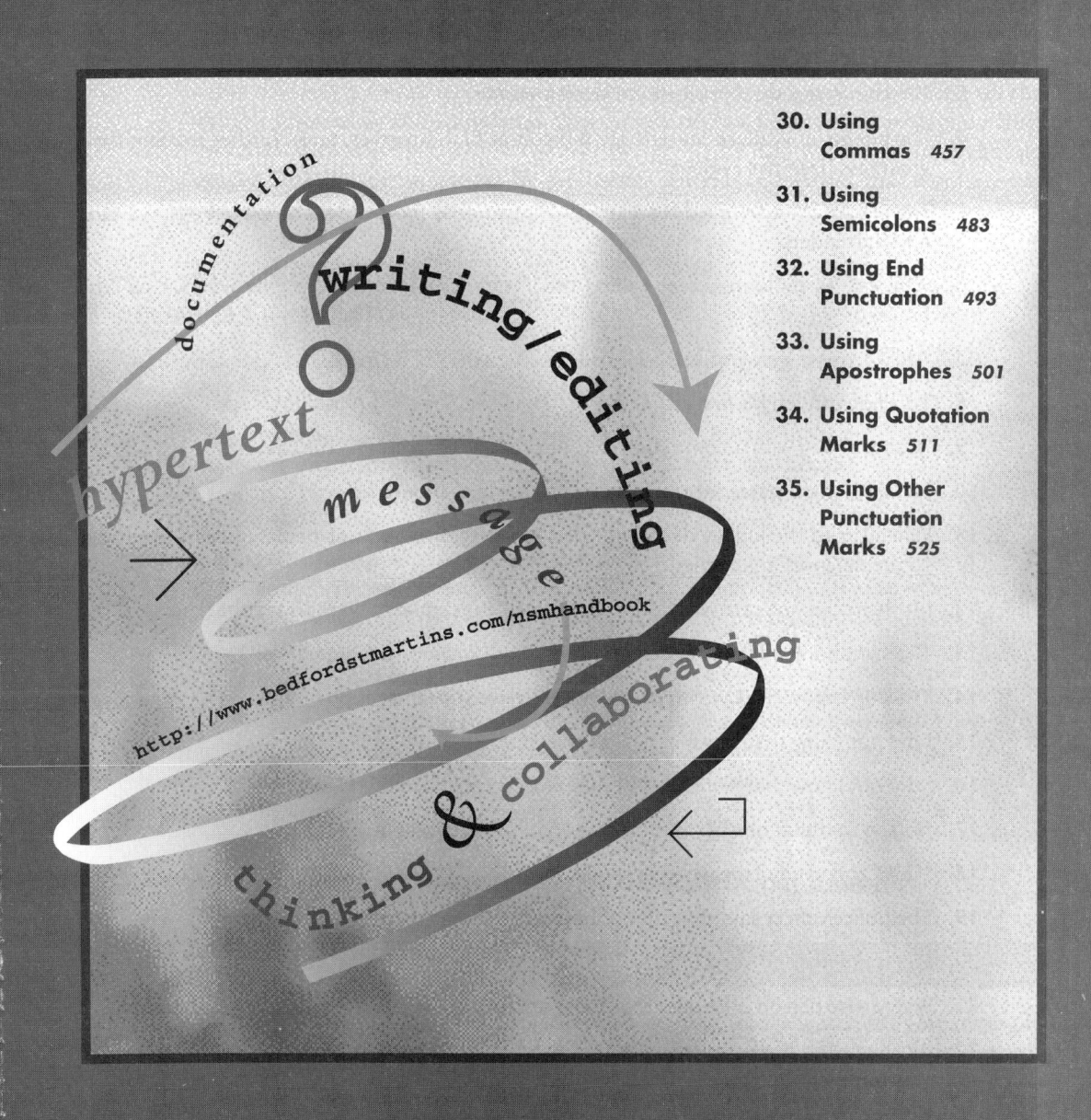

30. Using Commas 457
31. Using Semicolons 483
32. Using End Punctuation 493
33. Using Apostrophes 501
34. Using Quotation Marks 511
35. Using Other Punctuation Marks 525

Walter Mondale was the first presidential candidate to select a woman, Geraldine Ferraro, as a running mate.

Note that an adjective clause that begins with *that* is always restrictive and is not set off by commas. An adjective clause beginning with *which* may be either restrictive or nonrestrictive; however, some writers prefer to use *which* only for nonrestrictive clauses.

The sculpture that she entered in the competition won first place. [*Restrictive clause introduced by* that; *hence no commas used.*]

Crime and Punishment, which I have only started, is said to be the greatest novel in Russian literature. [*Nonrestrictive clause introduced by* which; *hence commas used.*]

To summarize: Use commas to set off secondary information. Omit commas to restrict or limit.

→ **COMMON ERROR: MISSING COMMA IN A SERIES**

Using commas to separate items in a series (30d)

Commas are routinely used to separate three or more words, phrases, or clauses in a series. Here are some examples:

Our order was for three boxes of computer paper, two boxes of typing ribbons, a stapler, and four rolls of tape. [*four parallel items*]

During the heat wave, some people bought air conditioners, others settled for fans, and some just drank glass after glass of iced tea. [*introductory element set off by a comma, then three parallel clauses*]

When the items in a series are long and complex or when they contain commas of their own, use semicolons rather than commas to separate them. For examples, see Chapter 31.

Coordinate adjectives are also separated by commas. Coordinate adjectives are adjectives that can be placed in any order in front of the noun they modify. In *Her straight, long drive took a large bounce and rolled another five yards,* the words *straight* and *long* are coordinate adjectives; their order can be switched without changing the meaning of the sentence: *Her long, straight drive took a large bounce and rolled another five yards.*

If two adjectives are not coordinate, they should be left unpunctuated: *Ellen is an accomplished free-lance ad writer.* In that sentence, *accomplished, free-lance,* and *ad* are all adjectives modifying the noun *writer*. However, changing the order of these adjectives plays havoc with the sentence's meaning: *Ellen is an ad accomplished free-lance writer.* Since these adjectives are not coordinate, no commas are used.

Using commas to set off interjections, direct address, contrasting elements, parenthetical and transitional expressions, and tag questions (30e, 30f)

Interjections and words used in direct address are routinely set off by commas.

INTERJECTIONS Well, this is an interesting turn of events.

Oh my, it is hot today!

DIRECT ADDRESS Beth, go give your dog some exercise.

Now, ladies and gentlemen, let us bow our heads.

Writers may also use commas to set off contrasting elements in a sentence.

CONTRASTING ELEMENTS Her days were numbered, but not her hopes.

Available credit, not ready cash, determines a consumer's purchasing power.

Parenthetical expressions are defined as relatively unimportant supplementary information or comments by the writer. **Transitional expressions** are words and phrases used to connect parts of sentences, including conjunctive adverbs such as *however* and *furthermore*. Parenthetical and transitional expressions are always set off by commas.

PARENTHETICAL AND TRANSITIONAL EXPRESSIONS That watercolor over the couch is, by the way, an original Mulvey.

The picture near the stereo, however, is only a reproduction.

A question that follows a statement and calls that statement into doubt is called a **tag question**. Use a comma to separate such a question from the rest of the sentence.

TAG QUESTION You ordered your hot dog with chili and onions, didn't you?

Using commas with dates, addresses, titles, place-names, and numbers (30g)

Commas also routinely separate parts of dates, addresses and place-names, titles, and numbers.

DATES She was born on Tuesday, July 31, 1952.

When only a month and year are given, the comma is omitted, as in *August 1987 was an unusually warm month*. Commas are also omitted when dates appear in inverted order: *31 July 1952*.

ADDRESSES AND PLACE-NAMES	Her address is Azalea House, 12856 S.W. Jackson Street, Cairo, Texas 66731. [*Note that no comma is used in street numbers or between state and ZIP code.*]
	He said he grew up in Malta, Montana.
TITLES AND NUMBERS	Danielle Smith, M.D., performed the surgery.
	Martin Luther King Jr. was one of the twentieth century's greatest orators. [*Note that the titles* Jr. *and* Sr. *are* not *set off by commas.*]
	She thinks Philomath's population is about 7,500. [*Note that the comma is used in numbers of five digits or more, but is optional within numbers of four digits. Do not use a comma within years or page numbers.*]
	The Scholarship Committee reviewed 12,000 applications in 1997.

Using commas with quotations (30h)

Use commas to set off quotations from words that introduce or explain those quotations. A comma following a quotation always goes inside the quotation marks.

"Autobiography," said Claude Simon, "is the most fictional of forms."

EXCEPTIONS

Do not use a comma after a question mark or an exclamation point.

"Are you planning to take the 6:05 train?" he asked.

Do not use a comma when a quotation is introduced by *that*.

The writer of Ecclesiastes concludes that "all is vanity."

Do not use a comma when quoted material in a sentence is both preceded and followed by other material.

His repetitions of "Please don't panic" failed to calm the crowd.

Do not use a comma before a paraphrase.

Mary Louise said that she would read the report this week.

Using commas to facilitate understanding (30i)

Sometimes using commas will make difficult sentences easier to read, as in these examples:

The band members strutted in in matching uniforms and hats.

The band members strutted in, in matching uniforms and hats.

Shortly after the rock concert began in earnest.

Shortly after, the rock concert began in earnest.

Realize that sometimes the way to cure punctuation problems is to rewrite the sentence. The awkwardness of *The band members strutted in, in matching uniforms and hats* can be relieved by revising the sentence to read *The band members strutted in wearing matching uniforms and hats*. The fact that a sentence is accurately punctuated does not necessarily mean that it is well written.

→ **COMMON ERROR: UNNECESSARY COMMA(S) WITH RESTRICTIVE MODIFIER**

Omitting unnecessary commas with restrictive elements (30j)

Sometimes using too many commas causes readers confusion. In fact, nowhere is correct usage more important than in sentences with **restrictive** elements which limit the meaning of the words to which they refer. Commas incorrectly used in such situations will radically alter sentence meaning. Consider this sentence, asking yourself whether its punctuation is accurate:

Candidates, who were selected as the five finalists, were to be interviewed beginning Monday of next week.

Now examine this grammatically identical sentence:

Candidates, who ranged in age from 22 to 60, were to be interviewed beginning Monday of next week.

Only one of these two sentences is accurately punctuated. Which one? Remember the guidelines:

1. Omit commas when your intent is to restrict or limit.
2. Use commas to set off secondary, nonessential information.

Clearly the sentence specifying the five finalists means *only* those five candidates. Thus that first sentence should not have any commas at all: *Candidates who were selected as the five finalists were to be interviewed beginning Monday of next week.*

EXERCISE 30.2 USING COMMAS TO JOIN INDEPENDENT CLAUSES

NAME _____ **DATE** _____

Study each of the ten sentences below. If commas are needed for accurate punctuation, insert them. Circle any comma you add. On the lines provided, indicate a grammatical representation of each sentence.

EXAMPLE   Before we leave for home, Alison needs to make sure the windows are tightly latched, and Jed needs to empty the refrigerator.

[Introductory element], [independent clause], and [independent clause].

1. My paper is due next week and I need to spend an afternoon in the library yet I'm still confident that I'll finish on time.

    _____

    _____

2. Our committee report is due next week so we need to finish the charts and graphs for the appendix.

    _____

    _____

3. The cafeteria always provides both a salad buffet and a low-fat entree in addition to the usual hamburgers and pizza slices.

    _____

    _____

4. New housing starts have increased again this year and the local economy is booming.

    _____

    _____

5. Although we are not finished discussing this material the bell will ring soon so let me give you the assignment for tomorrow.

    _____

    _____

6. New York's subway station mosaics are true works of art and we feel strongly that they ought to be preserved.

7. The Boundary Lakes area of Michigan boasts many miles of hiking trails and quiet water.

8. I did not mention that I had bought another Van Morrison cassette nor did I offer to lend it to anyone.

9. Since you haven't stopped nagging since last year I will take you to the Dodgers game and I will even get us box seats.

10. Despite hitting his head on the diving board Olympic athlete Greg Luganis went on to win a gold medal and the world's admiration.

EXERCISE 30.3 USING COMMAS TO SET OFF NONRESTRICTIVE, SECONDARY INFORMATION

NAME _____ **DATE** _____

The following sentences contain information that is either secondary (nonrestrictive) or restrictive. Read each sentence carefully, and add commas as needed. Underline the secondary or restrictive element in each sentence. On the line provided, indicate whether the information you have underlined is secondary or restrictive, and indicate whether or not you have added commas.

EXAMPLES The candidate <u>who seems most genuine and trustworthy</u> will get my vote.
<u>restrictive; no commas added</u>

Our firewood, <u>maple and fir</u>, should last us through the winter.
<u>secondary; commas added</u>

1. Most residents consider Terry Thornton a good mayor one who promotes the town and helps protect its economic base.

   _____

2. The *X-Files* episode that caused so much controversy will be repeated tonight.

   _____

3. Grandma's old rocker which traveled across the country in a wagon train remains a family treasure.

   _____

4. The soccer player standing at the end of the field is the team's goalie.

   _____

5. We were asked to bring fruit preferably some kind of melon to the picnic.

   _____

6. MTV which is carried locally on Channel 29 features the newest in music videos.

   _____

7. Trout that measure less than six inches must be released.

   _____

8. Razor clams which have grown increasingly rare in recent years still make the best clam chowder.

9. The doctor with whom you spoke was later sued for malpractice.

10. Blood and gore in the movies which doesn't bother me makes Sheryl queasy.

EXERCISE 30.4 USING COMMAS TO SEPARATE COORDINATE ADJECTIVES AND ITEMS IN A SERIES

NAME _____ **DATE** _____

A. The sentences below contain coordinate adjectives, noncoordinate adjectives, and items in a series. Add commas where needed, and circle any commas you add. Indicate whether the sentence contains coordinate adjectives or items in a series. If the sentence contains any noncoordinate adjectives, copy them on the lines provided.

EXAMPLE Jane arrived carrying a doll, a lollipop, and a large crayon picture she had drawn.

items in a series; noncoordinate adjectives: *large, crayon*

1. We're confronted with continuing drought a possible labor strike and the highest rate of bankruptcies in two decades.

   _____

   _____

2. The Alsea River bridge is a dramatic functional example of design that combines beauty and utility.

   _____

   _____

3. The moon circles the earth the earth revolves around the sun and out in space the sun is just one star among many in the Milky Way galaxy.

   _____

   _____

4. The new apartment looked clean smelled of fresh paint and had attractive blinds.

   _____

   _____

5. Last year Matt's little sister wore her colorful Spice Girls T-shirt everywhere she went.

   _____

   _____

B. Add needed commas to the sentences below, and circle the commas you add.

EXAMPLE   We were married on September 11(,)1971.

1. His birthday is next Saturday, April 18.
2. Angie, would you pick up the supplies for our project on your way home tonight?
3. Laura Williams, M.D., can be found in office 228 on the second floor.
4. Now we stitch the seam, right?
5. Last year, I am sorry to say, six elms had to be destroyed due to Dutch elm disease.

EXERCISE 30.6   USING COMMAS WITH QUOTATIONS

NAME _____   DATE _____

Add needed commas to the following sentences using quotations. Circle the commas you add. Cross out any unnecessary commas.

EXAMPLE   "Showers tomorrow, with a high near 50⊙" said the forecaster.

1. "Few Americans" she said "are able to understand the history of conflict in Northern Ireland."

2. "Yesterday" he said, "I disagreed with you. But after my experience today, I have changed my mind."

3. "The best defense" urged the coach "is a good offense."

4. Neville argues, that contemporary philosophy reflects the impact of both technological advances and the recurring devastation of warfare.

5. Mandel, after defining the importance of cultural differences, says "In Western society, these trends can be traced back as far as the 1860s."

6. Many writers have said that, *Ulysses* is the greatest work written in the English language but many Shakespearean scholars disagree.

7. Michael asked "Should we have tacos for dinner tonight?"

8. Bank tellers who take my check and say, "I'll be right back" make me worry that my account is overdrawn.

9. Lasswell then defines, "the decision seminar," and supplies examples of its possible applications.

10. Despite his many unhappy patients, the dentist maintained that, he always followed the best professional practices.

EXERCISE 30.7 DISTINGUISHING BETWEEN RESTRICTIVE AND NONRESTRICTIVE SENTENCE ELEMENTS

NAME _____ DATE _____

Underline the restrictive or nonrestrictive elements in each of the following sentences. Indicate whether the material you have underlined is restrictive or nonrestrictive. Punctuate the sentences correctly, and circle any commas you add.

EXAMPLES   The lab technician reports that the blood tests(,)<u>which were performed yesterday</u>(,) were negative. <u>nonrestrictive</u>

The lab technician reports that the blood tests <u>that were performed yesterday</u> were negative. <u>restrictive</u>

1. The grandfather you have visited every summer needs your help now. _____

2. Your lawn mowed and edged every week is the neatest on the block. _____

3. Dogs that are trained to assist people with hearing impairments learn how to alert their owners to ringing doorbells and telephones. _____

4. The cars recalled by the dealer need only one replacement part. _____

5. The evacuees some with only the clothes on their backs prepared to spend the night inside the high school gym. _____

6. The Dave Smith who is an accomplished poet and teacher lives in Richmond, Virginia. _____

7. Health care administration a field that has grown in recent years often attracts some of the best and brightest talents. _____

8. Tanita Tikaram whose songs are among the most provocative in music today always brings her own unusual perspective to a theme. _____

9. Grapes which grow on a hillside are the most delicious fruit. _____

10. Chain saws which make a great deal of noise are the most effective tool for clearing large areas of woodland. _____

EXERCISE 30.8 OMITTING COMMAS BETWEEN SUBJECTS AND VERBS AND BETWEEN VERBS AND OBJECTS

NAME _____ **DATE** _____

In the following passage, some sentences are punctuated correctly and some are not. Read each sentence carefully, paying close attention to the use of commas. Put an *X* through any misplaced commas. Be ready to explain your decisions.

Watching the stars, is an ancient interest, still engaging today. If you can leave the city lights behind, you will be able to use a night sky chart to identify groups of stars. These groups, called constellations, form distinct patterns. Ancient peoples supplied, the names for many of the constellations that we still see. As a result, the names used today include, mythological figures such as Hercules or Orion, imaginary creatures such as Draco the dragon, real animals such as Ursa the bear, and other objects or shapes. Of course, you need to use your imagination because the stars only suggest, the patterns of the names. You also, need to be prepared for the earth's movement changing the night sky. Once you figure out where to look, however, watching the stars, will give you a new sense of the enormity of the universe.

EXERCISE 30.9 OMITTING UNNECESSARY COMMAS

NAME _____ DATE _____

Cross out any unnecessary commas in the following sentences. If a sentence is correct as shown, write a C next to its number.

EXAMPLE For twenty-six straight days, the high temperature in Salt Lake City**,** reached over ninety degrees.

1. During midsummer one year**,** (on the fourth of July, in fact)**,** snow fell in Missoula.
2. Jim runs ten miles every other day, and he says he feels strong, healthy, and fit.
3. Two lanes (usually those on the far left side of the pool)**,** are routinely reserved for lap swimming.
4. Any list of living, well-respected poets would have to include Rich, Levertov, Kinnell, and Dove**,** (named poet laureate in 1993).
5. My favorite kinds of architecture are**,** Greek Revival, Federalist, and Art Deco.
6. On September**,** 1, 1939, Adolf Hitler invaded Poland**,** and defied the rest of the world to stop him.
7. Magician**,** David Copperfield**,** is known for being clever**,** and ingenious**,** in addition to being famous for spectacular tricks.
8. Once you are prepared for your clinic tour, call the office to schedule a date, return this form to your advisor, and follow the directions for writing out your goals for the visit.
9. The homemade fudge looked sweeter**,** than honey fresh from the hive.
10. The campus cinema series makes**,** for good entertainment**,** and**,** surprisingly energetic discussions about the strengths and weaknesses of the films.

EXERCISE 30.10 USING COMMAS CORRECTLY

NAME _____ **DATE** _____

A. The following sentences are punctuated correctly. Combine or revise each according to the specific directions. Make sure your new version is punctuated accurately.

EXAMPLE My father graduated from Portland's Washington High School in 1963. (Revise so that the sentence begins *In 1963* . . .)
In 1963, my father graduated from Portland's Washington High School.

1. Some writers like to read a bit before writing. Some writers make notes to themselves. Some writers are too terrified to do anything. Some writers just sit down and start writing whatever comes to mind. (Combine into one sentence with multiple independent clauses.)

   _____

   _____

2. You wake up in Los Angeles. You look out the window. It's so clear without the smog that you understand why everyone moved here. This happens on those rare April mornings after a heavy rain. (Combine into one sentence with an introductory element followed by several independent clauses.)

   _____

   _____

   _____

3. These orientation classes are designed for transfer students only. These orientation classes begin Monday morning at 9. (Revise to a single sentence containing restrictive information.)

   _____

   _____

4. Hanging your own wallpaper is an exacting project. Hanging your own wallpaper is a satisfying and inexpensive way to redecorate. (Combine into one sentence containing secondary, nonrestrictive information.)

   _____

   _____

481

5. Sociology studies people, as does anthropology. (Revise so that the sentence subjects are *sociology* and *anthropology*.)

———————————————————————————————

———————————————————————————————

B. On the lines provided, combine each of the following groups of sentences into one sentence of connected independent clauses. Join the independent clauses by using commas and appropriate coordinating conjunctions. Use pronouns as necessary.

EXAMPLE   Hay fever season has arrived. We had better buy more Kleenex.

<u>Hay fever season has arrived, so we had better buy more Kleenex.</u>

1. The center was elbowed repeatedly by the opposing team. He maintained the fast pace of the game.

———————————————————————————————

———————————————————————————————

2. You carefully chop the tomatoes and onions. You quickly grate the cheese. You love hearing the sizzle of the spicy meat. You cook tacos only once a month.

———————————————————————————————

———————————————————————————————

3. The laser printer is fast. The laser printer produces professional-looking documents.

———————————————————————————————

4. The laser printer is fast. The laser printer produces professional-looking documents. I still prefer to hand-write my memos.

———————————————————————————————

———————————————————————————————

5. We have confirmed our reservations. We have taken the dog to the kennel. The car is packed. Let's go.

———————————————————————————————

———————————————————————————————

31 Using Semicolons

Powerful effects can sometimes be achieved by juxtaposing more than one idea inside a single sentence. Semicolons can be used for such juxtaposition, both by linking independent clauses and by separating items in a complicated series. In the following example, the semicolon helps to emphasize how closely the two halves of the sentence are related.

> The brilliant rainbow glowed in the sky above the garden; the fragrance of moist earth rose to meet the deep scent of the roses.

SEMICOLONS IN EVERYDAY USE

Although semicolons are among the more formal punctuation marks, you can sometimes spot them working quite well in informal settings—as these two bumper stickers illustrate.

> Careful! Baby on board; driver on edge.
>
> Vote for Espy; he means business!

Try replacing these semicolons with commas and conjunctions, periods, or exclamation points, and you'll see how useful the semicolon is. Watch for everyday uses of semicolons—in ads, on billboards, wherever—and jot down the examples you find.

Using semicolons to link independent clauses (31a)

Chapter 30 discusses the use of a comma plus a coordinating conjunction to link two independent clauses. Using coordinating conjunctions allows you to indicate the relationship between the two independent clauses. Semicolons can also be used to link independent clauses, resulting in compound, complex, or compound-complex sentences. Linking independent clauses with semicolons often makes for succinct, even blunt prose. (For more on this topic see Chapter 15.) Here are two correct examples:

> Karen votes for a movie, so we are going to a movie. [*comma + coordinating conjunction* so *indicating cause and effect*]

Karen votes for a movie; we are going to a movie. [*semicolon linking the two independent clauses and resulting in a blunt, direct statement.*]

Remember that when joining two independent clauses, a comma *cannot* substitute for a semicolon; if a comma is used, it must be followed by a coordinating conjunction.

Semicolons are also used to link independent clauses when the second clause opens with a conjunctive adverb or a transitional phrase:

I know starting early means I will accomplish more; however, 5:30 in the morning is just too early.

We can expect afternoon temperatures to be cooler today; after all, it is midmorning, and the sun has yet to burn off the fog.

REVIEW

Common **conjunctive adverbs** include *also, anyway, besides, finally, furthermore, hence, however, indeed, meanwhile, moreover, nevertheless, otherwise, still, then, therefore,* and *thus.* Common **transitional phrases** include *after all, as a result, at any rate, even so, for example, in addition, in fact, in other words, on the contrary,* and *on the other hand.*

Remember that semicolons separate *sentences*. The last example given can also be accurately punctuated as follows: *We can expect afternoon temperatures to be cooler today. After all, it is midmorning, and the sun has yet to burn off the fog.*

Do not use semi-colons to separate a dependent clause from an independent clause.

INCORRECT   While we were walking the dog after dinner; the moon rose.

We were up until after 2 last night; because our group project is due this afternoon.

REVISED   While we were walking the dog after dinner, the moon rose.

We were up until after 2 last night because our group project is due this afternoon.

or

Because our group project is due this afternoon, we were up until after 2 last night.

Using semicolons to separate items in a series (31b)

Besides joining what would otherwise be complete sentences, semicolons have only one other use: to separate complex items in a series. Recall from Chapter 30 that commas are used in this way, too. Use semicolons whenever one or more of the items you are listing includes commas already.

Pitcher, catcher, short stop; goalie, center, right wing; tackle, quarterback, end—these are positions in baseball, hockey, and football. [*Here commas separate the individual positions, with semicolons separating the groups of positions.*]

In the attic of one rental house, we discovered a yellowed, still readable newspaper from 1945; a wicker, two-wheeled baby carriage; and fifty-five cents' worth of buffalo-head nickels. [*Here commas are used as part of the identification of items, with semicolons used to separate the items themselves.*]

As you can see, the semicolons in the preceding sentences serve the useful function of separating items. Those sentences require semicolons; commas used in place of the semicolons would be confusing to readers.

Remember to use a colon, not a semicolon, to *introduce* a series, as in this example: *The buffet featured several kinds of fruit: apples, pears, kiwis, mangoes, and persimmons.* For more on colon usage, see Chapter 35.

Checking for overused semicolons (31c)

Knowing the rules of semicolon usage presents writers with new choices: should I join two independent clauses or punctuate them as separate sentences? One thing is certain: the use of too many sentences joined with semicolons results in dull, formally repetitious prose. Using too many semicolons also deprives the writer of the clarity that dependent clauses can afford. *I see it has begun to rain; I'll turn off the sprinklers* is grammatically accurate, but its full meaning depends on readers' willingness and ability to see the connection between the two independent clauses. Subordinating one clause to the other spells out the cause-and-effect relationship between the observation and the action: *Since it is raining, I'll turn off the sprinklers.* In general, joining sentences with semicolons should produce some obvious and positive benefit. If you join two or more sentences with semicolons, you ought to be able to point to the resulting benefit.

Using semicolons with other punctuation (31e)

Occasionally, you may want to use semicolons with quotation marks, parentheses, or abbreviations. The following examples show you how to handle these situations.

- Semicolons and quotation marks. Semicolons are normally placed outside any quotation marks.

    Sometimes the British hesitate to speak in the first person, saying "one" rather than "I"; most Americans say "I" without giving it a thought.

- Semicolons and parentheses. Semicolons are placed after and outside parentheses. Semicolons never precede parentheses.

The actress was nominated for an Academy Award (her third nomination in three years); this year she may win.

- Semicolons and abbreviations. When a semicolon follows an abbreviation using a period, use both the period and the semicolon.

The unwanted package arrived C.O.D.; I politely refused to pay the charges.

EXERCISE 31.1 USING SEMICOLONS TO LINK INDEPENDENT CLAUSES

NAME _____ **DATE** _____

A. Carefully check the punctuation in the following sentences. If the punctuation is accurate, write a C on the lines provided. If it is inaccurate, write a corrected version.

EXAMPLE   The unwanted package arrived C.O.D., I politely refused to pay the charges.

REVISION   The unwanted package arrived C.O.D.; I politely refused to pay the charges.

1. Please hand in your exam booklet; when you are finished writing your answer.

   _____

   _____

2. Two games were rained out this season, however, the make-up games have been scheduled for next week.

   _____

   _____

3. Enriching on-campus classwork as it does; study abroad may be arranged for one semester or two; in order to allow for intensive language study, specific research projects using local resources, or cultural comparisons.

   _____

   _____

4. During much of the summer; I will be working as a lifeguard at my neighborhood pool.

   _____

   _____

5. The traffic safety office has mailed out forms to request parking stickers; completed forms are due back by October 1.

   _____

   _____

6. My current work-study job ends in two weeks. I'll need to find a new position; starting next term.

   _____

   _____

7. The invitation distinctly said R.S.V.P., even so, we lost the invitation and never properly responded.

   _____

   _____

8. Oak burns slowly and makes a hot fire; fir splits easily and makes superior kindling.

   _____

   _____

9. Raspberries, which are my favorite fresh fruit, ripen in late June and early July in addition, some years there's a smaller crop in September.

   _____

   _____

10. Carla complained that she hated country music, we put on our Conway Twitty album.

    _____

    _____

B. Use a semicolon and whatever other punctuation is required to combine each of the following sets of brief sentences into one longer sentence. You may revise the sentences slightly as needed. Make sure that your new sentence is punctuated correctly.

EXAMPLE We walked the dog after dinner. The moon rose. The moon shone round and white as a bone china saucer.

REVISION <u>While we were walking the dog after dinner, the moon rose; it shone round and white as a bone china saucer.</u>

1. A replacement key for your office costs $10. You might lose your office key. Lost keys are sometimes turned in at the front security desk.

2. There are fewer drive-in theaters than there once were. The Canyon Drive-In, for example, has been demolished for a shopping mall.

3. An anemic patient may feel tired or worn out. The patient may complain of dizziness, shortness of breath, or a headache.

4. My roommate and I went to the pet store. We were trying to decide between a chihuahua and a St. Bernard. The St. Bernard threw up. We took the chihuahua.

5. Many state laws do not require helmets to be worn by motorcyclists. Helmets should be worn at all times.

6. Nelson Mandela spent many years in jail. He withstood great discomfort and hardship. The years he spent in seclusion did not lessen his determination to fight apartheid.

7. Most people can make spaghetti sauce. We have a special recipe. Our delicious ingredients include garlic and green peppers.

8. Kodiak Island is a beautiful part of Alaska. It has scenic peaks and broad valleys. They were carved by glaciers.

9. New York has welcomed millions of immigrants. Many have been fleeing famine, poverty, and persecution in Europe. California, however, has been a gateway for those coming from Asia.

10. Matt caught a cold last week. He has a stuffy nose and a sore throat. He has finished all his reading assignments for the week.

EXERCISE 31.2 USING SEMICOLONS TO SEPARATE ITEMS IN A SERIES

NAME _____ **DATE** _____

Carefully check the punctuation, especially the use of semicolons, in the following passage. Cross out unnecessary punctuation, and add any missing marks. Circle your additions.

Landscape design is far more complicated than just planting a few shrubs and trees. The designer must begin with technical considerations such as length, width, and shape of the yard or planting area, its angle, direction, and rate of slope, and any required easement or access to utility boxes. Then the designer must consider the objectives of the homeowners. They may want certain features such as a patio for entertaining a walkway and bench for sitting near a rose garden or a fountain. They also may want the plantings and design to conceal an unattractive garage wall or air conditioner; to create a view, complete with colorful flowers and year-round greenery, from the dining-room window, or to supply cut flowers for bouquets every week. Other owners may want; low-maintenance plants, limited grass to mow, and low water usage. Once the technical requirements; and the personal priorities are clearly established, the designer can begin to prepare a plan.

EXERCISE 31.3 REVISING USING SEMICOLONS

NAME _____ **DATE** _____

Some of the sentences in the passage that follows are punctuated inaccurately. Others may be accurate in their punctuation, but you may not feel the current version to be the most effective one. Edit the passage, making whatever minor revisions you feel necessary. Copy your best version on your own paper, and make sure that your version is punctuated accurately. Also make sure that your revised version uses semicolons in at least three instances. Finally, underline your changes.

    Recovering alcoholics are some of the nicest people you'd ever want to meet, unfortunately, they also tell some of the saddest, most distressing stories. Many of them come from alcoholic families maybe the father was a functional, low-profile drinker for years; maybe the mother drank during the day and locked her own kids out of the house because she couldn't stand their noise; maybe the kids suffered from sexual abuse or other physical violence; when these kids reached adulthood, they hid their hurt in a bottle. Some of them didn't wait for adulthood. Some drank right along with their parents.

    Untreated alcoholics believe they have every reason to drink. Through treatment, however, they come to learn that no reason is a good enough reason for them to drink. For the alcoholic, that beer or wine or gin makes every problem worse, without fail, excessive, compulsive drinking creates new problems. Staying clean and sober doesn't do away with the alcoholic's problems; it does eliminate one pressing, overpowering difficulty, the sober alcoholic then has at least the opportunity to deal with other problems. Recovery isn't easy. Recovery is never complete. But with family support and the help of organizations like Alcoholics Anonymous, people do dry out, families do get better.

32 ▼ Using End Punctuation

Periods, question marks, and exclamation marks are called **end punctuation** because they end sentences. As they do so, they indicate whether the sentence is a statement, a question, or an emphatic exclamation.

> **END PUNCTUATION IN EVERYDAY USE**
>
> Periods, question marks, and exclamation points constantly appear in advertising, often used to create special effects. Look at the following ads, and consider how each one would be different without these marks.
>
> **Toshiba laptops: the desktop alternative.**
>
> **So you think you can't afford a new PC?**
>
> **Get Microsoft Word now, and receive this kit FREE!**
>
> Look for some ads that use these marks of punctuation for special effect, and write down what you find.

Using periods (32a)

Using periods correctly makes life easier on your readers. It is not a complex skill to master. A period should end any sentence that is not a question or an exclamation.

I expect your essays on Tuesday. [*statement*]

Turn in your essays on Tuesday. [*mild command*]

Periods are often used with sentences containing direct quotations, even if the quoted material is a question: *"Are you going home now?" she asked.* However, if the sentence is turned around, the question mark alone is sufficient; no period is necessary: *She asked me, "Are you going home now?"*

Some abbreviations also use periods:

Ms.	A.M.	etc.	Dr.	D.D.S.	B.C.	M.S.
Mr.	P.M.	et al.	Ph.D.	R.N.	A.D.	C.O.D.
Jr.	Mrs.	ibid.	M.D.	C.P.A.	M.A.	f.o.b.

See Chapter 37 for more on abbreviations.

493

Using question marks (32b)

Sentences that ask direct questions end with question marks. Sentences that report questions (that is, sentences that contain indirect questions) end with periods. Note the difference.

DIRECT QUESTION   Did you air out the house after the exterminators were finished?

INDIRECT QUESTION   I was wondering if you aired out the house after the exterminators were finished.

When quotation marks are used with direct questions, the order in which sentence elements are presented makes a difference.

I said, "What time will the exterminators leave?" [*Here the quoted question ends the sentence. In this case, the question mark is the sentence's end punctuation.*]

Did I just say, "Be there or be square"? [*Here the question mark applies to the whole sentence and so goes outside the quoted material.*]

Did I just say, "What time will the exterminators leave?" [*Here both the sentence itself and the quoted material are questions. A second question mark does* not *follow the quotation marks.*]

Writers also use question marks between questions in a series, even when the questions do not form separate sentences.

Is that dog a collie? a Labrador retriever? what?

Using exclamation points (32c)

Exclamation points close emphatic and emotional statements. Using too many exclamation points is like being the boy who cried wolf; after a while, nobody listens. Sparingly used, however, exclamation points can indicate subtle differences in tone or meaning. Suppose that you have just given someone an expensive present in a small box. This someone opens the wrappings, looks at what is inside, and says only one word. This word could be punctuated three ways: "*Oh.*" or "*Oh?*" or "*Oh!*" Which punctuation would indicate the most positive response?

Exclamation points are not followed by commas or periods. When part of a direct quotation, the exclamation point goes inside the quotation marks, as in "*Oh!*"

When informed that she had won the lottery, all Erin Johannsen could do was scream over and over, "I can't believe it! I can't believe it!"

The border guard yelled, "Halt!"

"Halt!" yelled the border guard.

EXERCISE 32.1 USING PERIODS TO SIGNAL THE ENDS OF SENTENCES

NAME _____ **DATE** _____

A. Read this paragraph:

Without periods and the spaces that conventionally follow them, readers would have no easy way of recognizing the end of a sentence instead of being able to read quickly and effortlessly, we would all be required to slow down and continually ask ourselves whether or not the words we have just read make a complete sentence in short, we would be analyzing the form of the writing as well as trying to grasp its content; we would be doing two things at once chances are we would not be entirely successful with either task the end result would be frustration and an unwillingness to read

Now go back and reread the paragraph, putting in a period every time you think you have come to the end of a sentence. Does reading the paragraph feel easier and more comfortable now?

B. Now read this paragraph:

Sometimes there can be. More punctuation than is really needed, and it can. Often be in the wrong places. What's more. Without periods and the proper punctuation. Your readers will be totally confused. By what you have written. The periods will make them stop reading. Even though you want them to finish a thought. And the places where you don't have the periods will cause your readers to go on indefinitely they will lose the ideas you are trying to convey that is why periods are so important they stop and start your readers. At the places you feel are most effective.

Now go back and punctuate this paragraph properly by putting an *X* through unnecessary periods and adding appropriate punctuation where necessary. Can you see where the periods are needed and where they are not?

ACRONYM	NASA's performance record [*the record belonging to NASA*]
INDEFINITE PRONOUN	everyone's choice [*the choice made by everyone*]
TITLE	the transportation secretary's speech [*the speech made by the transportation secretary*]
MULTIWORD NOUN	her father-in-law's car [*the car belonging to her father-in-law*]

What about plural nouns? Many plural nouns end in *-s* or *-es*. To form the possessive of plural nouns ending in *-s* or *-es*, simply add the apostrophe. With plural nouns that do not end in *-s* or *-es* such as *children*, add *'s* as you would for any singular noun.

> Walking along the rocky shoreline, we could see the *seals'* faces. [*the faces of more than one seal*]

> The *children's* room is here at the end of the hall. [*the room belonging to the children*]

Suppose that you wish to indicate joint ownership. The boat belonging to Mo and Ann would be referred to as *Mo and Ann's boat*. To indicate joint ownership, add *'s* only to the last noun. Suppose both Mo and Ann own their own boats. Then both of their names would carry apostrophes, as in *Mo's and Ann's boats are entered in the race on Saturday*.

Since missing or misused possessive apostrophes occur frequently, rereading your draft to look for such errors is a good idea. As you reread, watch for any nouns ending in *-s*. Is the noun meant to show ownership or possession? If so, it needs an apostrophe.

Finally, remember that possessive pronouns—*my, your, his, her, its, our*(s), *your*(s), and *whose*—are already possessive; they do not need apostrophes. *The stolen bicycles were ours* (not *our's*).

→ **COMMON ERROR: *ITS/IT'S* CONFUSION**

Remember, *its* is a possessive pronoun, as in *The bird watched its nest fall to the ground*. *It's* is a contraction for *it is*, as in *It's nearly time for lunch*. To check for this error in your own writing, reread your draft, paying particular attention to every use of *its* or *it's*. Use the apostrophe to indicate *it is*; use *its* to show possession. (In academic writing, it is best not to use contractions at all.)

Using apostrophes to signal contractions and other omissions (33b)

We also use apostrophes to form **contractions**, which are usually two words shortened to one. Some common contractions are listed below.

FULL FORM	CONTRACTION	FULL FORM	CONTRACTION
are not	aren't	does not	doesn't
cannot	can't	he had, he would	he'd
could not	couldn't	he has, he is	he's
did not	didn't	he will	he'll
do not	don't	I am	I'm
I had, I would	I'd	there has, there is	there's
I have	I've	was not	wasn't
I will	I'll	were not	weren't
is not	isn't	who has, who is	who's
it has, it is	it's	will not	won't
let us	let's	would not	wouldn't
she had, she would	she'd	you are	you're
she has, she is	she's	you have	you've
she will	she'll	you will	you'll

Note that certain contractions sound identical to other words—*whose/who's, theirs/there's, lets/let's, its/it's*—though they have quite separate meanings. Using the wrong spelling in a particular sentence is a common error; in fact, confusing *its* and *it's* is one of the top twenty errors found in student writing (see section 33a). The only sure cure is careful proofreading.

Apostrophes are also used in some common phrases to signal that letters or numbers have been left out. Thus *of the clock* becomes *o'clock* and *class of 1989* becomes *class of '89*. Occasionally writers trying to create the sound of spoken dialects will also use apostrophes to signal omitted letters. Thus *suppose* might become *s'pose*, or *probably* might be written *prob'ly*.

Contractions result in more informal prose; full forms make prose somewhat more formal and precise. Using contractions in formal situations will sometimes create an inappropriate tone. Here is an example:

> Let's assume the awesome responsibility of forging a peaceful world for our children to inherit.

Here the informality of the contraction seems to conflict with the seriousness of the responsibility discussed; the full form would be more appropriate. Some contractions are so informal (or incorrect) that they should not appear in college writing. These contractions include *ain't, who's ever* (for *whoever is*), and *'nother*. (For a fuller discussion of formal and informal tone, see Chapter 27).

Using apostrophes to form the plural of numbers, letters, symbols, and words used as words (33c)

An apostrophe plus *-s* is used to form the plural of numbers, letters, symbols, and words used as words.

PLURAL NUMBERS — All my psychology test scores have been in the 90's.

PLURAL LETTERS — Young children sometimes confuse *b*'s and *d*'s. [*Note that letters of the alphabet referred to as letters are either underlined or set in italics.*]

PLURAL SYMBOLS — When I looked at the page I was typing, all the $'s were 4's.

PLURAL WORDS REFERRED TO AS WORDS — Every one of her *separate*'s was spelled incorrectly. [*Note that words referred to as words are either underlined or set in italics.*]

The plural of years can be written either with or without the apostrophe; ask your instructor which form to use, and make sure you are consistent.

EXAMPLE The 1990's will see a rise in the number of high school students.

The 1990s will see a rise in the number of high school students.

EXERCISE 33.1 USING APOSTROPHES TO SIGNAL POSSESSION

NAME _____ DATE _____

The following sentences contain material in parentheses. Incorporate that material, using apostrophes correctly.

EXAMPLE   Several buildings (designed by Frank Lloyd Wright) are still used as private residences.

REVISION   Several of Frank Lloyd Wright's buildings are still used as private residences.

1. The night classes (provided by the university) are a relatively painless way to return to school.

2. I've been able to arrange my classes around the schedule (required by my company).

3. I also have been able to balance the requirements (determined by the department) with courses that meet practical demands (presented by my job).

4. Most other night students are highly motivated people and the goals (of whom) are clearly defined.

5. Like me, they want to learn the secrets (that come from a practitioner), but they don't mind being challenged to understand new topics and to build the thinking skills (that they have).

505

6. They, too, are tired and want the pace (of each class) to be efficient and objectives (of each class) to be clear.

7. Unfortunately, this time pressure means that I've often missed sharing dinner (with my family).

8. I also cannot always go to the soccer games (of my daughter).

9. Despite my being so busy, I feel that I am accomplishing the dream (of my parents) in finally finishing college.

10. More important, I'm accomplishing the dream (of myself).

11. Having a college degree is one of the requirements (of my company) for promotion to the position (of a manager).

12. When I'm finished, I'll be ready for those new responsibilities, and I'll be proud of achieving one of the major goals (of my life).

EXERCISE 33.2   USING APOSTROPHES TO CREATE CONTRACTIONS

NAME _____ **DATE** _____

Read each sentence below. If the sentence uses contractions, rewrite it so that it uses full forms. If the sentence uses full forms, rewrite it so that it uses contractions. Correct any improperly used contractions. Think about the sentence's meaning and its probable context. Then indicate which of the two forms of the sentence you consider more appropriate by placing an *X* next to it.

EXAMPLE   In the unlikely event of any accidental injury to your child, medical personnel'll be available immediately.

REVISION   In the unlikely event of any accidental injury to your child, medical personnel will be available immediately. *X*

1. The soup I am making is full of vegetables but will not include spinach.

2. Who'll receive the Academy Award for Best Actor in the last award ceremony of the '90s?

3. Is not that the newest Indian restaurant that has opened in Wichita?

4. The president'll arrive in five minutes.

5. Should not we have stopped at Dairy Mart for more milk?

507

6. You have been listening to several folks as they have described how the United Way has helped them; now will you not please take out your checkbooks and help your neighbors?

7. That guy who's been giving you a ride after work called about nine o'clock.

8. For the test you'll be takin' on Monday, you're required to have a pencil with a No. 2 lead.

9. The distributor informs me that you're order has not received it's required approval from the business office.

10. Who's ever responsible for an accident has the legal obligation to compensate any injured parties.

11. You've read the honor code; now raise your right hand and pledge that you'll accept your responsibility to uphold this trust.

12. Its true that a snake can shed it's own skin and can swallow much of it's prey whole.

EXERCISE 33.3   USING APOSTROPHES

NAME _____   DATE _____

The following passage contains numerous errors involving apostrophes. Circle any errors you find, and pencil in your corrections in the spaces between lines.

With the end of summer, college students begin to think about registration for the new term, course schedule booklets become hot items, and the rumor mill churns into operation. Whose had whom in which classes? Hows so and so in history? How many As did so and so give in psychology last term? Anyone heard how many 121s there'll be? Hallways buzz and the tables in the student union fill up once more. All over campus, department secretaries patience wears thin even as they politely answer question's about adding or dropping classes, changing majors, and so forth. Faculty members offices echo with the sound of typewriters or computer printers. Meanwhile, the bookstores lines stretch back from the cash registers all the way to the next years calendars, which are already on sale. Returning student's sometimes find its not possible to walk across campus without running into old acquaintances. They keep "Hows it going?" and "What's up?" at the ready.

By late November, the elms dont rustle; theyre bare. Maybe its even snowed already. Snow or not, much of the terms earlier anticipation has been replaced by specific challenges: the paper due tomorrow, the necessary B on the next test (after two Cs and a C-), the P.E. classes required twenty laps. But in August or September, all thats in the future. The sun shines, the summers moneys in the bank, and everyone secretly believes that again this term the registrars computer will be friendly.

Using Quotation Marks   34

Quotation marks show us when people speak for themselves, identifying their exact words. Notice in the following sentences how moving one of the quotation marks (and rewording accordingly) creates a very different meaning.

> "Stop!" the guard shouted.
>
> "Stop the guard!" shouted the museum director.

Quotation marks are also used to identify titles, definitions, and ironic or other special uses of words.

QUOTATION MARKS IN EVERYDAY USE

Some people seem to find quotation marks so visually appealing that they use them as a kind of verbal makeup, dabbing them in anywhere they feel a word or phrase could use a bit of sprucing up. Like cosmetics, though, quotation marks can have unfortunate effects if applied too freely. What is the effect of the quotation marks in the following advertisements?

> On a movie marquee: Coming "Attractions"
>
> In a supermarket: "Fresh" Asparagus

Look around you for similar misguided uses of quotation marks, and keep a list of them.

Using quotation marks to signal direct quotations (34a)

In our culture at least, words have a status similar to that of personal property; thus, we use double quotation marks to signal **quotation**—the reproduction of someone else's exact words. Doing so also helps ensure that readers understand accurately who said what.

> "I vote for eating breakfast out this morning," she said.

Use single quotation marks to enclose a quotation within a quotation:

"Mother says she feels 'a little better' this morning," James said.

Remember that quotation marks, whether single or double, identify someone else's *exact words;* when **paraphrasing**, changing someone else's words into your own language, do not use quotation marks.

PARAPHRASE	Lisa said that she thought it would be a good idea for me to speak to the accountants' organization. [*no quotation marks*]
DIRECT QUOTATION	Lisa said, "You know, I think it would be good for you to speak to the accountants' organization." [*quotation marks required*]

If the quoted material itself includes a quotation, use the usual double quotation marks to open and close your quotation and single quotation marks for the quotation within the quotation.

Hoffman remembers trying to explain his equations to Albert Einstein. "Then came the staggering—and altogether endearing—request: 'Please go slowly. I do not understand things quickly.' This from Einstein!"

Using quotation marks with other punctuation (34e)

Quotation marks are almost always used with other punctuation marks. Commas and colons are often (but not always) used to introduce quoted material. In general, a comma or a colon is used whenever there is a perceptible pause or interruption separating the writer's words from the quoted words. Verbs describing speech are frequently set off by commas, especially if the quoted material is a complete sentence.

- *Quotation marks with periods and commas.* Periods and commas always go before the closing quotation marks.

    The Coast Guard officer called the rescue "routine."

    "For Eastern Oregon, it should be fair but quite cold tonight," said the radio announcer. [*comma used to set off quotation from the verb* said]

    Martha said that she "wouldn't be caught dead in that place." [*no comma because quote is only part of a sentence*]

    "If you go in there," he threatened, "I'll walk away and you'll never see me again." [*commas used to set off material that interrupts the quoted material*]

- *Quotation marks with colons and semicolons.* Colons and semicolons go outside the quotation marks.

Mr. Ono smiled and said, "I have brought you one example": there before us was a watermelon almost the size of an oil drum.

The cowboy said, "Smile when you say that"; he reached for his gun as he spoke.

- *Quotation marks with exclamation points, question marks,* and *dashes.* These punctuation marks go inside when they are part of the quotation; they go outside when they are not part of the quotation.

    "Jack! Wait!" [*Exclamation is part of the meaning of the quoted material; thus, the exclamation point goes inside the quotation marks.*]

    Who was it who said, "There's a sucker born every minute"? [*The quotation itself is a statement. However, the entire sentence is a question. Hence, the question mark punctuates the sentence and is placed outside the quotation marks.*]

    Frankie called after her, "Wait! I need—" but she was already gone. [*The dash here indicates that Frankie stopped abruptly.*]

- *Quotation marks with apostrophes.* The quotation marks follow the '*s*.

    I distinctly recall Luigi saying, "We'll meet after work at Pizza Bill's."

Finally, footnote numbers and parenthetical citations always go outside quotation marks.

A NOTE ABOUT CAPITALIZATION

Capitalize the first quoted word when that word begins a completely quoted sentence set off by a comma or colon.

The Coast Guard officer called the rescue "routine." [*not a sentence, not set off: not capitalized*]

She said, "If he offers me a promotion, I'll accept a transfer." [*complete sentence, set off by a comma: capitalized*]

Quoting longer passages

If you use quoted material as part of an essay or an argument and that quoted material runs only four lines or less, use quotation marks and incorporate the quoted material as part of your paragraph. Quoted material that runs longer than four lines should be indented ten spaces from the left margin, without quotation marks. (Indented quotations are also known as **block quotations**.) When material from another speaker or source appears inside a block quotation, use double quotation marks. When quoted material runs to more than one paragraph, indent the first line of each new paragraph an additional three spaces. When typing block quotations, double-space them just like the rest of your paper. (Note: these guidelines follow the style set by the Modern Language Association. There are other styles, some of them specific to disciplines other than English. Ask your instructors in all classes whether they require specific styles of quotation.)

EXAMPLE

Lacking visitors due to the heavy storms and unable to journey to town for the same reason, Thoreau says he was forced to imagine his company. That is precisely what he does:

> For human society I was obliged to conjure up the former occupants of these woods. Within the memory of many of my townsmen the road near which my house stands resounded with the laughter and gossip of inhabitants, and the woods which border it were notched and dotted here and there with their little gardens and dwellings. . . . (*Walden* and "Civil Disobedience" 172)

Quoting poetry

The guidelines regarding indentation of quoted material hold true for poetry as well as for prose: four lines or less may be incorporated into the body of your essay (using appropriate quotation marks), and more than four lines should be indented without using quotation marks. When quoted within quotation marks, a slash mark (with a space on either side of it) is used to indicate the end of a line. Here, for example, are the opening two lines of the early American Anne Bradstreet's poem "In Memory of My Dear Grandchild Anne Bradstreet Who Deceased June 20, 1669, Being Three Years and Seven Months Old": "With troubled heart and trembling hand I write, / The heavens have changed to sorrow my delight." Because line breaks in a poem are often as important as the punctuation and the actual words, you must not omit the slash marks.

When quoting more than four lines in a block quotation, make sure that you accurately reproduce all the line breaks, indentations, capitalizations, and stanza breaks of the original.

Signaling dialogue

When writing dialogue, start a new paragraph to indicate a change of speaker. Sometimes these paragraph shifts will be the only indication readers need:

> "You're going," he said, as though it were a fact.
> "Yes." Her voice was quiet but firm.
> "And you believe you ought to have the Ferrari and the Picasso?"
> "It was my money that bought them."
> "So it was," he said. "So it was."

To signal that a single speech covers several paragraphs, use quotation marks at the beginning of the speech, at the beginning of every new paragraph continuing the speech, and at the end of the speech. The omission of quotation marks at the end of a paragraph signals to readers that the same speaker continues speaking in the new paragraph.

Using quotation marks to signal titles and definitions (34b)

Identifying titles

Use quotation marks to identify titles that are part of larger works, such as titles of individual poems, short stories, articles, chapters, and essays. In contrast, full collections of poems, short stories, articles, and essays should be either underlined or italicized (for more on underlining and the use of italics, see Chapter 38). Songs and individual episodes of television or radio shows are also identified by quotation marks.

SONG	Bing Crosby's "White Christmas" gets radio airplay every December.
TELEVISION EPISODE	John Cleese appears tonight in a *Cheers* episode titled "Simon Says." [*Note that the television series title is underlined or italicized.*]
SHORT STORY	Tim O'Brien's "Quantum Jumps" later became part of his third novel.
ESSAY	"Loren Eiseley, Student of Time," an essay by Erleen Christiansen, was published in 1987.
POEM	In Elizabeth Bishop's poem, "The Waiting Room," the speaker is an adult remembering herself as a young girl.
CHAPTER	This chapter is titled "Using Quotation Marks."

Note that titles are often used as appositives (as in the "Poem" example). In such cases, the quotation follows the same punctuation conventions as any other appositive; that is, the appositive is set off with commas.

When titles normally set off by quotation marks appear inside other quoted material, use single quotation marks to indicate the title:

What Professor Smith said was, "If you'd read Richard Hugo's 'Glen Uig,' you'd know that not all of his poems focus on shame or degradation."

Identifying definitions

Writers also use quotation marks to indicate definitions.

The word *radical* originally meant "root."

Forte comes from the Latin and originally meant "strong" or "brave."

Note that words used as words are italicized.

Using quotation marks to signal irony and coinages (34c)

Writers may also use quotation marks sparingly to indicate irony or skepticism. Such punctuation works only when used prudently and rarely.

Our "dinner date" turned out to be a fifteen-minute stop at a hamburger drive-in.

Used carelessly, quotation marks may actually communicate a meaning directly opposed to that of the words alone. For example, most readers will interpret the following example as ironic rather than emphatically sincere: *I "love" your mother's creamed broccoli.* For emphasis, use italics or underline:

I *love* your mother's creamed broccoli.

Quotation marks are also used to signal the invention of a new word or the use of an old word in an entirely new context. Here is an example:

Computer companies occasionally announce new software only to discontinue its development later; some people call such software "vaporware."

EXERCISE 34.1 USING QUOTATION MARKS TO SIGNAL DIRECT QUOTATION

NAME _____ **DATE** _____

A. Revise the sentences below, using quotation marks each time someone else's exact words are being used. Make sure that you use quotation marks with other punctuation marks correctly.

EXAMPLE   Your phone's ringing! yelled Phil from the end of the hall.

REVISION   "Your phone's ringing!" yelled Phil from the end of the hall.

1. Ultimately, our differences with management may result in the need to strike; the crowd shifted uneasily at those words.

2. Has everyone been informed that Ms. Jenkins said, For the duration of these training seminars, there will be no absences?

3. Emerson didn't say Consistency is the hobgoblin of little minds; he said, A foolish consistency is the hobgoblin of little minds.

4. I'm going to take the dog for a walk, said Robert as he picked up the leash, but I'll be back before ten.

5. Please write soon, he wrote, after wishing me a happy birthday.

B. Read the following sentences. On the line after the sentence, identify the quotation as either direct or indirect. Add quotation marks as needed.

EXAMPLE It was the American revolutionary Patrick Henry who said, "Give me liberty or give me death." _direct_

1. Call me Ishmael is the first sentence of Herman Melville's *Moby Dick*. _____

2. Most people like to characterize themselves as open-minded and flexible enough to change when the circumstances demand. _____

3. The county employment office's annual summary states that the current unemployment rate is 37 percent lower than it was five years ago. _____

4. Appealing to the public to help find her lost child, the little girl's mother said One minute, she was walking right in front of us. The next, she had vanished into the trees. _____

5. The principal said that she was pleased to have so many parents involved with their childrens school. _____

EXERCISE 34.2   USING QUOTATION MARKS TO SIGNAL DIALOGUE

The following is part of a scene from the famous American play *Waiting for Lefty* by Clifford Odets. Read the exchange between the two characters, then, on your own paper, rewrite it as dialogue, using quotation marks correctly.

A tired but attractive woman of thirty comes into the room, drying her hands on an apron. She stands there sullenly as JOE *comes in from the other side, home from work. For a moment they stand and look at each other in silence.*

JOE: Where's all the furniture, honey?

EDNA: They took it away. No installments paid.

JOE: When?

EDNA: Three o'clock.

JOE: They can't do that.

EDNA: Can't? They did it.

JOE: Why, the palookas, we paid three-quarters.

EDNA: The man said read the contract.

JOE: We must have signed a phoney. . . .

EDNA: It's a regular contract and you signed it.

JOE: Don't be so sour, Edna. . . . *(Tries to embrace her.)*

EDNA: Do it in the movies, Joe—they pay Clark Gable big money for it.

JOE: This is a helluva house to come home to. Take my word!

EDNA: Take MY word! Whose fault is it?

JOE: Must you start that stuff again?

EDNA: Maybe you'd like to talk about books?

JOE: I'd like to slap you in the mouth!

EDNA: No you won't.

JOE: *(sheepishly):* Jeez, Edna, you get me sore some time. . . .

EDNA: But just look at me—I'm laughing all over!

JOE: Don't insult me. Can I help it if times are bad? What the hell do you want me to do, jump off a bridge or something?

EXERCISE 34.3 USING QUOTATION MARKS CORRECTLY

NAME _____ **DATE** _____

Proofread the following sentences for correct use of quotation marks. If the sentence is correct, write a *C* on the line below the sentence. If the sentence needs to be repunctuated, copy the sentence and punctuate it accurately. Should you need a review, the first section of this chapter discusses the use of quotation marks with other punctuation.

EXAMPLE   "Under Stars and The Ritual of Memories" remain two of my favorite Tess Gallagher poems.

REVISION   "Under Stars" and "The Ritual of Memories" remain two of my favorite Tess Gallagher poems.

1. We need to read the last chapter, The Transition to the Post-War Era, by tomorrow.

2. After I finished the chapter about the transition from middle to modern English, I started reading Language Variations in Chaucer's Tales, an essay on reserve in the library.

3. The Marvin's mortgage contract specified penalties for paying off the loan within its first two years.

4. Listen," screamed the television character, if you say I'm going to leave you" one more time, I'll ask you to leave!

5. The episode I enjoyed most,' she said, was the one titled "Atomic Shakespeare; it was inventive and funny.

6. "As I was telling you, he sat there in his library, sipped his drink, and said, I find it delightfully reassuring to live among all these words."

7. "Who but the British," the guide remarked, "would knit 'sweaters' for their teapots?"

8. "Did I tell you," he said, that when Cary got here, the first thing she asked was, 'Well, are the hills alive with the sound of music"?

9. The opening line of her speech read, "It was Dean Herman who said 'Four score and seven days ago this college brought forth a new class.

10. The medical report came to this conclusion: "Patients who 'take responsibility for their own recovery' do indeed recover faster than those who see themselves as victims passively accepting treatment."

EXERCISE 34.4 IDENTIFYING AND CORRECTING ERRORS WITH QUOTATION MARKS

NAME _____ **DATE** _____

Below is the final draft of a brief essay. Read it first, then proofread it for errors involving quotation marks. Place a check in the left margin beside any line that needs correction. Cross out whatever should not be there; add whatever should. If some portion of the essay needs repositioning, indicate that in the margin.

One of the best-kept secrets about poetry is that reading it can be a wonderful, benign addiction. Poems, like anything else handmade, reflect their makers; they are as strange, exotic, thought-provoking, and beautiful as people. Who can deny a rush of adrenaline at taking a deep breath (a really deep breath) and saying (almost singing) some of the most gorgeous sounds in English: "Now as I was young and easy under the apple boughs / About the lilting house and happy as the grass was green, / The night above the dingle starry, / Time let me hail and climb /

        Golden in the heydays of his eyes,

        And honoured among wagons I was prince of the apple towns

        And once below a time I lordly had the trees and leaves

        Trail with daisies and barley

        Down the rivers of the windfall light."

So goes the opening stanza of Dylan Thomas's Fern Hill. Skeptics might say "Even if we grant that the language of Fern Hill is indeed gorgeous, as you say, it is also virtually impossible to follow.

Ah, pity the skeptics; they have an adversarial relationship with the world. Fern Hill is difficult only for readers who ask that it transmit its content as a newspaper does. Newspapers are read for their information. They're written to be read easily, quickly. The sentences are short, and individually they are forgettable. Who recalls last week's headlines? In contrast, Poetry, said Ezra Pound, is news that stays news.

The truth is, Fern Hill is made to be read slowly and even inquisitively. How, after all, can a house be called "lilting"? The word has more to do with song than with architecture. Could someone have been singing? How happy is happy as the grass was green? It's as happy as the night is starry. Is the pun on heydays (hay days) intentional? What can it mean to be prince of the apple towns? Could apple towns be rows of apple trees—an orchard? Does that tie in with the "windfall" of the last line?

And what does this add up to? Doesn't it add up to an intensity of feeling that makes the experience ours even though it's not? We don't know that farm, except we do. We've seen the imaginations of children; we've seen how they become queens or kings of their bedrooms, their toys, their dolls. The speaker in Fern Hill is prince of it all. The speaker owned that farm, that time, and owns it still.

What about the odd shape of Fern Hill on the page? Why insist on such an arrangement? Why is the second stanza arranged identically to the first? And how is it that Thomas could ensure that the first line of the second stanza contains precisely the same number of syllables as the first line of the first stanza? The same correspondence is true for the second lines of each stanza, and the third lines, and so on until the fifth stanza, which changes the pattern somewhat. What astonishing union of content and form are we looking at here?

Actually, Fern Hill is childhood distilled; all the frustrations and angers have been boiled away. What's left is the awe-inspiring precision of language and feeling. What's left is the exhilaration of childhood as time in the Garden of Eden, 'it was all / Shining, it was Adam and maiden, / The sky gathered again / And the sun grew round that very day.' If poems are indeed an addiction, they must be the very best kind.

Using Other Punctuation Marks   35

Parentheses, brackets, dashes, colons, slashes, and ellipses are all around us, setting off, inserting, or marking the absence of information.

According to the student guide to the library, "The new books (shelved near the entrance to the library [the main building]) reflect campus reading tastes . . . rather than the best-seller lists." Some of the current books include scholarly works such as *Perspectives on the California Gold Rush: Journals and Diaries of the Forty-Niners*, volumes of poetry such as *Him/Her: Golden Reflections*, and suspense novels—including the latest from Mary Higgins Clark.

OTHER PUNCTUATION MARKS IN EVERYDAY USE

Notice how *TV Guide*, for instance, freely uses punctuation marks such as parentheses, brackets, dashes, colons, slashes, and ellipses in its program previews. These marks help present information for viewers clearly and efficiently, as this example illustrates.

9 PM Movie (CC)—Biography: 2 hrs. A thoughtful screenplay by *China Beach* creator John Sacret Young and a moving performance by Raul Julia distinguish "Romero," a fact-based 1989 film about the heroic Salvadoran archbishop. [Time approximate after baseball.]

Check the newspaper, a magazine, or other reading material to see where you find these marks. Which marks do you see most often? Which ones less often?

Using parentheses (35a)

Writers use parentheses to set off supplementary information. Such information may be only a word or two or may form an entire sentence. Whatever this information may be, readers will view it as less important than the rest of the sentence. Any sentence containing parenthetical information should be grammatically complete and clear without the material in parentheses. Here are some examples of sentences containing parenthetical information:

Walt Disney's movie *Alice in Wonderland* (1951) remains a bright, weird tale even on television's small screen.

Stock analysts refer to IBM (International Business Machines) as a blue-chip stock.

Just as I rounded the corner (and I could tell something smelled funny), I saw flames licking at the Whittleseys' garage.

Occasionally, writers will place quite important information in parentheses. These writers count on the surprise value such information yields. Here is an example:

The taxi driver was finally persuaded (by means of $600) that the damage to his back seat could be repaired after all.

As with exclamation points and quotation marks used for irony, parenthetical explanations or additions should be used carefully. The following sentence makes two tactical errors. It contains too much parenthetical information, and that information is crucial, not supplementary:

Employees (by which is here meant all employed half-time or less) are not expected to resume work (that is, should not be physically present on company premises) until the last Monday of this month (when it is expected that line repairs will be complete).

Revising such a sentence may involve writing several smaller sentences. In this way, each important idea receives its due attention from readers:

Part-time employees (half-time or less) should plan to return to work on the last Monday of this month. Line repairs should be completed by that time. Until then, we ask these employees to remain off company premises in order to allow repairs to proceed.

The second version is only a little bit longer, but it is quite a bit clearer.
Writers use parentheses in only one other way: to set off numbered or lettered items.

Once you have finished dinner, I want you to (1) clear your place, (2) take a shower and wash your hair, and (3) give your old dog a walk before it gets too dark.

End punctuation goes outside the parentheses unless the parenthetical material is a separate and complete sentence.

Geri says she is smart because she has ESP (whatever that is).

We will meet at the lodge at noon. (Remember your lunch.)

When needed, commas follow closing parentheses; commas are never used before a parenthesis.

If we decide to climb Mount Rainier (or any of the Alaskan peaks), we will do so only with an experienced guide.

Using brackets (35b)

Writers use brackets in two quite specialized ways.

1. To set off a parenthetical element within an already parenthesized passage:

    The Republican party has not always been unsympathetic to feminist concerns (such as the Equal Rights Amendment [ERA], which the Nixon administration supported).

2. To insert explanatory words or comments into a quoted passage:

    Then she turned and said, "Will you [meaning my father] be joining us for dinner?"

In sentences like the one just given, readers attribute the bracketed material to the author of the sentence, not to the person who is quoted. (If your typewriter or computer lacks bracket keys, it is acceptable to write brackets in by hand.)

Using dashes (35c)

Dashes may be used singly or in pairs. A single dash indicates a sudden change or contrast; occasionally, the single dash can be used repeatedly to mimic the breathlessness or fragmentary quality of thought or speech. (To type a dash, you can always hit the hyphen key twice, leaving no spaces between the ends of the dash and the words on either side of it. Some word processing programs enable you to type dashes like the ones in this book.)

EXAMPLES We'll meet you at nine at Woodstock's for pizza—if Rob's aging Buick can get us there. [*single dash used to signal sudden change or contrast*]

"I—wait—no—don't shoot—I'll tell you—I'll tell you what you want to know." [*single dash used repeatedly to mimic the breathlessness or fragmentary quality of thought or speech*]

Writers use dashes in pairs to set off material from the rest of the sentence. You may recall that commas and parentheses also set off material from the rest of the sen-

EXERCISE 35.2 REVISING TO ENSURE CORRECT USE OF PARENTHESES

In each of the two passages that follow, parentheses have been overused or used inappropriately. Using your own paper, rewrite each passage so that parentheses are used sparingly and appropriately, making sure that crucial information does not appear in parentheses.

Where in the World Is Carmen Sandiego? (an ever-popular and hard-to-stock game program) has just arrived on our shelves. This program (it runs on any of the various PC's manufactured by IBM) teaches game players world geography (including such things as the various national currencies and flags, as well as the locations of major cities and rivers). This moderately priced program (so popular that new shipments sell out in days) is marketed by Broderbund Software Co. (San Rafael, California).

Our car was approaching the intersection from the west (we were arguing about which movie we were going to see, so maybe we weren't paying close attention) when somebody (maybe Judy, who was driving) yelled "No!" Just seconds after that (I think by then Judy had begun to swerve right to try to get out of the way), the station wagon hit our front end behind the wheel (the left one). As metal crunched and we spun around, it all seemed to be happening in slow motion.

EXERCISE 35.3 USING DASHES

NAME _____ DATE _____

A. Read the sentences below, paying particular attention to the use of dashes. If a sentence is acceptable as written, write a C on the line below the sentence. If the sentence needs revising, write your corrected version. Make sure your revision uses dashes correctly. Be ready to explain your reasoning.

EXAMPLE   Hamburg today the largest city—and busiest port—in West Germany—has twice risen from the ashes of fire and destruction.

REVISION   Hamburg—today the largest city and busiest port in West Germany—has twice risen from the ashes of fire and destruction.

1. Your term papers will be returned promptly grades are due Tuesday morning to the student basket in the science office.

   _____

   _____

2. After the rafting trip, I'll return your jacket if it isn't lost in the river.

   _____

   _____

3. Few recognize the name Sarah Josepha Hale; many know her poem titled—"Mary Had a Little Lamb."

   _____

   _____

4. Several kinds of lace among them Alencon, Honiton, and Maltese—take their names from their place of origin.

   _____

   _____

5. Their sophistication, their perceptual abilities, even how they feel about themselves children's pictures can tell us much—about the children who drew them.

   _____

   _____

535

B. Combine each group of short sentences, using dashes appropriately as needed.

EXAMPLE Chicago's Sears Tower contains 110 stories. It rises to a height of almost 1,500 feet. It measures 104 feet taller than New York's World Trade Center. It is the country's tallest building.

REVISION <u>Chicago's Sears Tower—rising some 1,500 feet, containing 110 stories, and measuring 104 feet taller than New York's World Trade Center—is the country's tallest building.</u>

1. You should escape from your landlord. You should decorate as you please. You should begin to build your own assets. You should save your money. You should buy your first home.

2. Pets should be treated like animals. They should not be treated like family members!

3. Paul Klee was a renowned graphic artist, painter, and art theorist. He died some fifty years ago. He remains an influential presence for contemporary artists.

4. Twice, Knoxville served as Tennessee's state capital. This occurred from 1796 to 1812 and again from 1817 to 1818.

5. Renata Scotto is famous. She is an opera singer. She was born in Italy. She is still remembered for her debut in Milan in 1953. She is particularly recognized today for her performances of Puccini's *Madama Butterfly*.

EXERCISE 35.4   USING COLONS

NAME _____   DATE _____

A. Combine the following sentences, using colons in each one. There may be more than one way to combine these sentences; for this exercise, however, make sure that your versions use colons.

EXAMPLE   Check the *Encyclopaedia Britannica*. The volume to check is volume 3. The page number is 187.

REVISION   Check the *Encyclopaedia Britannica* 3:187.

1. Bill's decision was a difficult one, but he stuck to it. Bill quit smoking for good.

2. Ellen Gilchrist has a fourth book. It is titled *Drunk with Love*. It is subtitled *A Book of Stories*.

3. I like the Book of Proverbs. I especially like Chapter 12. I especially like verse 8 in that chapter.

4. Although the trip was only for a weekend in the mountains, the family stuffed supplies for a week into the car. They packed fishing poles, tackle boxes, a large cooler, food, swimsuits, towels, parkas, and even some deck chairs.

5. The server displayed the dessert choices. The desserts included chocolate torte, cherry crepes, and blueberry cheesecake.

B. Read each of the sentences below, paying particular attention to the use of colons. If the sentence is punctuated accurately, write a C on the line below the sentence. If the sentence needs revising, write your revision on the lines. Make sure your revision uses colons correctly.

EXAMPLE Advertisers assume that we all want to be: beautiful, protected, stylish, and trendy.

REVISION Advertisers assume that we all want to be beautiful, protected, stylish, and trendy.

1. During the 1930s, Academy Award winners for Best Picture included the following movies. *Grand Hotel, Mutiny on the Bounty,* and *Gone with the Wind.*

2. You listen to me right now, shape up or ship out.

3. Now, now, sweetie: what's the matter?

4. Leonid Telyatnikov has done something he hopes no one else will have to do he has: commanded a fire crew attempting to extinguish a nuclear reactor fire.

5. Recognized as perhaps the nation's best prison newspaper, the *Prison Mirror* of Stillwater, Minnesota, publishes articles on: stress management, the alternatives to execution, smoking, and education.

6. The list of John Huston's movie credits includes: *Moby Dick, Prizzi's Honor, The Maltese Falcon,* and *The African Queen.*

7. Lucille Boone Berry, a genuine descendant of Daniel Boone, suffered a fate that seems right out of the history books: when she was a young girl, her father and brother rode out hunting one day and never returned.

8. Every town has restaurant ads proclaiming: "All You Can Eat" or "Home-Cooked Food."

9. I am: annoyed, exasperated, sorely tired, and: fed up.

10. You must remember this: a kiss is still a kiss, a sigh is still a sigh.

EXERCISE 35.5 USING ELLIPSES

NAME _____ **DATE** _____

Read the following passage. Then copy it, leaving out the underlined portions. Make sure that you use ellipses correctly.

Not all states allow the public to remove elected officials from office by recalling them. <u>Even among</u> the fifteen states that do provide for recall, <u>requirements differ. States</u> have their own formulas for determining the required number of signatures to be collected. <u>If the formula is based on the number voting in the last election for office involved, the number of signatures could vary considerably depending on the intensity of the contests that year or the other offices on the ballot.</u> Simply filing the required number of valid signatures might <u>in itself</u> be sufficient to require a recall election. On the other hand, the petitions might need to spell out specific grounds <u>that would justify a recall election.</u> Other differences might occur in registration procedures for petition carriers, signature requirements, <u>and so forth; similar variations might exist in</u> filing deadlines, petition formats, and other details.

PART 7

UNDERSTANDING MECHANICAL CONVENTIONS

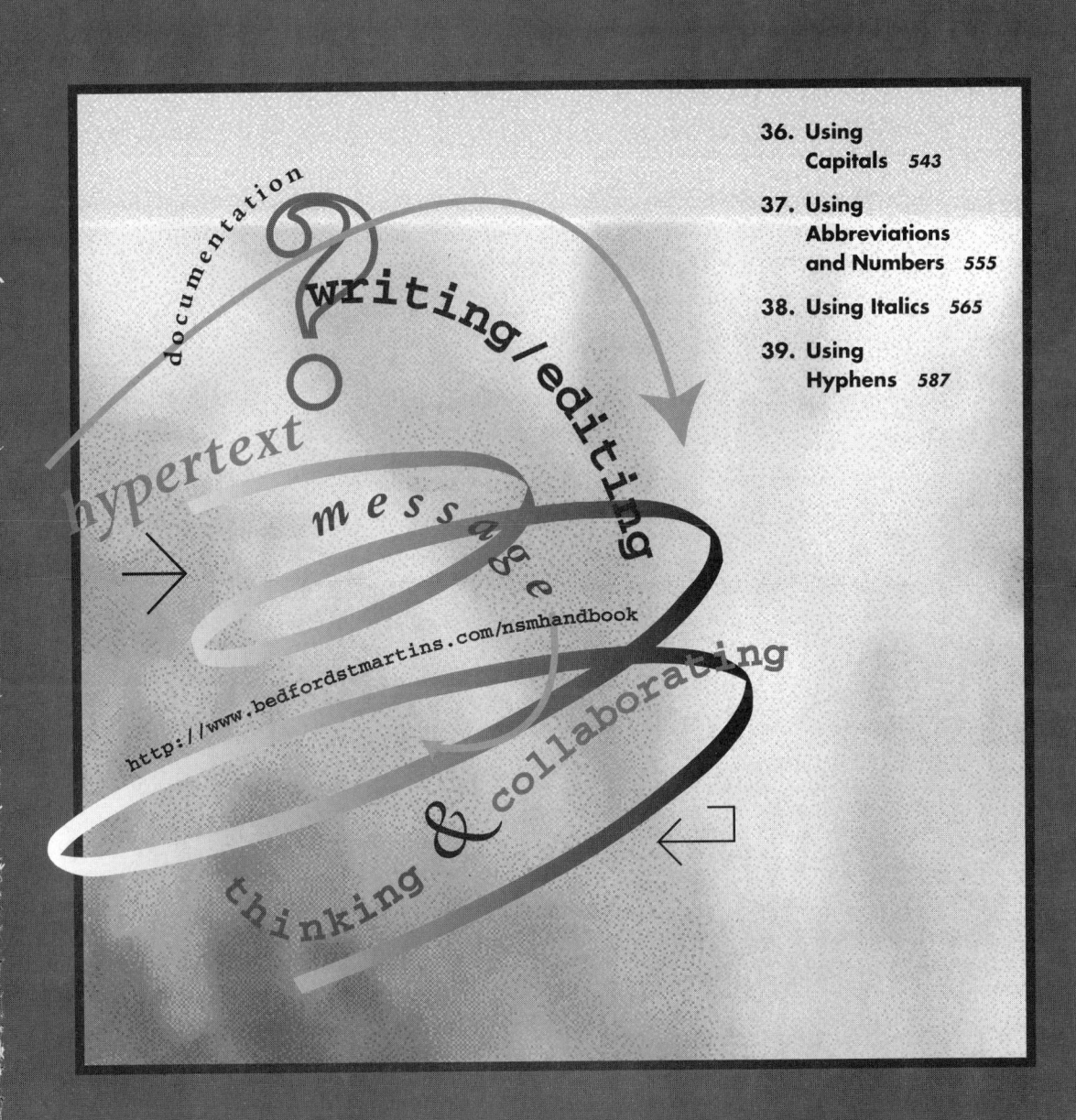

36. Using Capitals 543

37. Using Abbreviations and Numbers 555

38. Using Italics 565

39. Using Hyphens 587

PART 7

PREVIEW QUESTIONS

These questions are to help you, the student, decide what to study. Correct any mistakes in capitalization, abbreviation, use of numbers, use of italics, or hyphenation that you find in the following sentences. If there are no mistakes, mark a C next to the sentence.

1. we will be going to Northwestern France in two weeks.
2. These books—They all cost under a dollar—are available inside.
3. Michael Dukakis, governor of Massachusetts, ran for president.
4. We used to live on First Avenue, but then we moved uptown.
5. A common misconception among students is that the renaissance was man-centered whereas the middle ages were God-centered.
6. Anne Fisher is a doctor and an M.D.
7. First Kay got her B.A., then she decided to become a social worker so she applied for an M.S.
8. Boethius composed the *Consolation of Philosophy* sometime between AD 480 and 524.
9. Whenever you go to Jane's Bakery, you must take a #.
10. My parents live in Cal., but I now go to school in Ariz.
11. 6 people came to hear the lecture.
12. He has about 10,000 records.
13. The *Hebrew Bible*, the *Gospels*, and the *Koran* are all sacred books.
14. Stephen Greenblatt's chapter on "King Lear," "Shakespeare and the Exorcists," appears in his book "Shakespearean Negotiations."
15. Roland Petit's ballet, *Notre Dame de Paris,* will be performed next week.
16. Every night I tune my radio to NPR and listen to *All Things Considered*.
17. Spenser's epic, *The Fairie Queene,* begins "in medias res," "in the middle of things."
18. In the Renaissance, "poetry" did not just mean verse, but all fiction.
19. "Annie Hall" is my favorite Woody Allen film.
20. Although Beethoven wrote many works for piano, his *Moonlight Sonata* is the best-known.
21. We depend upon oil for approximately seventy-five percent of our energy.
22. Although they said that it would be cloud-less, it rained all afternoon.
23. He was always such a happy-go-lucky person.
24. None of the television stations had better-coverage of the election.
25. Only one-third of the class showed up today.
26. This anthology contains poetry from eighteenth- and nineteenth-century manuscripts.

Using Capitals 36

Capitalization depends almost entirely on convention—the customary habits writers follow and readers expect. Once we understand these conventions, we expect capital letters to mark each new sentence, to help name Aunt Fran or Seattle, to distinguish a Xerox machine from just any copier, and to help us understand how one might drive south in order to reach the South.

> **CAPITALS IN EVERYDAY USE**
>
> Writers often capitalize words or even whole passages to add special emphasis (WOW! ZAP!). The writer Dave Barry uses this technique in his humorous newspaper columns: "Today I saw a chicken driving a car. (I AM NOT MAKING THIS UP.)" Look through your local newspaper, noting examples of capital letters used to name products, to identify people, to emphasize points, or to otherwise engage a reader's attention.

Capitalizing the first word of a sentence or line of poetry (36a)

One of the oldest conventions regarding capital letters is the capitalization of the first letter of the opening word in a sentence. This holds true for quoted material as well as for your own words. Every sentence on this page provides you with an example of this capitalization convention.

Here is an example of a quoted sentence appearing inside another. The first word of the sentence is capitalized; so is the first word of the quoted sentence:

Mark yelled, "Will you be in early tomorrow?"

When a sentence follows a colon, capitalization is optional. Either version of the following sentence is acceptable:

Writers speculate that Lindbergh's aerial tour of the United States contributed to his interest in conservation: he [*or* He] saw firsthand the still unspoiled beauty of his country.

If your sentence contains a sentence set off by dashes or parentheses, the sentence inside the dashes or parentheses does *not* begin with a capital letter. Here is an example:

All requests—please keep them to one page—should be on Jennifer's desk by noon Friday.

When writing or typing a letter, capitalize the first word of the salutation (*My dear Angela*) and the closing (*Very truly yours*).

Finally, if you are quoting lines of poetry, follow the poet's wishes when it comes to capitalization. If the poet capitalizes the first letter of every line, follow suit. If the poet has chosen not to capitalize the first letter of every line, again, follow suit.

Capitalizing proper nouns and proper adjectives (36b)

Whenever you name specific persons, places, or objects, those names are **proper nouns** and should be capitalized. For example, in the sentence *Marilyn lives in New York*, it is accurate to capitalize both the *M* in *Marilyn* and the *N* and *Y* in *New York* because both are proper nouns.

Proper adjectives (made from proper nouns) are also capitalized. Thus the adjective *New Yorker* (made from the proper noun) is capitalized in the sentence *Marilyn is a New Yorker*.

When a title precedes a name, in effect becoming part of the name, both are capitalized, as in *Aunt Bernie, Grandma Berry, Senator Boxer,* and *Police Chief Harrington*. However, when these titles follow the name or are used instead of the name, the titles are not capitalized. The only exception here is for very high officials, such as *president* or *prime minister*; these titles are sometimes capitalized even when used alone.

EXAMPLES

Senator Boxer	Barbara Boxer, senator from California
Police Chief Harrington	Penny Harrington, the police chief
Aunt Bernie	Bernardine Matusek, my aunt
the Prime Minister	John Major, Prime Minister of Great Britain

The names of products, corporations, and businesses are also capitalized, as in *First Interstate Bank; American Express; Floating Point, Inc.; Wheaties;* and *Campbell's Soup*.

Specific geographic sites and formations are capitalized, as in *Patterson Falls, Fifth Avenue, Europe, the Flatiron Building,* and *the Great Salt Lake*. Note that although the articles *the, an,* and *a* usually accompany proper nouns or proper adjectives, they are not normally capitalized.

Common nouns such as *road, brook,* and *avenue* are capitalized only when they form part of a proper name or an address. The same is true of directional words such as *west* and *southeast*.

Southeast Missouri State University	the southeast corner
Ponderosa Road	the road to town
Fairhaven Brook	the rocky brook

Consider this sentence: *The <u>Waterfall</u> at <u>Alsea falls</u> forms the focus for a <u>Picnic Ground</u> and an overnight camping area.* Should all the underlined words be capitalized? Should other words be capitalized? *Waterfall* is not part of a proper name; hence it should not be capitalized. *Alsea* is part of a proper name, so its capitalization is correct. *Falls* is also part of the proper name, so it should be capitalized. *Picnic Ground* is a common noun; hence, it should not be capitalized. Thus the sentence should really look like this: *The waterfall at Alsea Falls forms the focus for a picnic ground and an overnight camping area.*

Many other names and titles are also routinely capitalized. Here are some examples.

- Days of the week, months, and holidays

    Monday   October   Columbus Day   Easter   Ramadan   Passover

- Historical events, movements, and periods

    the Civil War   the Victorian Era   the Battle of Hastings

- Government or public offices, institutions, and departments

    West Slope Water District   the U.S. Senate   the Commerce Department

- Organizations, associations, and their members

    United Auto Workers   Rotarians   The Crazy 8's   the League of Women Voters

- Races, nationalities, and languages

    Hispanic   Filipino   Dutch   Haitian   Arabic   Russian

(Note: The terms *black* and *white* are not usually capitalized when used to refer to race.)

- Religions and their adherents

    Judaism/Jews   Protestantism/Protestants   Hinduism/Hindus
    Islam/Muslims   Buddhism/Buddhists   Roman Catholicism/Catholics

- Sacred persons, places, or things

    Allah   Rama   the Koran   the Angel Moroni
    God   Jesus   the Bible [*but* biblical]   Saint Peter's Basilica

- Trade names

    IBM   Pepsi   Bartles & Jaymes   Charmin

Some trade names have become generic and hence are not usually capitalized; an example is *aspirin*. When in doubt about a trade name, consult a dictionary.

- Academic units, colleges, departments, and courses

    College of Mechanical Engineering   Department of Art   Writing 121

Do not capitalize the name of a subject area unless it is a language: *I was bumped from both psychology and French.* The name of a specific course is capitalized, as in *Writing 121.*

Capitalizing titles of works (36c)

Important words in the titles of books, articles, essays, poems, songs, paintings, musical and dance compositions, films, plays, short stories, documents, and television series are capitalized:

Interview with the Vampire	"How I Found My Runaway Husband"
"A Modest Proposal"	"Ode on a Grecian Urn"
"Stand By Me" [the song]	*The Peaceable Kingdom*
Great Mass in C Minor, K. 427	*Swan Lake*
Schindler's List	*Death of a Salesman*
Stand By Me [the movie]	Treaty of Versailles
"The Lottery"	*I Love Lucy*

As in the case of poetry, an author or artist will occasionally decide not to capitalize the title of a work—the poet e. e. cummings made a stylistic statement by avoiding capitalization in most of his works, for instance. Another example is the television series *thirtysomething.* Always check to see how the title of a work is capitalized in its original form and follow that styling when in doubt.

A, an, and *the* are not capitalized unless they are the first word of the title itself. *The* is not capitalized when it is the first word in a magazine or newspaper title, even if it is part of the title itself. Prepositions and conjunctions are not capitalized unless they are the first or last words in the title. Remember to capitalize the titles of your own works as well as others'.

Capitalizing *I* and *O* (36d)

The first person pronoun *I* is routinely capitalized whenever it is used. *O* is an old and stylized version of the word *oh*.

> Whenever I feel sad at her being gone, I try to remember what the pastor said: "And remember, O ye of little faith, that justice and mercy shall attend thee at the end of thy days. . . ."

Checking for unnecessary capitalization (36e)

Inexperienced writers sometimes punctuate sentences almost solely according to the thought process that produced them: any pause in the process produces a punctuation mark (usually a comma), and a long pause produces a period. These writers then capitalize the first word of the "new sentence." The results might look something like this:

> Any discussion of the death penalty, makes me uncomfortable. Because it goes against everything I believe. Namely, that life is sacred and no government has the right to kill.

In such instances, writers cannot correct their punctuation until they are able to distinguish between sentences and fragments. For review in this area, see Chapter 16. Accurately punctuated (and only slightly rewritten), the same passage looks like this:

> Any discussion of the death penalty makes me uncomfortable because it goes against everything I believe. In my opinion, life is sacred, and no government has the right to kill.

Overall, good writers recognize that capitalization is not a matter of style or emphasis. Capitalizing for emphasis, as in "The test subjects did NOT respond as we had predicted," is not helpful to readers or appropriate in most writing. Capitalization is, rather, a matter of following generally accepted conventions. Some of the most common capitalization errors are detailed here.

- Seasons, academic terms, and academic years are not capitalized.

    spring   fall quarter   summer semester   junior year

- Compass directions are not capitalized unless they refer to the accepted name of a geographic region.

The wind blew fitfully from the southeast.

The West was hit by an unseasonably early frost.

- The names of family relationships are not capitalized unless they substitute for a proper name.

My father took me to my first circus when I was six.

I asked Father if he would buy me cotton candy.

The letter said my uncle had open-heart surgery.

The letter said Uncle Herman had open-heart surgery.

Worrying about capitalization too early in the writing process can distract you from concentrating on what you want to say. Try saving such concerns for proofreading—usually the last stage of the writing process. Here is a capitalization checklist you can use as you proofread.

- Are the following words capitalized?

    proper nouns and adjectives

    names of people, places, events, institutions, products, and businesses

    titles of works of art, music, and literature

- Have capitals been used incorrectly for any of these words?

    seasons

    compass directions

    family relations

EXERCISE 36.1 CAPITALIZING THE FIRST WORD OF A NEW SENTENCE

NAME _____ **DATE** _____

The following passage sometimes uses capitalization incorrectly. Capitalize any words that should be capitalized, and substitute lowercase letters where necessary. Make your revisions in the space above each line.

Basically, she was shy. as a child, she had always been quite a bit shorter than her classmates, Leading to a certain amount of teasing. Sometimes the teasing was quite severe—Once a dozen or more of her fifth-grade class had circled her, chanting "you're short, you're short, you're short." when the playground monitor broke up the circle, She was on her knees in the middle of the group, tears on her face, Her hands held tight over her ears. "no, no, no, no," She'd been screaming, trying to outshout her tormentors.

Then, in eighth grade, finally she grew: she grew six inches in six months, she gained fifteen pounds, and the teasing stopped. her classmates quickly forgot about it, but she did not forget. for years, she had to teach herself to join the group. She had to persuade herself that she would be accepted, not teased. How do I know this? i am that girl, or rather she is a part of me. And if I am no longer shy, It is because I have worked hard. I don't want to forget those experiences. I do want to keep them in perspective, To learn from them rather than be victimized by them.

EXERCISE 36.2 CAPITALIZING PROPER NOUNS AND PROPER ADJECTIVES

Words are underlined in each of the sentences that follow. Analyze how each underlined word is used, and decide whether it should be capitalized. Then rewrite each sentence so that it uses capitalization accurately. Write your analyses and your revised sentences on a separate sheet of paper.

1. The <u>Chief Executive Officer</u> of the <u>Company</u> encouraged <u>Investors</u> to be patient until the <u>Fall</u> sales figures were complete.

2. When I have a headache, I never know whether I should take an <u>aspirin</u>, a <u>tylenol</u>, or an <u>advil</u>.

3. <u>Dr. Lambert</u> is <u>Chair</u> of the <u>department</u> of <u>Political science</u> at the <u>University</u>.

4. Columbia, <u>south</u> Carolina, lies on the <u>Congaree</u> <u>river</u> and boasts a <u>Population</u> of nearly 100,000.

5. <u>Screen Actress</u> and later <u>Princess</u> of <u>Monaco</u> Grace Kelly died when her car (which was headed <u>North</u>) left the road and plunged down an embankment.

6. Salt Lake City <u>Business</u> <u>leaders</u> consider <u>american</u> <u>express</u> one of the <u>City's</u> most important corporations.

7. On <u>tuesday</u> we'll go to the <u>art institute of chicago</u> and look at the <u>Exhibits</u> of <u>picasso's</u> works.

8. Bill Clinton, <u>President</u> of the <u>United States</u>, is an <u>arkansas</u> man.

9. The <u>civil war</u> devastated the <u>south</u> and took quite a toll on the <u>union</u> <u>soldiers</u> in the <u>North</u>.

10. <u>New York City</u> has an incredible mix of cultures: on almost any street one will pass <u>jews</u>, <u>blacks</u>, <u>hispanics</u>, <u>chinese</u>, <u>indians</u>, and scores of other nationalities.

EXERCISE 36.3 MORE PRACTICE WITH CAPITALIZING PROPER NOUNS AND PROPER ADJECTIVES

Some italicized words in the following sentences are capitalized; others are not. On a separate sheet of paper, analyze how each italicized word is used, and briefly note that analysis as shown below. Then rewrite the sentence so that it uses capitalization accurately.

EXAMPLE That *Botany* 201 *class* looks tough, but not as tough as *french* or *physics*.

Botany; title of actual class; capitalize
class; not part of a title; do not capitalize
french; name of a language; capitalize
physics; not the title of a specific course; do not capitalize
Revision: *That Botany 201 class looks tough, but not as tough as French or physics.*

1. Although *Presidents Day* is now celebrated on *a monday* in *february*, some years ago, the actual *birthdays* of both *Lincoln* and *washington* were holidays.

2. At *Bill* and *Dana's Wedding* at *Neighborhood Church*, the guests began hunting for their *kleenex* when the soloist began to sing.

3. Theatre lovers dream of an annual *London* or *new york trip* to see the new *Plays* and *Musicals*.

4. *The Division Of* Language and Literature is happy to announce that it is the recipient of a grant from the United States Department of *education*.

5. Cub *scouts*, Rotarians, members of the *league* of Women Voters, and *Members* of various fraternities and *Sororities* joined forces yesterday to publicize the need for more blood donations.

6. The *biblical* injunction to *honor* one's parents is echoed in *the koran* and can also be found in the *various* sayings attributed to *Confucius*.

7. After *Senator* Ben Nighthorse Campbell spoke quietly with the *Senator* from Wyoming, the two left for lunch.

8. If *i* win the *Lottery*, I'm going to buy a giant *Red Cadillac*, a house in the *caribbean*, and a color *t.v.* so I can watch *the tonight show* in style.

9. The *Apollo theater* has been a testing ground for many of this *Country's* greatest *Musicians* and *Dancers*.

10. I don't speak *spanish*, *italian*, or *french*, but I do speak *"the Language of Love."*

Ms. Barbara Hogg   Mr. Gregory Pfarr   Rev. John Dennis
Dr. Erret Hummel   St. Theresa of Avila

Other titles follow the name:

Alan Palmer, D.D.S.   Suzanne Clark, Ph.D.   Hank Williams Jr.

Use *Ms.* as the common title for women, just as *Mr.* is the common title for men. In current usage, neither of these terms relates to an individual's marital status. Substitute *Miss* or *Mrs.* only when you know that a particular woman prefers to be addressed that way.

Other religious, military, academic, and government titles may be abbreviated whenever they precede a full name; if they appear before only the last name, the title should be written in full.

Sen. Nancy Kassebaum *or* Senator Kassebaum

Rev. David Olivier *or* Reverend Olivier

Prof. Laura Rice-Sayre *or* Professor Rice-Sayre

Gen. Amos Halftrack *or* General Halftrack

Note, however, that *Dr.*, like *Mr.*, *Ms.*, or *Mrs.*, may precede a lone surname: *Dr. Spock* is as correct as *Dr. Richard Kimble.*

Do not abbreviate these titles when used without any names.

INCORRECT   My Dr. said the lab results would be ready Wednesday.

The Sen. took the floor.

CORRECT   My doctor said the lab results would be ready Wednesday.

The senator took the floor.

Spell out *Reverend* and *Honorable* whenever they are used with *the* and precede an individual's name, as in *the Reverend John Dennis.*

The abbreviations for educational degrees are commonly used whether attached to particular people or not.

B.A. (Bachelor of Arts)   B.S. (Bachelor of Science)
M.A. (Master of Arts)   M.S. (Master of Science)
Ph.D. (Doctor of Philosophy)

EXAMPLE   He is finishing his M.A. work this spring.

Using abbreviations with years and hours (37b)

Some abbreviations—for example, *F* for *Fahrenheit* and A.M. for *ante meridiem* ("before noon")—should be used only when preceded by numbers, as in *75°F* or *6:45 A.M.* In general, these abbreviations deal with units of measure—temperature, size, quantity, time, and the like.

ABBREVIATION	MEANING	EXAMPLE OF USE
B.C.	before Christ	399 B.C.
A.D.	*anno Domini,* Latin for "year of our Lord"	A.D. 49
A.M.	*ante meridiem,* Latin for "before noon"	11:15 A.M.
P.M.	*post meridiem,* Latin for "after noon"	9:00 P.M.
r.p.m. *or* rpm	revolutions per minute	2,000 r.p.m. *or* rpm
m.p.h. *or* mph	miles per hour	55 m.p.h. *or* mph
F	Fahrenheit scale	212°F
C	Celsius scale	100°C

Writers traditionally capitalize *B.C.* and *A.D.* but use lowercase letters for *a.m.* and *p.m.* Printers and publishers often use small capitals for all four of these abbreviations.

The common symbols on the top line of your keyboard are also abbreviations. With the exception of the dollar sign ($), which is allowable in formal writing so long as it is followed by a number, none of the other symbols should be part of formal essay prose. (Graphs, charts, and other modes of visual presentation do sometimes employ some of these abbreviations in captions or identifications, but such charts or graphs are typically parts of memos or technical reports, not essays.)

Using acronyms and initial abbreviations (37c)

Countries, companies, and a variety of other organizations regularly shorten their own names to initials. The National Broadcasting Company advertises and identifies itself as NBC; Mothers Against Drunk Driving regularly refers to itself as MADD. MADD is an example of an **acronym**—a set of initials that form a pronounceable word. NBC, by contrast, is simply a set of initials that do not form a pronounceable word. Sets of initials and acronyms are typically written in capital letters and without periods separating them. (If you are unsure about the use of periods in a particular abbreviation, consult your dictionary.)

How can you know whether or not an organization's name can be shortened? Two factors should guide you here. If the organization itself uses initials or an acronym, chances are that you may acceptably do so as well. Examples here would include IBM and AFL-CIO. Be sure that your readers will recognize any initials or acronyms you use. For example, the initials COLA probably suggest a soft drink to most people. Only a very few readers (those involved in labor-management contracts) may recognize those initials as standing for *cost-of-living adjustment*.

When in doubt, write the name or title in full and enclose the initials or the acronym in parentheses immediately following the title.

> In the 1950s and early 1960s, doctors commonly prescribed the drug diethylstilbestrol (DES) for pregnant women. However, it was not until the late 1970s that researchers discovered its dangers for female children. Since 1973, over 70,000 "DES babies" have been diagnosed with cervical cancer.

Here is a short list of common acronyms and initial abbreviations:

NATIONS

UK	United Kingdom
UAE	United Arab Emirates

CORPORATIONS

AT&T*	American Telephone and Telegraph
UPI	United Press International

ORGANIZATIONS

OAS	Organization of American States
UN	United Nations
NASA	National Aeronautics and Space Administration
ACLU	American Civil Liberties Union

SCIENTIFIC OR TECHNICAL TERMS

DNA	deoxyribonucleic acid
ROM	read-only memory
AIDS	acquired immune deficiency syndrome
ABM	antiballistic missile

Checking for appropriate use of abbreviations (37d)

In composing notes, rough drafts, informal letters, and the like, writers will often abbreviate in order to write quickly. Such abbreviations can be quite helpful, but they should generally not appear in the final draft of a college essay.

- Units of measure should be spelled out, not abbreviated.

---

*This example illustrates one of the few instances where an ampersand (&) is acceptable in college writing.

Our smooth collie weighs ninety-two pounds. [*not* 92 lbs.]

Deke's Harley gets over fifty miles to the gallon. [*not* 50 m.p.g.]

- Names of days, months, and holidays should be spelled out.

    Sunday turned out warm and cloudless. [*not* Sun.]

    October 21 was our first day of heavy rain. [*not* Oct. 21]

- Geographic names should be spelled out.

    New York boasts several major-league sports teams. [*not* N.Y.]

    The Columbia River empties into the Pacific at Astoria, Oregon. [*not* Col. R., *not* Astoria, OR]

- Academic subjects should be spelled out.

    Psychology and economics are proving to be my most difficult subjects this term. [*not* Psych. and econ.]

    Chemistry laboratory sections are scheduled in the afternoons. [*not* Chem. lab sections]

- Divisions of written works should be spelled out.

    One of the most famous chapters in *Moby Dick* is Chapter 32, "Cetology." [*not* chs., *not* Ch. 32]

    Those twelve or so pages begin on page 116. [*not* p. 116]

- Company names should be spelled out exactly as used by the company itself. Use *Co., Inc., Ltd.,* and the ampersand only when used by the company itself.

    Arrowood Book Company is a small, regional publisher of literary titles. [*not* Arrowood Bk. Co.]

NUMBERS

Spelling out or using figures for numbers (37e, 37f, 37g)

Suppose that you are writing about the time of day, weight loss plans, or the cost of various products, services, or programs. Should you spell out the numbers you use, or should you use numerals?

The conventions vary from discipline to discipline. For instance, most scientific or technical journals stipulate that numbers be identified with numerals rather than spelled out in letters. Journalists follow their own set of conventions. College essay

EXERCISE 37.4 WRITING NUMBERS

NAME _____ **DATE** _____

Read the passage below for any errors in the presentation of numbers. Underline any errors you find, and make your corrections in the space above each line.

Readers have either loved Ernest Hemingway or hated him. Either way, they have bought his books. By October nineteen twenty-nine, his then new novel *A Farewell to Arms* had sold twenty-eight thousand copies in less than a month. By November, it was number 1 on the best-seller list—its nearest competitor a book by a German titled *All Quiet on the Western Front*. Since that time, Hemingway's books have continued to sell. His name is still a household word.

Ernest Miller Hemingway was born at 8 o'clock in the morning in his parents' house at four thirty-nine North Oak Park Avenue in the town of Oak Park, Illinois, a suburb of Chicago. The date was July twenty-first, 1899. Hemingway weighed in at 9 and a half pounds. In the next 60 years, he would live enough and work enough to write a score of books, 4 or 5 of which will be read as long as people read English. Curiously enough, one of the best of them, *The Garden of Eden,* was first published fully 25 years after his death.

Using Italics

38

Italic type—type that slants like *this*—is used by word-processing programs and by printers in a variety of conventional ways. If you write and print your work using computer equipment, you may be able to produce actual italics. Otherwise, underlining is the standard substitute. If you can't produce italics, you should mentally translate every mention of italicizing to mean underlining.

ITALICS IN EVERYDAY USE

Look around, and you'll see italics used in many ways: on signs, in pamphlets, on the sides of trucks. On a recent visit to Chicago, a student looking for good, cheap food found this listing in a visitor's guide.

Gold Coast Dogs (418 North State). Chicago is serious about hot dogs. A good Chicago hot dog is an all-beef critter with natural casing, in a steamed bun and topped with your choice of the following (aka *everything*): yellow mustard, relish, raw chopped onion, tomato wedges, a dill pickle sliced lengthwise, maybe jalapeño peppers if you're perverse, and celery salt. A good Chicago hot dog *never* touches catsup, brown mustard, cooked onions, cheese, or sauerkraut.

For what purposes are the italics used in this listing? Look around you for some examples of italics in use, and write down two or three interesting examples.

Using italics for titles (38a)

Writers identify titles either through italics or through the use of quotation marks. In general, italics are reserved for the titles of long or complete works, whereas quotation marks identify titles of shorter works or sections of works. Thus in a manuscript, a book title is underlined, but a chapter title is placed in quotation marks. The title of a book of poems is underlined, whereas the title of a particular poem is placed in quotation marks. The name of a television series is underlined, whereas the name of a particular episode is identified by quotation marks. (For a review of the use of quotation marks, see Chapter 34.)

- Underline book, magazine, journal, pamphlet, and newspaper titles.

BOOKS	*Native Son, The Awakening, Ulysses* [Note that sacred books (the Bible or the Koran, for example) are not underlined, nor are the divisions within them. In general, writers do not underline the titles of public documents such as the Constitution, the Camp David Accords, or the Magna Charta.]
MAGAZINES, JOURNALS, PAMPHLETS, AND NEWSPAPERS	*Newsweek, Journal of the American Medical Association, North American Review,* the *American Scholar, Common Sense,* the *New York Times,* the *Chicago Sun-Times* [Note that *the* is not italicized or capitalized before the name of a magazine even if it is part of the official name. Similarly, the word *magazine* is not italicized or capitalized following the name. Only when the name of a city is part of the official name of a newspaper is the city name italicized (thus *New York Times,* New York *Daily News*).]

- Underline the titles of plays, long poems, long musical works, choreographed works, paintings, and sculptures.

PLAYS	*A Midsummer Night's Dream, Cats*
LONG POEMS	*Paradise Lost, Paterson*
LONG MUSICAL WORKS	*The Joshua Tree, The Wall, La Bohème, Messiah* [Note that classical works identified by form, number, and key are not italicized (for example, Sonata in F Minor).]
CHOREOGRAPHED WORKS	Martha Graham's *Frontier,* Agnes De Mille's *Rodeo*
PAINTINGS	*Starry Night, The Peaceable Kingdom*
SCULPTURES	*David,* the *Pietà*

- Underline the titles of television series, other television programs, and radio programs.

TELEVISION SERIES AND PROGRAMS	*Mister Ed, Nightline*
RADIO PROGRAMS	*Morning Edition, A Prairie Home Companion*

Using italics for words, letters, and numbers referred to as words (38b)

Use italics whenever you want readers to see that you refer to a particular word, letter, or number not for its meaning but for itself.

How many *m*'s are there in *accommodate*?

In the inscriptions on some old buildings, the *u*'s look like *v*'s.

The binary system contains only *0*'s and *1*'s.

Also use italics to indicate a word you are about to discuss or define.

The word *prognosticate* has Latin origins.

Using italics for foreign words and phrases (38c)

Sometimes writers wish to use foreign words as part of English prose. Words or phrases such as *Gesundheit* (German) and *gracias* (Spanish) are commonly understood by many English speakers and writers, even though these expressions are not part of English itself. When you do use words such as these, italicize them (except as noted in the discussion that concludes this section).

Recently, *pro bono* work has been added to course requirements for law students studying at the University of Pennsylvania. [Pro bono *is a shortened version of* pro bono publico, *which means literally "for the public good." Thus* pro bono *legal work is done without charge.*]

In the Gorbachev era, the key word in Soviet-American relations was *glasnost*.

That puppy has more energy and *joie de vivre* than it can handle.

However, notice this example: *The way the clerk treated me, I felt like a peon.* In this example, the word *peon* is not given special treatment. Some originally foreign words are now so commonly used that they do not need to be italicized simply because of that foreign origin. When in doubt about whether or not to italicize a particular word, consult a good dictionary.

Using italics for the names of vehicles (38d)

Italicize the names of specific ships, trains, aircraft, or spacecraft but not generic names such as cruiser, battleship, fighter plane, or subway. The names of specific production models are capitalized as products, but not italicized. The initials S.S., U.S.S., H.M.S., and so on are capitalized but not italicized. Do not italicize the word *the* before the name of a vehicle.

SHIPS	the *Golden Hinde,* the U.S.S. *Missouri,* the trawler *Alice III*
TRAINS	the *Golden Zephyr,* the *City of New Orleans*
AIRCRAFT AND SPACECRAFT	*Columbia, Echo I,* the *Graf Zeppelin*
SPECIFIC PRODUCTION MODELS	Learjet, Volkswagen Rabbit, Stealth bomber

Using italics for special emphasis (38e)

Especially in informal writing and in writing dialogue, italics can be used sparingly to help readers actually hear the intonations of a person speaking. Note the differences in the following sentences:

The workers insisted they could not finish until at least Monday afternoon. [*no special emphasis*]

The *workers* insisted they could not finish until at least Monday afternoon. [*The workers insist one thing, but perhaps someone else is saying something else.*]

The workers insisted they could not finish until *at least* Monday afternoon. [*This version suggests that the job will take longer than the Monday afternoon deadline.*]

Here is another example; this time the emphasis is straightforward:

If we want to achieve our objectives, we *must* vote, and together we *will* win.

EXERCISE 38.1 USING ITALICS FOR TITLES AND FOR WORDS, LETTERS, OR NUMBERS REFERRED TO AS WORDS

NAME _____ DATE _____

Most (but not all) of the following sentences contain titles or other words that should be italicized. Underline these words. If the sentence is correct as written, simply go on to the next sentence.

EXAMPLES   As a result of his extensive travel covering events like the Olympics for television's <u>Wide World of Sports</u>, Jim McKay has seen the world.

The word <u>separate</u> is one that many people misspell.

1. When I go to the dentist's office, I catch up on People magazine.
2. Our first reading assignment was the novel Fathers and Sons.
3. Russell's poem, "The Lone Seal," was published in Bylines magazine.
4. I often confuse the word affect with effect.
5. TV Guide's cover story discussed some of the old westerns: Bonanza, Death Valley Days, The Lone Ranger, and others.
6. After the fire, we had to replace our copies of the Symphony No. 5 by Beethoven as well as those of the Messiah by Handel.
7. Arthur Miller's play Death of a Salesman opened in 1949; today it's a classic of the American theater.
8. When Kate Chopin wrote The Awakening, she couldn't have realized how many college students would respond to the book.
9. Native English speakers in French or German classes finally find out the difficulties nonnative speakers encounter here in the United States.
10. Boys' Life, Sports Illustrated, Better Homes and Gardens, the Saturday Evening Post, Redbook, and Life—all those magazines arrived in the mail when I was a kid, and I read them all.
11. Last year we saw one of the four original, handwritten, fifteenth-century copies of the Magna Charta on temporary display at the Huntington Library.
12. Overlooking the town, a large M is painted on the face of Mount Sentinel.

EXERCISE 38.4 USING ITALICS SPARINGLY FOR EMPHASIS

NAME _____ DATE _____

A. Using your own paper, briefly analyze the emphasis created by the use of italics in the following sentences.

EXAMPLE   *I* heartily agree with you.
Italicizing *I* suggests that although the speaker agrees, someone else disagrees; italicizing *I* implies and highlights a contrast.

1. In case of hydroplaning, effective skid control requires that you *immediately* remove your foot from the accelerator, not slam on the brakes.
2. Will you ask the Johnsons to bring hamburgers *and* a potato salad?
3. When the scores were shown, it was clear that the judges could not find *anything* wrong with her diving performance.
4. With perseverance and care, we *will* defeat AIDS.
5. Sven's vacations are more like days *on* if you think about all the work he does at home.

B. Read the following passage, noting the use of italics for emphasis. Underline any other words that should be in italics; circle any words that should not be italicized. Keep in mind the likely context for this kind of writing.

The Vikings were *dreaded warriors* who disrupted trade routes, seized valued treasures, and *terrorized* those they attacked. Because they were *excellent seafarers*, the Vikings often *attacked quickly*, arriving by ship from the sea or from a river. Then they left equally quickly, carrying the *spoils* of the day. Given their remarkable success, it is not surprising that some histories now hail this period as the *Viking Age*.

Using Hyphens

39

Writers use hyphens to divide words at the end of a typed line, to form compound words (such as *after-school* in the phrase *my after-school activities*), to write out fractions (*one-half*) and two-digit numbers (*twenty-two*), and to prevent misreading. This chapter will discuss each of these uses.

> **HYPHENS IN EVERYDAY USE**
>
> Hyphens play a number of roles in our everyday lives. On any day, we might order a medium-sized Coke, wear a Dodgers T-shirt, buy gasoline at a self-service station, worry about a parent-child relationship, or listen to some fifties rock-and-roll. Make a list of some of the hyphenated words or phrases you run across in a day.

Using hyphens to divide words at the end of a line (39a)

One of the very last things writers do is produce a final copy. Often this copy is typed; more and more frequently, it is printed from computer equipment. Most computer software will take care of the problem of end-of-line hyphenation by eliminating it either through justification or word wrap (moving the whole word to the next line). However, if you are typing, you may find that you do not have enough room to fit a word on a line. If you must break a word, use the following generally accepted writers' conventions:

1. Place the hyphen after the last letter on the line, not at the beginning of the next line.
2. Divide words only between syllables, and never divide a one-syllable word; either squeeze it onto the end of the line, or shift it to the next. If you are not sure about the syllabic breaks for a particular word, check your dictionary.
3. Whenever possible, begin the part of the divided word on the new line with a consonant (*medi-tate* rather than *med-itate*).
4. Divide words that contain doubled consonants between the doubled letters (as in *occur-ring*) *unless* the doubled consonants are part of the root word (not *cal-ling* but *call-ing*).

5. Never divide the last word on a page. (Thus you will never begin a new page with part of a word.)
6. Never leave a single letter at the end of a line or fewer than three letters at the beginning of a line.
7. Do not divide contractions, numerals, acronyms, or abbreviations.

UNACCEPTABLE Though the eclipse was scheduled to begin at 9:-38 A.M., a heavy cloud cover made observation impossible.

Ellen called to let you know that she would-n't be able to meet with you until after 2 P.M.

After an exile that lasted several years, the AFL-CIO allowed the Teamsters Union to rejoin.

8. Words that already contain hyphens should be divided only at a hyphen.

UNACCEPTABLE The corporate plane seated twelve and was equipped with a jet-prop-elled engine.

ACCEPTABLE The corporate plane seated twelve and was equipped with a jet-propelled engine.

Using hyphens with compound words (39b)

English is full of **compound words** (such as *backpack*, *underline*, and *payday*) that frequent usage has joined together to make single words. In other cases, such combination words are formed using hyphens, as in *simple-minded*. And sometimes these combinations retain the normal space between words, as in *lame duck* and *mountain range*. When it comes to specific compound words, you may simply have to consult a dictionary. If your compound word is a noun and your college dictionary does not list it, the compound word is probably two words and should be written as such. However, you may sometimes wish to construct and use compound words as modifiers; to do so correctly, see the discussion that follows.

Forming compound modifiers

Suppose you wish to describe a picture that you are sending to family or friends. You are in the picture, and the look on your face is not exactly cheerful. You might write, *Don't worry about that down-on-my-luck expression*. You have strung four words together with hyphens. By so doing, you are telling your readers that these four words combine in one meaning. In theory, you could replace *down-on-my-luck* with a single adjective such as *sour*, as in *Don't worry about that sour expression*.

Note that a series of compound modifiers sharing the same word (or words) can be shortened by using suspended hyphens:

This summer, the eight-, nine-, and ten-year-old campers were placed in a single group.

- Hyphenate a compound adjective appearing before a noun; do not hyphenate such an adjective when it follows the noun. In the example, *down-on-my-luck* (an adjective) precedes *expression* (a noun). The hyphens are appropriate in that example. However, if you rewrite the sentence so that the adjective follows the noun, hyphens are not used.

That expression makes me look down on my luck—don't worry about it.

- Never use a hyphen to join an adverb ending in *-ly* to another word.

Her radically different approach produced excellent results.

A crowd of morbidly curious onlookers gathered at the accident scene.

- Do not hyphenate a compound modifier if the first word is a comparative or a superlative, such as *more, better, best*.

The second course provides more extensive coverage.

Using hyphens to create your own compounds for special effect

When speaking or writing informally, we often create our own spur-of-the-moment compounds. Although informal (and hence not always appropriate in formal writing situations), such compounds do add flair and can make for more interesting prose.

We enjoyed another August-in-October day.

After four hurry-up-and-wait hours in the airport, I was ready to fly anywhere.

Again, note that the hyphens connect words that form essentially a single modifier positioned in front of a noun. Sometimes the same words use hyphens when functioning as a modifier but use no hyphens when functioning as separate modifiers and nouns.

The stained glass cast colorful shadows on the pews. [stained glass = *adjective + noun*]

Stained-glass artistry made the church distinctive and inspiring. [stained-glass = *single adjective*]

Officials estimate we need a month of rain to replenish the city's water supply. [water supply = *modifying noun + noun*]

The plumber says our water-supply pipe has corroded and needs replacing. [water-supply = *single adjective*]

Using hyphens with fractions and compound numbers

Writers conventionally use hyphens to spell out fractions. The fraction *3/4* would be spelled out as *three-fourths*. Here the hyphen acts (as it always does) to connect separate words in order to form one unit, one thing—in this case, one fractional number.

Compound numbers from *twenty-one* to *ninety-nine* are also written out using hyphens. Numbers higher than *ninety-nine* are not hyphenated, no matter how long they may be when written out, except for parts from *twenty-one* to *ninety-nine*. (Remember that numbers expressed in more than two words can also be written using numerals.) For example, to reproduce the number *300,354* in words, write *three hundred thousand three hundred fifty-four*. Note that the one hyphen occurs only with the part of the number between *twenty-one* and *ninety-nine*.

Using hyphens with prefixes and suffixes (39c)

Over the years, many **prefixes** (letters added to the front of a word) and **suffixes** (letters added to the end of a word) have so frequently been attached to some words that now no hyphen is used to connect them. *Unusual, disinterested, predestined*—these are all examples of words containing prefixes and no hyphens.

However, several prefixes and suffixes do commonly take hyphens. Prefixes attached to numerals or to capitalized words always take hyphens, as in *pre-1914* and *un-Christian*. When a prefix is attached to a compound word, use a hyphen, as in *pro-civil rights*. Other prefixes that commonly take hyphens include the following:

all- as in *all-inclusive*.   *quasi-* as in *quasi-complete*
ex- as in *ex-softball player*   *self-* as in *self-employed*
half- as in *half-convinced*   *twenty-* as in *twenty-odd*
quarter- as in *quarter-hour*

Such suffixes include the following:

-elect as in *treasurer-elect*   *-odd* as in *forty-odd years old*

Unfortunately, there are a number of exceptions to this general guideline. *Halfback* and *quarterfinalist* are exceptions; over time, the hyphen has been dropped from these words. The only way to be certain of such exceptions is to consult a dictionary.

Finally, some suffixes, such as *-like* and *-wise*, sometimes take hyphens and sometimes do not (for example, *warlike, giraffe-like*). Again, your surest bet is to check a good dictionary.

Using hyphens to clarify meaning

Suppose that you are reading this sentence:

> Kevin sells men's clothing for Macy's, and Michael is a bus-
> boy at the Ringside.

For at least a moment, the word *bus* appears to be part of that sentence; for just a moment, it sounds like Michael is a transportation vehicle. Although such hyphenation follows the guidelines presented earlier in this chapter, in this case it still leads to confusion. Whenever you hyphenate at the end of a line, make sure that you do not inadvertently send a confusing message. Here is another example:

> When I get up late and have early morning appointments, I may care-
> lessly skip breakfast.

In the two examples just given, end-of-line hyphens create momentary confusion. However, sometimes hyphens are crucial to meaning. Consider these sentences:

> The couch needs to be recovered after the flood.
>
> The couch needs to be re-covered after the flood.

The first sentence says that the couch is lost (perhaps washed away) and needs to be found. The second sentence says that the couch's upholstery needs repair. There are similarly significant differences between *procreation* and *pro-creation* and between *re-create* and *recreate*.

Hyphens are also commonly used to separate suffixes from their roots whenever the combination would result in three identical consonants in a row. Thus *skill+less = skill-less*.

When adding a prefix results in the repetition of a vowel (anti-imperialist, for example), a hyphen is often used. However, this practice is violated too frequently to be considered a reliable guideline (consider *reenlist, cooperate,* and the like); when in doubt, consult your dictionary.

Combinations of single letters and roots are nearly always hyphenated, unless they form the names of musical notes or keys. Here are some examples: *T-shirt, I-beam, F sharp, B major.*

EXERCISE 39.1 USING HYPHENS TO DIVIDE WORDS AT THE ENDS OF LINES

NAME _____ **DATE** _____

Many of the following sentences employ unacceptable hyphenation. Read each sentence and underline any improperly hyphenated word; make your correction in the space above the line. On the line below the sentence, explain briefly what is wrong with the use of the hyphen. If the sentence is acceptable as written, write a *C* on the line below the sentence. (Note: Treat proper nouns like all other nouns.)

EXAMPLE Ellen called to let you know that she <u>would-</u> *wouldn't*
n't be able to meet with you until after 2 P.M.
<u>Contractions should not be hyphenated.</u>

1. If between now and the end of the month no precipitation falls, this will be the driest October since 1895.

   _____

2. Weather forecasters are predicting heavy rains and hur-
   ricane-force winds for this afternoon.

   _____

3. The very first books, those printed during the fif-
   teenth century, are known as *incunabula*.

   _____

4. Some fish possess modified muscle tissue that is capable of generating 450 to 600 volts of electricity.

   _____

5. The widely acclaimed actress Gertrude Lawrence had a career that spanned more than two decades.

   _____

6. The first set of ratings figures for the fall season shows NB-
   C leading its two network rivals.

   _____

7. Baseball trivia buffs will recall the 1987 St. Louis vs. Minnesota World Series as the first in which the home team won every game.

8. We spent the afternoon driving the overheated car slowly through the mountain pass.

9. Because he loves to argue, people sometimes find Fred abrasive and oblivious to other people's feelings.

10. When news of the accident reached Kansas City, Nick was stunned, as was his family.

EXERCISE 39.2 USING HYPHENS WITH COMPOUND WORDS AND COMPOUND MODIFIERS

NAME _____ **DATE** _____

Many (but not all) of the sentences below use hyphens or compound words incorrectly. Read each sentence. If hyphens and compounds are used correctly, write a *C* on the line below the sentence. If the sentence needs revising, write your version on the lines.

EXAMPLES   Michael spent his afternoon entertaining the six-year-olds, seven-year-olds, and eight-year-olds.
Michael spent his afternoon entertaining the six-, seven-, and eight-year-olds.

Stained-glass artistry made the church distinctive and inspiring.
C

1. The well-done pork roast was perfectly prepared, but the pumpkin pie was dried out and far too well-done.

2. This is a beautifully-decorated home.

3. From a long-term perspective, the stock market has consistently outperformed other popular investments.

4. An Albany youngster was hospitalized yesterday after consuming a still to be determined quantity of mothballs.

581

5. When you drop off your completed form, we will check to make sure that you have an up to date file.

6. Several drop offs of over sixty feet make the Eagle Creek Trail a potentially dangerous one.

7. My grandparents left the mother-country in 1908.

8. Almost everything about U.S. elections is geared to the two party system.

9. Many argue that abortion is not just a two-sided or three-sided question.

10. After two days of pitching and yawing on a fishing boat, I feel weak-kneed, windburned, and weather beaten.

11. He decided his I don't care attitude was too easy; besides, it left him feeling empty.

12. Jack limped up the mansion steps and plopped his badly-bruised arm onto the mantel.

EXERCISE 39.3 USING HYPHENS WITH PREFIXES AND SUFFIXES AND WITH FRACTIONS AND COMPOUND NUMBERS

NAME _____ **DATE** _____

A. Each item below is either a number or a word with a prefix or a suffix. Construct sentences that use the specified words correctly. Consult your dictionary as needed.

EXAMPLE thirty-six+odd
After thirty-six-odd years, she trusted her own judgment.

1. post+high school _____

2. 3/4 (write using words) _____

3. all+consuming _____

4. pre+1980 _____

5. semi+finalist _____

6. half+back _____

7. self+control _____

8. trans+continental _____

583

9. machine+like _____

10. mid+stream _____

11. anti+freeze _____

12. un+important _____

13. 405,222 (write using words) _____

14. 4,000 (write using words) _____

15. president+elect _____

B. Check the words in the following passage for the correct use of hyphens. Make any needed additions in the space above the word; cross out any extra hyphens.

   The college's annual essay-contest creates both excitement and pressure. Most junior-year students who enter want to win the unusual prize—dollars equal to the year for first place and one half that amount for second. In 1994, the president elect awarded $1994 to the winner while the outgoing president awarded $997 to the second-place contestant. Most of the entrants are half convinced that they can win and half afraid that they will lose. Despite their fears, they all troop at mid morning on the appointed day to one of the large halls. By mid-afternoon, nearly everyone is finished writing, ready to await the results. By mid week, the announcement is scheduled. By the week's-end, the results are publicized, the awards presented, and the all encompassing suspense ended for the year.

EXERCISE 39.4   USING HYPHENS TO CLARIFY MEANING

NAME _____ **DATE** _____

Use each of the specified words below correctly in a sentence. Consult your dictionary if necessary.

   EXAMPLE   pro-creation <u>The pro-creation camp has definite opinions about how science ought to be taught.</u>

1. procreation _____
   _____

2. re-cover _____
   _____

3. recreation _____
   _____

4. re-creation _____
   _____

5. re-form _____
   _____

6. reform _____
   _____

7. recount _____
   _____

8. re-count _____
   _____

9. recoil _____

_____

10. re-coil _____

_____

11. protesting _____

_____

12. pro-testing _____

_____

13. cooperate _____

_____

14. co-operate _____

_____

EXERCISE 39.5 USING CORRECT HYPHENATION

NAME _____ **DATE** _____

Proofread the sentences that follow for confusing end-of-line hyphenation or other inaccurate hyphenation. Underline the errors you find, and correct each in the space above it. Consult a dictionary whenever necessary. If the sentence is acceptable as written, write a C after it.

EXAMPLES   When I get up late and have early morning appointments, I may <u>care-lessly</u> skip breakfast.   *carelessly*

I have never learned how to find B sharp.   *C*

1. Several people have told me that the lead cabinet holds a radio-active substance.

2. The lakefront was dotted with log cabins and A frames.

3. I was driving home in a soggy coat when I saw the most beautiful rain-bow I've ever seen.

4. B flat and C-major are both musical keys.

5. With candy, cookies, cakes, nuts, and cider, our Halloween festivities were definitely high in calories.

6. I'd love to see your chest-nut antique dresser.

7. I was really hoping we could be pen pals.

8. When the mower crossed the field, the prairie dogs ran underground to escape the noisy intruder.

9. We've just heard that the new manager will supervise the production line.

10. The angry cat tipped over the milk, jumped to the floor, and spattered the carpet with milky spots.

PART 8

FOR MULTILINGUAL WRITERS: MASTERING THE NUANCES OF ENGLISH

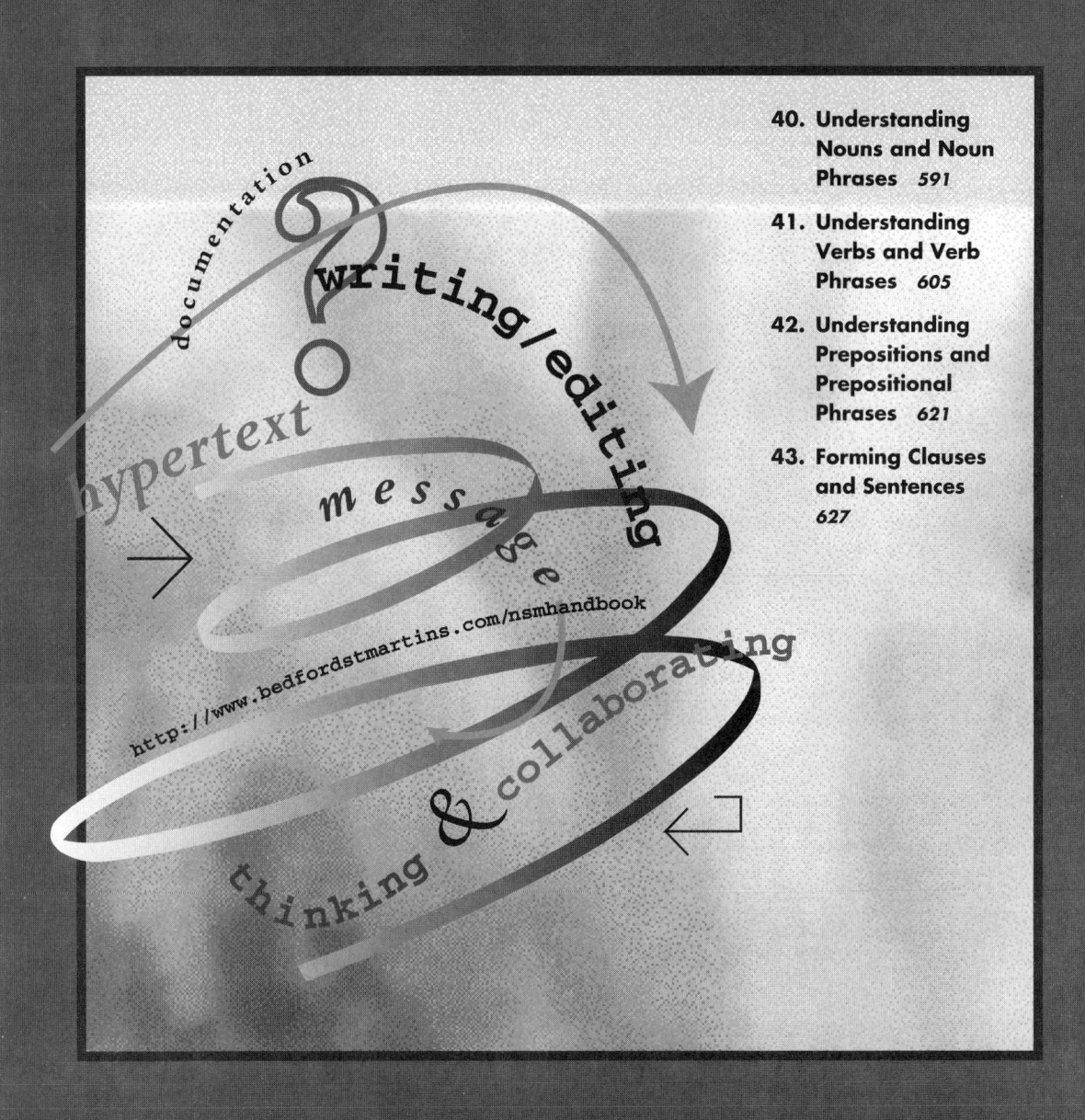

40. Understanding Nouns and Noun Phrases *591*

41. Understanding Verbs and Verb Phrases *605*

42. Understanding Prepositions and Prepositional Phrases *621*

43. Forming Clauses and Sentences *627*

http://www.bedfordstmartins.com/nsmhandbook

PART 8

PREVIEW QUESTIONS

These questions are designed to help you, the student, decide what you need to study. Read each sentence, and underline the correct word or words from the choices provided within the sentence. (Answers to preview questions are found at the back of the book.)

1. He wrote (a or some) check to pay for (a or the or no article) dinner he had just eaten.
2. She drove (a or the) family's car to (a or the or no article) Northampton to look for (a or the or no article) new shoes.
3. This chili needs (the or some) onions and peppers.
4. Dinner included (rice or rices) and (bean or beans).
5. This room needs a (large crystal or crystal large) vase of (fragrant red or red fragrant) roses sitting on the piano.
6. Since I have begun taking business courses, I (learned or have learned) much more than I (expect or expected).
7. During World War I, doctors (cannot or could not) use antibiotics to treat wounds because penicillin (have or had) not yet been discovered.
8. Just as we left the theater, the storm (begins or began).
9. The salt is (in or on) the shelf (in or on) the kitchen.
10. They met for breakfast (at or on) the coffee shop (at or on) the corner (at or in) seven (at or in) the morning.
11. The paper is due (in or on) Monday, but the exam will take place (in or on) the first Wednesday (in or on) December.
12. (No meatloaf or There's no meatloaf) left for tomorrow.
13. We went to the bakery and (bought or bought a cake).
14. Katherine (books reads or reads books) as often as she can.
15. I agreed (to open or opening) the store on Monday.
16. My mother appreciated (to receive or receiving) the invitation.
17. This large pot is the best for (to make or making) soup stock.
18. (Who is wearing the blue dress the woman or The woman who is wearing the blue dress) is a reliable worker.
19. If it rains for several days in a row, the roof (may leak or would have leaked).
20. If I finish my paper, I (watch or will watch) a video.
21. If you were to buy the car, you (need or would need) to paint it.
22. If my family had gone to Australia instead of the United States, we (would live or would have lived) near koala bears instead of prairie dogs.

▼ Understanding Nouns and Noun Phrases

40

Whether speakers and writers refer to *books, pens, rice, milk*, or *philosophy*, nouns are primary components of English sentences. Because nouns are so important, their forms in English require particular attention. This chapter identifies some of the complexities of using count and noncount nouns, specific singular and plural forms, appropriate articles, and modifiers in English.

> **ENGLISH NOUNS AND NOUN PHRASES IN EVERYDAY USE**
>
> Sometimes English speakers use noncount nouns as if they were count nouns in the rapid verbal exchanges of everyday life—for example, in coffee shops ("Two coffees to go, please") or supermarkets ("That's two breads and a cottage cheese"). Listen for exchanges like these, and record some examples. Then try revising these exchanges to the more expansive style of written English. Two examples are supplied below.
>
> two coffees → two cups of coffee
>
> two breads and a cottage cheese → two loaves of bread and a container of cottage cheese

Distinguishing count and noncount nouns (53a)

In English, distinguishing count and noncount nouns is important. These two types of noun may differ in their own forms (singular and plural), and they also may require different articles or other determiners. **Count nouns** identify individuals or things that can be counted. They usually have both singular and plural forms: *child/children, rabbit/rabbits, house/houses*. **Noncount (or mass) nouns** identify masses or collections without individual or separable parts. Noncount nouns usually have only a singular form and include many abstract nouns (*sincerity, honor*), feelings (*anger, love*), foods (*flour, sugar*), beverages (*coffee, tea*), groups of items (*equipment, food*), substances in the various states of matter (*air, water*), and natural events (*lightning, snow*).

COUNT	tree/trees	chair/chairs	bean/beans	word/words	fact/facts
NONCOUNT	wood	furniture	rice	vocabulary	information

the following sentences from a generalization (*first love*) to a hypothetical instance (*a first love*) to a representative instance (*the first love*).

> *First love* is rarely true love.
>
> *A first love* may be a romantic introduction to dating relationships.
>
> *The first love* may be intense and romantic, but the second love is more likely to incorporate reality as well.

The third sentence uses a formal style, common in academic papers. *The* would not be used in this way to generalize in conversation or informal writing.

Arranging modifiers (53e)

Positioning modifiers correctly is an important part of using English smoothly. Modifiers in a noun phrase can precede or follow the noun head. Some modifiers that precede a noun have an **obligatory position** and must always be placed in a certain position; others have a **preferred position**, generally but not always following a commonly accepted sequence. Modifiers that follow a noun are most likely to be phrases (the house *across the street*) or clauses (the house *that Sam rents*).

Guidelines for obligatory modifier positions

BEGINNING THE NOUN PHRASE

Place determiners at the beginning of the phrase.

> *My* new apartment is right here.

Place *all* or *both* before any other determiners.

> I carried *all* my clothes up the stairs.

Place numerals after any other determiners.

> These *three* pictures are my favorites.

AFTER DETERMINERS AND BEFORE NOUN MODIFIERS

Place adjectives between the determiners and any noun modifiers.

> (see preferred positions below)

IMMEDIATELY BEFORE THE NOUN HEAD

Place nouns that are modifiers immediately before the head.

The large *living room* window has a view of the lake.

Guidelines for preferred modifier positions after determiners and before noun modifiers

Place subjective adjectives (indicating the writer's attitude) first.

Those three *charming* photographs capture the spirit of my classmates.

Place objective adjectives (adding descriptive detail) second. Describe size early.

My mother's lovely *large* Chinese ceramic vase is in the hallway.

Place adjectives without a preferred sequence in the middle (separated by commas).

That gorgeous, *sparkling*, diamond necklace is her favorite.

Describe color late.

The soft, fluffy *pink* pillows were tossed on the couch.

Place a proper noun derivative after color and before noun modifiers.

The deep blue *Mexican* floor tiles have lively accent colors.

Describe materials after color and before noun modifiers.

Those heavy, old-fashioned green *velvet* bedroom curtains still hang.

EXERCISE 40.1   IDENTIFYING COUNT AND NONCOUNT NOUNS

NAME _____ **DATE** _____

Underline each of the common nouns in the following short paragraph. Then identify each as either a count or a noncount noun. The first noun is marked for you.

In his <u>book</u> *[count]* *Hiroshima*, John Hersey tells the story of six people who survived the destruction of Hiroshima on August 6, 1945. The bomb detonated at 8:15 in the morning. When the explosion occurred, Mrs. Hatsuyo Nakamura was looking out her window and watching a neighbor at work on his house. The force of the explosion lifted her into the air and carried her into the next room, where she was buried by roofing tiles and other debris. When she crawled out, she heard her daughter, Myeko, calling out; she was buried up to her waist and could not move.

EXERCISE 40.2 USING APPROPRIATE DETERMINERS; STATING PLURAL FORMS EXPLICITLY

NAME _____ DATE _____

Each of the following sentences contains an error with a noun phrase. Rewrite each sentence on the lines provided.

EXAMPLE They made a important linguistic breakthrough.

REVISION <u>They made an important linguistic breakthrough.</u>

1. Lost by the end of the eighteenth century, the language of ancient Egypt was rediscovered through the lucky discovery.

2. Because France and England were at war at this time, Napoleon, a French ruler, invaded Egypt.

3. French army engineers went to Rosetta, a city located near the Nile River, not too many mile from Alexandria.

4. While they were building a fort, some soldiers found stone half buried in the mud.

5. They made an historic discovery—the Rosetta Stone.

601

EXERCISE 40.4 POSITIONING MODIFIERS

NAME _____ **DATE** _____

Possible modifiers for each of the following nouns are listed alphabetically in parentheses after the noun. Indicate the order in which the adjectives should precede the noun.

EXAMPLE   <u>Popular New Orleans jazz</u> album (jazz/New Orleans/popular)

1. _____ team (coed/volleyball)

2. _____ subway (hectic/New York)

3. _____ rental (movie/X-rated)

4. _____ freeway (congested/endless)

5. _____ program (educational/worthwhile)

6. _____ encyclopedia (multivolume/valuable)

7. _____ question (surprising/trick)

8. _____ park (amusement/deserted/large)

9. _____ cloth (batik/orange/unusual)

10. _____ novel (new/Spanish/well-received)

41 Understanding Verbs and Verb Phrases

Along with nouns, verbs are crucial sentence components in English. Unlike some other languages, English requires that every sentence have a verb. If a sentence does not have a verb that adds lively action to it, the sentence must include a form of the verb *be*.

The students *read* their books.

The children *skip* along the walk.

The rain *falls*, and the thunder *booms*.

The boy *is* very tall for his age.

ENGLISH VERBS AND VERB PHRASES IN EVERYDAY USE

Everyday interaction, especially in making requests, calls for a delicate balance between the need to get things done and the need to show consideration for other people's feelings. Modals—auxiliary verbs that show possibility, necessity, and obligation—are an important device for softening the bluntness of a message. You can direct someone to do something (*Close the window*), but it's more considerate to say *Could you close the window?* Note also the difference between saying *Let's go* and *Shall we go?* The first is more of an order, while the second is an invitation.

Notice the kinds of requests people make, both those containing modals and those formed in other ways. For example, if someone says *The phone is ringing*, is the actual meaning "Please answer the phone"? Record some of your observations. Identify any patterns you notice, too—for instance, in the ways teachers make requests of students, customers make requests of sales personnel, or men and women make requests of people of their own or the other gender.

Forming verb phrases (54a)

Verb phrases include the **main verb** (the base form of a verb or a past or present participle) and one or more **auxiliary verbs**, also called helping verbs, which are added to show the intended tense and form of the verb. The most common auxiliaries are forms of *be, have, do, will,* and *shall.* (See also Chapter 9.) In English, the words in a verb phrase must follow a particular order.

> The children *play* soccer.
>
> The children *are playing* soccer.
>
> The children *have been playing* soccer.
>
> The children *may have been playing* soccer.

Notice that you cannot rearrange *The children have been playing soccer* as *The children been playing soccer have.* A new order is possible only if you change the original statement to a question: *Have the children been playing soccer?*

The sequence of auxiliary and main verbs

Up to four auxiliary verbs may precede a main verb, but the use of four is quite unusual. The auxiliary verbs must be placed in this order in a verb phrase:

> modal (such as *can, could, may, might, shall, should, will, would, must,* and *ought to*)
> perfect (*have,* which must be followed by a past participle)
> progressive (indicated by a form of *be* and followed by a present participle)
> passive (indicated by a form of *be* and followed by a past participle)

If *be* or *have* is the first auxiliary verb in a verb phrase, it needs to indicate present tense or past tense. Its form should also agree with the subject. (In contrast, a modal auxiliary does not change form.)

In the following discussions of various auxiliaries, notice that the sentence pairs show how adding an auxiliary (in the second sentence) necessitates a shift in form.

Modal + base form

Modal auxiliary verbs include *can, could, may, might, shall, should, will, would, must,* and *ought to.* These verbs do not change form (always *can,* not *cans*) and are followed by the base form of the verb (not, in English, by an infinitive form). Only one modal at a time can be used in a sentence.

> The dog *growls.* (main verb with -*s* ending)
>
> The dog *can* growl. (*can* + base form)
>
> The cook *has* been working.
>
> The cook *should have* been working.

Perfect *have, has,* or *had* + past participle

The students *went* to class.

The students *have gone* to class all day. (*have* + past participle *gone*)

The baby *will be* crying all day.

The baby *has been* crying all day. (*has* + past participle *been*)

Progressive *be* + present participle

Progressive verbs include a form of the auxiliary *be* (*am, is, are, was, were,* or *been*) followed by the present participle of the verb (ending in *-ing*). If the word *be* is itself used as an auxiliary, it must follow a modal such as *can, could, may, might, shall, should, will, would, must,* or *ought to.* (If *be* indicates the passive voice, it is followed by the past participle, not the present participle ending in *-ing.*)

We *eat* sandwiches for lunch every day.

We *are eating* sandwiches for lunch today. (form of *be* + present participle *eating*)

We *could be camping* by tomorrow night. (*be* itself + present participle *camping*)

Passive *be* + past participle

Passive verbs include a form of the auxiliary *be* (*am, is, are, was, were,* or *been*) followed by the past participle of the verb (never ending in *-ing*). If the word *be* is itself used as an auxiliary, it must follow a modal such as *can, could, may, might, shall, should, will, would, must,* or *ought to.*

The dog *chases* the cat. (active voice)

The cat *was chased* by the dog. (passive voice)

Using present and past tenses (54b)

A complete sentence in English has to include a verb or a verb phrase (main verb + auxiliary verbs), each indicating a **tense**—the time at which the action of the verb takes place. The main verb in a sentence cannot be a **verbal**—an infinitive (*to walk*), a gerund (*walking*), or a participle (present *walking* or past *walked*) without the auxiliaries needed to form a verb phrase.

After the earthquake, many homes *collapsed.*

My parents *call* every week; they *called* last night.

My uncle rarely *calls.*

When you use the third person singular in the present tense, be sure to add the *-s* ending (he *calls*). When you use the past tense, be sure to use the *-ed* form (they *called*) or the appropriate irregular form for the past tense (they *ran*).

Understanding perfect and progressive verb phrases (54c)

Some sentences require a perfect or progressive tense rather than a simple present or simple past tense. These complex verb phrases are formed using perfect and progressive auxiliaries with present tense verbs, past tense verbs, or modals.

The simple present and the present perfect

The simple present conveys current action or a current situation.

> His dog *barks* every night.
>
> She *lives* in Apartment B.

If a sentence describes ongoing activity beginning in the past but continuing in the present, the verb tense needs to include both the past and the present, using the present perfect or the present perfect progressive.

> His dog *has barked* every night during the past week.
>
> She *has been living* in Apartment B for two years.

The simple past and the present perfect

The simple past conveys actions that happened at a definite time in the past.

> He *bought* his books on Wednesday.
>
> Last summer, she *ate* lunch at the deli every day.

If a sentence describes ongoing action beginning at an indefinite time in the past, the verb tense used should be the present perfect or the present perfect progressive.

> Ever since he started working in the bookstore, he *has bought* his books early.
>
> Since last summer, she *has been eating* lunch at the deli every day.

The simple present and the present progressive

The simple present conveys actions that happen during a period of time, possibly including the present but not necessarily happening at the moment.

She *enjoys* skating.

She *goes* to the mountains every winter.

On the other hand, the present progressive conveys an action continuing at the present moment.

She *is going* to the mountains this week because she *enjoys* skating.

The simple past and the past progressive

The simple past conveys actions that happened at a definite time in the past, even if those actions continued for a period of time.

She *attended* summer school during June and July.

He *bought* his new car last month.

Even when this type of past action endures over a period of time, English speakers would be unlikely to use the past progressive tense unless the ongoing past action occurred at the same time as another past action.

She *was attending* summer school when she *received* the scholarship offer.

He *was buying* his new car when his old car *was stolen*.

Using modals appropriately (54d)

The modal auxiliary verbs include *can, could, may, might, shall, should, will, would, must*, and a few other words such as *ought to*. Used for making requests, giving instructions, revealing doubts, expressing possibility or probability, and predicting, modals express a writer's assessment of available options.

The final exam *might* be very difficult.

You *could* begin studying now.

Would you like to borrow these books?

Modals referring to the past

The modal auxiliary verbs generally indicate the present tense or the future tense. Adding a perfect auxiliary verb to a modal allows you to indicate past tense. (However, *had to* needs to be substituted for *must* to indicate past tense.)

If you want to get to work on time, you *should* catch the next bus.

If you had wanted to get to work on time, you *should have* caught the next bus.

You *must* finish repairing the roof before it rains.

You *had to* finish repairing the roof before it rained.

Modals making requests or giving instructions

Modals are used in both statements and questions that make polite requests and supply instructions or directions.

Can you walk the dog?

Would you please pass the spaghetti?

Could you fix the salad for dinner?

Although these requests are arranged in an increasingly polite order, all three of them allow for the possibility that the request cannot be fulfilled. As a result, they are less assertive and more polite than they would be using *will*: <u>*Will* you walk the dog?</u>

The choice of modal controls the degree of assertiveness expressed, as the following instructions illustrate. Notice how they move from more demanding to less demanding.

1. You *will* report to work tonight.
   (requires that instructions be followed)
2. You *must* report to work tonight.
   (acknowledges no option besides following instructions)
3. You *should* report to work tonight.
   (strongly urges following instructions)
4. You *may* report to work tonight.
   (somewhat formally allows but does not require following instructions)
5. You *can* report to work tonight.
   (less formally allows but does not require following instructions)

Modals revealing doubt and certainty

Modals can also express the degree to which a statement is likely to be accurate or true. Notice how the following sentences move from most assertive or definite to most tentative.

Please join us for lunch; you *must* be hungry.

Please join us for lunch; you *may* be hungry.

Please join us for lunch; you *might* be hungry.

Using participial adjectives appropriately (54e)

Certain verbs form adjectives that describe emotions created by circumstances. For such verbs, the present participle (*disappointing*) and the past participle (*disappointed*) express very different meanings. The past participle is used to describe the person who feels the emotion involved; that person feels *bored, depressed, excited, frightened*, or *satisfied*. The present participle is used to describe the person or thing that creates the emotional response: that person or thing is *boring, depressing, exciting, frightening*, or *satisfying*.

> The *fascinated* crowd watched the magic show.
>
> The *fascinating* magic show attracted huge crowds.

Because words such as *interested* and *interesting* are used so often, be sure to use them correctly or use alternate phrasing that expresses what you intend.

> I am *interested* in economics.
>
> Economics *interests* me.
>
> Economics is *interesting*.

Watch out for incorrect forms, as in *I am interesting in economics*.

EXERCISE 41.1 USING THE PRESENT, THE PRESENT PERFECT, AND THE PAST FORMS OF VERBS

NAME _____ **DATE** _____

Rewrite the following passage by inserting the appropriate form of the verb in parentheses. Remember to use *have* with main verbs to form the present perfect. The first answer is supplied as an example.

As I <u>have improved</u> (improve) my English, I _____ (begin) to take reading more seriously. I _____ (discover) that I enjoy a great range of books. Some books _____ (be) fairly easy to read—what I _____ (call) "practice books" in high school. Others (be) more difficult—what my current teachers _____ (call) "college-level" material. Although some books _____ (assign) by my teachers, I also _____ (find) short stories, mysteries, and biographies of famous people at the library. Since I _____ (read) much more, my family also _____ (read).

EXERCISE 41.2 USING SPECIFIED FORMS OF VERBS

NAME _____ **DATE** _____

Using the subjects and verbs provided, write the specified sentences on the lines provided.

EXAMPLE subject: Bernie   verb: touch
sentence using a present form: <u>Bernie touches the soft fur.</u>
sentence using the auxiliary verb *had*: <u>Bernie had touched a squid before.</u>

1. subject: I   verb: arrange
sentence using a past form:

_____

_____

sentence using an auxiliary verb + the present participle form:

_____

_____

2. subject: they   verb: agree
sentence using a present form:

_____

_____

sentence using an auxiliary verb + the past participle form:

_____

_____

3. subject: bears   verb: hibernate
sentence using a past form:

_____

_____

sentence using an auxiliary verb + the present participle form:

_____

_____

4. subject: we   verb: request
   sentence using a present form:

   _____

   _____

   sentence using the auxiliary *had* + the past participle form:

   _____

   _____

5. subject: children   verb: play
   sentence using a past form:

   _____

   _____

   sentence using the auxiliary verb *were* + the present participle form:

   _____

   _____

6. subject: dogs   verb: jump
   sentence using a present form:

   _____

   _____

   sentence using an auxiliary verb + past participle form:

   _____

   _____

7. subject: rice   verb: cook
   sentence using a past form:

   _____

   _____

   sentence using an auxiliary verb + present participle form:

   _____

   _____

8. subject: Dodgers   verb: lose
   sentence using a past form:

   _____

   _____

   sentence using an auxiliary verb + a present participle form:

   _____

   _____

9. subject: pizza   verb: taste
   sentence using a present form:

   _____

   _____

   sentence using an auxiliary verb + a past participle form:

   _____

   _____

10. subject: racers   verb: drive
    sentence using a past form:

    _____

    _____

    sentence using an auxiliary verb + a present participle form:

    _____

    _____

EXERCISE 41.3   IDENTIFYING TENSES AND FORMS OF VERBS

NAME _____ **DATE** _____

From the following list, identify the form of each verb or verb phrase in each of the numbered sentences.

> simple present   past perfect
> simple past   present progressive
> present perfect   past progressive

EXAMPLE   Judge Cohen considered the two arguments. <u>simple past</u>

1. She had forgotten the assignment. _____
2. This morning in class he is explaining his project. _____
3. My mother has driven the same Mazda for ten years. _____
4. Paul required special medical attention for years. _____
5. I have attempted that math problem several times now. _____
6. Just as we took our seats, the movie began. _____
7. As guests were arriving, Cheryl was still getting dressed. _____
8. She is exercising to reduce stress. _____
9. The elephant's floppy ears were delighting my son. _____
10. The twins Emily and Sarah befuddle their teachers. _____

EXERCISE 41.4 USING VERBS APPROPRIATELY

NAME _____ **DATE** _____

Each of the following sentences contains an error with verbs. Rewrite each sentence on the lines provided.

EXAMPLE Linguists cannot interpret hieroglyphics before they discovered the Rosetta Stone.

REVISION <u>Linguists could not interpret hieroglyphics before they discovered the Rosetta Stone.</u>

1. The Rosetta Stone was discover in Egypt in 1799.

   _____

   _____

2. A decree carved on the stone in three versions—ancient Egyptian hieroglyphics, Greek, and the Egyptian language spoken when the stone was carved.

   _____

   _____

   _____

3. The French who had discovered the stone have circulated copies of it to scholars.

   _____

   _____

4. Language experts at that time can read Greek but not hieroglyphics.

   _____

   _____

5. They were exciting about the opportunity to decode the hieroglyphics.

   _____

   _____

6. By comparing the Egyptian writing with the Greek writing, the scholars interpreting the former.

7. The scholars were praise for their work.

8. They have carried out their work almost two hundred years ago.

9. Museum goers visit the stone for more than a hundred years.

10. We have visited it in 1966.

42 Understanding Prepositions and Prepositional Phrases

Prepositions are words that indicate the relationship—location, direction, time—of a noun or pronoun to another part of the sentence. They distinguish putting a chair *near* the fireplace or *in* the fireplace, serving chicken *under* the rice or *over* it, and wearing a skirt *above* the knees or *below* them.

> **ENGLISH PREPOSITIONS AND PREPOSITIONAL PHRASES IN EVERYDAY USE**
>
> In many fields, you will find phrasal verbs that are a part of their specialized vocabulary. Examples include *log on* (computers), *blast off* (space exploration), and *kick off* (football or soccer). Make a list of some other phrasal verbs that are used in these or other fields.

Using prepositions idiomatically (55a)

English prepositions may be especially troublesome because they are often used idiomatically. For example, a cup may be placed *on* the table, the dog may jump *on* the sofa, a ring may be worn *on* the finger, your friend may live *on* the second floor of an apartment *on* First Street, or you may invite someone for dinner *on* Saturday night. Here are some guidelines for using some potentially confusing prepositions.

In expresses the idea of enclosure, while *on* expresses contact with a surface. Notice how the following sets of examples move from literal to more figurative applications of these prepositions.

The laundry is *in* the washer.

My brother works hard *in* the heat or *in* the rain.

Paula has fallen *in* love.

The cereal is *on* the shelf.

His hat is *on* his head, and his coat is *on* his back.

I found several books *on* American history, but I will also look for information *on* the World Wide Web.

In is used with locations in space (enclosing a place) or locations in time (enclosing an event).

> *In* 1989, my aunt arrived *in* Los Angeles *in* April.
>
> I take math *in* the morning.

On must be used with days of the week, days of the month, and street names (though not with exact addresses), just as if a date is placed on a calendar or a location is placed on a map.

> My appointment is *on* Thursday.
>
> The final paper is due *on* May 11.
>
> Brad is moving to a small house *on* Maple Avenue.

At specifies an exact location—in space or in time.

> I will meet you *at* the museum *at* noon.
>
> He lives *at* 4919 College Way.
>
> *At* home, I always watch the news *at* ten.

Notice that *at* is used with *night*, even though *in* is used with other times of day.

> I take classes *in* the morning, work *in* the afternoon, and study *at* night.

Using two-word verbs idiomatically (55b)

Phrasal verbs are two-word verbs that may look like a verb plus a preposition.

> I *dropped* the carrots *into* the stew.
>
> (*Into* is a preposition; *into the stew* is a prepositional phrase.)
>
> Sheila *ran into* Nan.
>
> (*Ran* and *into* form a two-word verb.)

Phrasal verbs have their own idiomatic meanings. In this case, *ran into* means *encountered* or *met*. English has hundreds of these expressions; here are just a few examples.

TWO-WORD VERB	DEFINITION
ask (a person) out	arrange a date
blow up	explode
call (an event) off	cancel
drop (a person or thing) off	leave at a certain place
put away	place something back where it belongs
shut off	turn off or stop a flow
wear out	reduce to shabbiness or inefficiency

There are several ways to distinguish between a preposition and a two-word verb. A preposition introduces a prepositional phrase, and other words can be added between a verb and a prepositional phrase. A phrasal verb, however, is a two-word unit. This unit cannot generally be separated by other words except for the direct object of the verb. (Some types of two-word verbs are exceptions, however.) Notice the word order in the following sentences.

I made up a bedtime story for my son.

I made a bedtime story up for my son.

A bedtime story is the direct object of *made up*. This direct object can follow the phrasal verb, or it can be placed between the two words of the verb. Should the direct object be a personal pronoun, however, the pronoun has to be placed between the two parts of the verb: I *made* it *up* for my son. Other words, however, cannot divide the two parts of a phrasal verb: *I made for my son up a bedtime story* does not make sense in English.

In contrast, a prepositional phrase can be separated from the verb and can be moved around within the sentence. Other words and phrases can also be added freely between a verb and a preposition.

<u>For my son</u>, I *made up* a bedtime story.

I *made up* a bedtime story with wild animals <u>for my son</u>.

I *made* a bedtime story *up* last night <u>for my son</u>.

Phrasal verbs are complicated because some types do not follow this pattern. Sometimes the second word acts like a preposition and may be separated by other phrases. In other cases, the preposition cannot be separated from the verb, even by the object of the verb.

I *came across* this information yesterday.

I *came* unexpectedly *across* this information yesterday.

(*not* I *came* this information *across* yesterday.)

Sheila *ran into* Nan.

(*not* Sheila ran Nan into.)

Whenever you are uncertain about what an expression means or how it functions within a sentence, check it in the dictionary. The *Longman Dictionary of American English* includes detailed information about the various types of two-word verbs.

EXERCISE 42.1 USING PREPOSITIONS IDIOMATICALLY

NAME _____ **DATE** _____

Insert an appropriate preposition into each of the following sentences. If there is more than one appropriate preposition, insert all of them.

EXAMPLE   We read the article _in_ the newspaper yesterday.

1. Newspapers and magazines report problems _____ high schools with disruptive students.

2. Some articles say that teachers frequently are distracted _____ disruptive students.

3. Other articles report on schools _____ areas of poverty and crime.

4. These articles say that schools can't solve problems _____ themselves.

5. Families need to encourage students to work or participate in sports or other activities _____ school.

6. Every evening, students need to do the homework assigned _____ school.

7. Local businesses need to encourage students so that they are prepared _____ jobs or higher education.

8. Students need to come _____ school ready to learn.

9. They should get to school precisely _____ time.

10. Once _____ the school building, students should be ready to learn.

EXERCISE 42.2 RECOGNIZING AND USING TWO-WORD VERBS

NAME _____ **DATE** _____

Identify each italicized expression as either a two-word verb or a verb + preposition.

EXAMPLE   *Look up* Jeremy the next time you're in town. <u>two-word verb</u>

1. The angry cat *struck at* the baby. _____

2. The troops *fell back* to the base camp and radioed for help. _____

3. I *gave up* chocolate for a week. _____

4. My sister *took back* all the clothes she had loaned me. _____

5. I *looked at* all the fruit in the market, but I only bought strawberries. _____

6. The camp counselor *handed* the candy *out* as if it were gold. _____

7. *Put* the garbage *out* on the sidewalk, please. _____

8. Don't *put* yourself *out* on my behalf. _____

9. The frog *turned into* a prince. _____

10. The car *turned into* the driveway. _____

Forming Clauses and Sentences   43

In English, sentences are built from one or more **clauses**, groups of words containing both a subject and a predicate.

> *He opened the door* <u>which was painted red</u>.
> (independent clause + dependent clause)
>
> *She just left for the airport* <u>because the flight is late</u>.
> (independent clause + dependent clause)

A sentence itself can be called an independent clause. An **independent clause** has a subject and a predicate; it must be grammatically complete and express a thought. An independent clause can stand alone as a sentence, but a **dependent clause** cannot. Instead, a dependent clause must be connected to another clause that can stand independently. (See Chapter 7.) Because clauses are the basic building blocks for English sentences, they sometimes require special attention—making sure that all their required elements are explicitly stated in the sentence and that they are logically positioned and correctly connected with each other.

ENGLISH CLAUSES AND SENTENCES IN EVERYDAY USE

Signs and newspaper headlines often omit sentence elements that are otherwise required, as these examples illustrate.

> **NO HOT WATER TOMORROW**
> (*There will be no hot water tomorrow.*)
>
> **JUDGE REBUKED FOR STATEMENT TO JURY**
> (*A judge has been rebuked for making a statement to the jury.*)

Collect other examples like these, and see if you can formulate general rules about what elements can be omitted and what elements cannot (for instance, articles can, but prepositions cannot).

Expressing subjects explicitly (56a)

In English, every sentence must have an explicit subject and an explicit predicate. The subject position in a sentence must be filled, if only by "it" or "there."

> The *temperature* is dropping.
>
> The *rain* continues to fall.
>
> *It* is cold and rainy tonight.
>
> *There* are few people outside.

Although "Went to the mall" or "Running late" might be left in a note to a friend or family member, neither expression would be acceptable in college writing. (See also Chapter 16 on sentence fragments.)

> *Letty and I* went to the mall.
>
> *We* are running late.

Expressing objects explicitly (56a)

Transitive verbs are those that generally require a direct object. Even if this object is clear from the context, it needs to be stated in the sentence. Although your dog may respond to "Give!" a written sentence needs to include more information. (See also Chapter 7 on types of verbs and sentence structure.)

> Give me the *ball*.
>
> Give her the *receipt* for her purchase.

Using English word order (56b)

Because word order shows how sentence elements are related in an English sentence, make sure that you leave subjects, verbs, and objects in their typical positions in the sentence. (See Chapter 7 for the typical patterns of sentences using transitive, intransitive, and linking verbs.)

> We ate spaghetti for dinner.
> (subject + verb + direct object + prepositional phrase)
>
> The spaghetti was delicious.
> (subject + verb + subject complement)
>
> Dinner gave us an opportunity to talk.
> (subject + verb + indirect object + direct object)

Using noun clauses appropriately (56c)

When a sentence is built from several clauses, the clauses within the sentence can act in place of individual nouns. These **noun clauses** can act as subjects, subject complements, direct objects, and objects of prepositions. They are generally introduced by a **relative pronoun** (*who, whom, whose, which, that, what, whoever, whomever, whichever,* and *whatever*) or by *when, where, how, why,* or *whether*. Rather than just adding on a dependent clause to a sentence, these words can be used to integrate a dependent noun clause within the independent clause.

> *Whoever ate the cake* left crumbs all over the kitchen.
> (noun clause acting as subject)
>
> The auditorium was *where the concert was held*.
> (noun clause acting as subject complement)
>
> I asked *what was going on tonight*.
> (noun clause acting as direct object)
>
> I will look under *whatever magazines are stacked there*.
> (noun clause acting as object of preposition)

If a noun clause at the beginning of a sentence is long, a native speaker is likely to relocate the clause later in the sentence. In such a case, *it* or some other word needs to fill the subject position.

> *That the gym wall collapsed during the earthquake* made everyone on campus worry.
>
> *It* made everyone on campus worry *that the gym wall collapsed during the earthquake*.

Choosing between infinitives and gerunds (56d)

An **infinitive** is the base form of a verb preceded by *to* (*to play, to sleep, to read*). A **gerund** is the base form of a verb with *-ing* added (*playing, sleeping, reading*). Although these forms are easy to distinguish, it's not always easy to tell which one fits into a particular sentence. Usually when an infinitive follows a verb, it conveys an expectation, a hope, a wish, or an intention; on the other hand, a gerund following a verb is likely to convey a fact.

INFINITIVES

I expect *to receive* my check after work today.

The committee agreed *to present* its report on Friday.

Robert decided *to buy* a car.

His brother refused *to go* to the grocery.

GERUNDS

We appreciated *getting* a round of applause from the audience.

Margaret enjoys *playing* tennis.

The teacher began *scheduling* appointments right after class.

Although many verbs are followed either by infinitives or by gerunds, some verbs can be followed by either of the two. In some cases—with verbs such as *continue, prefer, start,* or *like*—the choice of infinitive or gerund has little effect on the essential meaning of the sentence.

I like *to eat* tacos.

I like *eating* tacos.

In other cases—with *remember, try, forget,* or *stop,* for example—the choice of infinitive or gerund will completely change the meaning of the sentence.

I stopped *to practice* the piano.

(*Stop* with an infinitive means "in order to do something," that is, in order to practice.)

I stopped *practicing* the piano.

(*Stop* with a gerund means that the activity—in this case, practicing—ended or was discontinued.)

After a preposition, however, a gerund, not an infinitive, is always used regardless of the intention-fact distinction used with verbs.

These shoes are my favorites *for* running.

This sentence cannot use an infinitive placed directly after the preposition:

These shoes are my favorites *for* to run.

Using adjective clauses carefully (56e)

When a sentence is built from several clauses, a clause within the sentence can act in place of an adjective, modifying a noun or a pronoun. Such a clause should be placed close to the word it modifies and is often introduced by a **relative pronoun** such as *who, whom, whose, which,* or *that,* or by *when* or *where.* (Sometimes the relative pronoun is understood and can be dropped, but do not drop a relative pronoun that is the subject of a verb.)

The <u>children</u> *who attend that school* wear uniforms.

INCORRECT	The <u>store</u> *that Janet's mother owns* it is across the street.
CORRECT	The <u>store</u> *that Janet's mother owns* is across the street.
INCORRECT	The <u>office</u> *that Mark works* is across the street.
INCORRECT	The <u>office</u> *Mark works* is across the street.
CORRECT	The <u>office</u> *that Mark works in* is across the street.

Understanding conditional sentences (56f)

Conditional sentences are those in which one situation depends on the occurrence of another situation (expressed in a clause introduced by a word such as *if*, *unless*, or *when*). Conditional sentences can indicate different degrees of confidence in the likelihood or truthfulness of the possibility expressed in the *-if* clause.

If the statement in the *-if* clause is very likely to be true, then both verbs can be in the present tense or in another appropriate tense.

> If you *sneeze*, you *are* allergic to the cat.
>
> When it *snows*, driving *is* difficult.
>
> If you *have studied* all semester, you *have learned* what you need to know.

If the *-if* clause predicts the future and is likely to be true, the *-if* clause uses the present tense. The independent clause, however, uses either the future tense or a modal that shows future time.

> If you *watch* the film again, you *will decide* what to say in your review.
>
> If we *eat* at China House tomorrow, we *may order* the won-ton soup.

If the statement in the *-if* clause is doubtful, it uses *were to* with the base form of the verb or a past subjunctive. The independent clause uses *would* with the base form of the verb.

> If you *were to bake* bread every day, kneading the dough *would seem* easy.
>
> If he *played* tennis all year, he *would win* all his matches.

If the statement in the *-if* clause is not possible, it uses the past subjunctive. The independent clause uses *would* plus the base form of the verb.

> If you *wore* a diamond necklace, you *would sparkle* more than the jewels.
>
> If you *were* tall, blond, and handsome, you *would have* no more friends than you already do.

If the statement in the *-if* clause is not possible and also is placed in the past, it uses the past perfect. The independent clause uses *would* with the perfect form of the verb.

If you *had lived* in ancient Rome, you *would have worn* a toga.

If you *had invented* the traffic signal, you *would have collected* a fortune from your patent.

EXERCISE 43.1 EXPRESSING SUBJECTS AND OBJECTS EXPLICITLY

NAME _____ **DATE** _____

Revise the following sentences or nonsentences so that they have explicit subjects and objects as necessary. If a sentence does not contain an error, write *C* on the line below.

EXAMPLE   Is a coffee bar in my apartment building.
REVISION There is a coffee bar in my apartment building.

1. Is of great importance that I know Yiddish.

   _____
   _____

2. Snowed during my entire vacation.

   _____
   _____

3. No hot water tomorrow.

   _____
   _____

4. Having a great time; wish you were here.

   _____
   _____

5. We were losing patience with her because was always late.

   _____
   _____

6. There's no difference between us.

   _____
   _____

7. The poster publicizing the charity said "Give!" in big letters.

8. We walked to the mailbox and mailed.

9. "I will now go to my chambers and consider," explained Judge Cohen.

10. Was even windier in Chicago than I'd expected.

EXERCISE 43.2   EDITING FOR ENGLISH WORD ORDER

NAME _____ DATE _____

Revise the following sentences as necessary. If a sentence does not contain an error, write C on the line below.

    EXAMPLE   On vacation she wants to go.

    REVISION   <u>She wants to go on vacation.</u>

1. Chocolate eats the baby messily.

   _____

   _____

2. To sleep he wishes to go now.

   _____

   _____

3. "Speak fluently English," ordered the instructor.

   _____

   _____

4. John watches videos incessantly.

   _____

   _____

5. Desserts some restaurant guests would like to begin with.

   _____

   _____

6. She not can pronounce all English sounds.

   _____

   _____

7. A week's vacation he expects.

8. Put on the table the silverware.

9. Slow and easy wins the race.

10. Comes in first the runner from Kenya.

EXERCISE 43.3 USING NOUN CLAUSES, INFINITIVES, AND GERUNDS APPROPRIATELY

NAME _____ **DATE** _____

Revise the following sentences as necessary so that each contains an appropriate noun clause, infinitive, or gerund in the proper position. If a sentence does not contain an error, write *C* on the line below.

EXAMPLE It pleases me you like me.

REVISION It pleases me that you like me.

1. Makes me very proud that my English vocabulary is expanding.

2. It annoys the teacher we don't practice conversation.

3. What he has to say is of great interest to me.

4. Is important that we think in English.

5. I enjoy to study the slang expressions of native speakers.

6. I expect understanding more as I proceed with my studies.

7. We appreciated to get the invitation.

8. I agree to invest at least three hours a week in improving my English.

9. Her mother stopped to drive on her ninetieth birthday.

10. It is obvious that she made the right decision.

EXERCISE 43.4 USING ADJECTIVE CLAUSES WELL

NAME _____ DATE _____

Revise the following sentences so that each includes an appropriate adjective clause positioned well. Make sure the sentence does not include unnecessary words or omit necessary relative pronouns. If a sentence does not contain an error, write *C* on the line below.

EXAMPLE   The doctor prescribed medicine for her headache that was no help.

REVISION   <u>The doctor prescribed medicine that was no help for her headache.</u>

1. Who has red hair the young man is picking up English very quickly.

2. The textbook that I am using it contains many examples of English sentences.

3. The class in that I enrolled has only a few students.

4. The class dinner we cooked together represented food from a dozen countries.

5. The chef works at my club helped by lending us pots and pans.

6. A reporter attended the dinner and wrote an article which he praised the chefs in it.

7. The results of the test, which we all prepared for, demonstrate the progress that we have made.

8. I want that is the newest the textbook.

9. The book that is the biggest is not necessarily the best.

10. The student practices the most gains the most.

EXERCISE 43.5 WRITING CONDITIONAL SENTENCES

NAME _____ **DATE** _____

Revise each of the following sentences so that both the *-if* clause and the main, or independent, clause contain appropriate verb forms. If a sentence does not contain an error, write C on the line below.

EXAMPLE   If you had loved me, I would stay.

REVISION   If you had loved me, I would have stayed.

1. If the Rosetta Stone was not discovered, it would have been much more difficult to decipher hieroglyphics.

   _____

   _____

2. If I win a fellowship, I would go to graduate school.

   _____

   _____

3. If you had read the instructions, you had been finished assembling the desk by now.

   _____

   _____

4. If John Kennedy were alive today, he would question what we see as progress.

   _____

   _____

5. If he did not wear a seat belt, he would not have survived.

   _____

   _____

6. When you feel the flu coming on, you should consider getting more rest.

7. She will face months of therapy if the tests were positive.

8. If I'd known you were coming, I would bake a cake.

9. When she is good, she is very good, but when she is bad, she is horrid.

10. If it stopped raining, we will go biking.

Answers to Preview Questions

PART ONE 1) F 2) F 3) T 4) F 5) F 6) T 7) T 8) F 9) T 10) T 11) T 12) F 13) T 14) F 15) T 16) T

PART TWO 1) Meryl, car, supermarket 2) Washingtons, pet, doctor 3) will get, finishes 4) might speak, going 5) Anybody, those who, his 6) Which, you 7) Until, under, up 8) I 9) whom 10) Whom 11) he, she 12) me 13) am 14) doesn't 15) gave 16) lay 17) would 18) wants 19) its 20) a 21) travels 22) have 23) is 24) well 25) most 26) really 27) nicer, nicest

PART THREE 1a) no 1b) no 1c) no 1d) yes 2a) yes 2b) no 2c) yes 2d) yes 3a) yes 3b) no 3c) no 3d) yes 4a) no 4b) yes 5a) no 5b) no 5c) no 6a) no 6b) yes 6c) yes 6d) yes

PART FOUR 1a) yes 1b) no 2a) so 2b) but 3) no 4a) When the rain started 4b) who gave me this watch 4c) even though she left an hour early 5a) no 5b) yes 5c) no 6a) wordiness 6b) C 6c) passive verbs, wordiness 6d) weak verb 6e) passive verb

PART FIVE 1) Their (They're) 2) definately (definitely), desert (dessert) 3) herd (heard), developped (developed) 4) rein (reign), righters (writers), dyed (died) 5) nucular (nuclear), treatey (treaty) 6) Latin, *adjudicatus*, past part. of *adjudicare*, to judge 7) premature dementia, schizophrenia 8) trend, drift, current, inclination, tenor 9) six-ten 10a) *for instance*: biology, biography 10b) *for instance*: jurisdiction, jurisprudence, justice, justify 11) *-ly* 12) *-ive, -ic, -able, -ful, -ish* 13) eludes (alludes) 14) stink (*fragrance, aroma,* or *scent* would be better) 15) continuously (continually), continual (continuous) 16) C 17) X (*tons* is informal language) 18) (sentence acceptable) 19) X (*he's just wrong* is too extreme; readers who disagree may feel offended)

PART SIX 1) . . . shared much, they . . . 2) . . . cousin, lives . . . 3) . . . china was totally . . . 4) . . . at first; however, upon further reading, . . . 5) . . . positions: short-order . . . 6) . . . a "bookhouse," I . . . 7) . . . Marisa asked. 8) T. S. Eliot . . . J. Alfred . . . 9) . . . one's writing?" they . . . 10) . . . shouted, "Stop!" 11) . . . judges' . . . defense's . . . 12) . . . just doesn't want . . . 13) . . . eight o'clock . . . 14) C 15) . . . was theirs. 16) "I did not know . . . evening," Peter said. 17) . . . was 'very taxing,'" Vincent . . . 18) . . . windy," the . . . 19) . . . robbers "are now in custody." 20) C 21) . . . literature: good . . . 22) . . . sixty dollars' worth . . .

643

Part Seven 1) capitalize *We*; do not capitalize *northwestern* 2) do not capitalize *they* 3) C 4) C 5) capitalize *Renaissance* and *Middle Ages* 6) "a doctor" and "an M.D." say the same thing; use one or the other when referring to a single person or group 7) C 8) AD (A.D.) 9) # (number) 10) Cal., Ariz. (California, Arizona) 11) 6 (Six) 12) 10,000 (ten thousand) 13) *Hebrew Bible, Gospels, Koran* (none of these should be italicized) 14) "King Lear," "Shakespearean Negotiations" (italicize; do not use quotation marks) 15) C 16) C 17) "in medias res" (italicize; do not use quotation marks) 18) C 19) "Annie Hall" (italicize; do not use quotation marks) 20) best-known (do not hyphenate) 21) seventy-five (75) 22) cloud-less (do not hyphenate), rain-ed (do not divide) 23) C 24) better-coverage (do not hyphenate) 25) C 26) man- uscripts (do not begin a new line with a vowel)

Part Eight 1) a, the 2) the, no article, no article 3) some 4) rice, beans 5) large crystal, fragrant red 6) have learned, expected 7) could not, had 8) began 9) on, in 10) at, on, at, in 11) on, on, in 12) There's no meatloaf 13) bought a cake 14) reads books 15) to open 16) receiving 17) making 18) The woman who is wearing the blue dress 19) may leak 20) will watch 21) would need 22) would have lived

Index

Note: A page number beginning with E *indicates that the entry refers to an exercise.*

a, an, 595
abbreviations, E563
   for acronyms and initials, 557–58, E563
   checking for appropriate use of, 558–59
   in everyday use, 555
   for personal and professional titles and academic degrees, 555–56, E561
   semicolons and, 486
   with years and hours, 557, E562
absolute phrases, 111
academic degrees, abbreviations for, 555–56, E561
acronyms, 557–58, E563
active readers, 412
active voice, 50, 172–73, E193–94
   memorable prose and, 369–70, E375–76
   shifting from passive voice to (or vice versa), 254–55
addresses
   commas used with, 462, E475–76
   numerals for, 560, E562
adjective clauses, 630–31, E639–40
adjectives, 223–29, E231–36
   adverbs distinguished from, 223–24
   comparative form of, 227–29, E233–36
   coordinate, separated by commas, 460, E473–74
   in everyday use, 223
   after linking verbs, 224–25
   participial, 611
   positive form of, 226
   possessive forms as, 141
   predicate, 108
   proper, capitalization of, 544, E550–51
   recognizing and identifying, 102, E117
   suffixes indicating, 412
   superlative form of, 226–29, E233–36
adverbs, 223–29, E231–36
   adjectives distinguished from, 223–24
   comparative form of, 227–29, E233–36
   conjunctive, 105
      coordinating conjunctions distinguished from, 271–72, E281
      linking independent clauses with, 270–71
      semicolons for linking independent clauses and, 484
   in everyday use, 223
   after linking verbs, 224–25
   positive form of, 226
   recognizing and identifying, 102–3, E118
   suffixes indicating, 412
   superlative form of, 226–29, E233–36
advertising, 62
age, references to, 450
agreement. *See* pronoun-antecedent agreement; subject-verb agreement
allusions, 422
alternating comparison, 33
analogies, 422
antecedents, 101. *See also* pronoun-antecedent agreement; pronoun reference

antithesis, for memorable prose, 370–71
apostrophes, 501–4, E509
   for plural of numbers, letters, symbols, and words used as words, 504, E505–6
   quotation marks with, 513
   to signal contractions and other omissions, 502–3, E507–8
   to signal possessive case, 501–2, E506–7
appositive phrases, 111
   as fragments, 289
appositives, pronoun case with, 144, E157–58
argument
   appealing to logic and, 64–66
   characteristics of, 61–62
   credibility in, 63–64
   emotional fallacies in, 67, E73–74
   logical fallacies in, 66, E73–74
   purposes of, 62
   reasons for, E70
   recognizing arguable statements, E69
   Toulmin system for, 67–68, E75
Aristotle, 29, 62–63
articles, 100–101, 594–96, E603
   definite, 594–95
   indefinite, 595
   zero, 595–96
assignments, analyzing, 13–14, E21
audience, analyzing, 13–15, 17–19, E25–26
authority, citing, 64–65
auxiliary verbs, 100, 110, E115, 162–63, E178, 605–6

645

auxiliary verbs *(continued)*
    modal, 606, 609
    sequence of main verbs and, 606

backward reading, as editing strategy, 50–51
bad/badly, 225–26, E232
bandwagon appeal, 67
be, 161–62, E177
    + past participle, passive, 607
    + present participle, progressive, 607
begging the question, 66
block comparison, 33
brackets, 527, E533
brainstorming, 27–28
broad reference, 241

capitalization, 543–48
    in everyday use, 543
    of first word of a sentence or of a line of poetry, 543–44, E549
    of *I* and *O,* 547
    of proper nouns and proper adjectives, 544–46, E550–51
    quotation marks and, 513
    revising for, E552–53
    of titles of works, 546
    unnecessary, 547–48
case
    with appositives, 144
    in elliptical constructions, 144–45
    possessive
        apostrophes to signal, 501–2, E506–7
        pronouns, 141–42, E151–53
    of pronouns. *See* pronoun case
cause-and-effect relationship, 65
cause-effect organizational pattern, 32
cause-effect paragraphs, 83, E91–92, E94
-ceed, -cede, -sede, 388
chronological organizational pattern, 32
class, references to, 450
classification, organizing information by, 34
clauses, 627
    adjective, 630–31, E639–40

dependent, 111–12, E135, E137–38
independent, 111, E135, E137–38
noun, 629
recognizing and using, 111–12
subjects of. *See* subjects of sentences and clauses
clichés, 423, E434
climactic order, 326–27, E329–30
coherence of paragraphs, 79–80, E89
coinages, quotation marks for, 516
collective nouns
    pronoun agreement with, 216–17, E219–20
    subject-verb agreement with, 200–201, E207–8
colloquial language, 419
colons, 528–30, E537–39
    quotation marks with, 512–13
commas, 457–65, E482–83
    with addresses and place-names, 462
    in compound sentences, 458–59
    with dates, 461
    in everyday use, 457
    to facilitate understanding, 462–63
    after introductory elements, 457–58, E467
    to join independent clauses, 458, E469–70
    joining independent clauses with, 273, E278
    with numbers, 462
    quotation marks with, 512
    with quotations, 273, 462, E477
    with restrictive elements, 463, E478
    to separate items in a series, 460–61, 465, E473–74
    to set off nonrestrictive elements, 459–60, E471–72, E478
    between subjects and verbs and between verbs and objects, 464, E479
    with titles, 462
    unnecessary, 463–65, E480
comma splices, 267–73, E275–83
    in everyday use, 268
comment portion of a working thesis, 30–31

common ground, building, 63, 447–50, E451–53
    age, class, sexual orientation, and physical ability references and, 450
    in everyday use, 448
    gender references and, 448–49
    race, ethnicity, religion, and geographical area references and, 450
companies (corporations), acronyms and abbreviations for, 558, 559
comparative form, 227–29, E233–36
    double comparatives, 229
comparison/contrast organizational pattern
    in essays, 33
    in paragraphs, 83, E91–92, E94
comparisons, complete, consistent, and clear, 312–13, E321
complete grammatical structures. *See* consistent and complete grammatical structures
complete predicate, 106
complete subject, 106
complex sentences, 113, 114
compound antecedents, pronoun agreement with, 215–16, E219–20
compound-complex sentences, 113
compound numbers, hyphens with, 576
compound objects, 143–44
compound-predicate fragments, 289–90, E295
compound sentences, 113, 358
    commas in, 458–59
compound subjects, 143
    subject-verb agreement with, 199–200, E205–6
compound words, hyphens with, 574–75, E581–82
conciseness, 327–28, E331–32, E333
conditional sentences, 631–32, E641–42
conjunctions
    coordinating. *See* coordinating conjunctions
    correlative, 104
    parallel structures and, 346–47

recognizing and identifying, 104–5, E120
subordinating, 105
conjunctive adverbs, 105
   coordinating conjunctions distinguished from, 271–72, E281
   linking independent clauses with, 270–71
   semicolons for linking independent clauses and, 484
connotations, 419–20, E429–30
consistent and complete grammatical structures, 309–13, E315–22
   comparisons, 312
   elliptical structures, 311–12, E319–20
   in everyday use, 310
   garbled sentences, 309, 310, E315, E316
context clues for new words, 412, E416
contractions, apostrophes to signal, 502–3, E507–8
contrasting elements, commas to set off, 461, E475–76
coordinate adjectives, separated by commas, 460, E473–74
coordinating conjunctions, 104, 335
   commas before or after, 458–59, 464–65
   conjunctive adverbs or transitional phrases distinguished from, 271–72, E281
   linking independent clauses with a comma and, 270, E278
   parallel structures and, 346–47
coordination (coordinate and subordinate structures), 335–38, E339–40
   to relate equal ideas, 336
   for special effect, 338, E343
correctness, checking for, 50–51
correlative conjunctions, 104
   parallel structures and, 346–47
count nouns, 591–92, E599
credibility, establishing, 63–64
critical thinking, 61. *See also* argument
   in everyday use, 62

cumulative sentences, 358

dangling modifiers, 300–301, E305–8
dashes, 527–28, E535
   quotation marks with, 513
dates
   commas used with, 461, E475–76
   numerals for, 560, E562
days of the week, capitalization of, 545
declarative sentences, 112, 113
deduction, 65, E72
definite article, 594–95
definition essay, 33
definitions, quotation marks for, 515
demonstrative pronouns, 101–2
denotations, 419–20, E428
dependent-clause fragments, 290, E295
dependent clauses, 105, 111–12, E135, E137–38
   misplaced, 298
   who, whoever, whom, and *whomever* to begin, E155–56, 143
details in paragraphs, 80–81
determiners, 592–94, E601–2
dialogue
   fragments in, 291
   paragraphing, 83–84
   quotation marks for, 514–15, E519
dictionaries, 399–401, E403, E407–8
   specialized, 401
   unabridged (unabbreviated), 401
diction (word choice), 419–25. *See also* English language
   appropriate for college essays, 419, E427
   balancing general and specific, 420–21, E432
   denotations and connotations, 419–20
   editing, 49–50, E58
   in everyday use, 419
   figurative language, 421–23, E433
   shifts in, 256–57, E265–66
direct address, commas to set off, 461, E475–76

direct objects, 107, E125
   pronouns as, 140
disruptive modifiers, 299–300, E307–8
division, organizing information by, 33
draft, final
   format of, 52–53
   proofreading, 53
drafting, 34–35, E44, E56
   in writing process, 4, 7

editing
   most common errors, 51–52
   strategies for, 48–52
editing checklists, 51–52, E59
educational degrees, abbreviations for, 556
either-or fallacy, 66
ellipses, 530–31, E540
elliptical constructions, case in, 144–45
elliptical structures, 311–12, E319–20
emotional fallacies, 67, E73–74
emphasis. *See also* special effects
   italics for, 568, E572
end punctuation, 493–94, E497–98
   proofreading and revising, E499
English language. *See also* diction
   other languages in academic writing than, 441, E446
   standard academic, 439, 441, E443–44
   varieties of, 439
   ethnic, occupational, or regional, 440, E445
errors, most common, 51–52
ethical fallacies, 64
ethnicity, references to, 450
ethnic varieties of English, 440, E445
etymology, 400
examples
   paragraph development by, 81
   providing, 64
exclamation points, 493–94
   quotation marks with, 513
exclamations, fragments as, 291
exclamatory sentences, 112, 113
exploring a topic, 27–30, E37–40
fairness, demonstrating, 63–64

fallacies
    emotional, 67, E73–74
    ethical, 64
    logical, 66, E73–74
familiar language, 423, E435–36
faulty predication, 310–11, E318
field labels, in dictionaries, 400
figurative language, 421–23, E433
figures of speech, 422
flattery, 67
foreign words and phrases, italics for, 567, E570
formal language, 424–25, E437
format, 52–53
fractions, hyphens with, 576
freewriting, 28–29
fused sentences, 267–73, E275–83
    in everyday use, 268
future perfect progressive tense, 170
future perfect tense, 170
future progressive tense, 170
future tenses, 169–70, E186

garbled sentences, 309, 310, E315, E316
gender references. *See also* sexist reference to gender
    building common ground and, 448–49
general-to-specific paragraphs, 81
geographical area, references to, 450
geographic names
    capitalization of, 544
    spelling out, 559
gerund phrases, 110–11
gerunds, 110, E131, 141–42, E637–38
    choosing between infinitives and, 629–30
good/well, 225–26, E232
grammatical functions, in dictionaries, 400

had + past participle, perfect, 607
has + past participle, perfect, 607
hasty generalization, 66
have, 161–62, E177
    + past participle, perfect, 607
helping verbs. *See* auxiliary verbs
holidays, capitalization of, 545
homonyms, 384–85
hours
    abbreviations with, 557, E562
    colons used to separate minutes, seconds, and, 529
hyperbole, 422
hyphens, 573–77, E587
    to clarify meaning, 577, E585–86
    with compound words, 574–75, E581–82
    to divide words at the end of a line, 573–74, E579–80
    in everyday use, 573
    with fractions and compound numbers, 576
    with prefixes and suffixes, 576–77, E583–84

idiomatic use of prepositions, 621–22, E625
illustration, paragraph development by, 81
illustration essay, 33
imperative mood, 174
imperative sentences, 112, 113
indefinite article, 595
indefinite-pronoun antecedents, pronoun agreement with, 217, E221
indefinite pronouns, 101
    subject-verb agreement with, 201, E207–8
independent clauses, 105, 111, E135, E137–38
    comma splices and fused sentences, 267–73
    commas to join, 458, E469–70
    linking
        with commas, 273, E278
        with commas and coordinating conjunctions, 270, E278
        with a semicolon, 269
        with a semicolon and a conjunctive adverb or transitional phrases, 270–71, E279
    recasting as a dependent clause, 272–73, E284–86
    recasting as a single independent clause, 272, E284–86
    semicolons used to link, 483–84, E487–90
    separating into two sentences, 268–69

indicative mood, 174
indirect objects, 107, E125
    pronouns as, 140
induction, 65, E71
infinitive phrases, 110, E131
    single-word modifiers between *to* and the verb in, 300
infinitives, E637–38
    choosing between gerunds and, 629–30
    perfect, 171
    present, 171
    split-infinitive constructions, 300
informal language, 424, E435–36
information
    gathering, 31–32
    organizing, 32–34
initials, 557–58, E563
interjections
    commas to set off, 461, E475–76
    recognizing and identifying, 106, E120
interrogative pronouns, 102
interrogative sentences, 112, 113
intransitive verbs, 108–9, E129
introductions, editing, 48, E57
introductory elements, commas after, 457–58, E467
inverted order, for memorable prose, 371
irony, 422
    quotation marks for, 516
irregular verbs, 163–65, E181–82
it, vague and ambiguous use of, 241
italics, 565–68
    in everyday use, 565
    for foreign words and phrases, 567, E570
    for names of vehicles, 567, E571
    for special emphasis, 568, E572
    for titles, 565–66, E569
    for words, letters, and numbers referred to as words, 566–67, E569
its/it's, 502

knowledge, demonstrating, 63

language. *See also* diction; vocabulary
    familiar, 423, E435–36
    formal, 424–25, E437

informal, 424, E435–36
  levels of (registers), 423–25, E437
languages, capitalization of, 545
language variety (varieties of English), 439–41
  in everyday use, 439
letters
  apostrophes used for plural of, 504
  italics for letters referred to as words, 566, E569
lie/lay, 165–66, E182
linking verbs, 108, E127, E129
  adjectives and adverbs after, 224–25
  subject-verb agreement with, 202
listening, in writing process, 6–7, E11
litotes, 422
logic, appealing to, 64–66
logical fallacies, 66, E73–74
looping, 29

major premises, 65
mass nouns, 100
memorable prose, 367–72, E373–80
  changing nouns to verbs and, 369
  in everyday use, 367
  special effects for, 370–71
  strong verbs and, 368, E373–74
  voice and, 369
metaphors, 422
minor premises, 65
missing words, checking for, 312, E315
modals (modal auxiliary verbs), 163, 606, 609–10
  making requests or giving instructions, 610
  referring to the past, 609–10
  revealing doubt and certainty, 610
modifiers
  compound, hyphens for, 574–75, E581–82
  dangling modifiers, 300–301, E305–8
  disruptive modifiers, 299–300, E307–8
  in everyday use, 297
  limiting modifiers, 298

misplaced or dangling, 297–301, E303
nonrestrictive, commas to set off, 459–60, E471–72
phrases and clauses, 298
positioning, 596–97, E604
  restrictive, unnecessary commas with, 463
squinting modifiers, 298–99, E304
months, capitalization of, 545
moods of verbs, 174–75, E194
  shifts in, 254–55, E261–62
Ms., 555–56

narrative paragraphs, 83
nationalities, capitalization of, 545
noncount nouns, 591–92, E599
nonrestrictive elements, commas to set off, 459–60, E471–72, E478
non sequitur, 66
noun clauses, 629, E637–38
noun phrases, 109, 591–97
  in everyday use, 591
  as fragments, 288–89
nouns, 591–97
  appositives, 144
  changing to verbs, 369
  collective
    pronoun agreement with, 216–17, E219–20
    subject-verb agreement with, 200–201, E207–8
  count, 591–92, E599
  in everyday use, 591
  mass, 100
  noncount (or mass), 591–92, E599
  plural, 100
  possessive, 100, 142
  predicate, 108, 140
  proper, 100
    capitalization of, 544–46, E550–51
  recognizing and identifying, 100–101, E115
numbers
  apostrophes used for plural of, 504
  commas used with, 462, E475–76
  compound, hyphens with, 576
  in everyday use, 555
  italics for numbers referred to as words, 566, E569

spelling out or using figures for, 559–60, E564

object complement, 107
objective case, 140–41, E149–50
objects
  commas between verbs and, 464, E479
  compound, 143–44
  direct, 107, E125
    pronouns as, 140
  explicitly expressing, 628, E633
  indirect, 107, E125
    pronouns as, 140
offensive references or terms, 447, E451. *See also* common ground, building
omissions, 312, E315
  apostrophes to signal, 502–3
organizations
  acronyms of, 557, 558
  capitalization of, 545
organizing information, 32–34, E44
outlining, as revision strategy, 47
oversimplification, 66

pairs, parallel structures with, 346–47
paragraph breaks, finding, E85
paragraphs (paragraphing)
  cause-effect, 83, E91–92, E94
  choosing a pattern of development for, E91–92
  coherent, 79–80, E89
  comparison/contrast, 83, E91–92, E94
  definition and characteristics of, 77
  details in, 80–81
  editing and revising, 49, E58
  in everyday use, 77–84, E85–96
  general-to-specific, 81–82
  illustration and examples in, 81
  main idea in, 78–79
  narrative, 83
  problem-solution, 82, E91–92, E93
  process analysis, 82, E91–92, E93
  question-and-answer, 82, E91–92, E93
  quoted dialogue in, 83–84
  special-purpose, 83

paragraphs *(continued)*
    specific-to-general, 82
    summary exercise, E95–96
    unified, 78–79, E86–87
parallel structures (parallelism), E89, 345–47, E349–54
    in everyday use, 345
    including all necessary words in, 347
    with pairs, 346–47
    paragraph development and, 79–80
    in a series, 345–46
parentheses, 525–27, E533, E534
    comma before an opening, 465
    semicolons and, 485–86
parenthetical expressions, commas to set off, 461, E475–76
participial adjectives, 611
participial phrases, 111
participles, 111, E131, 141–42. *See also* past participles; present participles; present perfect participle
parts of speech, recognizing and identifying, 99–106, E121–22
passive *be* + past participle, 607
passive voice, 50, 172–73, E193–94
    memorable prose and, 369–70, E375–76
    shifting from active voice to (or vice versa), 254–55
past participles, 111, E131, E132, 161, 172
past perfect progressive tense, 169
past perfect tense, 169
past progressive tense, 169, 609
past subjunctive, 174
past tenses, 161, 168–69, E185, 607–8, E613
perfect *have, has,* or *had* + past participle, 607
perfect infinitive, 171
perfect verb phrases, 608
periodic sentences, 358
periods, 493–94, E495
    quotation marks with, 512
personal pronouns, 101
    as predicate nouns, 140
personal titles. *See* titles (of people)
personification, 422
persuasion, good reasons and, 62–63

phrasal verbs, 622–24, E626
phrase fragments, 288–89, E293–94. *See also* sentence fragments
phrases, 109–11, E133–34
    absolute, 111
    appositive, 111
    definition of, 109
    gerund, 110–11
    infinitive, 110, E131
    misplaced, 298
    noun, 109
    prepositional, 110, E119, 130
    verb, 110
    verbal, 110
physical ability, references to, 450
place-names, commas used with, 462
planning, in writing process, 4–5, 6–7, E44
plural nouns, 100
plurals
    apostrophes used for, 504, E505–6
    explicitly stating, 592, E601–2
    spelling of, 388
poetry, capitalization of first word of a line of, 543–44
possessive case
    apostrophes to signal, 501–2, E506–7
    pronouns, 141–42, E151–53
possessive nouns, 100, 142
post hoc fallacy, 66
predicate adjectives, 108
predicate nouns, 108, 140
predicates, 100, E123
    consistent subjects and, 310, E318
    of sentences, 106
prefixes, 410–11, E417
    hyphens with, 576–77, E583–84
    spelling of, 386–88
premises, 65
prepositional phrases, 103, 110, E119, 130, 621
    as fragments, 288
prepositions, 621–24
    idiomatic use of, 621–22, E625
    pronouns as objects of, 141
    recognizing, 103
    wrong or missing, 104
present infinitive, 171
present participles, 111, E131, E132, 160, 171

present perfect participle, 171–72
present perfect progressive tense, 168
present perfect tense, 608, E613
present progressive tense, 168, 608–9
present subjunctive, 174
present tenses, 167–68, E183–84, 607–8
problem-solution organizational pattern, 33
problem-solution paragraphs, 82, E91–92, E93
process analysis paragraphs, 82, E91–92, E93
progressive *be* + present participle, 607
progressive verb phrases, 608
pronoun-antecedent agreement, 215–21
    with compound or collective-noun antecedents, 215–17, E219–20
    in everyday use, 215
pronoun case, 139–58
    with appositives, 144, E157–58
    in compound subjects or objects, 143–44
    in elliptical constructions, 144–45
    in everyday use, 139
    objective, 140–41, E149–50, E151–53
    possessive, 141–42, E151–53
    of relative pronouns *(who, whoever, whom, whomever),* 142–43, E154–56
    subjective, 139–40, E147–48, E151–53
pronoun reference, 239–43, E245–52
pronouns
    agreement between antecedents and. *See* pronoun-antecedent agreement
    case of. *See* pronoun case
    demonstrative, 101–2
    as direct objects, 140
    indefinite, 101
        pronoun-antecedent agreement with, 217, E221

INDEX

subject-verb agreement with, 201, E207-8
as indirect objects, 140
interrogative, 102
as objects of prepositions, 141
as objects of verbals, 141
paragraph development and, 79, E89
personal, 101
as predicate nouns, 140
recognizing and identifying, 101-2, E116
reflexive, 101
relative, 102, 112, 143
    noun clauses and, 629
    subject-verb agreement with, 201-2, E209
sexist, 217-18, E221
shifts in, 255, E263-64
as subjects of sentences and clauses, 140
as subjects of subordinate clauses, 140
pronunciation
    in dictionaries, 400
    spelling and, 385
proofreading, 53, 384, E392
    end-punctuation errors, E499
proper adjectives, capitalization of, 544
proper nouns, 100
    capitalization of, 544-46, E550-51
punctuation. *See also specific punctuation marks*
    end, 493-94, E495-99, E497-98
purpose of writing, 13-15, 17

question-and-answer paragraphs, 82, E91-92, E93
questioning
    exploring a topic by, 29-30
    as revision strategy, 46, E55
question marks, 493-94
    quotation marks with, 513
questions
    fragments in answer to, 291
    tag, commas to set off, 461, E475-76
    who and *whom* to begin, 142
quotation marks, 511-16, E521-24
    for coinages, 516
    for definitions, 515
    for dialogue, 514-15, E519

for direct quotations, 511-12, E517-18
for irony, 516
with other punctuation, 512-13
semicolons and, 485
for titles, 515
quotations
    commas used with, 273, 462 E477
    of longer passages (indented or block quotations), 513-14
    of poetry, 514
    quotation marks for, 511-12, E517-18
quoted dialogue, paragraphing, 83-84

races
    capitalization of, 545
    references to, 450
reading
    aloud, 50, 53
    backward, as editing strategy, 50-51
real/really, 225-26, E232
reasoning, inductive and deductive, 65, E71-72
reasons, good, 62-63
recursion, 4
redundant wording, 327-28
reflexive pronouns, 101
registers, 423-25
relative pronouns, 102, 112, 143
    adjective clauses and, 630-31
    noun clauses and, 629
    subject-verb agreement with, 201-2, E209
religions
    capitalization of, 545
    references to, 450
repetition, E89
    for memorable prose, 370
    paragraph development by, 79
rereading, 46
    as editing strategy, 50-51
restrictive elements, commas with, 463, E478
reversed emphasis clauses, 273
reversed order, for memorable prose, 371
revising, E56
    capitalization, E552-53
    end-punctuation errors, E499
    with semicolons, E492

strategies for, 45-47
in writing process, 4-7
rise/raise, 165-66, E182
root words, 409-10, E415

sacred persons, places, or things, capitalization of, 545
salutations, colons after, 529
Santiago, Robert, 441
sarcasm, 422
-sede, -ceed, -cede, 388
semicolons, 483-86
    in everyday use, 483
    linking independent clauses with, 269, 270-71, E279, 483-84, E487-90
    with other punctuation, 485-86
    overused, 485
    quotation marks with, 512-13
    revising using, E492
    to separate items in a series, 484-85, E491
sentence fragments, 287-92, E293-96
    compound-predicate fragments, 289-90, E295
    definition of, 287
    dependent-clause fragments, 290, E295
    in everyday use, 287
    phrase fragments, E293-94
    for special effect, 290-91
sentence patterns, 107
sentences, 627
    complex, 113, 114
    compound, 113, 358
    commas in, 458-59
    compound-complex, 113
    conditional, 631-32, E641-42
    declarative, 112, 113
    effective, 325-28, E329-33. *See also* sentence structure
    in everyday use, 99
    exclamatory, 112, 113
    forms of, 113, E135-36
    functions of, 112-13, E135-36
    fused, 267-73, E275-83
    in everyday use, 268
    imperative, 112, 113
    interrogative, 112, 113
    length of, 49, 355-56, E361-63, E365
    openings of, 356-57, E359-60, E365

sentences *(continued)*
  parallel, E89
  parts of, 106–12
  simple, 113
  subjects of. *See* subjects of sentences and clauses
  topic, 78, E86–87
  transitions between. *See* transitional words and phrases
  types of, 357–58
sentence structure
  climactic order, 326–27, E329–30
  closing and opening positions for emphasis, 326
  conciseness, 327–28, E331–32, E333
  coordinate and subordinate structures. *See* coordination (coordinate and subordinate structures)
  editing, 49, E58
  emphasizing main ideas and, 326–27
  parallel structures, 345–47, E349–54
  varying, 355–58, E359–66
    in everyday use, 355
    sentence length, 355–56, E361–63, E365
    sentence openings, 356–57, E359–60, E365
    sentence types, 357–58
  verb type and, 108–9
series
  commas to separate items in, 460–61, 465, E473–74
  joining independent clauses in a, 273
  parallel structures in a, 345–46
  semicolons used to separate items in a, 484–85, E491
sexist reference to gender, 448–49
sexist usage of pronouns, 217–18, E221, 243
sexual orientation, references to, 450
shifts, 253–57, E259–66
  in mood and voice, 254–55, E261–62
  in person and number, 255–56, E263–64
  in pronouns, 255–56

in tense, 253–54
in tone and diction, 256–57, E265–66
in verb tenses, E259–60
similes, 422
simple future tense, 169–70
simple past tense, 169, 608, 609
simple present tense, 167–68, 608
simple sentences, 113, 358
sit/set, 165–66, E182
slang, 256, 419
slashes, 530
special effects
  coordinate and subordinate structures for, 338, E343
  for memorable prose, 370–71, E377–78
  sentence fragments for, 290, E295
  subordination for, 338, E343
special-purpose paragraphs, 83–84
specific-to-general paragraphs, 82
spelling, 383–89, E391–97
  commonly misspelled words, 384, E393
  in dictionaries, 400
  in everyday use, 383
  homonyms and other similar-sounding words, 384–85, E394
  personal spelling chart, 389, E397
  pronunciation and, 385
  proofreading and, 384, E392
  rules of, 386–88, E395–96
  unpronounced letters or syllables and unstressed vowels, 386
  words with more than one form, 385–86
  writing habits and, 383–84
squinting modifiers, 298–99, E304
stance, 15–17, E23–24
stereotyping, 447, E451
stock phrases, 423, E434
subject complements, 107, E127
subjective case, 139–40, E147–48, E151–53
subjects of sentences and clauses, 100, 106, E123
  commas between verbs and, 464, E479
  compound, 143
  subject-verb agreement with, 199–200, E205–6

consistent predicates and, 310–11, E318
explicitly expressing, 628, E633
pronouns as, 140
subject-verb agreement, 197–213, E205–13
  with collective-noun or indefinite-pronoun subjects, 200–201, E207–8
  with compound subjects, 199–200, E205–6
  in everyday use, 197
  with linking verbs, 202
  with relative-pronoun subjects, 201–2, E209
  with subjects that are plural in form but singular in meaning, 203
  with subjects that follow them, 203–4
  with third-person singular subjects, 198
  when separated by other words, 198–99
subjunctive mood, 174
subordinating conjunctions, 105
subordination, 336, E341–42
  to distinguish main ideas, 336–37
  for special effect, 338, E343
suffixes, 410–12, E417
  hyphens with, 576–77, E583–84
  spelling of, 386, E395
superlative form, 226–29, E233–36
  double superlatives, 229
symbols, apostrophes used for plural of, 504

tag questions, commas to set off, 461, E475–76
talking, in writing process, 6–7, E11
Tan, Amy, 441
that, vague and ambiguous use of, 241, 242, E251–52
the, 594–95
thesaurus, 401, E405–7
thesis, 30
  working, 30–31
they, indefinite use of, 242–43, E251–52
this, vague and ambiguous use of, 241

time
    abbreviations for, 557, E562
    numerals for, 560, E562
titles (of people)
    abbreviations for, 555–56, E561
    capitalization of, 544
titles (of works)
    capitalization of, 546
    colons to separate subtitles from, 529
    commas used with, 462, E475–76
    editing, 48, E57
    italics for, 565–66, E569
    quotation marks for, 515
tone
    editing, 50
    shifts in, 256–57, E265–66
topic portion of a working thesis, 30–31
topic sentences, 78, E86–87
Toulmin, Stephen, 29–30, 67
Toulmin system for argument, 67, E75
trade names, capitalization of, 546
transitional words and phrases, 80, E95
    commas to set off, 461, E475–76
    coordinating conjunctions distinguished from, 271–72, E281
    linking independent clauses with, 270–71, E279
    semicolons for linking independent clauses and, 484
transitive verbs, 108–9, E129, 165, 628

understatement, 422
usage labels and notes, in dictionaries, 400

varied sentence structures. *See* sentence structure, varying
vehicles, italics for names of, 567, E571
veiled threats, 67

verbal phrases (verbals), 110. *See also* gerunds; infinitive phrases; participles
    as fragments, 288
    pronouns as objects of, 141
verb phrases, 110. *See also* auxiliary verbs
    in everyday use, 605
    forming, 605–7
    perfect, 608
    progressive, 608
verbs, 159–96, 605–11
    agreement between subject and. *See* subject-verb agreement
    auxiliary, 100, 110, E115, 162–63, E178
    base form of (present form), 159–60
    be and *have*, 161–62, E177
    changing nouns to, 369
    commas between objects and, 464
    commas between subjects and, 464
    common errors
        lack of subject-verb agreement, 197
        wrong or missing endings, 160
        wrong tense or verb form, 166–67
    in everyday use, 159
    forms of, 159–62, E179–80
    intransitive, E129
    irregular, 163–65, E181–82
    linking, 108, E127, E129
        adjectives and adverbs after, 224–25
        subject-verb agreement with, 202
    mood of, 174–75, E194–95
    phrasal (two-word verbs), idiomatic use of, 622–24, E626
    recognizing and identifying, 99–100, E115
    regular, 163
    strong, 368, E373–74
    suffixes indicating, 412

transitive, 108–9, E129, 165, 628
    voice of. *See* voice
verb tenses, 166–72, E613–20. *See also* future tenses; past tenses; present tenses
    in sequence, 170–72, E187–92
    shifts in, 253–54, E259–60
vocabulary, 409–13. *See also* diction; dictionaries; language variety
    active reading and building, 412–13
    colloquial and slang, 419
    context clues for new words, 412, E416
    denotations and connotations, 419–20, E428–30
    prefixes, 410–11, E417
    root words, 409–10, E415
    suffixes, 410–12, E417
voice, 172–73, E193–94
    memorable prose and, 369–70, E375–76
    shifts in, 254–55, E261–62

well/good, 225–26, E232
which, 242, E251–52
    vague and ambiguous use of, 241
who, 242, E251–52
who, whoever, whom, whomever, 142–43, E154–56
word choice. *See* diction
word division, in dictionaries, 400
word order, 628, E635–36
words used as words
    apostrophes used for plural of, 504
    italics for, 566–67, E569
wordy sentences, 327–28, E331–32, E333
working thesis, 30–31, E41–43
writing process, 3–7, E9–11

years, abbreviations with, 557, E562
you, indefinite use of, 242, E251–52

zero article, 595–96